# BIBLION

## Stephen Leonard

A Falcon Book

First published in 1997 by Falcon Books
An imprint of M&N Publishing Co. Ltd
1 Northumberland Avenue Trafalgar Square LONDON WC1N 5BW

Paperback ISBN 1 899865 92 6

i

# TABLE OF CONTENTS

# FOR GRACE

'Mit einer schönen Wunde kam ich auf die Welt;
das war meine ganze Ausstattung.'

- Franz Kafka

# VOLUME ONE: ALBION

## *BOOK ONE: Country Matters*

Hamlet: Lady, shall I lie in your lap? (lying down at Ophelia's feet)
Ophelia: No, my lord.
Hamlet: I mean, my head upon your lap?
Ophelia: Ay, my lord.
Hamlet: Do you think I meant country matters?
Ophelia: I think nothing, my lord.
Hamlet: That's a fair thought to lie between maids' legs.
Ophelia: What is, my lord?
Hamlet: Nothing.

# Once

In 1912 or thereabouts two young men, sons of a Derbyshire farmer, set out across that broken limestone plateau which, cut by dales and capped by outcrops, makes up most of the Peak District. It was a wintry day and they were cold to their bones, and their bones, grown brittle from the bite of the wind, seemed to jangle and shake as the harness shook, carrying them forward to the Staffordshire side, there to pick up their father's new bride, a girl of nineteen, a mere slip-of-a-thing really, and bring her back to the little church in Elmsworth, where, without father or mother present, she would be married to Alderman, much older than she. Thus, herself coming from a family of six, she would at nineteen - and she had never seen the world - become the step-mother of the two boys.

The two boys themselves were not at all alike: Tristan, the elder, was his mother's son, with a dark-haired, narrow, Celtic head, a ruddy complexion and an easy laugh; Cecil, his brother, was taller, more intense, with already at that age a tendency to stoop. Neither of them relished the journey very much, but Alderman Dakin's word was law and he had decreed that they should go and fetch Jessie. And so they had set out on that February day in the pony-and-trap, this time into Staffordshire and not, as was their early morning wont, to Bakewell station with the milk.

They could count on no enchantment for the day. It was bleak and bare, as February days are, with the trees like fingers, stiff and cold, pushing up black and naked from the earth. They rumbled into Crowdecote, down Derbyshire, up Staffordshire, across the Dove, which for much of its course forms the country boundary. They arrived in Longnor, where they asked for directions and were told that their destination, Weatherall, a clustered clump of houses and farm-buildings, lay a few miles south on the way to Hulme End.

Doubters of Destiny, beware! These young men were able and were able to prove it. They arrived thick and solid at Weatherall, where the bride's father, complaining of lumbago, took them in and fed them bread, brawn and tea.

- Come in, lads, you must be starving, he said. The wife's gone to Leek but she'll be back any time.
- We've got no time to waste, said Cecil. It's a tidy way back and it'll be dark afore long.
- But you must wait a bit: she'd be sorry to 'ave missed you.
- Not 'alf as sorry as we'd be if we dinna get back.

And the old man, who was rather a complainer anyway, had to admit to the exigencies of the moment and call upon his daughter, Jessie, to leave. She was all packed up ready and demurely, daintily, as befitted a young woman about to be married, she got into the trap, while her father from below handed up her hat-box and a travelling-rug. Thus demurely, unimpeachably she sat, while her father said to the world at large:
- I should love to 'a' come, but tha knows 'ow it is. Your mother'll never forgive 'erself for not comin'.

Jessie was speechless to interject; she knew how easily her mother forgave herself, what privileges of pleasure devolved to her in Leek. What a gullible old fool her father was! In his weak, pathetic way he said:
- I s'll miss thee, Jess.

Then the trap set off back, with the three of them in it: Jessie and Tristan and Cecil, his brother.

1

Alderman Dakin was not pleased: he thought they'd be back the same day, but they weren't. He went to the window several times, looking down the farm-track and on to the road. In his fussy way he was anxious about the future, about his new bride and what she would be like. It is something of a stand-off with Fate for a man of fifty to marry a young woman of nineteen. 'A farmer needs a wife,' or so the saying goes, and that was probably the long and short of it. Jessie's father was more than happy, having been glad to find a husband for his daughter, who, whatever the mortgage, still had a farm. A suitable 'bottom drawer' had been assembled, and the wedding-day was fixed for 29 February, the whole event being, as Jessie's father put it, 'a stroke of luck, a proper good turn.'

But still the party had not arrived. Should Alderman, he, like Oedipus once, go down to Crowdecote and meet his fate? This waiting, for an agitated man like he was, became with every passing moment more infernal. It was a slow death-passage among the souls of the dead.

Then, on the second day, they came: a wheel had splintered and they had had to stop at Longnor, where a cousin of Jessie's had put them up. Nothing more was said and they all went inside. But the air that lay about the house had altered, the air that for generations had been whole. It seemed now rent, as if all of a sudden a flaw had appeared in a piece of shot silk.

- Come in, all of you, Alderman said. There's none t' much room but we'll all have our place.

And indeed there was ample room for them all, in spite of the fact that Alderman's sister was living there with him most of the time and also they employed a cook and kitchen-maid.

- Minnie, be getting some tea, will you, Alderman said.

And, as she put the kettle on the fire, attempting to stir the ashy coals, they took down Jessie's things from the trap and were soon themselves installed in the dining-room, whose windows faced out over falling fields to the concealed Wye valley and the moors beyond.

- Do you think as you'll like it? Alderman asked.
- I think I might, said Jessie, like a lady.
- I'll show you your room, then, Alderman said, after they were finished with their tea.

He brought her to the threshold of the small back room and stood there, hesitant, waiting for a sign. But no sign came: she felt barren and bleak, lost among aliens like an unwanted waif. Seeing her thus quiet, withdrawn, aloof, he kissed her on the cheek and went back downstairs.

- Gormless bugger! she said to herself.

She too was waiting, evidently; she had no hold, no prision, no place. Suddenly she had been cut adrift and was floating in the Underworld. A bottomless Chasm was opening up, through which she fell, head-down, unwanted. Darkest demons leeringly stretched out bloodless, white webbed hands. She wanted to scream but her scream was silent; it was

3

strangled in her throat by cold white hands. And, as well as the angst, she had something on her mind, which she conveyed in a letter to her sister at Weatherall.

28 February, 19...

Dear Else,

I am to be married tomorrow - this you know - but just the fact of it, not the impending sense of doom. He will know after the wedding, then where shall I be? What shall I do, Else, in any case?

It happened last night when we stopped at Longnor. The trap broke down and we had to change a wheel; we stayed at our Jimmy's for the night. I was forgetting you weren't there when they came to pick me up - they came in a pony-and-trap from Brewston. Tristan he's called and he's younger than me, but - I don't know why - I fell for him. As soon as I saw him I felt, 'This is it!' I felt my belly fall away. After that it was easy really, easier than I could ever have imagined. His brother Cecil got on with the repair and I'm sure he never noticed a thing. Good job, too - I'm sure I was flushed! Tristan was very shy as well - must have been thinking about Alderman, his dad. I thought of him, too, but not for long. It's a bit of a contract for our dad: now he doesn't have to provide for me. Sounds sad, but there it is. Both of them would kill me if they knew! So, please, not a word - you're my 'confidante'.

Tomorrow is my wedding-day - ha, ha! You're the only one I wish were coming. It's cold and complex here already, and Tristan is avoiding me. He doesn't want Alderman to find out, either.

Your loving sister and bride-in-white,

Jess

There was no reply from her sister Else to Jessie's letter of the 28th., and the wedding took place in the little church at Elmsworth, and it was cold and damp and bleak and bare. A brother of Alderman's gave Jessie away. There were photographs afterwards on a hummocky mound, for all the world like an incipient grave. Alderman was proud and nervous, and at the reception, after a few drinks, he gave vent to the adage, 'Marriage maketh man,' to which all agreed and to which some added, 'Aye, and tha'll be provin' it again toneet!' 'Enough o' that, enough o' that!' Alderman said, solicitously turning to his bride, the gorgeous, dark, desirable Jessie, whose blood was mounting to her face. 'I correct myself,' he said, resuming: '*Some* marriages make *some* men,' while the eyes of the dark, desirable Jessie sought out the face and the form of Tristan.

He had wanted to avoid the whole thing: it was a torture and a nightmare to him, the whole thing. He had slipped into the church and stood at the back, while his brother Cecil acted as usher, showing the meagre congregation, all local people, to their seats. The wedding itself was a further turmoil, for wasn't Jessie now rightfully his? She belonged to him in body and blood. And yet she was going through with it. When it came to the moment when the vicar asked, 'Wilt thou take this man to be thy lawful wedded husband, to have and to hold, in sickness and in health, till death you do part?' she answered, 'Yes.' And what else could she have answered, pray?

But he was thrust into the pit of himself, into the place where no holds hold. It was bleak and sepulchral like the day outside, like the dark wind moving among the trees. He was back to the narrow bed of himself, the unholy place from which he wanted to escape. And, momentarily, he *had* escaped, had been drawn up into something else. But the seal of the grave was on him again, the blank foreboding of dissolution. It warred in him with his new-found love, that moment plucked from time and trouble, when, spare and vulnerable and tender as a shoot, he had lain with Jessie on the bank beneath the trees. It was coming back to him now, the memory of it; it was flooding and flushing the greyness out. And yet here she was, saying yes; she was being literally given away. How far was she being given away? Whose death was it that would keep them apart? Everything turned and churned in him: he was connected now; there was no way out.

## 2

Mrs. Alderman Dakin accepted her husband, as wives had to, like it or not. On their wedding-night he was quite a different man from what he had been the day before: he was relaxed, jovial, self-assured, with none of that daylight twitchiness about him. He seemed to have entered into himself, to have become in himself what he was outwardly: a farmer, a landowner, with a beautiful young bride. And she in her turn was moving towards him, dimly, darkly, unexpectedly. She liked it when he picked her up and carried her over the threshold of their room; she liked his hale strength, blue eyes, fresh complexion. Taking her gently by the shoulders, he said:

- You're a fine lass, Jess.

But there was no response. Though her shoulders were beautiful, rounded to his touch, there was within herself no response. And, as she stood there - head lowered, waiting -, as she seemed aloof, adrift, withdrawn, he said:

- Where are you, lass?

- I don't know, she replied. It's all so new to me.

- I know it is, lass. An' I can wait.
- O, no, she said. You don't have to wait.

There was within her the urge to say yes, to say it from soul-depths up to the sky. It wasn't something she waited for, pondered over, conjured through her mind: it was the chord of her, the nerve, the essence, which by the enunciation she became. Yes she was from top to bottom, and that was her beauty, her passion, her fate. Standing there meekly, absently, roundly she compelled his desire in spite of herself. And he wanted her blindly, like a man possessed, for whom at this moment the time had come. In entering her he entered himself, he entered into full possession of himself. It was as if, until now, he had never quite arrived; he had never been a man four-square on the earth. Now he was here-and-now with her, caught up in the fire's flame licking the sky - so much so that he hardly noticed her: he performed on her an *act* of love. And she was prone, parting, dark, accepting, feeling him inside her like some distant thing. She had to fake the blood, that was all, which she did with a bodkin concealed about her clothes. Involuntarily she held him to her, pulled his huge, mute strength into her. She was Mrs. Dakin now, in deed as well as word.

The effect on Tristan was instant and impelling: he felt even more of an outcast now. The new situation tortured him, as Jessie, become strategic and ambiguous, avoided him - or so he thought. He mooned and moped about the place, as young men will, who are basically unsettled, while the forked seed of Jessie's destiny grew, mutely, immutably, in its own other way. He began to talk constantly of leaving home: he could go to Agricultural College, he said, marry, settle down, find a place of his own. Alderman seemed happy with this initiative and actively encouraged him to go. He had become aware of Tristan's restlessness and attributed it to growing pains or the susceptibilities of adolescence. Life was catching up with him, and where could he go and what could he do to prepare himself for the adult world? School was a bore - he had already left - and the only option open to him was farming. He would take it, of course; he would go away.

Life, however, has its own take to tell, different from this tale I am telling. With late June came hay-making time: there was that ancient richness in the land. Tristan revived; his spirit revived. He was quite looking forward to going now.

One evening, as they were coming back from the fields, Jessie caught hold of his arm and said:
- Tristan, I'm going to have a baby.
- What's that to me? he said surlily.
- It might just be yours, that's all, mightn't it?
- But we 'anna seen each other for months.

6

And he strode away from her briskly, across the land.

That night Jessie did not sleep: her feigned indifference crumbled in on her. It had all been a fake and a sham, a deception: she felt herself a liar deep down. As she lay adrift in her foreign bed, the walls came down and she was thrown out, exposed. Sharp shards of sunlight blenched her like a weed. Where was she now? She was nowhere. She was in one of those bowges of the soul which Dante and Virgil visited once - except that now it didn't belong to any inverted Hieratic Order: it was the sum of Nothing, a No-place, a Void. And she went down through it, her soul stripped bare, what she called herself scraped down to the bone. It was only in her witness-soul that she survived.

The torment of the world was her torment, too, and it poured into her like an agony. She was on the inverted downward Spiral, the Journey-in-darkness in the temple-dark Wood. Wherever she looked it was gnarl and seethe, tree-trunks broken and paining from the light. The roots of the trees had been worked and stretched, and they lay now taut across the earth like knotted veins. No Way-markers here, no Signs, no comforting, commanding, corresponding 'Thou shalts'. For all was bleakness and darkness here, in this universal Undercountry of the Blind, this terrible, sheer, shorn, blank Golgotha, the unfed Garden before the Cross.

She reached the bottom of the Pit about dawn, when a pale light was streaking the eastern sky and tears and sleeplessness had worn her out. She turned to Alderman, who was sleeping still, and threw her arms like a child around his bulk. She slept then softly, as a child might sleep, whose instant tragedy has been dissolved. She dreamed of a place, an Open Space, into which she walked, uncluttered, nude. Surrounding it was a grove of trees, an oval of them, and she was in the Egg. It stretched away from her as she went, opening up to the parallel sky, and the two natures, the white and the yolk, blended in her from earth to sky. She was, in her own earth-nature, whole - young, ripe, tender, luscious as a fruit - and also she possessed the nature of heaven: it was plain, strong, clear as an open book. And she walked in That, as she walked upon the earth: she was naked and undivided in herself. The Clearing was peopled - she noticed it now -, it was opening up in the mind's space always. All people always were flowing through it, like tiny atoms or motes of light. Imperishably moving, they came and went.

Then, on a small mound, she caught sight of Tristan; he was beckoning to her through the scales of the light. The scales fell away and he was naked, pristine, holding out a slender arm to her. She knew then, in her soul of souls, that her whole existence lay with him; the essence of her existence lay with him: he was the primordial other reality, herself. And what had happened in the deep-wound night, on the bank beneath the

7

trees in February, was as final and absolute as Death itself. There was no returning from that place.

She awoke to find herself thrilled and cleansed, as if a million volts had passed through her. The hair on her forehead was matted with sweat, and she turned through the phases of a lateral gyre to the place where Alderman had got up and gone.

Tristan, however, held aloof, having solved, if only superficially, the question of turmoil for himself. The outer action was good enough. Time dilated; the summer season passed . . .

They had been together in the fields behind the house, where the corn now stood in patient stooks - Jessie, Alderman, Tristan, Cecil and an Irishman called Patrick, hired for the season -, when the harvest moon came up over Haddon, its red meniscus bursting into view. The very intensity of it made a space, as when a hand moved unwanted objects from a table, and Jessie and Tristan walked into it, while the rest of the party, dusty and aglow, made for the house, a wash and a drink.

But the two of them made a fused column of their own; they made a track for the moon to rise. And it rose in them, rich, red, ripe, rotund; it climbed all heaven in orange and gold. They were its secret investiture. The tides of heaven were touching the earth; they were swelling and coming in through the moon. And the moon, like an eye, was the place of passage, its silver light shining on the patient earth; it was a place, in the furling of its silvery tide, of transmutation from form to form. They were rising in it as the tide might rise, as the moon did rise in its round, white tract. Colossally, deeply the earth heaved; the harvest rotated in Jessie's eyes. She was giving herself up utterly, as the good earth gives, unstintingly, to this, her really first nuptial night, her rite of passage in the sacred moon. She watched her discarded daylight self go by like flotsam, broken sharp shards. Was this herself - what she called herself - , this jagged amalgam of bits and pieces? And where was she now, if not in that?

She was somewhere, surely, between heaven and earth, in the moment of passage between the two. The earth was yielding up its rich harvest secret in dark exhalations on the September night, and they were held suspended between heaven and earth, feeling out, obeying, following the rhythm that drummed in them silently, tide upon tide. They were back, it was true, to the Clearing in the trees, to the parallel, infinite sky, the First Place. And she had the thrust and the truth of him now; she had the Knowledge of him, ancient and dark. They possessed it together like some ancient secret, like an unspoken oath wedding heaven and earth. And they carried it thence forever in their hearts, as an affirmation of having been 'there', in that timeless Place which hovers behind the world and from which all lives and loves derive.

8

It was with them now from that night on; it was living and palpable in the air. Even Alderman noticed it, and he said as much to Jessie:
- The lad's looking better.
He had already, on more occasions than one, sought her counsel on how Tristan was, encouraged her even to 'speak to him'. To avoid suspicion she had generally declined, but now she saw - it was quite transparent - that he regarded her as an intermediary, the means through which he might know his own son. He was a simple man, this Alderman, a countryman bred up to farming, for whom human complexity was just too much. And so he began to defer to Jessie, partly out of a kind of gallantry, seeing the woman as superior, and partly because he felt he blundered whenever relationship became too dense. 'How is the lad?' he had asked very often, not even calling him by his name. But now he could see he was looking better and, as a fond father, he felt quite glad.

The migrant time of autumn came; it was time for Tristan to go to College. Jessie was holding on to herself, she, who until now, in spite of herself, had been encouraging him to leave and make his way. Everyone came to the station with him, leaving Gyp, his beloved dog, behind, to slink away quietly, as dogs do when we go. Alderman, on the whole, refrained from advice, though he did say something about 'managing your money', 'being careful', Polonial precautions. Cecil made sure he had all he needed and even bought his ticket for him. Jessie affected cheerfulness.
But here was the train he was due to take, and here he was, saying good-bye to them all. The train puffed in with its small caravan; passengers alighted; the milk was put in. Nothing would be quite the same again: he knew it evenly, like a stratum in the soul. One can never go back to the same place again, for everything changes, ineluctably. And he felt in his heart, as he said good-bye, in that little death which is saying good-bye, that the texture of his life, rich, fulsome and fraught, was being pulled ineluctably apart. He would come back, of course, quite soon, it wasn't that; in no time at all he'd be there again.
The train gave a whistle, a snort and a huff, and, like some errant animal, it chugged away.

3

On 30 November, right on cue, Jessie gave birth to a bouncing baby girl. She was a child unusual from the start. The muscular midwife came over from Elmsworth and was ready with forceps, hot water, soap. There were, however, no complications and the new-born mite nearly raised the roof.

Behind and beyond the house is the Moor, a largely untenanted tract of land, a freak gritstone cap in the limestone terrain. Across it and dipping to the nearest neighbours', it is said by the locals - and local people know - that the cry on that night was unlike any other: though the last wolf in England had been shot dead at Wormhill 150 years ago, perhaps it was him again, perhaps it was the wolf. In any event it was strange, it was unworldly. A kind of legend grew up around her, that she wasn't wholly a natural child: somehow she had been superin.posed. Was ageing Alderman her father, too? Didn't 'that woman' frequent other places? Was *she* all she was supposed to be? Thus, a net was flung about the child almost as soon as she was born, a net of rumour and superstition, the only answer to which was flight. She found her flight on the waiting Moor, on that lonely, denuded, unwanted piece of ground.

And yet, in the unwitting world of the child, she was happy enough, as she grew day by day. She followed Alderman about the place, as he fed and watered hens, collected eggs; she sat with him and Cecil as they did the evening milking. Or, around the house, she followed her mother, this child of forked Fortune, Emma Dakin.

4

Tristan hated Stiff College at first. It stood on a bluff overlooking the Trent and was said to be the finest place in the Midlands. The lecturers came from here, there and everywhere, and it fostered a sort of Public School cloisteredness. Indeed, many of its students were ex-Public School men, possessing acres of land between Humber and Severn, and they talked frequently and blithely of stocks and shares, motor-cars and going up to London. For a Derbyshire lad, with his close, cornered life, it was all a bit much and he kept to himself; he tended to be only nominally there. And yet, as Alderman wrote to him, it was a golden opportunity; he should make the most of it.

There was a battle going on inside him, the contour of which he was ignorant of, and it was as dramatic and real as the coming Great War. For it was still possible, at that time, to live off, by and through the country as the stem and source of one's existence, without worrying all-too-much about stocks and shares, investments, politics. There was still some wholeness in the land. This, mutely, he felt was being threatened: indeed, it was going under rapidly. It was not so much in the machines themselves, which in many ways were a blessing and a help, but in the implacable march of mechanical Progress, the nineteenth century monster-god. Though about to reach its first nemesis, it was strident, unquestioned, apocalyptic, strong and no-one, seemingly, could get to the flaw, no-one could tell it as it really was. Nor did Tristan have words for it. Yet he felt it dumbly, at unfathomable depth; it worked in him, inarticulately. One could not go back - that much was obvious - and how would he connect with all this, this rapidly moving, dry outer world? It was a mystery and a torment to him.

Then there was Jessie, the world of home, the close and intimate sphere, that bond. He wanted her often through the darkening days, though it was quite impossible; her time was drawing near. Quite impossible, and here was the card: it was a baby girl and they had called her Emma. He hadn't the faintest what would happen now. He tried to phase himself out of that mode, away from the place he had been to with Jessie. And yet it was in him and of him like his blood: it was there objectively, beyond his will. The lost world turned about the two of them; they were thrown up, illumined, as above a Waste Land.

He realised then that he had travelled very far, much further than his fellows on the outward trajectory. He was shocked by the way they talked about women, their weekend escapades in Nottingham and London. That all belonged, for him, to the same waste world, to the world that was coming, inevitably. Its shadow was darkening, deepening, spreading; their talk was the chatter of dying men. They were like overgrown schoolboys, smutty and vulgar, these young men who thought they owned the world. And was it he alone who felt uneasy, sensed the discrepancy, saw the flaw? Or was it something about men's minds, that they had to have it proved by several million dead? He wondered then what *he* could do: was this blank, unfathomable Slough of Nothing, this wash of ruination redeemable? He didn't feel it was, for himself. He wanted to escape the glare, go back to a place which was warm, rich and whole.

'No, I am no hero,' he thought, as a farm-hand drove him towards the grey stack of buildings, Christmas nearly come now, up the rough-rocked track. Yes, this was Brewston, the sycamores in a ʄan, and here was Gyp, come running forth to meet him. She leapt into the trap, then ran round and round the yard, always coming back to make sure that he was real. And real he was, indubitably, as ancestral in his way as stone, grass and tree. And yet there was a minor shift, a scarcely perceptible change of key: the same world certainly, always the same, but in it now a new catalyst, a furthering, invisible, subtle eye - his.

Jessie noticed it straight away: he was simultaneously there and not - at once a part of their daily life and away, aloof, an observer looking on. It was as if he had wandered into a theatre and were, at one and the same time, actor and spectator. He still took his cues but not always, as before; he sometimes now didn't answer as before but took one step further in the travel of his mind, stopping and sensing the unlettered pause. By this she knew that he had been elsewhere, he had been away from the close-knit fold.

Her attention, however, was very much on Emma, who was a gurgling little bundle just a few weeks old. She drank solidly at the breast every four hours or so, slept abundantly and, when awake, had a thousand small noises of pleasure and delight. She cried very rarely but, when she did, it was like a repetition of the night of her birth, so loud it brought the whole household running. Then she was quiet again for days on end.

Tristan never loved her as Alderman did (perhaps it was simply that he was too young and had so much growing of his own to do). In the end, the Dakin signature notwithstanding, she really resembled none of them and was from the start, even physically, her own person, original her. A little blessing she was, come to stay with them.

They all got into the Christmas spirit, foraging in drawers for streamers and things, cutting down a small fir-tree in the copse. Soon there were sprigs of holly along the mantelpiece, showers of tinsel down the corners of the room, then coloured streamers strung diagonally across it, fastened to the lamp which hung over the table. Shiny, bright baubles hung in the tree, and these were the delight of Emma's eye, as she stretched out a tiny mite's hand to touch them. The light on them glanced and danced in her - with the steep flames' flicker, at the opening of a door, or when the soft sun, from the mirror opposite, passed across them like a gentle hand. For she was herself that very light.

She was really the focus of everything, so much so that it was by accident that Jessie and Tristan, looking for holly, found themselves together in Gladwin's Copse.

- What's happening to you? she asked him point-blank.
- I dunno, he said. I suppose I'm growing up.
- Is that what you call it? Seems like estrangement to me.
- Strange, but not exactly estrangement: it's like being in two places at once.
- You were and are such a boy, you know.

She said it not unkindly and took his arm: it was her way of re-establishing parity with him. If he had grown in reflection and detachment, then so had she in motherhood. He was no whit or way her superior, with his hooded looks and lofty disengagement. She wasn't going to have any of it!

- We have to be very careful, she said.

It was as if she were giving him a sign. Both of them might go their own ways now, might spread like two streams from a common source, but nonetheless it was here and that they *were*, in this now nude place beneath the trees. It was a chaste Station where, singly and as one, they met in a flame which was soft like the sun. The frosty grass crackled, the holly shone, and they walked arm in arm back up to the house.

When Christmas Day came it was a jolly affair, and Alderman was in his element. There were presents all round, a roaring fire in the grate and, crisped and roasted, a turkey on the table. Cecil, who had invited a girl up from town, was his usual active, attentive self, while Alderman officiated at the carving of 'the bird', very much like the vicar at the Eucharist. It was, 'A bit of breast, Jessie?' or, 'How about a leg for you, Cecil?' and, 'What would the young lady care for?', etc. The 'parson's nose' caused quite a stir, and among the florid faces, innuendo and good cheer there was a wealth of crackers going off, home-made elderberry wine being drunk, and finally, brought in by Martha, the cook, steaming and flaming in its sauce, the Christmas pud.

The Christ-child, Emma, gave her blessing to the event, as, with her twenty-five days' worth of wisdom, she lay in her cot in the corner by the tree, periodically shrieking with joy in that inchoate way which children have, who still enjoy the bliss of pure Being. She conducted that joy and spread it among them, a blessing of Grace, a gift of the Tree. It was there, soft and lambent, like a gentle flame, and it informed their hilarity and underpinned their good cheer. They did not know and could not have said what it was that made that particular Christmas special, how everything in that lambent light was transformed into a higher power of itself. And yet it was real, and more real, than things, the material concretions solidified there. It leapt up, bubbling, with the wine and the light; it danced in and among them, cogently. It was the harmonisation, suddenly, of discord, where discord - *all* discord - unresolved falls to a level in its secret source. Step then over, Dakins-of-a-Day. Take the Journey to your secret Source.

And, indeed, there were resolutions in plenty, when Christmas was succeeded by New Year. It was a time to change and put things right, a time to be new and different again. But how can one change and what can one do, how can one travel to a different Ground? It seems, since resolutions are always broken, that it lies outside the power of Man. It is a gift of the strange gods, suddenly, like the Visitation on Christmas Day. And, even then, it is precarious; we sense, even in the enjoyment of it, the moment of enjoyment slipping away.

So it was with Jessie and Tristan - with Tristan, in particular: he ached and burned to be away with her, along some trajectory all their own. But she, though with him in her heart of hearts, was circumspect as women are, who bear the burden of generation, the day-in day-out sustaining of things. And, like an irritant, this made it worse: it chafed him, like a yoke about his neck. He was wild to take some instant action, to go off somewhere, anywhere.

- What about Emma? Jessie said.
- We'll take her with us.
- Where to?

Stop. For, indeed, there was nowhere for them to go. Unlike John Manners and Dorothy Vernon, the legendary lovers of Haddon Hall, they could not in the wraiths and sweep of night be carried thence on some princely charger. There was Emma to feed, the cows to milk, and they were living, for God's sake, in the real world: they were real. No clap of midnight thunder for them, no lightning on the bridge, no facile exit.

And yet he ached and pined for it, and, not getting it, he became morose. For Jessie, also, it was a torment, though she was more pinned down by necessities, pushed by necessities to draw on reserves, the like of which he didn't know: channels and focuses women know. She saw in him that she must go to him, she must actually save him from himself. The cast of doom had come over him; he wore it upon him like a brooding mask.

And so the task was on her again: that of making real what was like a ghost. She could not bear him like this, insubstantial, moping and drifting about, unmade. She would force him and free him from himself.

They packed Alderman off to the Monday Cattle Market, amid much shouting and coming-back-and-checking, until finally he felt that things were all right; he had the right stick, the right clothes on: all right. Minnie, the kitchen-maid, would look after Emma, who was sleeping quite soundly - all right for an hour. They would go and check the sheep down by Gladwin's Copse.

And there Jessie filled him with herself, taking the Void from him into her, replenishing him and restoring his blood. He didn't want it in a way, not the actual renewed engagement: he rather liked being an absent Hamlet, brooding and storming about the place, suicidally engrossed in himself. But, for her, all that was mere masturbation, the fay place in him which hadn't grown. She was going to push him through that place; she was going to push him to such a pitch he would never, ever be able to retract. He would *have* to become the man he was.

And she wanted the totem strength of him, the phallic power to touch and taste, the surge and the seethe of it, deliciously. She didn't want the love of him, no human conjunction, no making love, but only to feel his pulse and power, as he stood above her, his back against a tree. And as he stood there, hard against the tree, he was moved by the unutterable beauty of her, of her body bursting from its sheath of clothes. It curved and stretched all over him, covering him with its warm, wide mouth.

14

There was nothing in the universe except her mouth, the juices of it flowing over and around him, himself ingested and lost in her. It passed under, through and round him, like the sea. Shards of his Void were falling on her, in the form of bark scratched from the tree, as she locked her hands in behind his thighs and led him towards his ecstasy. For they were out of the human element altogether: they were transposed to a mode of Cult-Priestess and Lingam. But slowly, carefully it had to be done, as the long, primeval Rite required. It had to be laid on with flowers and oaths, with cries of, 'O, God!' from Tristan now. He was her deity and she had completed her ritual, making, not love, but more a form of worship, an opening on an unwindowed World.

He could barely accept it, nonetheless, this primal sexuality of the woman: he was disturbed by it, as men often are. It was too much, too strong, too undisguised. He felt his blood come back towards her; he wanted the human link with her. But this was at quite a diffurent level: it rubbished all the human pretence. It was a consummation of its own strong kind, at the Place where all fires flame and flare, where Beauty boundless calls to its own and the blue vein in the rock is the salt sea's vein.

But she was out and away already: the very intensity had cast her forth. While he came uneasy, craving, trailing, her mind was on Emma and the rest of the day. He followed her almost on the way back, oblivious of everything but her, the root-connectedness he had with her. And she was magnificent, cutting the air, laying the air back in swaths like sheaves. She was suddenly the potency of all the earth, its patient heaving, its clovenness. It was there in the rocking and the swaying of her limbs, in the tossing of her head, the black hair billowing; it was there in her face, which flushed in the wind. How could a man forbear to love her, when her breasts were the aching acres of the earth, rich, ripe, round to the kiss of the sun, and her arms were beautiful, moulded, firm, that took him in and gave him home?

It would not be easy, nevertheless. For here they were now, back at the farm, and Jessie was holding Emma in her arms. She was back now in that sainted World. The child was gurgling, laughing, sucking, and Jessie was utterly and completely with her. This was the thing that made her special: the fact that what she did she did wholly, without residue, totally absolved from the future and the past. And with it, of it, surrounding this absorption, was a haloed focus of radiance, as if the very lack of overspill had harnessed the energy lost in dispersion. She was crouching now, putting Emma, fed and warm, back in her cot for another long sleep. 'It won't be easy,' thought Tristan at the door.

Alderman came back earlier than usual and Jessie greeted him affectionately, standing up on tip-toes to kiss him. As if by magic Emma awoke, and he threw her up, shrieking and shouting, in the air. 'Up just once!' he said - she knew what he meant -, though he threw her up always three times or more. He'd had a good day: bought some young beef stores. He seemed to be on very good form.

Thus, the circle of husband-wife-child closed around them and Tristan was cut out. He was the alien, after all. The glow which had hung about Jessie since morning, which, foolishly, he had thought derived from him, was there with lambent intensity still. It was there for Emma, awake or asleep; it was there for Alderman, jolly, bluff or stupid. It wasn't her (or his) possession but, seemingly, a light of its own, a light of Nature, indifferent and free. It was there with her; it seemed it *was* her. Yet the beauty of her body did not compose it.

Jessie was free and at ease in it, as a fish is free and at ease in water. It was her subtle element. Did her actions, then, belong to her - or were they merely random offshoots, swift fish-dartings in a glancing world, a world which, in spite of its apparent solidity, appropriated itself at every moment, shot through with light, transparent really, and having its being in Consciousness? It might seem so, she was so detached.

Tristan watched them go up the stairs, and a sea of fury broke in him. Where was their special relationship now, where love's linking? Upstairs: she was there. She was there in the creaking of the green sycamores, as they bent about the house in the soughing wind. She was there, striding forth still; she was there, lying down. It was her mouth, the wind's mouth, drawing in the night. Then that silence, which was worst of all. He picked up a mug and threw it against the wall.

- Are you all right, lad? came Alderman's voice.

- Yes, dad, I'm all right. I just dropped a mug.

But still she was there, in the broken mug's lip. It was leering at him, unequivocally. It mocked his juvenile outburst of rage, his self-contracted war with himself. If she were free and happy, then what was wrong? He saw it, but only with part of himself. The rest of him sought the refuge of the night.

He closed the kitchen door quietly, leaving Gyp inside. She didn't make a murmur: good girl. The trees seemed quieter now, more gathered, though the wind still moved in them like a hand. Some of the rage of the night had gone, dispersed in the space between heaven and earth, and the stars looked coolly down on him. He could take a long walk; it would be the best thing. And where should he go to but the Moor, that crisp and protrusive rock terrain, which occupied the summit of their land like a fastness? It was always a couple of degrees colder there, and he buttoned up his coat against the prospect.

From the Moor he could see the lights of Bull Close, the nearest neighbour to Brewston Farm. He would have liked to be down there suddenly, to have vaulted the space with its trees and walls; he would have liked to be in a different ambience. But this, equally, was juvenile, he knew: it was a place made up from his own scattered reactions. The Marriotts were misers - everyone knew that.

And yet he needed a resolution. He found it by simply looking up, the straightforwardest thing he could have done. And there was the moon, ancestral and bold, its blank, bland face a quarter averted; there was the dark side, the hint of her. It was Jessie becoming his Teacher again. This time, she was saying, he shouldn't stir; he should simply allow himself to be absorbed, as the moon itself absorbs another's light. The swath of the dark-side-of-the-moon, which was her hair, fell across his face like the soft fall of the night. And he was with her, absolved, in her falling hair, as, into and through her, she released his desire.

There was nothing left now but to go back to the farm. He had reached some Station of Peace within himself; precariously, temporarily he was absolved from Darkness. Yet it still moved about him in a swirl, like the night which reasserted itself when the cloud banked up and obscured the moon. He walked round and round in a circle on the Moor, as if by that he might abjure the tumult, or bury, kill, obliterate, put to flight the swarm of madness which threatened him. Slowly, slowly it was ebbing away, as when at evening the rooks behind the house gathered cacophonously and then were still. Slowly it was subsiding, like that. And here he was, walking erect on the Moor, the rooks in their nests now, waiting, obscure.

He climbed the back- (or servants') stairs to his room, Gyp, who had lain in a curl by the door, coming up after him as she always did. She lay at his feet as he lay in bed, and when he awoke, quite refreshed, the next morning, his first sensation was of her warmth. Things warm were always a pleasure to him: they fed him what was lacking in the bleak, damp place. And then he thought he had not done too badly; he had salvaged something from the previous day. He was feeling really quite pleased with himself.

One look at Jessie was enough to disconcert him, as she moved about swiftly in the coming morning light: she was helping Minnie put out the breakfast things. She hardly seemed to notice him, so much was she assumed by the task at hand. 'I love you, Jess,' he said to her awkwardly in the kitchen, but the Edge of her, their sharp Situation cut him off without a glance. She skipped past him into the dining-room, saying over her shoulder for all to hear:

- Bring the knives out, Tristan, dear.

He was back in the uncontoured, the insubstantial World, the place where Measure has lost its hold. He was calling to her, but she wasn't there. The shortfall, however, was basically his, since he wanted the continuity of her, the always-being-there in some paradisal place. He

17

could not accommodate the shift of levels, the way she moved from each to each, leaving nothing of herself behind. For him there was always some residue, a bag he would have to come back and collect: he could never quite finish with anything. This made him vulnerable to the vicissitudes of life and, in response, he made up little schemas, which would help him cope when the moment arrived. When it did arrive, however, it was always slightly different, and what was intended to be pertinent action was always slightly false in fact. His mind slewed off, it missed the nuances; he didn't quite manage to be there at the time. And so his life had a frayed-edge quality. He was almost here-and-now, but never really quite.

In through the gap came the tumult of his feelings, as if there were nothing left of him, only this vacant gap of ground, which urgent urges rushed to fill. Gladwin's Copse it would have to be, whatever the time-lag, whenever the time. Jessie also knew it for herself, as she waited and watched him seething there, dovetailing her actions, letting him boil. There would be no complacency, no pause, no peace.

Again Time spread in its wanton way, as Jessie, intact still, watching, wary, kept her hold on everything and everybody: Emma, Alderman, the servants, Tristan. And had she not had her special gift, that poise of soul between heaven and earth, ancient as both are contiguous and holy, she certainly could not have managed it all, and the whole thing would have exploded long before it did.

In the end it was almost time for him to go; the January days were picking up. The Cattle Market called Alderman away, and everyone was busy with something or other. They were going to 'check the sheep' again, to count them in the greyness of mist and wall, the bundly bodies looming and lumped. They were going down to Gladwin's Copse.

But the balance was tipping away from them, from any precarious hold they might have had. Tristan was agonised within, as lovers are who soon must part. And he was bearing his agony boyishly, badly: he was angry, he was lustful, he was determined to hurt. His eyes were dark like the dark spears of the ash, as he smote the silent air with an ash-wand's swishing sound. It was only his tenderness holding him back.

He could not admit it to himself, and yet the impulse was coming from her: she wanted him, *all* of him, every last drain. And that included everything he was, from highest heaven to deepest earth: she wanted every resonance. Her own deep-point, the point of guilt, through which everything becomes allowable, was opening up like a wound in her. It was wanting him to do everything to her, anything and everything he wanted to do. Still he held back, hesitant.

It was she who prompted him, urged him, compelled him to do to her as she had done. Vengeance was his now, compounded with desire. He exacted it justly, blindly, strongly, from some primitive hidden corner of himself to which she had led him, inexorably. He had assumed the god he was for her, the god imperious, implacable, furious, the fire-eating Yahweh whose slave she was. It was wonderful, also, to be his slave, to feel his hot tongues pressing her, to be so abased she was nothing to him: simultaneously agony and bliss. And the bliss licked up in new, fine tongues, as slowly he took her on the ancient earth, gave back the self he had held above, became so infused with her they could not stop but ran on and on in the body's subtle reaches, past every milestone of sensation, great and small, till they heaved up, laughing and crying, both, on the rich, red pasture of the Further Field. From then on and for ever they were linked, they were conjoined. Neither of them spoke on their way back to the house.

5

Tristan's youth was disintegrating and he was becoming much more fully a man. They noticed the difference when he got back to Stiff: he moved with a confidence and spoke with a directness, which hitherto he had not possessed. In the company of the landed Public School men, with their præternatural self-assurance, he no longer felt phased and clammed, closed down: he could talk to them on equal terms. Only of Jessie did he mention nothing, while they talked loudly of their Christmas conquests.

He lived suspended between Night and Day, between the daytime world of markets and prices and the night-time mystery of love with her. He pulled her body over him like a cloak, and her body was night's mantle, with its thrill of steady stars. She ached and echoed through him like the call of ancient night; she had left her rainbow spectrum in the weather of his heart. It lay there, arched, her seal, her signature.

He threw himself into college work. The Market opened its secrets to him, as he studied its fluctuations and cycles (pig-, short- and long-term and others besides). Based on these and ignorant of the magnitude of, first, the Great War and, then, the Depression, he came up with a fifty year forecast for farmers. The life of grains and grasses was specially attractive, and his suggestions for hybridising certain strains of wheat, so as to produce an earlier-cropping variety, were adopted unaltered in 1943 by the wartime Ministry of Agriculture and Fisheries. His thesis on the subject, 'The A to Z of Grasses', while not so encyclopædic as the title suggests, is nevertheless a classic of its kind and holds pride of place on the library shelves at Stiff.

Meanwhile, the international situation worsened. In this small community, as well as more generally, the consensus of opinion was in favour of war. It would clear the air and do away with superfluities;

also, in a post-Darwinian sense, it would decide who the finest and the fittest were. For farmers, too, there would be special benefits: the government would cosset them and prices would soar.

Tristan, on the tightrope between Outer and Inner, barely balanced above the Abyss, considered the situation, albeit vaguely. The Triple Alliance, of which the papers talked constantly, was a source of strength, as was the Entente Cordiale. Really it was Germany that was causing all the trouble, committed as she was to the build-up of her navy, which would challenge Britain's supremacy on the seas. Then, related, was the matter of the Balkans, where the creaking-gate Austro-Hungarian Empire - and a good job, too: they were Monarchists, at least! - was holding out against the surge for independence on the part of Bosnians, Croats and Serbs. Obviously a work of necessary containment, with the Great Powers, heavy as dinosaurs, moving and manoeuvering precariously.

When on 28 June, 1914, Gavrilo Princep, the young Serbian revolutionary, shot Archduke Ferdinand dead in Sarajevo, there seemed little hope of a reprieve. The moves were set, the Schlieffen-Plan in place, and even the Socialists supported their governments by voting war credits: the flag-wavers had won. Grey, his high-wire agility notwithstanding, laboured in vain for a settlement but was forced to conclude, some five weeks later, that 'the lamps are going out all over Europe.'

The polarities, Tristan's metaphor, continued, highlighting the tension between Possibilities and Worlds: joining up, farming; the Land, the War. Some of his contemporaries at Stiff were gone already; they had been among the first to go. And wasn't it, surely, the honourable thing to do? Wasn't it, in some sense, the *clean* thing to do? The Field of Honour had returned to human life, that instantaneous human engagement which elevated one to the status of a hero and did away, at one fell swoop, with all the pettiness, misery and filth. Yes, it was good and noble to go; he would be going soon. And yet he didn't go.

Some other movement turned in him, some other necessity of mute indwelling, some navel-nurturing: the Love of the Land. He could always feel the pull of it. Even at Stiff it was not the same: one was learning to manage, direct, control, while his heart-of-hearts abhorred all that. He wanted and felt the flame of the land - its dark, unspoken, secret places, its abiding rhythms, the cycles of its seasons. These nurtured and sustained him as nothing else did, as nothing in life - he knew it dimly - ever would. It broke over him, as Jessie broke, in wave-upon-wave of sheaves of earth thrown back, when the plough moved patient inwards from the headland and threw back the purpling swaths of earth, riddled and lifting like pages turned. There was a Knowledge upturned from the waiting Earth, a Knowledge which only She possessed, something which glanced and danced in the soul, a kind of deep, dark, iridescent Magic, which issued in the glyphs with pictorial Power and was lost in the linear stridings of Thought. The land was patient, infinite, mute: to those who could listen it could and did tell all. And yet it was becoming more and more of a commodity, a usable, wastable, downtrodden thing. It was crying out for the reciprocal link it once had with Man, his sense of Being Here.

The War, in a sense, was only part of it, like the final term of an argument. It all began much further back and deeper down. The conflict was there in daily life: nations and neighbours were sparring all the time. Within him, too, as within a given Field, contradictions and stand-offs barely ceased. Any harmony was temporary and precarious, the likelihood of break-up and breakdown strong. The War - *all* war - was the mirror-image of what one lived anyway, day-in day-out. Not that this meant he shouldn't go, but certainly it put a brake on it. By this first quiet, almost involuntary involution he turned his eye, spiralling, in upon himself. He was inchoate, imperfect, barely born - it was, nonetheless, a seeing permanent and real. The enemy was us - he had an inkling of it - and it dwelt in each one of us, down beneath the skin. The enemy still, subcutaneous, endemic, when the War with Berlin and Vienna was at an end.

No, Tristan wasn't going yet, in spite of 'Your Country Needs You,' etc., in spite of that early and most provocative of public questions: 'What did *you* do in the War?' No, he was beginning to work through No, beginning to explore its fled-from Contour. He was picking up a pebble on the Infinite Beach. And that was the beginning or everything, for him.

Of all prognostications, buoyant and innocent, 'It'll all be over by Christmas' is the saddest. It was not over by Christmas, nor by the next, nor the next. It slogged on relentlessly for four whole years, revealing the destructive innards of the Model, the massive Machine which no-one could turn off. The Earth was savaged and pitted by its pounding: volumes and clusters and shot sods of earth. And then there were the trenches, her scars, bleak refuge, where, groaning and rotting, men lay in winter mud. Howitzers, mortars, bayonets and rifles - these were the tools of the Death Machine. And more tragically, more blindly, men were its tools, dispensable as they were, turned into numbers.

There was an uneasy silence about it at first, as if no-one could really believe it were true. It was true, though; the penny was dropping: a million dead Frenchmen could hardly be ignored. The call of King and Country went on, but, in a vein not dissimilar to Tristan's, its 100% self-assurance had gone. Doubt was moving in around the edges.

Tolstoy makes much of impersonal Forces, random encounters, Unforeseeables. In time of War these are much more apparent, as the little parameters are blasted apart and decisions are taken, literally, Elsewhere. We seem to inhabit a larger Theatre, where, in the stark exposure of the Stage, a heightened awareness comes to us - the logic of it all, the Unseen Hand: cables, wiring, lighting, props - and we capture for a second Life's secret Immensity, that breathing and enfolding-unfolding Action which permeates, informs and structures all we are. Then, of course, we get our little bit to do.

For Tristan the first move was leaving Stiff. In the darkening and lengthening days of the War the place was closed down: it was a luxury. Unexpectedly, then, he came back home, to the ever-patient, waiting farm. It stood in its settled eternity, as it had always stood, clustered on the hill, and it invited him, opening, back into itself, as it had known him always as boy and young man.

Nothing about it had changed at all. He could slip easily back into the established rhythm of rising at 5:20 with his brother Cecil, doing the morning milking (they had a dozen cows), then the two of them taking the milk to the station. It was all set down somewhere, running on fixed lines.

But he was no longer the person he had been before: he was driven by new imperatives. One of the things he noticed, for instance, was that the established order was utterly arbitrary. Alderman employed men but didn't use them. While he and Cecil had been toiling through the dawn, the live-in farmhand (there was always *one*) was 'tidying up', more often doing nothing, so that they arrived exhausted at school and could only scrape through in a makeshift fashion. Such unwitting injustices were plain to him now. Nor could Alderman change his ground: he was committed to this arbitrary, 'ad hoc' tack. He had no gift for organisation at all, did everything pell-mell in a kind of florid fluster, raged, stormed, cursed and gave everybody hell - everybody, that is, except the farm-men, who seemed, if anything, to be running him. Tristan realised quite simply that he was weak. In this fresh stand-off of father and son, this next necessary turning and cleaning of the lens, he had his father quite clearly in his sights, the mystique of his authority vanished and gone, while his father, he, unaltering and unaltered, did everything still in the same old way.

It was going to be uncomfortable, obviously, the Volcano working and ready to burst. A realignment of family forces was required to reintegrate the returning element. What would happen, actually? For there had been a spread, an easing, even; even Jessie had slotted back in. Cecil had his own room and liked it. Their different natures had blended in. Now Cecil would have to share again. It didn't really matter - but, then again, it did.

Alderman was the Hollow Head, like the emperor of a forsaken land. He operated on lines well-established, long-accepted, in which there was tacit faith, mute concurrence. Father was Law now, wasn't he? And yet that very Father was going; he was crumbling like a statue in the weathers of Time. Out there in the Empire he was going, too, and in all the battles from Flanders to Verdun. Whatever the outcome of the War, it was the End. Time was ticking over Him, like some unexploded bomb.

But here, at Brewston, he still went on: he had his own way of doing things. Jessie, for instance, was given no money and had to fiddle the grocery account, whenever she wanted anything for herself. She did it, of course - he never knew - though occasionally he might, when the spirit moved him, say, 'Here, lass, go and get yourself a dress.' More often than not, though, she would make it herself, pocket the difference, keep mum to him, then buy Tristan or Cecil a little gift. She was quite a mother to them, in a way.

He, meanwhile, strutted about the place, issuing orders where they weren't really needed, failing always to take the one step back which would have shown him where the reality lay. Circumstances were forever falling over him, coming in too quickly when he had a plan of sorts. For he *did* make plans, little ones, often, but they never quite cohered with what was going on. He would shout out, 'Cecil!' with a farmhand standing near, for all the world like a child in danger, who can only turn to his nearest and dearest. Ultimately, he was like a child himself, and his rule - if one can call it that - was amiable, at best.

Tristan brought tension to the family scene: it seemed stagnant to him; he was restless again. Jessie had gone back into herself, as if she had accepted her wife-and-mother lot. Cecil simply got on with it, drawing his own lines, independently, creating thereby a small pragmatic island, on which he was safe from the circumambient upheaval. It swam around him, nonetheless. It was there in the news coming back from the Front, in the April music of the sullen rain, in the tendrils of the lovers growing together again, in Alderman's fraught and swarming head. It romped and stirred and seethed around him, while he, on his own course, set due north, went on with his work, ignoring everything. He would sail through life, successful and blind.

Not so Tristan, whom Fate had singled out: his life's line and Jessie's were crossed from the start. Though spring was here once more and the flowers in Gladwin's Copse - primroses, violets, white wood anemones - were calling, freshly blinking, like a galaxy of stars; because of it, almost, the tide was on the turn. For them, as for the slaughtered, Death's note hung on the air.

It was as if their lives were wedded to the millions; and f⌐r them, too, there was no reprieve. They had walked into the Valley of the Shadow of Death, quite unawares, quite unprepared, as when one crosses a saddle in the mountains and is suddenly, dramatically, in a different place. The view stretched out before them, as it had always done, and yet it was different; everything was different. As when the sparse sun goes, the rain-clouds threaten: sharp rocks, deep drops, hard ridges, hung space. It was the land of bleakness and austerity, by entering which, along the little track, one becomes 'ipso facto' Death's familiar. And they were already there, so it seemed: they had loved one another into that Place.

Everything hung on the immediate moment, of what they could cull of ecstasy. There was no gentle letdown in amiable pastures, no link with the timed world of yesterday. If they failed they failed by a million miles and for Tristan, in particular, it was inner ruination: a blank, black icepool where the sun's blue eye had shone. For Jessie there was always the other interface, the one which, whatever the ups-and-downs, carried her forward through the seasons and the years. She was at home in it, also, in some way: in some intangible way her marriage was right. Commercial travellers, arriving at the door, would often ɔsk, 'Is your father in?' To her it was an enormous joke, and, disdaining to disillusion them, she would go and fetch him from the sheds or the fields. He was *not* her father, nevertheless, amiable duffer though he was. Even, at times, it seemed he was her child.

And she loved him also in some ancient way, in the way time-honoured by Country and Church, on a rhythm venerable, profound, osmotic, which she had absorbed initially in her childhood days at Weatherall: something to do with the land and its ways. She had brought it with her when she came to Brewston and she lived by it willy-nilly, impersonally. It was *out there*, somehow, like the dry stone walls, constructed by men's hands over centuries. Yet she also nurtured and pressed to her heart the Rose of Tristan's love, like a fatal wound.

- I've been thinking a lot about the War, he said, when they were out one day, walking among the fields. It seems, after all, it's a fellow's duty to go.
- Even when he's wanted at home
- Wanted who by?
- You know who by.

Of course he did: they were caught; they were twinned.

- I'm not sure it's best for us, either, he went on. And I can't fit back into the old routine.
- Not even with me here?

- Not even with you.

He didn't want to say, 'Especially with you,' though the words were on the tip of his tongue. He didn't want to tell her that, because of her, his life had been transposed to another pitch, one where all the ancient restraints and definitions had been thrown off like some unwanted corset. He could never have said that he didn't want her there, and he hated himself for even thinking it.

- It's different now, he said anodynely. I can't seem to gel with dad and his ways.

- He cares about you, you know, in his way.

- I know he does, but that doesn't help matters. I just can't function the way he does.

- Then function in your own way, if function you must.

- It isn't allowed.

- Am *I* allowed?

She was getting hot and angry with him: he was still such a cowering, unmade boy.

- Perhaps you'd better go, she said finally. It's none too safe here, either, after all. And I don't actually like deceiving him. I'd even thought of telling him.

- No, don't do that: he'd never understand.

- I know he wouldn't; that's the sad thing about it.

- So there *is* no solution, is there, really?

- There's Life, there's the Present, there's everything we are.

- And Death, my darling. Don't forget Death.

It was as if the grey ash-trees in Gladwin's Copse, the peeking primroses, the antic anemones had captured them, drawn them into themselves (for that was where they went now, tired of talking), elevated them, even, by a brush-stroke of their own into some more permanent Image of themselves, a haloed and facial counterpart of Love's Body flowing through the Universe. They lay there, naked, composite, redeemed, in a World which is always calling to itself, a World rich-pastured, rural, right, at the rim of which, as at the limit of sight, Light lies beckoning, balancing the Twain.

Jessie held the Icon in her heart, bathed in the tenderest and palest blue light. It was something, surely, which transcended Death: it subsumed, consumed and made them what they were. It was stronger by far than common mortal life, higher and freer than all Man's devising.

And yet there was Tristan going away, the virtual certainty of his going now. She didn't believe in freak events, in things just happening, even in wartime. No, there were subtle correspondences, avenues of meaning without a name, down which one walked, knowingly or not. Thus, Death was not some sudden Abyss but a perfectly plottable Co-ordinate, the points on which were the features of one's life. And she held him to her in that vein, not only to prevent his dying on the Field, but also, more inwardly, really, deeply to foster their Being and free them from Time.

In the end the decision was taken for him. Conscription was introduced in 1916 and, as a consequence, his call-up papers came. He was of an age to go, whereas Cecil was not. And it was estimated that, for the acreage they had, their present manpower was quite sufficient; if required, an old odd-job man from Elmsworth could help with the feeding and mucking-out.

So, in a sense, the tension was relieved: the larger Theatre had settled it. The War itself, meanwhile, had rumbled to a standstill, with neither side holding the initiative. Its whole death-or-glory ethic was at an end, as the poetic laurels, those spare spoils of war, passed from the now dead Rupert Brooke to the disillusioned (but still living) Wilfred Owen and Sassoon. In Tristan's system it was the same: he could and did also, sometimes, in a flight, go out in a white death-rush to the Beyond. More probably, however, he would simply go, treating it all as a job to be done, and slog through in muddy boots as if it were the farm. This, in the end, was the more likely option, Conscientious Objection, considered cowardice, being too insubstantial, like a distant language.

The die was cast for Jessie, too, as she knew now for certain that he would be going. It operated in her, graining the Rose. She had no time for caution any more but fled through the bleak and narrowing fields to every high pasture where Tristan could be found. Love's urgency impelled her, ask anyone. It was some faint fall or drop of soul, some passing-by of warnings, desperate and dire. She saw them, she knew them, but they were flying from her eye; they were going, centrifugally, out and away. All that mattered now was the instant's possession, that last quarter-inch of flamed intensity, the bliss-born burying and losing of oneself. It was the focusing-in of all energy, the double unsheathing of the lotus bloom, its finding and coming and merging in itself. It was the Flower of Bliss at one with itself. And they came to that, they cupped it in their hands, holding it braided or twinned, as they were. For their being had entered and folded into That, into a this-life's figure of the Other Ground, that palpable, moving, fecundating Genius, in and through which we live and are sustained.

They were not now reaching out to the Field but were in it and of it, as their element. It moved in and through them like a sound, like the Sound which is when all sounds cease. And in it, scarcely moving, hardly breathing, they were held; they were suspended, mutely, turning through the gyre. It was as if their tryst in Gladwin's Copse had been raised to a Place beyond itself, to a higher Power of itself, as if it existed in the Heart's Eye as a form of the Return from brokenness to Bliss. It was the

26

old, dumb, stupid, fractured world going back and down an Avenue of Light, like some film projected much too slowly and which, all focus wanting, blurry, botched, now by a natural, fine-tuned acceleration attains to its actual, made, precise speed. And they held to it there, in that focus of Light, in that new-found precision of body and blood, that tumultuous red-rose flowering of themselves, their new inherence in the Tree. They lay there naked, nothing-knowing now.

Thus, Tristan was made ready for the War, by the quiet Indwelling of the immutable Point. He would go out ready for the world-as-it-is. In the early summer of 1916 he was recruited into the Royal Staffordshire Regiment and ordered to report to Wellington Barracks. Six weeks later he sailed for France.

7

At first there was no news of him: somehow, he neglected to write. Then, towards autumn, a letter came, in which he said he was basically all right; the worst of it, at the moment, was the mud and the rats. There was talk of a fresh offensive in the spring, masterminded by the French general, Nivelle, but for the moment it was a matter of digging in, of endless waiting, scrappy fighting. He had never really thought it could be like this, 'but then,' he added philosophically, 'everything's different when you're at the Front.'
In fact, his letter was a deal less stirring than the one he received from Jessie in return. He opened it in his trench, down a hole in the ground, near a town since immortalised, Passchendaele.

Tristan, my dearest,

The first think is, HE KNOWS. In fact, he has known about us for some time and was only waiting for you to go away. As he says, it made things easier - now he has only me to deal with. It can't be that long since he found out, what with me being careful right up till the end. In the end, though, I think I gave myself away: I hardly sleep and I've lost a lot of weight. He must have put two and two together and made four. There must have been things I neglected in the end, little tracks and traces I covered before.

He says I'm a whore and that he's going to divorce me. He says the whole of Elmsworth thinks I'm a whore. And he can't bear the shame of it, not at his age. I tell him we didn't want to cause him shame, but he just looks and laughs in that funny way of his. He says I'm just a whore, that's all.

If there is a divorce he's sure to get Emma, and that would be the last straw for me. She's such a little girl now and we have real conversations. Yesterday, for example, she asked me about God; I said I didn't know and I almost broke down. Would a loving God make us all suffer like this, even a 'fallen woman' like me? Would Alderman call me a whore if he loved me? I loved him once - that much you know.

He has also said you are no longer his son, that you have no home here, etc. Tristan dearest, I'm sorry - it's all because of me. Perhaps it would have been better if we'd never ... you know. Only, I can't really feel that in my heart. I wish I could touch you and be close to you again. It already seems an eternity.

Different people ask after you. Old Sam and Mrs. Sam send their loving regards. They've moved to larger premises down in Bakewell, but they run it just the same as the little shop in Elmsworth. So, you see, some things just go on as before.

Do you remember when we talked of running away, of taking little Emma and just running away? Why, in heaven's name, didn't we do it then? Now it's too late and you've gone, anyway. I'm sorry, my darling, I really am - I've ruined your beautiful, rich, young life. It's not right of me even to write this letter, with you in the trenches and the bullets flying. You're risking your life for your country and me.

Tristan, my dearest, just try to forget me; forget you ever heard of me. I shall love you till the day I die, I swear it. May God forgive me and keep you safe.

    Jess

Tristan responded immediately.

My darling Jessie,

Your letter was a shock. Not that I didn't expect him to find out - I did, of course, but much, much later - after this bloody war is over, at least. He's been canny about it, as country people are. And you're suffering for both of us, that's the worst thing.

'Thy two breasts are like two young roes that are twins.' I wish I could touch them and touch you again - it's all I can think of most of the time. I wish I could walk with you again and lie with you in Gladwin's Copse. I wish I could hear Gyp's bark and Emma's laugh. It all seems so very far away, in this filthy, muddy trench, with the mortar-shells flying - and then the awful silences till they fall. Of late things have picked up considerably. We're going to try a late-autumn offensive, with a view to testing the enemy's lines. Then we'll move in in strength, come the spring - that's the word from Top Brass, at least.

The man next to me is giggling wildly. It's a kind of delirium, we're told, occasioned by shell-shock and OTT. The latter is a grisly business, really. Sometimes you go over and there's nobody there; sometimes it's a death-trap, with bodies everywhere. There's no means of knowing or of counting the dead, and there are enormous, anonymous cemeteries already. It really is a bloody nightmare, with the land so flat and ugly, too - what a contrast with the moors, the deep-cut dales, the sloping fields and the sheep I used to see.

My love, you haven't ruined my life. On the contrary, you have *made* my life. Nothing that I am is there without you: you are branded, imprinted in my every nerve and cell. Far from destroying, you have made me what I am - whatever I am, which is all that I am.

We shall be going over fairly soon - we've just had the orders, down in this hell. And when we go over, whenever we go over - there can sometimes be a delay of weeks - I shall be thinking of you, as I am now and always, as the one constant solace and beauty of my life. We are both sealed together in the language of the heart, and surely one day we shall speak it again.

Tristan

At this point it hadn't occurred to him that the wildest possibility might be the best: that of simply going AWOL. The punishment, of course, would be death by firing-squad. But what of the private Terrain he was forsaking? The War, after all, was easy, in a sense, in spite of its horrors: the slog and mud and death. It relieved one of the agony of living, with its terrible turnings, vicissitudes, blanks. One simply took orders and carried them out.

Tristan, however, was inchoate: he had launched himself on the Sea of the Unknown. And because of this he had become the arena, the open focus of a deep sea-change. It welled up in him hotly in the night, in the fretful slumber of the frightful Front; it turned in turmoil in his brain. He couldn't resist it or push it off, for actually and really it had become him. He was being called to let it be, to let it grow up hotly from the depths, with all its passion and organic strength. The rind of him was being cast aside.

And yet he could not fully surrender: the pull of the plain world was strong in him. It was Thee, my Country, he was fighting for, with all its ancient stitched-in ways; it was some kind of mystical Body to him. The War raged in him, with the intensity of the Field.

He could not resolve it by himself but only acknowledge the fighting factions, which fought for supremacy in his brain. His character, he thought, was basically flawed, that he could not see a simple truth, then act upon it decisively. He was flawed like Hamlet and doomed to die. And yet the flaw went out and away: it was not just his flaw, though he felt it now. It was something like a rift or a fault in the earth, which at any moment might open up, revealing its deadly, angst-filled Maw. It was here in flat Flanders, being spun out, between the daft trenches like scars in the ground. The world, seen this way, was an open wound, growling and festering and seething at depth. And it had the weight of aeons behind it: in some sense, it had been always like this. What was happening in Flanders and at Brewston now was a large- or small-scale explication. Deeply, he found, the psyche was flawed, and when one touched it, inflamed its wound, it flared up in brutalities, rank atrocities; nothing could assuage the secret core of rage. It might simmer sullenly, as Alderman's did, or it might be an all-out Theatre of War: trace it back to its hidden, unspoken source and one would find the same seared, blackened Crack.

This revelation of common consciousness produced in Tristan no direct action. He hovered, wavered, Hamlet-like. He had reached the point, the possibility of Not-being. He was again between polarities, but this time he was neutered, as if he were sexless, as if he had been shorn of what he was. In that Hollow Land, that noughted space, he looked for indicators but found none. It was, at one and the same time, nemesis and despair, a point of dead arrival in himself.

He could see nothing beyond the Dead Point, as he floundered without parameters. Predictably, romantically, he thought of putting an end to himself: to make his quietus with his own rifle, to go up in a puff of self-drawn smoke. It was too much to bear, this blank in the soul, this vast Hall of Nothing into which he had been drawn. What had pushed him there had been real enough (it had all the arrows of freedom to its bow), but now that, too, had petered out or lay in abeyance, unflowering, unfree. It was dreadful here, where nothing cohered, where the unlovely, clattering, machine-fed War banged in the vacuity of Nothing unresolved. He couldn't decide. On the basis of what? There was no firm footing anywhere.

Then a second letter from Jessie came.

Brewston Farm
- December, 1916

Tristan, my dearest,

The doctor called today. He says my fever is quite serious; it may even be typhoid - he doesn't know for definite. He took blood and urine samples, which will go to a hospital, though which one he meant he didn't say. It looks as if I shall just have to wait.

If I have made your life I'm glad of that, though my own part in it now seems faint and distant, as you are distant, with my life in yours. I am enfolded in you really, I think, as the land is enfolded in winter snow. I seem to have no substance without you. When you went to the War I thought to myself it was just an extension of your going to College, but it wasn't, of course; it was different altogether. Alderman hardly speaks to me now, and I live by myself in the downstairs room. He tells me I'm lucky I'm not on the street, which is where, I suppose, he thinks I belong. Emma is all I have left here now. She keeps asking what's the matter, and I tell her it's the 'flu. She'll learn soon enough what a horror-hole it is.

I could not have imagined what it would be like, nor how I would suffer when you went away. It was like a deep wound opening up, some fatal fissure in the bottom of my soul. Through it my life is ebbing away, it is going from me - and I want it to go. Even for Emma it would be best: she will grow up without the stigma of me.

Do not write or grieve for me, it isn't worth it - not now, not any more. There is so much in life for you to do and I'm sure, when the War is over, you will find it. I only wish I could see you once more and walk with you again through Gladwin's Copse. I've hardly been down there since you left.

How strange life is, how vulnerable! With all its wretchedness, such a tender thing! The cows are coming in for the evening milking, and the work of the land goes on as before. Keep Brewston in your heart, in a corner of your heart, where I shall be always, my darling, with you. Think of me sometimes.

Your loving,
Jess

8

Existentially, Tristan had nowhere to go but into the Pit of his own angst and void. Circumstantially, however, he had to be careful; he had to time it to a T: any false move, and he would be shot. Nevertheless, today was the day; it was written already in the greying dawn: today, at dawn, they would go OTT. The Dutch barn was only a hundred yards away.

The order was given and over they went, each man helmeted, heavy laden, carrying a rifle with a fixed bayonet. Immediately, it seemed, they were in a fog, laid for them by enemy smoke. Absurdly, Tristan thought of the Moor, of the frequent fog up there and how it felt. But it gave him the chance he was looking for. While his section stumbled forward like sheep in a fog, he detached himself from it and made off towards the barn. He was there in a jiffy, no distance at all. And by that one act of praeternatural folly (or justifiable daring) he had cut himself off: he no longer belonged with any of them. The pain and the guilt of it stung him, standing there.

Back at the Front, the smoke had lifted; the rare draught of a breeze was blowing now. It disclosed a dreadful reality. His section was stranded in No Man's Land, half-way between its own lines and the enemy's. And for reasons which, even years later, he couldn't fathom no-one had given them the order to crawl. They were all just fixed there, grey, bleared, adrift, bald and defenceless as mannequins. He wanted to shout out, 'Ted, Joe, get down!' But, in the event, he just averted his eyes. The pillar he was leaning on vibrated in his ear, as a spitting volley of gun-shot split the air. When he looked again there was not a man standing, and in his mind he compiled a list, to the names on which, had he not deserted, History would have added his own:

Lieutenant J.C.O'Flathery-Berke
Sergeant H.S.Lansdowne
Corporal S.J.Smith
Lance-corporal D.M.Socks
Lance-corporal O.R.Best

Private B.H.T.Plant-Smythe
Private B.J.Stills
Private T.M.Beckett
Private M.P.Henshall
Private W.G.Shakespeare

Each one, singly, like a homing bird would fly back to the town or village whence it came, there to be chiselled, along with other names, on a monument of stone to the home-come dead. Except that they would never lie in their native soil: it would be merely a Memorial of names, their lives and their bodies gone out here, shot to pieces on the fractured Field. And he wondered there, in that fall and fling of limbs, why he had been spared, why only he?

There were no solutions, public or private. Though Jessie's love was his impetus, that, too, was only part of it. At the core of it was the nameless Nothing, the deep-scored Hole, the endless Drop. And, somehow, he had let himself down into it; he was walking around in it, lampless, in the Cavern. This little skirmish, these ten men dead, were of no account in the Theatre of War, like some side-show that no-one even bothered to look at. They would be struck off the list, and that would be that. It bothered him as much as their single, separate deaths: this group statistic, this nullity. He found it frightening in a different kind of way - in a way that changed the contour of Life for ever. For there was no doubt in his mind that, in this hell of hells, a total reshaping of Life was taking place. Out there among the metal, already rusting, was the spiked statuary of the Modern Age. It was coming alive, giving birth to itself, and its birth was an ache and a scream of Nothing. How would it grow up? What would it *do*?

No, there were no solutions in the Field, only endless tunnelling, fathoming, searching: it went on and on, the more one looked. We had lived on finalities all these years, on hard-rod Certainties, infallible Laws, and they were thrown up now as aspects, merely, as finite and relative, not Absolutes. And, of course, the Great Yardstick had gone, sucked into the Void along with the rest. He was flailing about, a dying thing with dying men.

And yet the Call was on Tristan now. He felt it mutely in the funereal rain, which swept on the wind through the open barn; the cold lash of it told him that he must move. He felt in his pocket, found a few notes and coins: enough, he thought, to get him to the coast. The coast couldn't be that far away, by train. He would jump a train going west or south.

The railway station wasn't far away, up a slight incline beyond the town, a single-street straggle of small-brick Belgian houses. He walked towards it, skirting the town. The rain continued to fall in slanting pencils, and he was glad of it: it provided camouflage. Mortars were

33

going off in the distance - obviously there was fighting further up the Front - and the shells fell like stones falling into a well, with sporadic drops and plops, then final finished splashes. How strangely easily he had stepped out of it and was watching it now like some blurred, jerky film. It was all going on in some parallel World, not touching his now, but of its own kind.

He jumped into a goods train that had been shunting back and forth, with that lazy, going-nowhere air such trains have - it was now, quite decidedly, filled and ready - and crouched down low in a wagon carrying coal. Large lumps of it glistened silver-black in the rain, and a slurry was forming on the wagon floor. He pushed himself in among the coal, pulling his greatcoat collar up around his ears and squatting on his haunches, his feet cocked. He supported his back against the rear wall and looked, as the train began to move, at a skyscape of telegraph wires and boxed cloud. The train didn't seem to need to stop; he dozed a little, then the night came on.

He had never, throughout the whole cold night, imagined that he would end up in Paris, but that is exactly where he did end up, somewhere around six o'clock the next morning. The train pulled into Gare de l'Est and, after walking down the interminable goods ramp without being suspected or even seen, he found himself somewhere near the Odeon, in a stir and a clank of early-morning café owners and ribbed steel frontages being flung up. He slipped, shivering to his marrow, into the Bar Henri IV and ordered a large bowl of coffee and a slice of buttered bread. To try to staunch the trembling, he leaned against the zinc, while the proprietor, a domino of dapper black-and-white, put the coffee machine through its gargling exercises.

- Monsieur est en permission? he asked.
- Oui, replied Tristan, astounding himself.
- Vous savez, nous, la guerre . . . he went on. And he launched into a verbal essay on the War, which seemed to require no other response than the occasional nod, 'oui' or 'non' from Tristan. It was one of those pronouncements flung out upon the air, which exist for the benefit of the speaker alone but which require, nonetheless, that a second person be present. Tristan listened patiently, sipping his coffee and nibbling his 'tartine', as he slowly warmed inside his greatcoat. He was anxious to learn - if he could cross the Divide - what trains or lorries might be running to the coast. As he paid for his breakfast and left the mandatory tip, he asked simply:
- Pour Calais-Boulogne?
- A la Gare du Nord, Monsieur.
- Merci.
- C'est moi . . . Et au revoir, Monsieur!

34

Back on the street, he felt better; he was warmer. He walked back in the direction he had come from: Gare du Nord.

The day was still bleary and incipient, as he walked into the large concourse in front of the platforms. A posted printed sheet gave details of train departures, and he saw that there was a train to Calais at nine. Time to wait and time to blend. He walked over to a kiosk and perused the newspapers, looking - camouflage criteria - for the biggest and the cheapest he could find. He bought a copy of 'Le Peuple' and shut himself behind it.

It was one of those enormous station clocks, which seem to be a symbol of Time itself. Minute by minute the big hand jerked forward, and at five to nine Tristan went to the booking office and purchased himself a platform ticket. Holding it out, he passed the barrier and walked, slinking almost, alongside the train. With the signal-light green and the train shuddering into motion, he leapt on swiftly and, as luck would have it, found a lavatory immediately to his left. He dived into it, locked the door and waited.

The train moved off slowly, clankingly, stopping several times in the first few hundred yards, as if it were really not quite sure whether it wanted to go or not. The lavatory window had frosted glass, which made it impossible for Tristan to see out. He contented himself with counting the stops, an arbitrary exercise, at best, but one which, nonetheless, encouraged him: he was getting closer, whatever the outcome.

He realised it was dangerous to stay too long where he was and, regretting his haven, as he always did a safe place, he opened the door and peeked down the corridor. There was no-one there, as far as he could see. He was about to walk the length of the carriage, when the door of one of the compartments slid open and a duo of disputants stepped into the corridor. One of them was obviously the ticket inspector, and he was giving the other man a grilling about the non-validity of his ticket. The passenger was protesting that his ticket was in order, the word 'supplément', in various registers of rage, being flung back and forth any number of times. It was one of those Gallic fast flare-ups, which seem to come from nowhere and which Tristan, certainly, expected to result in bloodshed on the train. He stood gaping at the end of the corridor, oblivious of everything but the scene before him, so that when he got back to his haven, the loo, he found it doused in the odour of unflushed excrement, with an acrid overlay of smoke of Gauloises. He pulled the chain and got that dead, shocked sound. He pulled again, harder: the cistern was empty.

The dispute was over; the man had paid up, and the ticket inspector descended on Tristan. He was holding his nose, as well as his breath, in the hope that the inspector, an odious functionary - with eyes, now it seemed, in the side of his head -, would simply walk by and ignore the closed door. But he didn't; he stopped and, in spite of the LIBRE (he'd seen it all, anyway, a thousand times before), rapped out:

- Votre billet, s'il vous plaît, Monsieur!

It was only partly simulation and deception that Tristan, the vomit rising in his throat, flung open the door and, with a right-shoulder-charge, knocked the punctilious Frog to the floor, escaping therefrom with shouts of 'J'ai mal!' along the path the little man had just come, while he, all confusion and broken glasses, anxious above all to salvage his dignity, accepted, though not without bluster and protest, the amiable assistance of his erstwhile adversary, a gentleman among gentlemen in an Age of Gentlemen, whom he had stung, moreover, for an extra twenty francs. They proceeded without further hindrance to Calais.

The extensive use of the U-boat tactic, which the German High Command had been suing for for months, was delayed by a sense of moral opprobrium and the risk of America's entering the War till 9 January, 1917. Tristan slipped in under the net around the middle of December, 1916, at a time when there were regular ferry crossings, most of them troop vessels of one description or another. He mingled in with the crowd around the docks.

There was a ferry, 'The Isolde', leaving at five. He saw the bold letters on the white vessel's side, she cleaving to the sea with her massive metal volume. Then there was the sea itself, frothing in a surge to the stiff walls' side. It, too, was massive, eternal, imperturbable, pushing like cold molten metal at the land. Staved off here by these stiff stone walls, it yet was basic, fluid, elemental; it could at any time, he felt, overrun the land. And yet it was the land we were fighting about in those thousands of squalid squiggles in the ground; it was the right to possess and to stick a flag up there. No-one could actually possess the sea.

He mingled in with the khaki crowd, milling and moving like a second sea: he sought to become anonymous. The soldiers around him were friendly enough, talkers all of them, Geordies in fact.

- Where do you come from? one of them asked.
- From the North, like you, replied Tristan evasively.
- Aye, but where?
- North Derbyshire.
- Derbyshire, where's that?
- Next to Staffordshire. I'm in the Staffordshire Regiment.
- How come you're on leave then? I thought the Staffs were at the Front.
- Special dispensation: a bereavement.
- Oh! A family matter, is it, then?

- My step-mother's dying, Tristan said, as if the pressure of being put on the spot had made him admit to the fact of it.

- My mother died not long ago, the man said, as if in his mind the very statement lodged them together on the same plane. But Tristan refused the affinity, averting his gaze and saying nothing.

- She may recover, he said finally.

The anonymous crowd had melted away, the pink face addressing him become a blur. He was back in the fields of home with Jessie, her black hair sweeping in a swath across her face. He still did not and could not believe that that rich, royal body was wasting away. He remembered the blood flaming up in her cheeks and her eyes which were dark, quick, live black coals. Her passionate action was more than his: cleaner, more incisive, less riddling and worked. He, by contrast, was grey and thought-bound, meandering through life like some sluggish river, needing always to be prompted and stirred. With her he had lived along a revivifying axis, in a constant, deep-dredged, accelerated probing of everything that lay in him, crystalline and dormant. And now he was going back to her, as to the centre of his own search.

There was a tug in him like the tug of the sea, an undertow of unspoken necessity, and it worked in him strongly like a furled tide. Its volume was such he could not have described it; his mind could not have encompassed it. But it was throwing him up, irrevocably, onto a waiting and now changed Shore. There were no limits now, he saw actually, save in what we choose to call ourselves. The need in his love, which is the growing-point of love, was calling him out and away across the Tide. Even dying, she would be waiting for him there. He had no connection, except with her.

From two o'clock onwards it had started to go dark, in that peculiar crepuscular late-autumn way, which heralds out the day almost before it's begun. Everyone was waiting, talking, smoking, though the ship was in dock now, the cargo being loaded. Large hoists swung it across the flank of the ship, then suddenly, arriving at a certain point-of-poise, it was sucked down into the hold and disappeared. The hoists ran on tracks along the quayside and in a hole of sky, as he lifted his gaze, Tristan saw above the khaki mass a passenger-ramp being slowly lowered down into the space between the ship's flank and the tracks. They would soon receive the order to embark.

Tristan was wondering what he would do, if he were stopped by some assiduous MP. He couldn't cut and run, not in these circumstances. He thought of answers he might give to a whole panoply of possible questions, then reflected as he made them up, both question and answer, that they simply wouldn't come like that. The whole time-frame would be slightly altered, the juxtaposition of sea, land, sky something other than what it was now. It would require and would inevitably occasion a different instantaneity. And would he be there at that moment, then, in the way he was present to his own mind now? The mind of planning, forethought, control ran on straight lines like the tracks on the quayside. But the Moment was always deeper and wider: it had contexts incalculable homing in. He felt in the pit of his stomach the angst which is the necessary concomitant of any choice, the leap-in-the-dark which presages Freedom. It was like being out on some final Ground, the gut-and-thunder message driving in on him. It was elemental like the washing sea, like the angst which must have welled up in Adam, when he stood alone in the fateful Garden and asked himself the question: 'To eat or not to eat?'

The moment came, and they were walking up the gang plank. Tristan turned, as if by reflex action, to scan the darkening waterfront. It looked bleak and cold and barely lit, like a limitrophe outpost in the Country of War. 'If I were shot now,' he thought, 'I doubt if I would notice.' It was the way he was feeling, to himself. Blank.
The MP's were there, two of them, one on either side at the top of the ramp. They looked scrubbed, invulnerable, shining like hardware, with their strong, peaked caps and white belts and gaiters.
- Where's your kit-bag, laddie? barked one of them.
- In the hold, sergeant, Tristan replied.
- In the *hold*?
- In the hold.
This was it! The sergeant was scrutinising Tristan's features, as if the clue to the kit-bag's whereabouts - it was an answer he certainly hadn't countenanced - lay in the lineaments of the latter's face. The Sword hung between them, hovering ...
- Are you *lying* to me, laddie?
- No, sergeant.
- Then carry on! What do you think this is, a Christmas pantomime?
Tristan stepped on board between the two MP's, whose stature had now, instantaneously, shrunk to that of the rest of the innocuous crowd. With any luck now . . . There was only Dover.
Since he had no papers of any kind on him a check at Dover could still be fatal, though in the melee of wives, mothers, sweethearts and children it was highly improbable that anyone would stop him. Improbable, but not totally out of the question. The question was really, where was he now? In the comparative ease of the unwatched ship, and with his own mood eased, he considered it thus:
He had broken ranks in more ways than one, as perhaps he had broken them from the first, in that first night at Longnor between Weatherall and Brewston. They had both been outsiders from the day they had met,

38

perhaps even before that, intrinsically. Their meeting had been the brief, fatal flowering of creatures whose essence was not in this world. Intrinsically they were like visitants; like aliens, a'lies, other-dimensionals: they had incarnated the nameless Rose. And because of that, surely, they had been born and met here, at this Crossroads of Gravity, Nullity and Pain. They had come in swiftly, as it were before their time, and the Time-Machine was exacting its dreadful retribution. Jessie was being broken on it now, her beautiful body wasting and failing, and he, also, was being cast out, losing the place where Beauty lay.

And yet there was the thrill of freedom to it: it was what they had done and dared to become. At the crux of himself, whatever the nightmare, was the twinned, resilient, red-become Rose. It was deeply implanted in him now; it had grown in their braided blood, the two of them. And the two rivers flowed, eastwards out of Eden, and lost themselves in the parched, scorched land.

He would have to fight on alone, he knew it: the vessel of Jessie's body was breaking. Tears of self-pity welled up into his eyes, and he felt himself the focus of all time-space. It had all existed, conjunctively, for him - not in some stagey, egotistical sense, but because all time-space, all past and present were incipient and flowing through him now. It was a wide field suddenly, this Field of the Rose; it went out and away from itself for ever. And yet it was contained, as the sap is contained, as the universe sits in the eyebright's little middle. It was terrifying, also, this Further Field, this unknown Country, where none had been before. It was strange and signless, like a wilderness. Having strayed into it, a Blank in Blankland, he could do nothing now but simply sit, looking at the parched, unirrigated Waste, the Territory after, which was his, which was him. He went out on deck to await the White Cliffs.

'The Isolde' docked about 7 p.m., having hit heavy weather fairly close in to port and sloshed around in a fermenting sea, the passengers, military men to a man, running green and bilious to the ship's side or divesting themselves in the sick-bay below (at the best of times an airless, fetid place) of their overload of French cuisine. He had been right about the reception in Dover: it was a melee of wives, mothers, sweethearts and children jostling on the quayside to get a sight of their loved one. And the radiance on their faces when the loved one appeared! He was like some descending deity, perched high above them on the balcony, and they were in the pit gazing up at him. He was like that, a Star, with a transposed existence, an elevated being returning to them. It mattered not, in that exaltation, whether thousands and millions of men had died, for here was Bert, Joe or Arthur come back, and his very presence translated their lives from their back-yard squalor of misery and rain to a term heraldic, a heightened Field, where they stood aglow, shining and shouting, beneath the Wings unfurled of Victory.

For others, of course, it was a different tale (with the best will in the world not every message got through): they came and looked and found not that face, that single appearance which would make and change all. Their loved one lay in Flanders' fields, in those sore, scored acres, that broken Plot. No tears of child, sweetheart, mother or wife could bring that body back to life again. It was sinking, or would be sunk, into a grave with the bodies of other soldiers, nameless and numberless, whose brief earthspan had come to an end. The indifferent wind would blow over it, the land bake hard next summer, the crinkled poppies grow.

Tristan was in neither case: he was like an Emissary from the Unknown, some spectral enterprise that just went by unnoticed. He walked blithely, like a wraith, through Dover Docks Station and found himself a corner seat on the train. It was cold again, clammy and damp, and he thought about his ride from Passchendaele to Paris, crouching on the coal with that box of weeping cloud. Here, instead, it was enclosed; it was sepulchral. He was moving with the bodies of the living dead. They were closing in on him with rank smoke, the heat of their bodies making the carriage window moist. He was suffocating almost, but he couldn't move: he could not draw attention to himself. Now, as then, he slumped back, he slunk down; he pulled his greatcoat collar up around his ears.

It was strange, this world of movement and stasis, this life of making, building brick by brick, which then without warning resulted in death: it made no sense, when one added it up. Everything was passing, inevitably; everything was perishing: it had no hold. Here was a man on a train in a station, itself a monument to Permanence. It was one of those smoke- and steam-filled Temples, which had sprung up throughout the Country and the Empire and whose tracks, like arteries running through a body, served and fuelled it from end to end. Ponderous, Victorian, bolted, severe, it embodied the Age of Industry, its logic, and provided proof positive, if any were needed, of the final arrival of the State of Stone.

This mute fixity, this end-of-the-line (the smoke and the steam now filling the whole place) was as much a metaphor as a physical fact. It was the state of mind of a culture arrived, but whose very arrival was a presage of its death. And Tristan is held there, unmoving and unmoved, in the space between two deaths, waiting for a sign.

9

Around Brewston Farm the sycamores are blowing, with that little sough of wind which makes a moaning sound. A bed has been moved down into the front parlour, which looks out and away across the dipping fields to the wooded slopes and moors beyond, like an eye with opens on Infinity. Jessie is entering her last few days.

It *was* typhoid, after all. The water, no doubt, was responsible. Minnie and Martha minister to her, with that sense of distanced urgency which comes with the knowledge that someone is dying. She sits with her back supported by pillows, a shawl round her shoulders, looking out. The view opens out in a wide funnel, from the window-sill to the vast, spreading moor. She receives it all; she is leaving it for good. There is no person left in her field of vision - even Emma has receded from it now. But, though she is still and reconciled, progressively detached from the dumb-show around her, part of her, thrown into bright relief, waits and watches for Tristan's return.

Somehow, her life had no meaning any more.

## BOOK TWO: THE BROTHERHOOD

For a' that, an' a' that,
It's comin' yet, for a' that,
That Man to Man, the world o'er,
Shall brothers be for a' that.


- Robert Burns


# Once More

What brings about that infinitesimal Click, the smidgen of oil that makes it all turn right? Does it come mysteriously on the wings of the morning, unasked-for, unbidden, altogether free of charge? Do strange gods simply bring it to us, if we are receptive and allow them to? And what takes place in the flurry of the Heart, in the flutter of the Dream, when it begins to take shape? Aren't we then walking where no man has trod, are we not totally out on our own, like the first explorers of a Dark Continent? The nineteenth century was full of such ventures - jungles, journeys, White Intrepidity - but now the wide reaches of the Earth are known; the Moon is known: we have set our foot there. What remains to us is the Unknown Tract, a labyrinth of meanings simple and sacred, a scatter of scored and ancient rocks, on which we may find - the Eye single and clear, cleansed at last of all pretence - those secret, magical, inner Correspondences that lead one to the Diamond Heart.

1

Emma was a Priestess from the start, drawing her lineage from her mother but in a different, bolder, starker way. The death of her mother moved her deeply, but not in any way she could articulate or express: no words, no tears, no tantrums, nothing. It was as if she had taken upon herself, not just the responsibility and the cause, but the intimate action of her mother's death: that is, she became Death's familiar. Whereas Death had come upon her mother suddenly, in bold opposition to the fraught brilliance of her life, with Emma it was there from the start, so that the phrase 'the Valley of the Shadow of Death' was not, for her, an agent of grief but simply a description of things as they were. She saw the shadow-side of everything, in a way that is rare even among the adult. Not that she was unfeeling or cold; merely, she looked into the Pool of Death as naturally as one looks into a mountain tarn.

After Jessie's death she became very quiet: the bubbling, once-Christ-child was gone. She still followed Alderman about the place, but less frequently now: she preferred to be alone. For his part, he had become quieter, too, trying to forget his marriage to Jessie and the pain of shame which had been its consequence. He no longer thought of Tristan as his son, yet sometimes, when he looked at Emma, he was sure he saw a hint of him there.

The old adage, however, proved perennial, and in a few months time he was married again, this time to a widow from Brassington who, even if she was unprepossessing in the extreme, gave him, at least, the tacit assurance that she would make him a devoted, faithful wife, there being scant temptation for her to do otherwise. Indeed, so grateful was she to have found a new man - and a gentleman at that, with a farm to his credit -, that she waited on him hand and foot, made Minnie, now married herself, redundant and placed such a cushion of comfort around him that he forgot the dark days of his marriage to Jessie, putting on a belly with his slippers and pipe and allowing the last edge of youth and passion to be dulled to disappearance like the sun in mountain cloud. It was left to Emma to be the repository of That Time, to digest its essence and, growing quickly, to make its acceleration her own.


The time had come for her to go to school; she would leave the small, intense world of the farm and begin her education in Elmsworth. Miss Salterbrook was the only teacher and Emma was amazed, on her first day at school, delivered to the door by her new mother, Marion, to find, in the classroom which was big like a yard, a boy called John reading from the blackboard. It was something about a farm and a horse, but it bore no resemblance to *her* farm and horse. Was it, then, possible that there could be others? There *must* be, since John, so confident, so real, was reading about them: there must be countless others.

Next morning she thought she could go out and play, but to her chagrin, about eight o'clock, her new mother told her it was time for school.

- What, every day? asked Emma, alarmed.
- Every day, replied no-nonsense Marion.

So that was that, then; that was Life. The haloed World had come to an end. The brilliant, rich, indwelling Spectrum, which had its own pauses, avenues, explosions was being reduced to the World of the Grey. It would go on, immovably, down the track of the 3R's, like a train into ever more greying distances, till the Original World was completely lost. Then came -ologies, -ics, the 'big school'.

Emma took it all in her stride and was, in fact, a success at school. The teacher liked her because she was bright and because, after twenty-five years in the job, she was fed-up of ministering to rustic boors, who had precious little interest in learning at all, save where it could be applied to country matters, in which arena they were extremely shrewd. Poor Miss Salterbrook! She had entered the profession with all the idealism it constantly calls forth and she had foundered, little by little, day by day, on the impervious rock of cloddish self-interest. This more than anything had got her down, and she was close to becoming an embittered old maid when Emma Dakin happed along. At last, a child with wit and wonder in her eyes, who related, *saw* and penetrated things, for whom learning was close to being a dance, glorious and beautiful in-and-for itself! She began to bring her special things - stories, little puzzles, all her own - and Emma responded gleefully, absorbing them quickly and moving on. Thus, they established a bond between them, which enriched Emma's life with new morsels of delight, while to Miss Salterbrook, on an almost daily basis, it gave back some of the sense of vocation with which she had set out a quarter of a century ago.

Predictably, there was envious talk of her being 'teacher's pet' and 'why not our Margaret?' But such sentiments are rife in common consciousness and are not restricted to hill villages like Elmsworth. The child needs to play, and to play is to learn. Such ideas were gradually gaining ground, notably in the work of Maria Montessori, and Miss Salterbrook was quick to seize on them and to bring them into focus with her bright new Button. In this way Emma remained an innocent, incorporating even the learning of tables (from 'twice times' up to 12x12) into the magical contour of the Play.

In fact, Miss Salterbrook so loved the child that she became for her a second mother, in the sense in which Jessie had been a mother: she gave her something to grow up into, a World not her own, which the other possessed. It had something of the upward Spiral to it, whereas the world which Marion inhabited and projected was unremittingly grey and dull: a flat walk to the duck-pond in Wellington boots. Yet she cared for the child in a routine sort of way, seeing to it that she was clean and neatly dressed, much as she cared for the ducks and geese and locked up the fowls after evening milking. She was happy in her new home and treated Emma as an extra, who had to be looked after along with the rest. That here she might have come across, albeit at that very early age, a free spirit, a Wild Goose, a Poet of the Moor never even occurred to her. She just took the girl in hand and got on with the job.

And because of her attitude towards Emma, Alderman's also began to change. When Jessie was alive he had been a jovial daddy, picking her up and throwing her into the air, with an 'up just once' which made her shriek with joy. Now - and it was not just her being older - he became more sedate and reserved with her; she was now no longer his 'little girl'. The wealth and the fire of his affections drained out, much as they had from his life in general.

Sensing this, Emma also withdrew. It wasn't that she became hostile or ugly; it was simply that now there was a new regime: things moved more smoothly now, with less turbulence and upset. But in the unfolding and the folding of the sharp-creased tablecloth, the systematic filing-away of the cutlery, there entered the house, as into its bloodstream, a current of bleak and unimpeachable banality: grey days strung out in infinite series.

This sense of a levelled-off, stepped-down existence, where something exceptional was never even on, entered Emma's soul and made it ache. On some days she almost fled to school, not just to find out what Miss Salterbrook had in store for her, but, more, to escape from that unbreathable World, where grey fluid swam and fed like an amoeba. Strangely, also, as time went by, it became the edge on which she whetted her Knife.

It is odd how an atmosphere gets established, how it then dictates what goes on inside it. There was no declaration on Marion's part, no platform from which she announced her programme. Yet her unquestioning 'this-is-how-it's-done' attitude gradually seeped into every nook and cranny, along with the new curtains and rearranged furniture. Subtly, daily she asserted her influence, till very soon it was difficult to tell where one regime ended and the other began. Things were being done properly now - that, robustly, was the implication -, whereas in the days of 'that young lady', as Marion called her, it had all been a rather haphazard affair.

Now Alderman was happy to take his ease, to be waited on hand and foot, day and night, with the consequence that Marion had soon established herself and was in charge, not just of running the household, but of the ambience and tone of their lives as well. In her ruthless, silent wordless way she set out to destroy everything that had been Jessie: through unobtrusive shifts, refurbishments, changed colours - 'little improvements', as she called them - she put herself irremediably in her place; more, she went further than ever Jessie had done to set her seal and stamp on Brewston. In all this Alderman acquiesced, being vague and foolish as regards women's wiles. He gave up, in short, as many people do, and ceased to believe in the Finer Thing. Because of this it receded from him; it let him sink into his own sloth and slough. He fell down to the base of the triangle with Marion, and it was left to Emma to soar towards the Apex.

All these domestic developments had pushed the War very much into the background. Nevertheless, of course, they did read the news and were aware that by July, 1918, the tide had turned in the Allies' favour. No mention was ever made of Tristan, who was permanently, dead or alive, 'persona non grata'. Emma picked this up and herself kept silent, though she would love to have known what had happened to 'Uncle T'.

On 11 November the Armistice was signed, and there was general peace again in Europe. The dead were buried, the POW's returned. The MOD took upon itself the task of accounting for all personnel. Consequently, in the spring of 1919, a note arrived at Brewston Farm to the effect that 'Private Dakin, T. of the Royal Staffordshire Regiment' had proved untraceable and that, therefore, inevitably, 'we regret to have to inform you . . . Condolences.' Alderman read the note out to his wife, who said:

- You must have been expecting it, weren't you?
- I suppose so, he replied in a muffled voice, as if his actual feeling were obscured.
- There must be millions like him, she went on.
- Millions, he repeated, backing off. And, drawn and anonymous, he gave up his ghost; he surrendered more of the spirit in him.

Shortly afterwards there was a Memorial Service for those who had fought and fallen in the War. Alderman took Emma with him; Marion protested she had too much to do. They took the pony and trap and drove to Elmsworth, to the little village church that leans against the hill. It was a lovely spring evening and the swallows were dipping; fresh tulips were out along the south-facing lawns. They pulled up at the lych-gate, leaving Dolly untethered: she was so quiet and good, she wouldn't even budge.

The organist was playing a soft-pedalled introit, as they walked reverentially to a seat, which, while not strictly speaking a family pew, seemed nonetheless to be the Dakins' by right. Alderman kneeled and Emma did likewise, not knowing what he was mumbling into his hands. They said prayers at school, too, but she didn't know why. And why, if one prayed, did one use everyday language and not god-language, so God could understand? Then again, God *did* understand: He understood everything, including one's thoughts. He travelled a lot, somehow, and yet He never moved.

These musings were drowned in the Service of Remembrance. The names of the Elmsworth dead were read out: sixteen young men, including Tristan, from a village of barely three hundred souls. The

Union Jack was unfurled from the ceiling and hung above the altar, almost touching it, in a mystical marriage of Church and State. The underlying political realities were ignored, as, in the velvet interior light, with the organ throbbing and the hymn intoned, the congregation gave voice to all its pent-up emotion, the stored agony and anguish of the past five years. Widows and mothers in black, veiled in black, let flow their tears abundantly, while fathers, brothers, masculine mates recalled their lost hero, the now silent one. Alderman was reconciled: he could think of Tristan now as one of these dead, redeemed from disgrace on the Field of Honour. He was one with Joe Spiggs' lad and young Arthur Mellors, boys any father could have been proud of.

So much did Alderman crave respectability, so deeply was family honour engrained in him, that he was prepared to go to any lengths to reclaim it. If Tristan had fallen it made good the account, he could look the whole village in the eye again. And, after all, that's what really mattered. Having a whore for a wife and a 'wild 'un' for a son had written him off the record for good. Now here on the hillside where he had buried Jessie he had this day, in his own mind, at least, been redeemed by the sacrificial death of his son. Thus, by these predetermined and self-deluding contortions, Alderman was able to re-establish his standing, which was in the order of things as he had always known them, and totally ignore the revolutionary upheaval through which the world had been passing for the last five years. This order was the work of a whole civilisation, built year by year and piece by piece, and it was that very civilisation which was in a state of collapse. By patching up one corner of it he had merely immured himself for the time being from the imminent ravages and wrath of its destruction. More was on its way, much more and very soon.

In the interim, however, came the twenties. The indefatigable human spirit, which had seen itself blasted during the War, broke through again in the so-called Jazz Age. The ending of the War was itself a celebration, but the sense of release it brought with it was greater. Tradition and Authority were everywhere in question, as, in place of the crumbling Old Order, there promised to be a New Liberation: educational, sexual, spiritual. Summerhill was founded by A.S.Neill, the Russian Revolutionaries abolished marriage and Krishnamurti dissolved the Order of the Star. We were not going to need leaders any more: each one would blaze a trail of his own, breaking down barriers of closeted convention, heralding in the Millennium. And the Millenium was, as always, just round the corner, almost within our grasp, in fact. It would only take the slightest shift, the merest murmur beneath the trees, the least of realignments, and we'd be there.

But onto that stage of Near-miss and Void, into that Field of lapsed Honour and Pride, there stepped the man who, to all intents and purposes, was its nemesis, its exemplar and its creatic.ı: 'Corporal Hitler', as Churchill called him. He was the product (and more than the product) of his Age, an upstart certainly, a madman and a tyrant, but a man who fitted his country's bill, who harnessed its energies and redressed its wrongs. He was also, quite clearly, a 'man of the people', in the sense in which the vulgar are redoubtable: no finer feeling held him back. Chiefly, however, he was the agent of Power and, as such, the dark Harbinger of World War II.

3

Emma was eight at the beginning of the decade and eighteen by the end of it. It was, thus, largely synonymous with her growing up - not that she ever considered it so. Decades themselves are not usually that neat, and this one might more reasonable be thought to have begun in 1919 with the Treaty of Versailles and to have ended in 1929 with the Wall Street Crash. If the latter was retribution for the former - and, from several points of view, arguably it was - it also marked the end of experimentation, that faith in being able to 'bust out and live', which would not re-emerge for another forty years and which sim:larly had its youthful wings clipped, by the manoeuvrings of Mammon, unemployment, Viet Nam.

Emma was part of her Age in a different kind of way. Certainly, she went to the cinema at Bakewell; she learned the Charleston and the Black Bottom with the other girls at school. Yes, but also she caught some of its free spirit, that space and freedom some generations enjoy to walk and wander in places unknown. And, quite literally, she did walk and wander: away from Brewston and onto the Moor. She became virtually estranged from her family, with whom she had now no relationship at all. Marion had so far established territory and pulled poor Alderman inside its pale that she was actually a stranger in her own home, the one in the three the couple left out. Nor had she a sibling left now, as some while ago her half-brother, Cecil, had married the undertaker's daughter from Bakewell and taken the lease of a farm in Nottinghamshire, where, as he put it, 'th' soil's summat like'.

The girl was left, then, to grow up alone and, in a way, this was no trial to her, as she had always been a creature set apart. In early adolescence she became particularly withdrawn, staying for hours in her room, then wandering off at night onto the Moor. She had powerful ınd intimate mystical experiences, in which she saw the Virgin emerging from the darkness and carrying her with her into the Light. She was folded up in the Virgin's blue cloak and swept away into another time-space, where

49

distinctions of class, colour, age, sex, race were suddenly of no consequence whatsoever, and everyone and everything was exactly what it is. She remembered the passage from the Epistles, where Saint Paul says that here on earth we see things 'as through a glass, darkly'. She remembered it because, in the Place to which she was taken, she saw things, not darkly, but radiant with Light, as they are truly, in-and-for themselves, when the Veil of the Nescience is removed. She soared at such times in the arms of the Virgin and saw vistas of Being which are closed to normal sight. The Scales of Ignorance fell from her eyes and she entered without demur, without a word, into the quiet Realm, the inner Body of the World, as into a brightly illumined Cave. This was the true Place, the Source of the world, the Heart-Cave from which it all derived. Here things were exactly what they are, without the least distortion or embellishment. Indeed, they needed no embellishment, for each thing was, being utterly itself, not only singularly and perfectly unique, but simultaneously equal with everything else: equal in Oneness, equal in Being. It was what it was, without gift or choice, clean-edged and complete, inherent, not made. And this mode of utterly intact Being was the repository of Creation from first to last. To be That, to Be There, was all that really mattered, since nothing existed outside of It. There Time stopped and Eternity began.

Gradually, she returned to normality, to what we call normality. It seemed to her now that she walked a different earth, one which was constantly unveiling itself, a world where Beauty came, nude and pristine. She was a first-and-last Intimate of it, an Initiate, and, though she never sought out her experiences, they came to her instantaneously, dramatically, when of an evening she was quiet and the day dimmed down and curdled in the moon. Then she would go out onto the Moor, to be the living companion of That Place, to draw in its sharp, clear ecstasies, to make a counterbalance to the terrible day.

For the day *was* terrible, however one construed it: narrow, stepped-down, imprisoned, routine. The life of the farm went its preordained way, now quite smoothly and without hiatus, much more efficiently than in the former time. Yet the spark of the improvisational had gone from it; it was no longer a place which contained within its flow that half-turn of the sluice-gate which lets the Miracle in.

And School was a further quarter of the Bastion of the Grey. Sloppy, unkempt and largely dispirited teachers went through the motions of 'teaching kids', overtly and covertly complaining all the time, as if it were the kids' fault they were a bore. Now also it was the Big Institution, with its long corridors and chapel-like ceilings, its wooden beams stretching and arching up in a naked display of their musculature. And everywhere, in every nook and cranny - under desks, behind books, hovering over light-bulbs - was the all-pervading reek of carbolic. It hit

them as they entered the place: This is School; this is your enchantment. Except that enchantment was a million miles away - away from the ranks of battered books, sticky ink-wells, smeared sweat and dust; away from the gym-slips, the asphalt yard, the spiked iron railings with the notice NO BOYS. It lay in the meadow of a thousand summers, by streams of running waters, beneath peaks high and holy; it lay where no man had ever trod. What went on here, in this prison-cum-factory, was nothing short of a travesty: it took young minds, not quite spoilt yet, and squeezed them into its frightful mould, so that never again would they have the wit and wisdom to do anything other than what they were told.
- Do as you're told!
That was the universal cry, uttered alike by fraught parents and teachers, victims themselves of the dreadful Machine. And, as a codicil, 'Freedom is frightening. Stay within the limits: don't venture across.'
The dominant inner colour was grey: the grey of fear, amorphous, inhabiting, the grey of continually sunless days, the grey of the stripe in the school uniform's tie, repeated in the ritual, formless skirt; then the grey of Marion's unimpeachable routine, the grey of her little, frightened world, hedged-in by its inhibitions and control, the grey of the milk-buckets and the enclosing stone walls. All this washed around Emma like a sea, bleak and cold like the slushing North Sea. It stung her like the frothing, searching sea; it pushed her to a quickening of heart and mind. 'This is no good,' it sang within her, like the myriad call of the siren sea. 'You must out and away from the bleak, cold sea, comb the skies for a different view. You will founder, my child, in this phlegm-grey sea, you will go down and under, rolling in its waves. They will not caress, they will bear down and break you. Step back, fly high and seek the stars!'

Thus, Emma lived in two different Worlds: by turns, in the world of the Day-to-day, then, in her Night-flight, out and away, like the Eagle from its eyrie, flown and gone. Her estrangement from her parents was now complete. Marion had taken her on as a chore and had never sought or even seen the point of any closer relationship, while Alderman, sinking daily further and faster, had neither time nor love for her. It had all gone, somehow, down the drain; he had let the continual flow of effluent wash him down and watch him fail. How, then, could such a father, if such he was, reach a daughter who had grown beyond his grasp? It wasn't just the energy he lacked: deep down he had withered in body and heart.
In consequence, Emma became a creature of the Moor: she inhabited it in an inner-outer synthesis, as the Brontë sisters inhabited the Gandal World. That is, it became the mirror of her soul, the locus and realisation of her spirit - as if it had been projected from her body and

was only secondarily the consequence of Evolution. To the Moor she went on those sharp spring evenings, when the cows had been let out and were frisking everywhere, when the sheep were cropping the drier, stony places. In its wildness she found a Correspondence, an unwalled, unfenced tract of land, where there were scarcely any trees; only shrubs and bushes grew. From this she drew quietness and sustenance, buttoning up her jacket against the wind. And into the wind she shouted her poems or snatches of verses from Shelley and Keats. It turned on the touch and the impression of the Word, the orderly imprint of the Logos, that intelligible substratum which informs the world and which it is the Poet's task to make manifest. Unknowingly, she had assumed this role, that of the Vestal set apart, whose vocation it is to serve and to speak and who, having absorbed, transmits again, as it were through a prism, the attendant Light.

That this had to do with words was not in doubt: she sought and researched them constantly, finding in their meaning and particularly their sound the pattern and resonance of her own soul-states. It was not a matter of mental jugglery or even of anything she could tell herself, but the quest for a connection sacred and binding - bardic, in the original sense - between the World of the Word, the subtle-universal, and the world of words, as we know it grossly here. This was her mission; it was given and regiven. Was it any surprise that she couldn't share it?

Yet the urge and the challenge to share is strong. It welled up in her from time to time and she yearned, as we all do, for a bosom-friend. Or she tried assiduously to write things down, to find a final form, but it didn't really work. What felt like poetry out on the Moor, what came to her in an unimpeded burst, seemed cold and brittle when set down on paper. In losing the context she also lost the meaning, allied as it was to the open ground, the shrubs and bushes bending, the furious winds. What she called her poetry was really an 'event', a random happening without preparation, sung or semi-shouted as it might have been six thousand years ago, before Gilgamesh. She liked it so, she liked its rhythm and urge, and she had a vague but powerfully intuitive suspicion that the writing-down of things, their Embodiment in Stone and their subsequent shoring-up of Tradition was one of the prime reasons she felt bored stiff now. Why should one live on the past and its givens? Where was the leaven in that heavy dough? Her education was all of the past, a block-book of concepts and received ideas: what some people thought about what other people said. Where is the originality in that? Tell me.

No, what she was looking for was a breakthrough, a way into the world that was not just information about it. And in the context of school, at least, the more she looked the less she found. Nobody was interested in the Being of the World, only in more and better ways of exploiting it. Wherever she looked there was deliquescence of Being, as if the soul of the world were being sucked out, as if gradually - and not too gradually at that - the world were withering from within like a dried-up fruit.

This realisation struck her with alarm, but it also gave her a kind of poise. Was it really as bad as she thought it was? Was the world really rotting from within? She looked again, many times, and it was. We had not yet had Ausschwitz, Buchenwald, Treblinka or the Stalinist Purges of the 30's, but the ground had been laid; it was already there. All that it was waiting for was to go public.

This loss of Being, to which Heidegger ascribes the general malaise and collapse of our culture, was, to Emma, no mere idea but a blistering reality. She could not have put it in so many words, and she had never heard of 'Sein und Zeit', but she felt she was living in a spectral world, a world of shadow-people and feigned solidities. What Marion did, for instance, was totally 'unreal' in Emma's definition of that term. Certainly, of course, it cohered and made sense at the purely practical, pragmatic level, but even that it achieved only by exclusion, by reducing everyone and everything to an object. Thus reified, how could one live or breathe? Which was exactly the position she found herself in.

No, there had to be a wider purchase, an entry into something - she knew not what - that would allow for and sustain a richer quality of living and, while taking care of the practical and pragmatic, give access at every moment to the deeper Source. But it was just this that was lacking from the world-as-it-was: no-one gave it credence or seemed to feel it was important. Even the vicar, when he spoke of 'the world to come', meant the place one went to after death. Which was no help, either, since postponement wasn't living.

These questions preoccupied Emma for years, right through her adolescence, in fact. Her mystical experiences became more infrequent, but she still continued to haunt the Moor and to shout her poems into wind, sun and storm. Eventually her sorties were noticed by a local, and a rumour began to circulate that she was mad. They talked about it in 'The Devonshire Arms', among the pink pint pots of Ind Coope Mild, and it passed over the counters of sundry corner shops, through the smug little cafes selling Bakewell Pudding, on out to the Cattle Market and back to Water Lane. Emma was a freak, a 'strange lass, that one', and probably the cure - it was getting time, anyway - was to fix her up with some nice young man: take her mind off her ramblings, bring her down to earth. Alderman and Marion, who at last were appraised, thought this was exactly what was required. They consequently invited a series of local young worthies to Sunday tea at Brewston Farm. They even, on one occasion, when they thought they had got it right, discreetly retired, to leave the 'young couple' alone. Neither of them had any idea what to say, though the young man, Alfred, had more of a clue, having been invited by Alderman to 'come and meet our Emma'. For Emma herself it was still rather a game: she didn't understand why, at frequent intervals, another young fellow - often much older than herself - would suddenly materialise at Sunday tea. She was innocent of boy-girl relationships and, though the girls at school talked about it all the time, it had hardly impinged on her consciousness. She would, indeed, have been very shocked, had she known about the machinations going on behind her back, the secret huddles between Marion and Alderman, and the counsel they took from the doctor and the vicar. She would have found it very intrusive and crass.

It was just this aristocracy of spirit that set her apart, not from peers and parents only, but from the common run of mortal kind. She wanted something beyond the average, to which there were clues but no clear Path. She knew in the secret recesses of her heart that she had to rise above mediocrity, but in a world that was becoming daily more and more mediocre this was no easy thing to achieve.

The self-styled 'well-intentioned efforts' to set her up with a young man failed. She was too rarefied, aloof and aquiline, and after some time they took their leave and went. The next ploy was to find her something to do. Pupil-teaching was the obvious option, since she had the mental capacity for it and, though vague, had a pleasant, engaging manner. She was appointed Assistant Teacher at the little school in Monyash, cycling the five miles every day, pushing over the plateau in all winds and weathers. And actually she quite enjoyed the work: the children, though dull, were amiable, and it gave her a certain independence. She had money in her pocket, time to herself and the promise of a place at Matlock Training College. All in all, things were not too bad.

But in the world at large they were not too good. The euphoria of the twenties was giving way to a new mood of apprehension and gloom. The Wall Street Crash was just round the corner and in October, 1929, it came. The chief consequences in Britain were rising unemployment, shrinking markets, industrial cut-backs. The political consequences, however, were more dire, as the Banners of Fascism darkened the horizon.

4

It was at this end-of-decade time that Emma received an unexpected letter. It was post-marked 'Edinburgh', and she wondered who she knew there. She opened it and read as follows:

- November, ...

54

My dear Emma,

It is now many years since I last saw you or, indeed, heard anything of the family and Brewston. You must be quite grown-up by now, and that is why I am writing to you. I would like to see you again, if it's possible.

I shall be taking the overnight train to London on Friday, 29th., and was wondering if we could meet up there. There is a small park next to Charing Cross Underground and in it is a bust of the poet, Robert Burns. For an almost-Scotsman like myself this is an auspicious place to be! I'll be standing by it on Saturday at 3 p.m. and again on Sunday, just in case. I do hope you can come - there is much to tell.

> Yours affectionately,
> Tristan ('Uncle T.')

Well, if the graves could open and reveal their secrets, here was a person risen from the dead! Emma read the letter over and over, and in a short time she found she had memorised it. There was nothing in it, really, to speak of, and yet its very brevity and just-enough-said made it irresistible to her. It was a few weeks before her eighteenth birthday, and it was because of this, no doubt, that Tristan had written then. He must have been waiting for years, she surmised, assuming that everyone thought he was dead. And now, like Lazarus, he had risen from the dead and was beckoning to her across the years.

Would she cross over? Of course she would! In fact, it hardly occurred to her that she might not go to the rendezvous. She had never been to London in her life, but that was a detail: she would take it in her stride. Then, of all things, she remembered a friend from school, who had recently won a scholarship to King's and who would probably be able to put her up. She wrote straight off to her and got the following reply:

- November, ...

Emma dearest,

How lovely to hear from you! Yes, of course, you an come for the end-of-November weekend. I shall be delighted to see you and I'll be very discreet, i.e. not ask too many impertinent questions! Things here move apace and there's a great deal to do - London is a constant hustle and bustle.

Incidentally, isn't it your birthday about then? Looking forward to seeing you lots.

Love,
Eunice

Emma showed Eunice's letter to her parents, and they were glad to see she was stepping out and no longer leading her strange, secluded life.

She took the early morning Saturday train and, after changing at Derby and again at Leicester, got into St. Pancras just before noon. She had never seen such a railway station! It was like some imperial Hallowed Hall. And then the Underground, with its trotting escalators and its musty, warm air, a thousand times breathed. She went to the hostel where Eunice lived and dropped off her night-bag, glad of the fact that Eunice, indefatigable as ever, was out playing hockey the whole afternoon. She was glad the whole afternoon was free.

Following instructions, she rode to the Embankment, where she investigated the little park and found the statue of Robbie Burns. Still an hour and a half till 3 o'clock! She walked up Villiers Street and into a small restaurant, 'The Nelson', where she ordered something exotic called Spaghetti Bolognese, partly for the fun of it and partly because it was cheap. The menu read, 'England Expects ...' No-one, she thought, could be more expectant than her. She began to quiver with anticipation, hardly touching her meal when it came and, as if to make up for it, drinking several cups of tea. The dark, quick waiter flitted back and forth, looking her up and down on the sly.

She frittered some time away in a bookshop, then directed her steps back towards the park. It was 3 o'clock precisely and, standing by the statue, was the figure of a man in his early thirties, neatly but not exactly well dressed, with a ruddy complexion and dark, receding hair. That was 'Uncle T.', all right; she recognised him immediately. At the same second it flashed across her mind that he had no idea what *she* looked like and that, consequently, she could simply walk away, leave him standing there, and that would be that. She walked across his field of vision at some distance, her auburn curls bobbing at the nape of her neck, then she tacked in firmly from his blind side and, tapping him on the shoulder, said:

- Tristan Dakin?
- Emma! he said, blushing, stooping, taking her awkwardly in his arms. There was a hole in the air where some pigeons flew up.

They walked around the park for some time, then Tristan suggested they go and have tea.

- Did you know it was my birthday? asked Emma.
- Of course I did! Don't you believe in Correspondences?

And it was the first time she had heard a remark like that from anywhere outside her own skull. A burden dropped from her instantly: at last, she might be on a wavelength with someone!

She took Tristan's arm and they walked up across the Strand, through that warren of streets which leads to Covent Garden. They found a little place to have tea and were soon ensconced behind its steaming windows.

- You said there was much to tell, said Emma, when the waitress had brought them their tea and cakes.
- There is, young Emma, said Tristan, there is. But what about you and dad and the farm?
- You first; after all, it was you who wrote to me.
- Where would you like me to begin, then?
- At the beginning, naturally . . . with all the details, if you please.

And so he began the tale of his return.


'It was round about this time of year. I went AWOL on the battlefields of Flanders, near a place which later became famous: Passchendaele. It was only a few months before our major offensive and we were trying Gerry out, testing the ground, so to speak. The day I deserted my whole section was slaughtered, so, if I hadn't, I wouldn't be here, talking to you. I wanted to get back to England, you see . . . to see your mother . . . she told me she was dying. You were just a little girl at the time.

'I got to Dover without much trouble and I was sitting in the corner of a railway compartment. I suppose I must have dozed off for a while, because a very peculiar thing happened. In my sort-of-dream I saw your mother, standing by the window of the front parlour at Brewston. A beam of White Light was coming from her heart, in a steady stream, right around the world. Nobody seemed to notice it, which was odd. When it came to me I wanted to touch it, but it passed straight through me as if I wasn't there. The radiant shaft of it was tinged along both edges with the most delicate pale blue, making it softer to the eye. It made me think of secret Brotherhoods, those who swear allegiance on a single Sword. It had power to strike and power to heal. Why on earth did no-one recognise it? Then I saw that people's eyes were blind, that they just walk around without knowing why or where.

'I asked to be guided by the Light, but it just kept on beaming disinterestedly. It didn't seem it was your mother any more, at least not in any personal sense. Perhaps it was the Mother of the World - this dawned on me, as the Light went through and through me. She was so much more than I had ever imagined, so much less a prisoner of her painful, dying body. I thought of the many times I had been with her; they were all subsumed and contained in this one Presence.

'Still I sought guidance from the Light: I wanted it to give me some vital clue. For a long time it seemed impervious, then I noticed that, without my even trying, my attention was being focused in a particular direction. There was a map in front of me and I was looking north. Up here? I said, but it was pushing me further - out onto a limb of Scotland somewhere. On reflection I thought it might be symbolic, but it turned out to be actually, factually true: it was pointing to the place I was destined to go to. The power of the Light began to fade, and the figure of your mother became more real. It was true, she was extremely weak and frail. I wanted to reach her before she died, and all my old feeling welled up . . .

'Then someone started coughing in the dream; I thought it was odd, because I didn't know the voice. As the coughing became more regular and insistent, I realised it was someone inside the compartment giving me the hint that I was far away. I must have been calling her name out loud: Jessie! Jessie! I heard the echo in my brain.'

A pause fell between them like a flutter-down of wings, like the hole in the park where the pigeons had been.

- What did you do then? Emma asked.

'I came to with a start and the train began to move. It was an uneventful, dark, bleak journey, and we got into London between nine and ten. I wondered what I was going to do for the night: I hadn't got the money for a hotel and, for obvious reasons, I didn't want to go to a serviceman's place. As I was close to the river I walked along the Embankment, past the park where we met this afternoon. I stopped for a while and watched the sleek black limousines drawing up at the back entrance to the Savoy. It doesn't seem to matter, I thought to myself, war or no war, there's always rich and poor.

'I could have slept with the dossers under Hungerford Bridge, but I didn't feel I belonged there, either. I kept wandering through various parts of the city, stopping here and there when I found an all-night caff. A mug of tea can take a long time to drink, and you learn a lot about a city if you're up all night. It takes on a completely different shape. The people you meet are not the same (even the same people are not the same). The night-side of the city is like the night-side of mankind: the busy bustle is over, the masks are off and you can sink into any identity you choose. Freaks of every description emerge - and many more sexes than the plain, straight two. It's as if there were a multiple Underworld waiting, as indeed there is, beyond the circumscribed light. I don't mean the World of Crime exactly but something to which we're all intrinsically heir, when our daylight definitions cease and business and politics shut shop for the day. It's as if we were standing on our heads - at night the worms and lice crawl out. And we've all got worms and lice, believe you me. It's important to see that we're not all-of-a-piece, that there are threads and strands only Night can reveal. How stiff and proud we are in the Day, with our upright, strutting, rolled-umbrella Control! How little it takes in the dead of night to bring us to our knees, begging to be loved! But you're too young to know the Night.'

- I don't know the Night, but I now the Moor.

- Ah, yes, the Moor; I was forgetting the Moor. It must have been very important to you.

- Very, said Emma. But please go on.

'I hung around in this way till morning, then made my way to St. Pancras Station, where I bought a ticket through to Bakewell. I came to the ticket barrier, the last hiatus, and the man looked greyly and distantly at my ticket.

- Change at Leicester and Derby, he said.

'I was through in my uniform; I was coming home. Except that it wasn't really home, of course, for reasons you couldn't have known at the time, for reasons I think you may understand now . . . On a December day almost fourteen years ago I walked through Bakewell and trudged up the lane that makes its way over to Monyash and Brewston. Fortunately it was a lousy day, with low-hanging cloud and cold, bleak rain. Nobody recognised or even noticed me, I think. The few people I saw went huddling by, their heads behind umbrellas or with coat collars turned up. I was on the last thrust of the Tidal Wave that had pushed me out of Passchendaele.

'On the track to the farm I hesitated - I wasn't supposed to be there, you see. Your mother had sent me a letter to the Front, and on an impulse I had gone AWOL, become by that action a deserter and a traitor. For Alderman, too, I was a traitor: he had said that I could never come back. But here I was on the old familiar track, whose every rut and bump I knew by heart.

'I drew near to the house, taking cover behind walls, and came in close to the small front parlour. There was no figure at the window, as there had been in my dream. The world-encircling Light had vanished, and up against the window were bleak, blank blinds. I wanted to scream and lash out against them, kick in windows, blinds, furniture, everything: destroy this little world of cosiness and dying. I tried listening at the window for the sound of her voice. From time to time there were whisperings within, but so very soft I could make nothing out. Nothing, I repeated to myself. Nothing.

'When the day dwindles down to nothingness, collapses in upon itself like a softly bursting drum, when the night slinks in, taking everything away, and the tread of your foot makes no mark or echo, then you know what it means to be reduced to Zero, to have nowhere to go and nothing's to be done. Then you might as well be in Hades with Aeneas, walking among the Shades of the Dead. And, in Hades with Aeneas among the Shades of the Dead, you might meet Dido, who died of love. That's what your mother died of, Emma, though the symptoms were typhoid and the autopsy said so. Your mother and I were lovers, you see.'

- O, said Emma, so that's what it was.

And she blushed very red, down into her cup.

- I thought you should know the truth, said Tristan.

- The truth sets us free, she said flatly, ironically.

And, as he sat there, fumbling and fidgeting:

- Go on!

'I spent three nights sleeping rough in my army greatcoat. I faltered and went down to Gladwin's Copse, hoping somehow to recapture the fragrance of what I had known with Jessie in the past. Nothing was growing: it was the deadest time of year. Only the grass bent back by the rain. I went over to that barn which is down near the road. There, at least, I had shelter from the elements; there were a few old hay-bales lying around. I stretched out on them and slept blearily.

'Then suddenly I was on my feet. Some unaccustomed lights were strafing the night and I surmised, correctly as it turned out, that it was Dr. McKenzie driving over from Elmsworth. I pulled body and soul together and went back up towards the house. The blinds were still drawn; there was no light inside. And when Dr. McKenzie came out of the house, followed by Alderman, who went with him to the car, I caught the faintest scrap across the night air of its being 'for the best', of there being 'nothing one could do'.

'"I've come too late," I said to myself, "too late, too late," and I sank to the ground. I lay in the dark round the corner of the house, not more than ten feet from where Jessie's body lay, her soul already departed and gone. And in the dead of night, as the lights moved away, throwing up the track in broken sections like glass, I had only one wish: to die myself, to be out and gone from this bleak, cold world. What was this world without her, after all? An endless White-out of incipient Death, Snow falling everywhere, killing the tread. Furiously I hungered for death, as a starving man might hunger for food.

'Alderman must have walked some way down the track or simply hovered about in the yard, because the lights of Dr. McKenzie's car had already vanished over the hill when I heard him close the back door and bolt it. It was a sound both familiar and unique, and that night it betokened the end of everything: youth, love, the future - everything. I wished that I could have been taken then, that Jessie and I had died together, but, of course, life isn't that simple - ever. I just lay there in the darkness, bleating and sobbing, a pitiably miserable spectacle. I heard Gyp bark from inside the house, then the sound of her snuffling at the door. Perhaps she recognised my voice. I would have called out to her but every Veil was rent, every last channel of communication blocked. Torn and vacant, I could neither look nor speak.

'Then I remembered something Jessie had said: about Love being perennial, stronger than Death. She had often come back to it, in fact, as if she were preparing me for a moment such as this. And, though it was configured in wraiths of words, some trickle of her meaning filtered through. I couldn't have said I saw what she meant, much less did I feel it, but somehow it stood up: it wasn't just part of the awful Flux that was sucking me down in its fathomless Maw. There was something else at the bottom of the Darkness, some other impulse than pure, blank Destruction. It was something that was neither hers nor mine, some Imprint or Possibility made real, an invisible Thread, a . . .'

- Place of your Own?

'A Place of our Own, exactly, that's it. And I understood, lying there, looking at the sky, why human beings are immortalised as Stars. It isn't that they're any better than others; in fact, as people, they may be much worse. What they do for us is to plant a trail, to say: This is what human potential can do, this is the Panoply, this the Explosion. You have it in you to Be Here also, for this is the Immortal made visible and snining.

'Nonetheless, I couldn't get up straight away. I was still wracked with the pain of absence, with having lost everything, come back for nothing. But even this null sense of pain, grief and loss was as nothing compared to the feeling of futility. "That it should come to this!" I muttered to myself, partly to articulate the unspeakable Void, partly, by stating, to exorcise it. But the Void lapped round me like the night, with its infinite intangibilities. It, like me, had nowhere to go; it lay, as I did, blank and still. It reminded me of the chemical description of a liquid: colourless, odourless, a catalyst at best. But, unlike that liquid, it drank of itself, fed on itself, was ubiquitous, amorphous. Whatever had seemed real was now drunk down into it, losing all shape, definition and meaning. The living tissue of Life itself, which is what we are made of, which is what we *are*, and which all the time seems so substantial - all this was suddenly washed aside, turned inside out and burst like a bladder.

'Nor was there any means of putting it back together. It had gone to join the infinite Blank, the impenetrable Darkness above and below. Worse, this was the nature of everything: instead of solid substance, this appalling No-thing, this vacuous Pit into which all must fall. When one looked more closely it was there without pause, and our non-awareness of it was a temporary sojourn, a holiday really, in the summer Fields of Time. It wasn't that Death came as the End, like the end of the holiday, so to speak. No, it was altogether more abiding, walked with you everywhere, holding your hand. And at any moment it might obtrude, suck into itself your vital substance and spew you out anywhere, further down the line - totally outside what you had ever thought or felt - in some minus Dimension of its own importance, which didn't rely on this one for reference: a similar mass with an opposite charge. And this non-substantial Beyond-Black-Hole had its own co-ordinates, functions and data; only, they were different from what one had been taught. One's gut reaction was to forfend it, by any means one could lay one's hands on. But always it was waiting, the Shadow-self, the unalterable Companion, the Same-as-you-but-different. Here it was now in the unspeakable darkness, the quintessential Crosspoint by our own house wall.

'I got up and walked round the corner of the house. A dim light was burning in the front parlour. I propped myself upright and, aware of my Shadow, I surrendered to the darkness and the death of Jessie. I knew I was at the real Crosspoint, that from now on, if I was to live at all, it would have to be from another Source. My whole world, perhaps *the* whole world, had crashed in: it would never be the same again. With her, I felt, I could have gone anywhere, done anything I set my sights on. Now it would be a different tale. The War - and not just the War - had changed it all.

'I kept my vigil by the window for most of the night, then I went back down to the barn beyond the Copse and, as the day began to warm through, I did sleep for a few hours among the hay. I kept this up for three nights. Then, on the third day, as I had suspected, the hearse arrived to take Jessie's body away. I crept up nearer to the house and saw the family of mourners, dressed in black, assembled in that small space near the back door. I had a violent impulse to run in on the scene, to shout: "Stop!" imperiously, "This is all a mistake." But there was no mistake: the dreadful ritual went on. The mourners shuffled back and forth, gathered round the body like so many crows, being themselves like so many translations, numerous Emissaries from the Realm of Death. I couldn't move among them, though I might want to: I could not pierce their coded strength.

'The hearse moved off and the mourners followed: first Alderman, with his hat in his hand, then the nearer and thicker Dakin family, and finally, in a diminishing straggle, a retinue of spurious spouses, cousins, progeny, half-related kin. I noticed Emma had been left behind, and Martha, who was standing crying in the doorway, with a handkerchief held up to her face - she gave it a wave as the hearse moved off -, had obviously been detailed to look after her.'

- Indeed, said Emma, I was much too young.

'They went down the track and, curiously enough, at that very moment the sun came out. It was one of those early December days when the whole of Nature seems at peace, when all is storage and waiting and calm. In many ways I like it better than spring. The very fact that nothing is moving spreads a mantle of quietness over the earth. I could imagine Jessie radiant again, preparing herself in the fullness of time for a strong and striding resurrection.

'I followed at some distance, taking a short-cut across the fields, so that I was already in position on that bank above the village when the procession arrived at Elmsworth Church. The vicar's surplice made a splash of white among the black and I followed the movement of his lips, as he pronounced the final ritual prayers and Jessie's body was lowered into the grave. Long after the mourners had left the churchyard to meet and take food at The Dale Hotel I stood looking down at that gap in the ground. It reminded me momentarily of the wound of the trenches, and the deaths I had seen and suffered there - not singly, specially, as on this day, but anonymously, martially, belonging to no-one. Death was telling us something all the time. How rarciy it was we woke up to it!

'But on this single day this special death had changed the course of my life for good. I could never go back to the old, banal ways, the million complicities and compromises. It was like a surgical operation: so much of me had been cut away that all that remained was a single limb, one node of growth only. I was inchoate, at best.'

- How did you know what direction to take?

- I didn't - that's just the point, said Tristan.

The waitress was making closing-time noises and, sitting up and taking notice, they realised that they had been there now for almost two hours.

- Shall we go somewhere else? he said.

- I think I'd like to go back to Eunice's, said Emma. But we can meet tomorrow, if you like.

- Did it shock you, what I said?

- It did at first, shocked and confused me. Then I began to see how it all fitted . . .

it explains a lot of what happened later.

- How - if you don't mind telling me?

- About my father and how he changed, how he ceased to be my father at all.

- You can tell me tomorrow, said Tristan tenderly, seeing the tears well up in her eyes.

- He married again, you see, Emma put in quickly; that's my little bit of history. After that it was never the same.

- It never is, said Tristan magisterially.

They got up, left the café and went their separate ways.

Next day, when Emma went back to the 'Ay'n-al- Thabita', she found Tristan waiting beneath the sign. Once inside, he continued his tale.

'After Jessie died I was, in a sense, free - except that I was suspect, impecunious and homeless. I didn't know where to go or what to do.

One thing was certain: I had to move quickly, since it was only a matter of time before someone spotted me.

'I decided on a train to Manchester, for which I had the money and a little to spare. I also had a friend in Moss Side, who had been a boarder at Lady Manners and who I thought might be able to put me up temporarily. This, however, turned out *not* to be the case, though it was in my mind when I boarded the train.

'For as long as I could remember we had sent our milk along that line, but I had never travelled along it myself. We went over the huge spraddled viaduct at Monsall, up to Miller's Dale and on to Buxton, where we changed. I got into Piccadilly Station late morning and was glad that it wasn't raining for once. That was my only consolation, since my erstwhile school chum - 'Bradder' we called him - had passed into the Land of non-stop Hallucination as a consequence of inhaling nerve-gas at the Front.'

- You wouldn't know him, his father said. Perhaps it's better if you didn't . . .

'And I went.

'I've never been particularly practical and, even in these circumstances, I couldn't be pragmatic. I hunted around for an inspiration, and then I remembered my dream in Dover, the one with Jessie pointing at the map. That was it, the subtle Correspondence, the Via Cordis I'd been looking for. I decided there and then to make my way up to Scotland, where no-one knew me and I could start again. It was a sudden Leap into the arms of Fate, and if Fate was against me I was surely sunk. But that was the nature of the engagement; there was no time left for equivocation. I felt impelled to shift myself and let the Higher Order take me on. Ready or not, I was Brother to the Eagle - due for flight or doomed to crash.

'I won't bore you with the details of my itinerary, though that in itself was quit interesting. I tracked up the Pennines via Saddleworth Moor and, though I had to come down for food, I stuck to the high ground as much as I could. In spite of the exposure I felt safer up there, among the tussocky grass and fierce rock outcrops. It's always people I've been most scared of.

'I went to Scotland with a message from the Heart and it was at that level that I wanted to pursue it. There was no-one, of course, for me to turn to or consult with; I was like Sir Gawain in the wilderness of the Wirrall. In other words, I had to learn to read Signs.

'At first there seemed to be none at all, as I wandered across enormous tracts of land, peopled by farmers, with the odd scant village. I ate frugally and infrequently and sometimes I begged - only, however, when I felt strong, when I felt I could take 'no' for an answer without demur. It isn't always easy to lay oneself open, to let what is happening simply be.

64

'I pushed on further north to Glasgow, then out of Milngavie over Lennox to Loch Lomond. I suppose it was one of those turns of Fate, which give one courage, the strength to go on, that I arrived there on a richly purple evening, the sun suffused over its south-western end. I stood looking at the loch for a long, long while, feeling for the first time since I'd left Brewston that I was at some point of fixity, a Node, into which different Currents might flow and lead me off in a new Direction.

'I made a fire at the water's edge and watched the last of the sun grow dim. I became aware of an island opposite me, as in the growing darkness a light appeared. Obviously it was some kind of lamp, because it was swinging, perhaps suspended from a pole, in the breeze which blew up from the southern end of the loch. I don't know why, but in that conjunction of circumstances, with the darkness beginning to shut out all else, it seemed that here at last was a Sign, that I had come to the right place at just the right time - especially as suddenly, in the fire's glow, I caught sight of a rowing-boat pulled back among the trees.

'Initially I thought I would row over in the morning, but then a strange imperative seized me: it was now that I should make the trip, NOW, without prevarication. I had never in my life used a rowing-boat before, but somehow I manoeuvred it onto the water and was soon making headway towards the island. And, as if in confirmation of my intention, the lamp on the island began to move - steadily and, seemingly, in my direction - to let me in at a convenient point.

'And so, in fact, it proved to be, for as I approached a small scalloped inlet the lamp and the holder of the lamp came to meet me. He was a man, I should say, in his early forties, wearing a cloak of sorts which lifted in the breeze, then fitted back softly against his body. He deftly helped me out of the boat and led the way up some thick-hewn steps to a stone cottage among the trees. We sat on either side of a fire, with the lamp on a table slightly behind us.

- So you're here at last, said the man. I'm glad you've come.
- You mean, you've been expecting me?
- We've been expecting someone from the South; we didn't know exactly who.
- It's taken me a long time to get here. I didn't really know where I was going.
- That's understandable: one rarely does.

'He acknowledged his secret, smiling, then said:
- You're very welcome. My name's Bolen, by the way.
- Bo ...?
- Bolen. Brother Bolen. And yours?
- Tristan Dakin.
- Ah! Tristan, Tristan ...

'He rolled the name over on his tongue, as if in the very savouring of it there lay some clue as to the character of the person.
- The sad 'un, he said eventually.
- Sad and broken, I replied.
- That's part of your life's pattern, my friend. All of us in this Work have reached the Cross.
- The Cross?
- The Point of No Return. So far you have moved along a horizontal Track, looking perhaps a little to left and right. But when the vertical Instance intervenes, falls like a sword across the line of your life, then you are noughted at the Intersection and a totally different Journey begins. You, so it seems, have come to that Point.
' I was taken aback; I was blank with astonishment. I had felt all this vaguely, indeterminately, but in a way which as yet had no purchase in my life. I had sensed deep down that there was something beyond the turmoil but, because of the massive Gravity of Existence, I had been unsure, indeed had often felt that it was just some hyperbolic whim of my own. Now here was a man who spoke freely, with assurance, about those things which were hazy, dim and inchoate.
- Don't you want to know who we are?
- I do, but . . .
- You're English: you shut yourself down.
 I suppose I do, I put in meekly.
- We call ourselves 'The Brothers', he went on. We're known to each other but, to
the many, very little. We have what you might call a Wavelength, an Understanding.
- Does it extend all round the world?
- It does, but not in any formal sense. We have no Organisation, no Great Expectation. Ours is a Path which walks itself.
- Without any help or guidance?
- With guidance, certainly . . . but not necessarily human guidance.
- What other kinds are there?
- O, many kinds. Guidance is never lacking: it is we who are blind. A child, for instance, may be one's Guide, or a flower or a mountain - it depends on you, how you look and listen to what's around you. You must have had guidance to bring you here.
- Of course I did! I said emphatically, realising on the instant and with surprise the hidden aspect of my relationship with Jessie.
- I was being guided all along.
- And you were lucky enough to recognize it.
- Lucky?
- Very lucky, my friend. Innumerable opportunities are missed, chiefly by people who think they know better. The first step is to perceive that

66

one really knows nothing. Then Life itself can shape one to its purpose, instead of one's trying to shape Life, which is folly.

- Is that the basis of the Brotherhood - or do you hold office, take oaths, swear allegiances?

- Our only allegiance is to Life itself, but that indeed is a great austerity. It implies the eradication of self-will and the certain trust that, if one looks and listens, further aspects of the Truth will be revealed. When this happens - and perhaps it is happening with you - one no longer needs offices and positions of authority. There are so many intimations and demands that in twenty lifetimes one could never meet them all. So much is required of each one of us, you have no idea; it is incalculably vast.

- But how do you decide who does what?

- Everybody has their aptitudes, capacities. I, for instance, am a solitary character. I came here unbidden, though the others knew. At another time it might have been somebody else.

- And then?

- Then he or she would have come. It depends on the Constellation of the Moment, which of us is ripe and ready for the task.

- Aren't there jealousies and rivalries over things, people who think they're ready when they're not?

- If they're not ready they won't hear about it. In your case, for instance, no-one told me that someone was coming from the South: I just picked it up and acted on it.

- I see, I said incredulously.

- It does seem strange at first, he said. In normal society one gets so inured to Power, Authority, Command Structures of every kind. You should know; you've just come from the War.

- How do you . . .?

'Then I caught myself, sitting there in my fat greatcoat. I laughed out loud and Brother Bolen laughed with me.

- As you have no doubt realized, he went on, war itself is only an intensification of the state of conflict we live in day by day. Hence the necessity for Authority and Command. Just suppose the war in oneself could end, as the so-called Great War surely will. Where, then, would be the need for Command? One could reach out then in a completely different way - without imposition, without control -, act immediately, non-ideationally, in whatever circumstances presented themselves. That is what the Brothers are about.

- And anyone can join you?

- Anyone who has come to the Cross. Such people do, in fact, choose themselves: there's no selection panel, no interview. It's the total opposite of bourgeois society, with its crude approximations and merit lists. It doesn't try to patch up the Inner, while all the time pushing for

67

the outer result. No, being at the Crosspoint means having direct access to the inward Disposition, the Skein of Things. Seeing how things are, one then knows how to act - just as a mother, when her baby cries, knows exactly what to do; she is intimate with her action. Starting from this end, with harmony, not conflict, with the subtle contagion of the Whole Body of the World, one moves discreetly, finely, swiftly to that disclosure of Beauty which is its Essence.

- Beauty, not Love, not Truth?

- Those too. but the connecting element, the physical and tangible, the plastic and actual - what we live in and by - these are all manifestations of Beauty and align us, if we let them, with the World of Truth.

- And through them, again, That World operates in us?

- Exactly. That is exactly the point. But you have to go through the Zero first.

'I was about to say, I thought I had, when I realized what an assumption and assertion it would be. Better to gather myself quietly at that Point, assume-assert nothing, simply wait.

- You can sleep here, Brother Bolen said, as if reading my immediate apprehension. The boat belongs here, anyway.

- Thank you, I said, looking round the cottage.

- Through there, he said, indicating a small bedroom.

'I must have been very tired by now. The accumulated fatigue of weeks of wandering, added to the relief of a roof and human company, had combined to bring me to a state of exhaustion akin to what a mother feels, when she has given her all and the well is dry. I felt blank and emptied of all emotion, as if I were really at the Zero Point, waiting to begin all over again.'

- I'm afraid I shall have to go now, said Emma, standing up. It's getting dark already and my train leaves at five.

Tristan realized that, for quite some time, he had been virtually talking to himself. 'I've been away too long,' he thought. He had also forgotten to what an extent he was still, for Emma, 'Uncle T.' and that she retained her adolescent privilege of keeping her life at one remove from his.

- I'll take you to the station, he said.

- No, I must go to Eunice's first, for my things.

- To the Underground, then.

There was an insistence in his voice.


5


It wasn't until he had watched her go, seen her single weight absorbed in the mass of converging bodies at the ticket barrier, that he began to wonder when, if at all, he was ever likely to see her again. Probably, he felt, he had talked too much and his very intensity had put her off. Still, she had needed to know the truth, first and foremost about her mother, but also about him.

For her part, it was all so new, so much of a departure from what she had known, that she would take some time to assimilate it. She was certainly capable of understanding at that level, had indeed been abreast of it all from the start, but the strength and the shock of Tristan's disclosures were forcing her into a fresh Acceleration, ~ pick-up of Meaning from a different Zone. She wanted it actually but, as the saint said, 'not yet'.

She waited for a letter or a sign from him, while he, back again among friends in Scotland, wondered if he had not overstepped the mark in recounting so much of his personal history. He felt he had offered so much, and yet . . . Finally, after New Year, he wrote again.

- January, ...

My very dear Emma,

Time has flown, and our meeting-and-parting is now two months in the past. I wonder how you are getting on, how you feel about what I told you? It wasn't until you had disappeared that I began to get a sense of its impact on you - not too calamitous, I hope.

I have also wondered about seeing you again, but before I do - before I even ask - I would like to finish my story to the present. Then, perhaps, you can decide for yourself whether, or in what way, we might meet again. For my own part, I would very much like to, but you must feel free to do as you please.

I think I was recounting two months ago the conversation I had with Brother Bolen, when I first met him on the island in Loch Lomond. I discovered, incidentally, some time later that the island had been the site of an early Christian community as far back as the sixth or seventh century and that the Brothers had been aware of this. They believe in sustaining certain aspects of Tradition and have an eye and a taste for special places, particularly Places of Transition: the confluence of rivers, for instance, or certain saddles in the hills at a watershed. In our culture such sites are often marked by a stone circle, even two, contiguously figuring in solid substance the basic inner transformation: from duality to Unity, the two becoming One. This is the truth the Ancients possessed, which now we have almost totally forgotten. It is still present, of course, the stub of it, in such public rites of passage as the marriage ceremony, though whether, even here, the meaning is felt is something that is open to doubt. Nonetheless, the basic truth exists. One can go to the Stones; it is palpable.

69

What Brother Bolen was trying to show me was that I was at the Gateway of this intuitive Knowledge, what he called the Cross or Crosspoint (+). The Ancients knew this as a Certainty: that the Way to Truth goes through the Eye of self-noughting. It is the Eye one finds on the Egyptian tombs; others call it the Eye of Infinity, since it opens onto Worlds unseen. Worlds more transparent, which guide and govern this one. Being at Zero was where we left off ...

I stayed for several days with Brother Bolen, as he had much to tell me about the Brotherhood. Its influence is world-wide but the Brothers work unseen, rather, he informed me, like the Dervishes in Turkey. They live an ostensibly ordinary life, refining their Attunement, pushing inward all the time. Sometimes they can see things before they happen, and many a potential catastrophe, which the world at large never hears about, has been headed off by some timely intervention. This doesn't mean they can prevent everything - witness the Wall Street Crash, for instance - but they can and do infiltrate many areas, where harmonious solutions just seem to come about. They work always for the Concert of Heaven and Earth, that festive Marriage of Heart and Mind which alone can bring true Peace to mankind. Do not, therefore, dearest Emma (and forgive me for even thinking you would) give in to the temptation to bleak despair. Much is happening that we know not of; many are the Emissaries, multiple the Callings. The time for nurture and growth is here, and all the help we need is at hand. That, in a nutshell, is what Brother Bolen said.

He had laid out the work of the Brotherhood before me, and I rather gathered, from the way he put it, that he was expecting me to know what to do. I must confess that, in his terms, I didn't, though in the back of my mind was always the possibility of being picked up and court-martialled as a traitor. Eventually this decided it, since, in the changed Arena where I found myself, death by firing-squad made less sense than ever.

It was up to me, then, to decide where I would go. I lit on one of the Hebridean Islands, the name of which I still prefer to keep secret and which is known, above all, for its whisky and wool. The journey from the mainland takes about three and a half hours, so you will have a rough idea where I mean. Apart from its remoteness, the chief attraction of the Island was that, living on it, was a Community of the Brothers. You can imagine that, after Brother Bolen's description, I was anxious to find out more about them: what they did, how they managed to live together. In spite of my gullibly optimistic nature, some part of me remained sceptical: I couldn't imagine a situation where people lived freely, without bossing or constraint, and simply picked up what needed doing. I was sceptical, but I was in for a shock . . .

The very first morning the entire Community - eight or ten people - had disappeared. In a considerable panic I looked everywhere, and it was only when they came back in mid-afternoon, dressed in oilskins, completely drenched, that I discovered they had been out since first light to rescue a stranded fishing-boat. I later found out that such things were common, that, appraised or no, radio or no, they seemed to be aware of what was going on and to have the knack of rolling up, fully equipped, in the direst situations. They had been nicknamed 'The Angels' by the Islanders, but they were certainly not weightless Intelligences. The could muck in with the best of them - fishing, sheep-shearing, even knitting woollen jumpers.

So I came and lived with them on the Island, no questions asked; I was simply there. I joined in with all their activities, though at first I avoided trips to the mainland. The Community was largely self-sufficient, living from the sea and home-grown fruit and veg. We also kept sheep for their wool and meat; except for these animals, we did not eat meat. A bakery stood next to the main building, and its warm wafts permeated the House at all times. The climate isn't dry enough to grow grain, and we had to bring our flour over from the mainland. Such was the quality of our own produce, however, that we were able to sell the surplus for cash.

At the time I went there, of course, the War was on, and there were no fit men of fighting age - except for a quite beautiful Conscientious Objector, called Brother Thomas, who subsequently died. Most of the Brothers were, indeed, women, which startled me, since I had imagined from the name and also because of our monastic tradition that 'brothers' meant just that - men. Not at all; in fact, I later learned that in the Brotherhood worldwide a clear majority are women.

The focus of communal life was the House, which served the dual purpose of home and parliament. All meals were taken in the dining-room-cum-kitchen, while adjacent was a south-facing parlour, large enough to seat a dozen people and where the whole Community met each day, initially in silence, then, arising from that, talked over the matters closest to its heart. If this might seem a lugubrious procedure, let me assure you that it was not. It never degenerated into a formality but was always alive with some fresh perception, a new way of looking at daily affairs. Inwardly, the Brothers never stood still, as the Door, once opened, can never be shut.

I can hardly express in clumsy words the sense of joy and release I felt. It was like walking into a different World, one which I might have dreamt about but whose substantial reality I had never touched. Yet here it was, the living thing: here were actual men and women living a life of total communion, without all the misery, back-biting and conflict which characterize most human relationships. Freedom was the air that came in through the door, whipping up off the freshening sea. Freedom was the Distillation of Desire, unthwarted, pure, given free range and play.

71

The odd thing was, they did it all without theorizing, without using other sources that the direct tap-in to Life. Hardly any books were there, and those the choicest from the world's literature. For music, the Brothers played themselves and, indeed, the fact that they played themselves not only kept the House vibrant and lively, it also gave them contact with the Islanders, with whom they performed at crofters' ceilidhs.

It was a life uncluttered by Furniture. Each person owned the necessary minimum in terms of clothing, toiletries, etc., but apart from that we held all things in common, and the place belonged to whoever was there. More importantly, we had no mental furniture, by which I mean that we strove at all times to eschew accumulation of any kind: any form of prestige or power, I-know-more-than-you-do-because-I've-been-here-longer stuff, or any sense of hierarchical authority. On the other hand, we were a hieratic society, tuned into and moving on a Mystery unfolding, that pristine Unnameable beyond Space and Time, whose Essence we never described, or tried to. Possession played no part in it. For just as the ineffable What Is is free, so must the mind be free to find it. Each member sorted out his own Room first and saw the immediate necessity of it. From that Focus the Brothers moved out to the physical and material needs of the day. Beyond those needs we kept and stored nothing: that, I think, was the Secret we all shared. To have and hold nothing is to *be* nothing, too, with all the austerity and deftness that enjoins.

This applied equally to the sphere of relationship, which had me rather foxed at first. Again, I imagined that because they were 'the Brothers' they had taken some vow of celibacy. When this turned out not to be the case - and the Brothers were always extremely discreet -, I had to realign my thinking. They spoke often, for instance, of the value of chastity, which I had taken to mean 'no sexual relations'. But that's exactly what they *didn't* mean: by 'being chaste' they meant an austerity of heart, a lack of complicity in possessiveness, which did not preclude any kind of intimacy, with the same or with the opposite sex. Relationship, intimate or otherwise, could be entered into at any time, and only its untimeliness or the risk of hurting someone might bring a word of censure from others. It did, of course, happen from time to time that a couple formed so strong an attachment that they chose to leave, at least for a while. This happened twice while I was there, and both times easily and without recrimination. The emphasis was always on the quality of the relationship, on how it might enhance and enrich the Whole, rather than on who-was-doing-what-with-whom.

There is no marriage as such among the Brothers, and it is possible for a woman to have several 'husbands', as it is possible for a man to have several 'wives'. Usually, however, where the long-term is concerned, partners choose to stay together for life and, where there are children, this is obviously preferable. Nor did I find, in my time with the Brothers, the kind of obsession with personal relationship which narrows and mars most people's lives. On the contrary, intimate, personal relations became more of an offering made to the Whole, some new-found flowering of its Heart-Potential, another aspect of its perennial Growth. In such an atmosphere of Austerity and Beauty is was marvellous, also, what things *did* grow, which the closed parameters of our living preclude. The instinctual urges and deeper feelings were not suppressed, nor were they exalted, and because of this people found one another in ways that were mutually restorative and healthy.

The Unconscious, thus mooted, was not a Cave of Devils but an untapped Reservoir of Riches and Wonders, the opening of which gave free rein and volume to the creative drive in its many forms and facets. For some it was a walk in the glen with a friend, for another a long study, a poem or a painting, for a third a scientific experiment. All were free and had ample time, beyond the exigencies of physical survival, to dig and further a vein of their own, to tap into Life the way it suited them. This gave everyone a sense of latitude and freedom, which society at large and communities in particular rarely, if ever, seem to provide. On the one hand, the capitalist-industrialist Structure; on the other, some final fixed Goal or Purpose. In both the individual goes to the wall.

With the Brothers the difference is this: you come when you please, you go when you please. Your entry to the Brotherhood is through your own spirit, and that spirit is always and inalienably your own, not in the sense of possession or holding, but because that spirit lives and breathes you. No-one can or should ever try to shape, make, mould or control it. For that Source is pure like a mountain spring and, if it is allowed, it will find its way; it will bubble along in a natural course, irrigating the whole Waste Land in the process. This the Brothers, unique among people, are inviting and allowing each person to do.

Having thus arrived and joined the Brothers, I continued to live with them for the next year or more. Then news of the Armistice began to filter through, and that made me feel a little bit easier - to the point where I contemplated leaving the Island. But, being banished from Brewston, I had nowhere to go; what's more, I was learning so much with the Brothers, I was moving at such an accelerated rate, that it seemed mere folly to cast myself anew on the turbid, troubled waters of the world. No, I would stay and continue to grow: what I had learnt so far was only a beginning. And so, in fact, it turned out to be.

It would take too long - it's inappropriate anyway - to go into detail about what happened later, in all the months and years till I wrote. I went abroad - to Paris, in particular - and there met a lady, remarkably like your mother, with whom I lived on-and-off for several years. I travelled through Italy and bathed myself in the cultural splendours of the Renaissance. In short, I completed my education, which now for the first time seemed important to me and on which the Brothers lay such emphasis.

To cut a long story short, I eventually returned and settled with a group of ex-Islanders in a large house in Salisbury Road, Edinburgh. We sustained ourselves by marketing produce from the Island and, at the same time, with a number of friends, I helped start a school on Rudolf Steiner lines. Such activities, however, were largely peripheral: I was waiting for something else to happen, a new Birth from a long Gestation.

Well, now you've heard my story, most of it, perhaps you can write back and tell me what you think. As I say, I would love to see you again, but you should really do what's best for you and not be persuaded or cajoled by me. That's another thing I learned from the Brothers: NO INFLUENCE. You alone can go through the Eye. But if you do and if you choose, that Eye opens up into everything: Love, Death, Beauty - everything.

Yours, with tenderest affection,

Tristan

It was again two months before Emma replied.

- March, ...

Dear Uncle T.,

Thank you for your letter. I have naturally been pondering my response to it, while continuing to work as a pupil teacher here. You say a lot but, in a strange way, very little - as if, in your love and devotion to the Brothers, you had laid your intrinsic life aside. I am sure this is just an impression I've picked up and not at all the truth of the situation. But then why, I wonder, do you want to see *me*? What is this freedom-from-the-past business? Isn't there - trailing, lurking in your guts; hanging, as it were, suspended in your mind - an unresolved hunger for the old blood-link?

You have lived, as you put it, 'freely', whereas I have lived a very sheltered life - without real communication, admittedly. But, in a peculiar way, this has given me strength: I don't crave things, as you seem to. I have built within myself the strength to live and, while I couldn't say that I was happy, nor fulfilled, nor in any way whole, I attend to what needs doing every day and in that way, perhaps, I attend in true vein. There are many Avenues of Service, I think, and what is right for one is wrong for another. Mine is a separate calling, I feel, and

74

one which I wouldn't want anyone to share. Which doesn't mean I'm unwilling to share - just that in my niche there isn't room for two. I know that sounds awful and heartless, but it isn't: it is simply, as I see it, a statement of fact. It is my Station, my Place, if you prefer. And, as such, I have no right to leave it.

You are a wanderer, but a wanderer is restless: he is always looking for the next Horizon. There is a hollowness and unfulfilled longing about him, a desperate craving for a new Dawn and Place. This you give off like an atmosphere, and there is a haunting and saddening quality about it. I felt it surrounding you when we met and it is there in your letter, poking through, in spite of your enthusiasm and sense of adventure. The search for stimulation is rife and, while this is so, you will never find peace.

I'm sorry if this letter sounds deadening - it really isn't meant to be - I'm merely telling you what I think. I come to my little bits of wisdom slowly, like watching a pot very slowly boil. But at the moment of boiling there is no doubt; the truth is out, all over the place! I don't know how else to put it to you.

I was fascinated to hear your story of the Brothers, and I'm sure it's a wonderful place to be. Yet somehow, again, I don't think I would like it, however loose a set-up it may be. And if you were to jeopardize your relationship with them - go astray, as it were - on my account, it would only lead to ambiguities and frustrations. Of these there are already plenty and I wouldn't wish to add to them. Also, to me, you are still 'Uncle T.', and I would like to keep that pillar in place. I'm glad we met and we shall always be friends. The things you have told me are locked in my heart and from time to time I take them out, admire them like jewels and store them carefully away.

Please don't think me remiss or cold - I shall always think of you with affection. I am still young, however, and you are much older. Please understand this and love me still.

Emma

6

There is nothing like the frankness of the young: it wakes one up like a bucket of cold water! This letter of Emma's sent Tristan reeling. He had not been expecting a letter like this, full, as he was, of his own intoxications; he had been expecting something adulatory and submissive, from a person flattered and already half-in-love. The mature tone and impartial observations brought him up short and made him think again. Obviously his vanity had been working double-time, when all along he had thought himself free. Also, he was lonely and wanted someone close. All this and more he had projected onto Emma, recasting her in the mould of his Vision, oblivious to the fact that she was an independent human being. Now, in no uncertain terms, she had let him know she was.

In the back of his mind had been the Family Saga, the rediscovery of the Lost Paradise. But it had been a folly and a false creation. Back to the drawing-board, Tristan, back to the Road!

## BOOK THREE: ASPERITIES AND ANGELS

And Jacob went out from Beersheba, and went toward Haran.

And he lighted upon a certain place, and tarried there all night, because the sun was set; and he took of the stones of that place, and put them for his pillows, and lay down in that place to sleep.

And he dreamed, and behold a ladder set up on the earth, and the top of it reached to heaven: and behold the angels of God ascending and descending on it.

And, behold, the Lord stood above it, and said, I am the Lord God of Abraham thy father, and the God of Isaac: the land whereon thou liest, to thee will I give it, and to thy seed;

And thy seed shall be as the dust of the earth, and thou shalt spread abroad to the west, and to the east, and to the north, and to the south: and in thee and in thy seed shall all the families of the earth be blessed.

And, behold, I am with thee, and will keep thee in all places whither thou goest, and will bring thee again into this land; for I will not leave thee, until I have done that which I have spoken to thee of.

And Jacob awaked out of his sleep, and he said, Surely the Lord is in this place: and I knew it not.

And he was afraid, and said, How dreadful is this place! This is none other but the House of God, and this is the Gate of Heaven.

Genesis, 28: vv.10-17


### The Heights of Abraham

It is only when a break in the cloud occurs and the sun pours through with all its strength that we get a clear picture of the landscape of our life. Emma found herself a short time later perched high over Matlock, where she went to Training College, on just such a sunny, sailing, white-rock promontory. It wasn't that she had been resistant or unwilling -

there had been plenty of opportunities for boyfriends - but, simply and easily, she had flown clear, landed here, following the dictates of her own 'daemon'. The girls at College were full of the topic, talking of weekends and prospective marriage partners, but to her, as yet, it was all remote, part of some other, foreign landscape. It was strange, too, she reflected, with what despatch she had written off Tristan - but he *was* too old.

She devoted herself to reading and her studies, with a broad and general spread of all subjects, such as befits a prospective Primary School teacher. Occasionally at weekends she went back to Brewston, but mainly she wandered the local hills, forging sometimes as far as Crich, then winding back slowly down to Cromford Meadows. She loved the countryside, with its odd perched pines, its deep-cut dales, its distant singing moors. Always she longed to be up there with the larks. But the world, with its weight and its need, called her back.

1

She began to wear her hair very straight, to push it back severely at the nape of her neck, so that the white skin there was always exposed. Her breasts were small, her body slim, and she began, in addition to her reveries and walks, to take up body-culture in a more serious way. She was developing a concept of the ideal human being, psychologically serene and physically perfect, as it appears in certain statues of the Greeks: the Venus de Milo, the Young Charioteer. And always behind it was the unseen push, the unspoken drive towards something sublime. She wanted to incarnate the Ideal, to make it present, live and breathing. She saw herself in her mind's eye Greek, with that potency of the Creative Imagination, which rediscovers and restores the hidden Harmonies and renders them living, instinct and tangible. She fired on this; it became her meat and drink.

She became in her own eyes a daughter of the Muses, dwelling on Parnassos, inspired by Apollo. She felt she needed *all* the accomplishments and not just the elements of meagre 'teacher training', which her lecturers laid out and the other girls accepted as the necessary passport to a job. No, as ever, she wanted more - some exaltation of body, mind and spirit - which would put her in touch with the Music of the Spheres. Modern Dance was just coming in, and insofar as she could, practising alone, she developed the taste and skill for it, loving the fluidity and dynamism of movement, the frank liberation from stiff-stuff ballet. She was seeking to find a synthesis of this free-wheeling, fluid drive and the fixed, unmoving laws of mathematics, the laws of musical intervals and harmonics. She was aware all along of an underlying Order, to which the human mind could aspire, which it could touch, apprehend, comprehend, perhaps live by, but which did not depend on its machinations. This she was constantly pushing for, attempting to realize it in her life, while all the time maintaining and presenting to the world the image of the Vestal, the unentered Shrine.

Inwardly, however, she was casting out the vestiges of mystical experience. She rarely, if ever, went to Church, though there was a church nearby with a statue of the Virgin. When she went there sometimes, silently, alone, it was more by way of an experiment; it was to find out what was left of her old religious leaning. She found she no longer burned with love of the Virgin, and what had once been the secret Charge of her life, those discreet, world-encircling Emanations, seemed more to her now like her own projections, phantoms of her own brain, fascinations, illusions. She no longer wanted to 'waft off', as she put it, but to be grounded, tensile, fibrous and real: a living node of connection between Heaven and Earth. Thus, she lived and shaped herself into her self-chosen Model of Perfection - away from Semitic inwardness and vision towards Hellenic clarity, the out-there Level Line. A new current began to flow in her life, which gave a fresh account of things and allowed for, indeed necessitated, some unforeseen and devastating changes.

Tristan wrote again, to Brewston, and his letter was forwarded on to her. He suggested meeting but again she refused. She really wanted to carve her own way, independent of family affairs. No - and, somehow, it came through the No - that was *not* the way for her. No nostalgia, no sentiment, no mush . . . So that when she made the acquaintance of Miss Rodd she was primed to fall in love with her, with the sort of violence and instant totality reserved for those of her caste and kind, who think themselves eternally above such things.

In the event, it was she who sought out Miss Rodd. Her work with Dance was proving unsatisfactory and, despite the meagreness of her funds, she advertised in the Derby Evening Herald for a dance teacher 'on an occasional basis'. She received a reply which specified immediately that dance tuition was 'on a regular basis', signed E. Rodd, R.S.D.T. She should come to Derby on 15 January for an interview and audition, 'then we can see'. Miss Rodd described herself as 'peripatatic', which in Emma's eyes added to her distinction. When she later discovered she had been in New York, her status was elevated even further.

On the said day in January, which was slushy and cold, Emma arrived at the dilapidated hall. Above the door hung an improbable sign, from which a number of letters were missing, with the consequence that it read, . . sick maket. M . n. She thought it might be some secret code, the cracking of which gained one access to the hall, but when she pushed the door and the frosted glass bent back she realised it was one of those literary devices which a maverick God occasionally sends down to torment, puzzle, amuse and let us past.

The hall was cold and the boards bare. What's more, Emma, in anticipation, had flung just an overcoat over her dance things, which meant that, after the ride in the unheated train, the wait for the trolley-bus and the search for the address, she was approaching a state of blue paralysis. Compounded with this and worsened by it was her high degree of nervous tension. In public, before a real dance teacher! She hardly thought she could move a muscle. Her agony, however, was somewhat attenuated by the presence of three or four other girls and a shy young man of elfin mien.

Miss Rodd took them all together from her podium, on which she beat out a merciless measure. The other girls - the shy young man, also, who throughout the session was called 'girlie number two' - must have had classical training, thought Emma, for at least they moved correctly in time, though their movements were no more 'modern' than her own. When she had twice almost fallen and the whole group affair had become so elephantine that performing elephants might actually have been better worth watching, Miss Rodd put an end to the ludicrous proceedings by beating three times very loudly on the podium. Everybody stopped and needed no verbal referent, before picking up their things and making for the door. Emma had long since given up hope and would have left earlier, had it been possible. Imagine her astonishment, then, when the close-clad, dark and imperious Miss Rodd said:

- You, I'd like to see you dance alone.

Nervously, Emma moved to her routine, which portrayed a rather Chaplinesque tramp, slouching through the streets in a down-and-out way and choreographed to the music - she didn't have it with her - of 'Saint James' Infirmary', rendered by the Hot Seven. And, somehow, this time everything was different. Perhaps because she was alone, her muscles warmed from the group work-out, her body, indefinably, began to flow, to seek and find its right moments and pauses.

She seemed, in a way, to be outside her body, as if the whole organism belonged to someone else and yet, in another, more intimate way, she was entirely centred and focused there. Her weight was right down and her weight *was* Sound, the unheard sound of that searing song. She was, as it were, in the belly of the song, living its breath and being breathed by it. As she turned and skipped and ran across the boards, she fell like Jonah into a new Becoming, a fresh unfoldment of her native spirit. She *became* the unheard music and the song, in a breath and vibration which none could hear but which, nonetheless, she made visible and real. And what she had choreographed became the bare structure, like the basic melody in jazz, around which she improvised spontaneously. It was a thrill to her - and the thrill eddied out - to be able thus freely to dig down and express what had been locked and throbbing inside her for aeons. She wanted to go on, to dance herself to death, like the sacrificial virgin in the Rite of Spring, but a voice within her - she thought it was within her - said: 'All right, that's fine': it was Miss Rodd's voice.

She found herself in a kind of Swan Lake finale, with her torso folded over her legs. Miss Rodd took her firmly, gently by the shoulders and raised her to her feet, standing slightly behind her.

- I'll take you on, she said finally, curtly.

- O, thank you! said Emma, with a little flush of joy.

- We can start on Wednesday, if you like.

- That would be perfect, Emma said, reflecting amidst the euphoria of acceptance that Wednesday was a sports afternoon and that she could, with permission, leave Matlock by noon.

She left the hall in an ecstasy, sweeping invisible along the street, conjuring up for herself Miss Rodd's last words:

- There's a lot of work to be done, but you have a gift.

Work was nothing if the gift was there. If it was, indeed, a real, true gift, work came naturally, easily, smoothly. Then it wasn't really work at all, in the sense of a frictional effort imposed, but an arm and aspect of Creative Labour, the unforced offering of oneself.

It took Emma some time to realize that part of her whirlwind intoxication was due to the fact that her Dance teacher was Miss Rodd. The Wednesday afternoon sessions began, initially at the Musick Hall, later (which was better for both of them) at a smaller place on the edge of town. Miss Rodd travelled over from Nottingham, where she had a much larger contingent of pupils. Derby she described as 'provincial and drab'.

Miss Rodd was always immaculately turned out, as if she were about to give a performance on the London or the New York stage. Her finely moulded, high cheek-bones gave the rest of her features an austere grace, and with her hair brushed back and her body trim, there was no part of her that did not cohere. She seemed invincible, made for any occasion, and like a true professional she spoke only of her work. There quivered yet beneath the skin the sensitivity of a startled deer; that shyness and wildness played about her eyes. She was never quite still, not even for a second, and her tell-tale eyes blinked vigorously. Nevertheless, she had a studied composure, an iron-and-satin imperious veneer.

When it came to the lessons she was very strict, absolutely rigorous about rhythm, never for a second allowing Emma the illusion that 'modern' meant undisciplined, disorderly or slack. Yet she had, she said, selected Emma precisely *because* she had no classical background. With

81

the others it would have been impossible: they already had too much to unlearn.

Emma threw herself into this phase of her life, which picked up on all her latent enthusiasm and offered her a path of self-development. She was assiduous to a fault, attentive and obedient, and practised three or four hours a day on her own. Perhaps it was this working love, this utter dedication, that moved Miss Rodd; perhaps it was simply Emma's beauty, which was such it might have made the stones sing: her sylph-like grace, her noble face, the woman in her rising through every pore. And such was her innocence, she didn't realize that whatever she did she was doing for Miss Rodd. This lady was now the pole of her existence, magnetizing and drawing her on.

Miss Rodd, for her part, encouraged and emboldened her, pushing her in movement and choreography to make original innovations and never to accept what was routine or predictable. It was a constant spiralling, a consistent joy, and the two of them arrived, after a certain time, at a point of Being, a mutual Plateau, from which there was no going back.

The stretched, soft evening swam about them, holding them, cupped, on a Height in that hall. Emma, vivid from the dance, was pirouetting with a silk scarf fluttering at her throat. Miss Rodd came up and, taking her by the shoulders, as she did so often, said:

- More like this.

But, thorough professional though she was, a hair-line crack had appeared in her voice, a faint tremble issued in her touch, so that she removed her hands rapidly and smiled obliquely, one of those half-apologetic smiles, which was quite out of character with her general demeanour.

- Like this? said Emma, carrying on.

But the snap in the air was palpable and, after making two or three turns more, Emma stopped and stood facing Miss Rodd, who was gazing at her from dark, dilated eyes.

- You're very beautiful, Emma, she said.

Then deliberately, smoothly, almost fastidiously she took the silk scarf from Emma's throat and kissed her strongly, passionately there. Emma, shocked, took two steps back and the thought occurred to her: 'I might just run.' But the new movement in her life was too powerful, the intimate blood of Miss Rodd too strong. All this it would be futile to reject; indeed, it was already part of her. She threw herself, as she had not done since a child, into Miss Rodd's open arms.

- I love you, too, Miss Rodd, she said. I have done ever since the first day!

- Call me Evelyn, my darling, said Miss Rodd. I have waited and waited for you to come to me.

She was kissing her face and neck over and over, oblivious of everything but the Height they were on. She pulled her to her, body to body, and she felt the flame run through both of them. It was a flame ubiquitous, light and dancing; it played in Emma's eyes, as she kissed them one by one. Emma's face, still flushed from dancing, drew deep blushes under her eyes. She nuzzled her head into Evelyn's shoulder and flung her arms about her neck.

- You won't ever leave me, will you? said Emma.
- Never, my darling, Evelyn said.

## 2

Miss Evelyn Rodd was originally from the Midlands and had been left a family house in the country, on the banks of the Trent, somewhere south of Notthingham. The following weekend she invited Emma there, and the girl arrived to early spring sunshine, primroses, wood anemones and celandines beneath the trees. She felt relaxed, warm and open, as if with the relenting of the winds of March her own inner being had lost its aridity and come supple into the white and yellow world. She wore an open coat, a light jumper and a pleated skirt, almost ankle-length. She had, on the strength of some money from home, bought herself a new pair of shoes, and they glistened brown in the welcoming sun, with sporadic shots of gold from their polished buckles. A red scarf blew back from her throat, as she ran to meet and embrace Evelyn, who had come to the station to pick her up.

They stood there, hugging and kissing like lovers, while the world of cars and pony traps went by and the train pulled out on its way to Nottingham. Evelyn had also dressed for the occasion: she was wearing a cap of purple velvet, the perfect counterpoise to her jet-black hair, then, over a white blouse, a dark navy loose jacket, the cuffs turned back, sleek black trousers, black shoes. It was like the marriage of metropolis and country - Emma with her fresh-of-face outdoors look, Evelyn of the city, a sojourner here.

They got in the car and drove to the house, Emma was completely enchanted by it; in fact, she had a feeling of 'déja` vu', so close was it to some region of her consciousness, partly illuminated, partly obscure, into which she had wandered unawares. It was an evocation of the classical Pastoral, with a small Diana on a pedestal, obelisks in 'trompe-l'oeil' open landscapes, vases flower-filled and vases closed, urns and arbours and lovers' trysts. Along trellis-work ran a scatter of vine-leaves (the fruit was a gesture, a suggestion, never picked) and they tumbled and spread into a half-acre orchard, which itself gave way to native woodland: willows, poplars and alders by the water. The leaves were just coming and on the light-of-limb poplars they were tinkling and

83

dancing, as they do in summertime. The Cultivated ran into the Wild and, in turn, the Natural ran back to the Sown, in a way which stated: 'Yes, we are here. Our proper place is here - *among.'*

The lichen-encrusted garden urns gave way to a smoother statuary indoors. From a wooden platform Hermes rose, with his loose, long locks and sandalled feet. His face had a feminine charm and grace, as do that of so many of the young gods and heroes, in whom some Marriage has taken place. A statue of Poseidon, copied from Athens, stood bearded and erect, his trident missing, in the centre of the sunny front-room, while, in a niche adjacent to the stairs, a small sculpted Venus represented and expressed that indwelling serenity which signifies Completion. The light ran in- and out-of-doors, reflected, echoed in the high ceilings, playing on the river in a million shifting sparks.

Evelyn and Emma were like two spring lambs, kicking off their shoes, and running barefoot through the grass. They ran through the garden, the orchard, the wood, back into the house, up- and downstairs, pausing in the kitchen, their Signature writ, with that sudden fall of seriousness lovers have, to embrace, hold and kiss, spin Love's loop away, in a World that is dawning, which was bursting from their hearts.

The deep, dark swirl of the Trent went by, and in the afternoon they took the rowing-boat out - upstream and, strangely, through green pastures, south. They sported straw boaters for the occasion and, though there was a chill on the river, they rowed strongly in turns, enjoying the movement of their bodies, watching each other's body unfurl. Already in their laughing, gambolling, playing, they were unveiling the Icon, the Secret of themselves.

They got back to 'Trentside' about five o'clock and took tea in the loggia at the south-west corner of the house. Evelyn had baked some special scones, with a whimsical whorl and cream on top. She asked Emma what she thought of them and Emma said they were 'utterly delicious', which made both of them laugh and Evelyn almost cry. Her belly was laughing but her heart was pressed, milled almost to silent ecstasy but afraid lest this delicate, fine-glass thing should suddenly shatter and its shards cut her flesh. She, who knew the world, who knew Paris and New York, who held London audiences spellbound by her performances, was more afraid than this slip-of-a-lass, this Vestal Virgin from Derbyshire. Emma was secure behind her tea, she was home and dry in her own Midlands; she had never been anywhere and she feared no-one. That, along with her praeternatural innocence, the open outpouring of her whole intact heart, made her unbearably desirable to Evelyn, who consequently feared at every step some slip which might ruin everything.

Emma found Evelyn simply wonderful - so poised, sophisticated and mistress of herself. She could prepare an elegant dinner from what looked like scraps, and it all tasted so exotic and refined that Emma was sure she had never eaten anything like it. She deferred to her in everything - helping her chop vegetables, laying the table -, keeping it somewhere in the back of her mind that this was Miss Rodd and she was Emma Dakin, pupil. When Evelyn asked her to taste the wine, she answered in all honesty that she had never drunk wine. Evelyn told her to try it anyway, filling their two glasses, the Cup to the Brim.

- My education is just beginning, said Emma.
- Mine too, said Evelyn. Mine too, with you.

The Angels in her life had been few-and-far-between. She had loved the theatre from a child and, as soon as she was old enough to leave school, she had gone to London and worked back-stage: stagehand, lights, props, tea-masher - anything. After some time and a lot of push and practice she began to get work as a chorus girl. Then an impresario from New York spotted her, took her out to dinner and made her an offer: she could dance with Martha Graham and sleep with him, and how about trying the second part first? She was streetwise enough to 'need time to think' and, realizing that progress depended on compliance, she duly accepted, though not until New York. The sexual aspect was 'rugged but unfulfilling', but the man kept his word about the Martha Graham troupe, in which she soon began to excel, to the extent that she was given solo dances. She 'kept house' in this way with a string of men, most of them generous, almost all of them married, till she felt she was well-known and well-off enough to be able to ditch them, which she did. But something had happened in the hard meanwhile, some part of her had been buried alive, so that now, some years on, she was desperate: behind her mask, deep-down afraid. She feared most of all to grab at good Fortune, to pluck the Fruit before it was ripe. She held on still to the Rope of the Living - but, my God, not another failure, please!

This all contributed to the heightened mood, the 'pétillant' feel of their first evening together. Emma was really very at home, thawing and giving in Evelyn's hands, feeling warm, expansive, nurtured and loved, in a way to which she had become a stranger since Jessie's death and Alderman's marriage to Marion. To that bleak, stone, philistine place of toil had succeeded this cultured house by the river, with its sentient trees and emergent flowers, its Hellenic contour of beauty and grace.

It was a World which Evelyn had created for herself out of the asperities of her existence. Because of the contractual nature of her dealings with them, men had lost all attraction for her; they had ceased to be able to make present in her life the higher, finer masculine principle: to embody, in a word, the 'animus'. To establish this counterbalance to herself, the clear White Light of the Other Half, Evelyn had turned more and more to the Greeks, finding in their sense of aesthetics and order some kind of compensation, albeit in stone, for the brutal, venal nature of her own intercourse. What she had sacrificed to becoming a success on the boards had come to rest, petrified, within her and she had cast it forth in its ideal image, finding therein a touchstone to live by, while abhorring its earthly counterpart.

Thus, she projected and made a World, whose very exclusivity had become a limitation. For she was far too human, too much a woman and an artist, to wish to remain forever immured, even in such a Chastel Merveil. She must and wanted to share her treasure, to make it shine in another human heart. And the danger, existentially, of coming up against another Blank Wall was as nothing compared to the misery and disenchantment of a life unproffered, a Child unborn.

The fire in the grate burned eminent and warm, and they were sitting on the floor with their after-dinner coffee. Emma's face had a ruddy, leonine glow, her forehead high and broad, her hair dipping like a mane. Evelyn looked at her in silence for a very long time, then she stroked her brow gently, running her fingers down her cheek, till she came to the mouth, which she parted with her index. Then, taking Emma's face in both her hands, she kissed her long, strong and deeply on the mouth. Emma opened her eyes wide and looked at her, then, mathematically almost and to the same degree, she returned the kiss, tasting Evelyn's mouth and pushing her back against the settee.

- I want you to teach me everything, she said.

- I shall, my darling, Evelyn said.

And it was then that their intimacies began. Evelyn was the quicker and the fiercer of the two, Emma the shy one but, when the mood was on, the stronger. She did not initiate but followed her teacher; yet at times she returned her play so strongly that Evelyn was wholly subjected to her, overmastered by her calm strength. And in Emma there was always something apart, some element watching, as when she danced. She didn't have Evelyn's impassioned drive, that whirlwind energy which breaks all restraint and in which there is always a corner of angst. No, she was, even in her nakedness, studied, something akin to a Greek statue herself, something like Michaelangelo's 'David'.

This enraptured and excited Evelyn, who found in her all the beauty of the Boy, the transposed evocation of the Ideal. In truth, her manhood's ideal was here: in this leonine, golden, almost abstracted young woman. Here was no fatal fall into fucking but a fresh, chaste, constant, quiet unveiling, a running-fire Journey to the inner sanctum, where the burning Deity sits supreme.

Emma's touch was very pure, like that of a child waking up in the world, so that Evelyn began to come alive, to let the deadness and coarseness which had been her sexual body drop away like so much

86

unwanted skin. Yet she hardly dared trust the wonder and beauty; the 'frisson' went through her: she was fragile like glass.

Emma's nude body was god-like, serene, and she gazed and gazed at it, murmuring:

- My beautiful Greek, my darling, my . . .

Then, convulsively, she began to sob, the tears flowing copiously down her cheeks, round the corners of her mouth and over her nipples. She clung to Emma and Emma held her firm.

- It's all right, she said. We're together now.

The nakedness of their first love-embrace had brought Evelyn up against herself, and the whole buried River of her ruinous life had burst its banks and come flooding out.

- I must have you near me, she said, choking on her tears.

And it really did seem to her that, without Emma there, without this strong, chaste, firm, young body she would simply disintegrate, her vulnerability was such.

Emma bent down and kissed the tears from her eyes, from her mouth, from her nipples, with the flesh of her lips, sensing a shiver of pleasure run through Evelyn, who smiled weakly, wanly, bleak counterpoise to the gut-wrenching spasms, which were the dredging of her life. It was the wounds of her history welling up, the Story of Sorrow which afflicts mankind: the iron-staircase mercilessness of New York, the innumerable loveless encounters in hired rooms, where he paid the rent and she paid the price. It came gushing out of her, wave upon wave, rising from some hidden depth of pain, in which everything human has its birth. She had tapped this reservoir of silent suffering, the tragic Underlay of things, and, what's more, she had tapped it unawares.

Emma had come to her innocently and she had wanted to penetrate that innocence, to make of her the girl-boy she wanted. She was not averse to hard-woman tactics and all day she had been thinking, among their carefree revels, of the moment when she would possess Emma. She had, in fact, had it all worked out. Losing her interest in men, she had turned to women, using her power and lithesome body to attract and seduce the sexually miserable, as well as women who just preferred women. But it had grown in her as a mannerism - largely the consequence of her glamour and success - to take the lead role, to master and dominate, and this was how she saw herself. Perhaps she was secretly taking revenge for all the humiliation she had suffered. Who cared, anyway, if from time to time her relationships involved a little SM? She could bring some dowdy, unloved wench to a pitch of passion she had never known. Then, what did it matter if she disappeared in the crowd? She had been the lover of Evelyn Rodd.

Although her feelings for Emma had been more complex and she had nurtured them over a longer time, she still had seen her as one of her conquests, a new Golden Flower on her red-and-pink Priapic Road. She had coveted the girl so constantly, been skin-to-skin with her in her mind's eye so often, that she could not have imagined their nakedness to be anything but an Orchestral Opening. But this girl - God bless and damn her! - was different. She had never been naked with anyone before and yet she had touched her at so many points at once, had disclosed to her, in her single rich presence, the skin-deep brittleness of her own emotions, that Evelyn had gone through a change unwonted, unprecedented in all her life. What she had thought to find in the younger woman - some quivering, sobbing, lovely pleading child - had instead come to focus in her own heart's pain, the seat of which was far, far deeper than anything she had known or experienced before.

She let herself go, her hardness fell away, and Emma, the auburn-haired country lass, held her, soothed, in her arms till Morpheus came. They had entered the same, dark, pristine, open World.

3

When Evelyn woke up the next morning, she found, in a blue ceramic vase by her bed, a yellow bobble-head of late daffodils. 'Emma's up and about already,' she thought. She lay back, thinking of yesterday, trying to reassemble the pieces in her mind; they had fallen out so singularly, the whole bright sequence had taken her by surprise. She felt, however, curiously cleansed, as if she had been dirty from the day she was born and had now only yesterday taken a bath. A great weight of filth had come rolling off her and she had slept like a baby, what was it? Twelve hours! She sat up, smiling, feeling very relaxed, allowing the impression from every side to work in and through her and bring her to life.

- Emma! she called, but there was no reply. The sunlight was licking the daffodils, bringing their throats up a deep, dark yellow. It fell across the counterpane, stroking Evelyn's face. 'I must get up,' she said to herself. But she was in such a mood of luxuriant ease, looking at every little flicker of light, every attribute of the April morning, that it took her some time to actually do it. She slipped on her housecoat and went downstairs.

Without thinking about it consciously, she was aware of Emma's absence, surprised not to find her. While the water was boiling on the hob, she went out into the garden to look for her. Not there, either. She came back inside. Then, propped against the milk-jug - how come she could have missed it? -, she noticed an envelope with her name written on it. She opened it and read the following:

Sunday,...

My dearest Evelyn,

This morning I tiptoed into your bedroom, where I had brought you the night before. You looked so lovely and peaceful asleep that I didn't want to wake you up. I hope you like the daffodils.

I also, in my peregrinations, came upon the House of Lesbos, which I looked at for some time. You are quite a lady! Don't think I was shocked - I wasn't really - but I must say I found it all a bit contrived. I'm a simple country girl, as you know. I found it in some way claustrophobic, and it awakened in me a strong desire to leave.

You are older than me and have led a very different life, and sometimes this surfaces dramatically. When you're not there in person to hold my hand, it seems we belong to two different worlds. I know it isn't so, actually, but at moments like this the switch is abrupt. I didn't want to wake you, thinking all this - and, then, you were sleeping so peacefully!

Think of me, dearest Evelyn, as a foolish child, or as you will, but think of me, do, as I am thinking of you.

Your Emma

And there she was - gone! Evelyn made her tea and lit a cigarette, allowing the smoke to waft around her and melt bluely into the atmosphere. The House of Lesbos, the sweet little fool!

The swallow-danced, lyrical Island of Lesbos rises from the Aegean at its eastern end. Fabled for its poetry in the preclassical period, it is better known as the Sanctum of Women. Here it was priestesses who initiated the rites, and it was on this basis that the Cult began.

Evelyn's attempts to recreate it reflected her own life more than anything else. Having no interest in Divine Origins, she had focused on the love-between-women which was her art. 'Ars Amoris' stood over the door.

There was a whiff, inside, of some dreamy narcotic, some pleasant, sense-enhancing substance, that permeated as much as it was burned or smoked. It wasn't just there, it *inhabited* the place, just as an atmosphere of strife or peace comes to settle in and define a home. Her perfumes, unguents, oils, her 'toys' lay strewn about the room as if waiting there, as if they too were animate. Here was no prospect of river or sun but a gaze inturned on thick plush purple curtains, soft sunk velvet cushions, satin black-and-white. One could go for black leather, one could go for gold - and surely, somewhere, there was a hint of both, intermingling, enriching, making dense. It was a World half-hinged, semi-coital, unfulfilled, but whose background persuasion was: 'Yes, it's O.K.'

Emma had stumbled into it half-awares and been taken aback by its rich ambience. She had wanted to close the door and walk away, but her watching self told her: 'No, you must look.' She took stock; she examined everything.

Peopled by dolphins, diving and playing, the Aegean was a deeper blue than any real sea. In the middle of the screen, among the ruins of a temple, two young women were kissing and caressing one another. Behind them a third woman played the lute, while to one side, fleshy and grape-laden, drunken Dionysos sprawled beneath a tree. The picture was called 'The little Theatre of Love.'

At the turn of a button the image changed to reveal an Allegory of Dominance, painted in the manner of the Flemish School. It depicted a so-called 'Mediaeval Master', dressed in the softer leathers of the period, with long blond hair, astride a suppliant victim. The whole thing was called 'The Gate of Salvation' and someone had written on it. 'attributed to B...g..l.'

The eighteenth century was the period of aristocratic seductions, voluptuous bosoms, wigs, masks, powders, the Dangers of the Dance. A chamber orchestra, that customary pretext, was dutifully playing on a small, curved stage. A raven-haired young beauty, red rose in hair, from whose delicate fingers a fan had just fallen, reclined on a couch, a flush upon her cheek, while her sovereign mistress bent across her and with dextrous digits gave pleasure to her charge. Title, tongue-in-cheek: 'For Your Eyes Only.'

This evocation of Evelyn's Unconscious was as much as Emma could bear for now and she didn't stop to watch the end. If she had, she would have seen a black-and-white photograph, greatly enlarged, like the detail of a painting, and in which a boy-girl with close-cropped black hair had pushed back the petticoat of her ash-blond lover and inserted her head between her thighs. The belly-bent blonde held her head for good measure, as if to ensure that no drop of pleasure should be lost from the lingual exercise, and her skin, thus vivified, textured, emboldened, looked powerful and soft like the smooth-stroked shore, when the hand of the sea passes over it. It was called, quite simply, 'Girl-friends: black-and-white'.

In spite of what she wrote, Emma *had* been shocked and had quickly sought the freshness of the outdoors. There was nothing left for it now but to leave, and this she did, carrying her bag to the station. In the event (its being Sunday) she had to wait a long time for a train and, if this had occurred to Evelyn, she could easily have driven to the station and retrieved her. As it was, she sat smoking and musing on the split, on the acreage of distance between their lives. And yet she felt revivified,

90

intensified, released; a new phase was opening up for her. One penny, however, had surely dropped: this was no ordinary, run-of-the-mill girl.

She slipped into slacks and took a look at the House, her private World of Erotica. She ran her hand across the surface of the photograph, almost feeling the flesh of the thighs, as they opened softly and strongly to the kiss. They seemed to be granulated, hot like sand, to resist and yet to invite the touch, as if all the flowering of the senses lay there and the entire woman's body - not just its parts - had become, in that instant, sexual. Did it really matter how the ecstasy came, so long as one knew it and had it in one's blood? To young Emma Dakin it might seem contrived, but would it still seem so when she had tasted it? Wasn't it great to be loved, no matter how?

For Emma, though, still it all hinged on the 'how'; she still kept her distanced view of things. Evelyn, the seasoned, the woman-of-the-world, trusted, in spite of everything, the shard-shot Waters of Experience, throwing herself into their fast-flowing Swirl and wondering later, if ever she had time, what secret Meaning had been lurking there.

Thus, they were poised at opposite Poles, awaiting the conjunction and explosion of their World. It was quite some time before it took place.

4

Tristan, meanwhile, had remained in Scotland, disappointed that his revelations to Emma had not resulted in closer acquaintance. He had mulled over carefully many times the words she had written in her letter of last spring, her bolt from the blue, in which she had exposed the hollowness and desperation of his Quest. This was the ground he had wanted to skip over, and the Pangs of Anguish he had felt at Emma's rejection of him were proof positive that she was right. When, in late summer, he had written again in the hope that she might have changed her mind, might be willing, at least, for him to call through and see her, he was naturally more circumspect and steadied for her 'No'. But, like most Doors shut in one's face, it hurt.

Her diagnosis was true, he had to admit. There *was* an unsatisfied Hunger about him, a wanderlust, a lack of deep peace. And he craved a warm Corner with one other human being. To this the Brothers, while not openly disparaging it, had obviously attributed secondary value, speaking always in more general terms of the virtue of Communion and Community. Because of this it had *become* Tristan's life; for the last fifteen years it was what he had known. Still - and there was no denying it - it was not a life of textural wholeness. Thanks to the percipience of a country lass, who might just be, come to think, his own daughter, the frayed-edge quality had become all-too-clear.

Having the Explanation, however, does not free one from the Cause. Tristan didn't know where his next move lay and, for all his mulling and thinking it over, it hadn't actually occurred to him that what was required might be *not* an action. What Emma had been pointing out to him was the perennial tendency - in particular, in men - to seek solutions in projects, in Doing. In spite of his heroism and generosity - and partly, perhaps, because of them - Tristan was prey to the time-honoured saying: 'Do good if tha can, but do *summat!*'

But summats and summits may themselves be illusions, after the scaling of which one looks for the next. The Secret, indeed, may lie elsewhere: in the transitional places, the passes, the cols. To find it one may need, not upthrust Effort, the strain of the snow-covered Lance, the White Whale, but a gentler, steadier, more lateral Poise, a shift of emphasis, a Passage through the Void. For, in moving, we go always from the Known to the Known, whereas in the Matrix of the Zero, the Heart, lies the generative Womb of the soul's new life. This utter Grey Wethers, these Stone Circles on the Moor, we constantly by-pass in our reach for the Top. By not standing still we miss the whole thing, for the Secret, indeed, lies Here, where Ways meet.

This, in a nutshell, is what Emma was saying, in her own words, more succinctly than I. It is easy, she was saying, to become luxuriant, to feed on the grist of one's own experience (and spiritual experience is still experience); it is easy to let oneself be defined by a particular Way, however noble, and become just another facet of that Way. A person like Tristan, who *was* noble, was all-too-susceptible to such a possibility. Add to that his vagabondage, his youthful-unhappy love-and-war, and one had a recipe for gratitude which had thrown him, without a moment's equivocation, lock-stock-and-barrel into the arms of the Brothers. Now *she* had thrown a salt-grain of Doubt into the stew of his unquestioning conviction, and he found himself milling and thrashing around, feeling cooked like a chick-pea and very ill-at-ease.

The one thing he needed was austerity, and her Grain of Salt was the beginning of it. Nobody likes not getting what they want, and not getting what he wanted, so far as Emma was concerned, had thrown him back to a place-among-himself, where he had to re-examine what it what it was he *really* wanted. Initially, he felt rebellious towards the Brothers, as if his idealism and ready-roving were *their* fault. Then he realized how puerile and foolish he was being, how much he had lived and learned with them, how much they were integrally part of his life. Still he was restless, anxious to *do*.

The small school he had been working in collapsed, due to the leading light's of the place falling in love with a Manchester Jewess, who became his obsession night and day and, demanding and commanding

92

as she was, left him no time for anything but herself. In addition, she owned a chain of draper's shops, which as a means of earning a decent living was streets ahead of pedagogic self-sacrifice. Tristan considered education more generally and his own potential role as a teacher. He looked and turned back from that Classic Clash, where the inner beings of teacher and taught are locked in a scrimmage without a ball and have only each other to torment and bludgeon.

No, incomeless again, but footloose and free, he filtered through the Edinburgh streets looking for a destiny to incarnate. The special spirit and openness of that city had attracted a group, called simply 'The Welkin', some of whom, initially at least, were an offshoot of the 'Münchener Kosmiker', that loose band of Spiritualists, Sensitives and Seers, who had gathered in Munich circa 1926 and who counted among them a house-painter-cum-writer, but actually a Medium, called Adolf Hitler.

Their unspoken leader was a lady of mature years, with white hair and a gentle manner, whom some called 'Jenny' but most 'Mrs Alpenstock'. She had grown up in Vienna towards the end of the last century and, as she came from a nightmare family, had become increasingly interested in the work of Sigmund Freud. When the split with Jung came, she had followed Jung, preferring his desexualized version of the libido and his wider interpretation of the Unconscious. This had helped her, not only with her schizophrenic brother, whom she had in a sense been able to cure, but also, significantly, with her own life, where she had overcome a number of identity crises by enlarging her view of the human personality and discovering its hidden Matrices. At the age of thirty she had married a Scotsman, who had come to Vienna to do medical research and who subsequently proved to be impotent, a condition she had thought she 'could help him with'. They were married in Vienna and divorced in Edinburgh, where Jessica ('Jenny') took her maiden name again, keeping for convention's sake the 'Mrs'.

Since then she had built up a steady reputation as a psychotherapist and interpreter of dreams and it was rather in the latter capacity that Tristan, who had come to hear the group, was going to see her that Thursday evening. He was met at the door by a young man called 'Dada', who took him through to a largish room, where cushions lay scattered about the floor and a number of people were already seated. Incense burned beneath the suspended left foot of Shiva Natarajan, the Lord of the Dance. He stood framed in the centre of the Cosmic Wheel, with twenty-three flickering flames upon it, while beneath his right foot lay the demon of the ego, the vanquished bit-of-child in all of us.

Mrs Jenny Alpenstock laid aside her stick and sat down in a chair against the wall, in a central position where everyone could see her. She would prefer, she protested, to sit on the floor, but her ageing, aching limbs prevented it. The title of her talk was 'The Dream Today'. She began by talking about 'the dreams we all have', which included visions of the future, versions of reality and all the plethora of Imaginal Worlds which accompany us on our Journey through this one. The whole thing she described as the World of the Dream: what we are, where we are, all of the time.

- Interesting definition, thought Tristan, who realized he had accepted all along a narrow and disparaging view of the subject.

'Joseph, with his coat-of-many-colours, was a Dreamer. But what he dreamed was another kind of truth, *the* Truth, in fact, waiting to *come true*. When he dreamed of the six fat and the six lean kine, his dream was symbolic, obviously, since it referred to six good and six infertile years. Not symbolic, however, in any fanciful way: it betokened something about to come true, in the concrete, material, everyday sense. That is, *it already existed as truth*. As such, it was a Veridical Dream, one which cuts through our ordinary miasma and puts us in touch with a higher plane, the Plane, one might say, of Things-as-they-are. The Journey of the Veridical Dreamer is vertical, up into this Source, this Reservoir. And in shamanism, of course, it is very well known (and an indispensable element in the preservation of the tribe) that the Shaman travels *upwards* through the Roof of the World to bring down the sustaining truth. It takes time for the Truth to work its way through and, as it descends to ever denser layers of Matter, it becomes more and more involved in the strictures of Time. Nevertheless, the breakthrough has occurred, and it is only a matter of patience and waiting, waiting with patience, until it is manifest.

'We are all, then, Dreamers all of the time - in the sense that we live simultaneously in a mutually sustaining sequence of Worlds, only the densest of which is tangible and visible to the mortal eye. At night, of course, something else takes place: the subtler bodies are liberated from their set detention in gross Matter, and we actually do visit other places in those forms. I'm sure, for instance, we are all familiar with such experiences as flying and falling. That is, we are freer and can move more freely than in our day-time consciousness, with its control mechanisms and customary constraints. These are the constructs of the ego and are absolutely necessary for its daily functioning. At night-time, however, their control subsides, our hidden promptings rise to the surface, and also we have access, if we follow Jung, to Areas outside our personal experience, to which he gave the name 'Collective Unconscious'. We become, if I may express it so, aquatic - in the sense that we join the Sea of Consciousness and have direct contact with its Waters. The Sea is a good image, because consciousness is fluid and cannot be contained within the brain. On the contrary, it is the brain which drinks of it, drawing its content and sustenance from that vast, ever-changing Reservoir. Because of the commonalty of consciousness we can dream dreams which had their origins thousands of miles away: in a Japanese garden or a Tibetan monastery. And also, as in the case of Joseph, the Dream can come from a Higher Plane. It is a question of Synchronicity.

'Dreaming, then, in the sense I speak of it, is completely different from phantasizing, because it has always a concrete referent: it focuses on a reality and it indicates a truth. That is why deep-dream analysis is important: through it we can find our own truth to live by. For, although the Reservoir of Consciousness is common, what we make of it is our very own, a responsibility we cannot shirk.

'What do I mean by the term 'deep-dream'? Obviously not those associations which drift up frequently when one is coming awake and are allied to our daytime preoccupations. No, I mean dreams of a deeper kind, the first of which are recurrent and admonitory and the second, well, rather difficult to define. An example will show what I mean by the first:

'An attractive young lady of seventeen, with plenty of escorts and great fun in life, came to see me because of a dream she was having. Apparently, she had been invited to a ball, because there she was on the threshold of the dance-floor, alone and looking up at the lights. These were arranged like chandeliers, in elegant, rather stately rows - except that they were feathery and soft and waved about gently in whatever breeze there was. Then suddenly, as, alone still, she began to take the floor, the chandeliers became crystalline and hard and fell all about her, destroying the floor. As the wood burst and splintered, she ran distraught among the lights, which continued to fall. She woke up in a sweat.

'I told her the dream was an indicator of her fear of sexual intercourse. For the moment her relationships were light and airy, and she could look on them without any sense of threat. Her subconscious, however, was prefiguring to her the actuality and the very real danger of penetration by a man. She *would* be destroyed (some part of her would be) and that would be the end of her carefree, light existence. Though she was a little shocked, she liked my explanation, and apparently, by virtue of making the fear conscious, it subsided some time later along with the dream.

'Such dreams, nonetheless, are fairly easy to fathom and form part of the classic psychoanalytical casebook. The second type are rather more testing. They involve snatches or elements of 'other-awareness' and are not necessarily - in fact, they rarely are - available to cause-and-effect diagnosis. For this reason they are difficult to talk about, as any explanation must carry the condition that it is provisional, for-the-moment, a wait-and-see kind of thing. The contrast is rather, if I may use an analogy, like that between classical and modern physics. In the

95

former there exists a direct, linear correspondence between the object observed and its origin. In the latter we speak rather of Fields of Force, Random Events and Action-at-a-Distance. In other words, it's not entirely clear how a given 'observed' took place. You can't draw a graph and plot its course. You know *some* things about it: that it took place, for instance - but not necessarily when or where. You never *see* it, physically, sequentially. It is open and hidden, both-at-once and neither.

'What relevance, you may ask, has all this to us? How does it affect the way we live? The difference lies, not initially in the particular, but in the general way we see ourselves. If we see the self solely as personal history, as Freud's critics say he did, we do in a sense create a prison for ourselves and, by exclusion, leave ourselves the only option of making the prison as comfortable as possible. If, on the other hand, we take the wider view and admit to the council of our considerations factors outside our personal ambit, we find that the human personality itself is, by virtue of this shift of emphasis, a very different animal. It is subtler, more plastic, and it no longer resides between the straight, narrow walls of a linear definition. It can receive hints from Elsewhere; it can explore Oceans and climb Mountains, in countries far removed in time and space from its own.

'What I wish to say and what is of vital importance is that it is *how* one looks which really counts. Depending on how you look, you will see a prison (and that very looking is itself a prison) or you will see yourself, wherever you are, as the immediate focus of all time-space, of humanity's experience, as well as your own, and therefore capable, responsible, intact, the growing-point of a singular node. A great deal, naturally, is implied in all this, since it allows for input from *all* the Matrices: the far-flung, oriental, unseen, as well as the intimate, family, personal. It allows you to become what you truly are, and that is why I am interested in it.

'The discovery of what you truly, not what you think, you are is a lifelong journey, and one is always on the move. It starts with the discovery of what one is not, which can in itself take many years, subject as we are to so many influences. Yet it is through the Not that the Journey begins. Then the whole Spectrum undergoes a change, and what began as patching up neuroses becomes a genuine psychological enquiry, a systematic and ongoing exploration of the ever-expanding Field of our life.

'And now, if there are questions . . .'

The speaker stopped. Her words still hung in the quiet air, while the audience, most of them quite young, took time to ponder what she had said. Asked for an example, she simply replied that *we* were the creators of the confusion in the world: that the Great War had produced the Treaty of Versailles, with its punitive demand for war reparations, and that this very sense of being 'stabbed in the back' was contributing to the rise in Germany of a nationalist-militarist regime, which was extremely dangerous to the future welfare of mankind. Some people - Sunday Psychdelics, mainly - were perturbed by this switch to the political arena, but for Tristan, who had seen war and the horrors of the War, it was all-too-real and palpable an instance. It impressed him that she was able to make this swift inclusion, and he left the place thinking that his own next move *must* take account of all levels of reality.

In the event (and this, perhaps, in itself was a confirmation of what Jenny Alpenstock had been saying) his next step forward involved a step back, not retrograde but geographical and inward. He bumped into one of the Brothers in Edinburgh, who had recently been fêted by the SNP for his mystical expositions on the Cross of St. Andrew and who had moved to the Capital on a permanent basis. He said the Islanders 'lacked leadership', which was a strange thing to say where the Brothers were concerned. What he meant by it was that the Light had gone; they seemed to have lost their intimate touch, to be struggling for any kind of Meaning, going through the motions but never really *there*. Wouldn't he, Tristan, long-standing Member that he was, like to go back and help sort it out? Tristan didn't think he would, but some element in his Force-field, of which he was unaware, took charge of him against his will, and a few days later he was on the boat.

It was true, the place was in a mess. People were praying at idiot Shrines, chiefly those of their own invention. What had seemed little more than a year ago to be a clear, hard, firm, unimpeachable Edge was now buried half-a-yard down in deep Mist, while the equally unimpeachable communitarians were groping and peering for the merest Clue. A sorry sight, indeed, thought Tristan. And he set himself to put it right.

But oddly - and, perhaps, with hindsight, inevitably - all his deliberate initiatives failed. He had never been a person to dwell on things, particularly things which had turned out badly, and this, together with an innate optimism, had grown over the years into a kind of conviction that by pushing and innovating all scars could be healed. That it was not so and that he must relinquish action as a means of bringing about change in the world was a lesson he learned slowly and with difficulty. People came and went; the bakery closed down; there was an open fist-fight between two of the Brothers. Nothing he suggested made any sense at all.

Facing the Unprecedented, what does one do? Tristan realized that he was stymied, that the only undertaking of any value was a shift in the level of his own inner being. He had hunted around frantically for ideas, which would get other people going again, but essentially they had just watched him hunting around, while he himself became ever more frantic. STOP! it seemed to say to him; look what you're doing, the futility of it. You are becoming a leader of the time-honoured type, and in the context of the Brotherhood it just won't work! He saw it on the instant, and he actually did stop.

And when he stopped he began to dream. It was a Dream that had been inside him for ever, which his own nuttiness had been obfuscating. While he had been obsessed (and he still had obsessions) with the outer mechanics of daily life, he had missed the Vision of himself, the elegant, ever-extending Ladder, on which, balanced on the Earth, he could climb upwards to the Stars. He had lived a life of arid disenchantment, missing his step and barking his shin; he had, in his naked aspiration, broken the cord between Heaven and Earth, seeking thereby some posthumous Nirvana. But the only nirvana had been the desert of himself, in which he had wandered these many years, wishing to break out on many occasions, but incapable always of any real thrust.

Now, magically, because he had stopped - it was an existential Stop, not an invention of his mind -, he found himself out of the blistering Desert, with its asperities, rugosities and endless sand. He was on the delectable Borderline, the empty, invisible Place-between, feeling, being and seeking nothing. It was not a state of atrophy: on the contrary, it was full of sunlight and air, the delicious Crossroads of the Breezes of the Nile.

There he stood and there his Ladder rose. Like Jacob's, it had angels ascending and descending, files and choirs and choruses of them, and they went from the earth to the pivot of the sky. The sky seemed to be *his pivot*, too: that is, it was the focus of his being, the Very Place from which he derived. It was as if his body were a piano (he had all the notes, and all the notes were he) and the music kept playing up and down, continuously, from one to eighty-eight - though that in itself was a modicum, a metaphor for the angelic range. He was everything and everywhere at once, without distinction or separation, and yet he was always and only himself. And that, as the music played and swelled, was, he realised, the Secret of it all. He had always suffered, as everyone did, from not being fully what he was, from being cut down to a few puny notes. This thought- acknowledgement came from afar, it was only peripherally part of him, so absorbed was he in the Ocean of Sound, in hearing and perceiving the Music of the Spheres.

The Angels descended and ascended the Scale; they formed an everlasting Chain. They were like dancing sunlight on a fast-flowing river and, though perceptible only by their reflections, there was absolutely no doubt that they were real. They sang through Tristan and he sang in them, he in his body becoming rich and deep, they incorporeal, somehow responding, the light of their intelligences flaring up, becoming incandescent and bright. He was only dimly aware of his body - as if that, too, reached upwards and down -, as if its frontiers were hard to define, or rather, as if the body itself were just a part of the larger Orchestration, in which it was included like an instrument. He stood, the Gamut of Light-sound through his spine, at the very Centre of Eternity.

6

Evelyn and Emma were at a different Place. Since the interrupted weekend they suffered a hiatus and, as so often when this occurs, external circumstances came flooding in to blur the focus and keep them apart. Evelyn went away on a ten-week spring tour and Emma went back to her studies at Matlock, reflective but unbruised, awaiting her return. The other girls asked her what it had been like, but she answered rather primly that 'Miss Rodd' was 'very nice'.

Then, in mid-term, a telegram arrived, informing Emma that Alderman was ill and asking her to come home a.s.a.p. She packed her bag and took the train, excusing herself from classes for that week. A deferential and quite handsome young farm-hand, who was sporting a red neckerchief for the occasion, met her at the station in the pony and trap. On the way up the steep hill from Bakewell to Brewston he told Emma the news about Alderman:

- 'e's 'ad a stroke, Miss, about three or four days sin'. 'e were in 'ospital for two nights, but they've let 'im come 'ome.
- How is he in himself? asked Emma.
- 'e's none t' good, Miss. 'e 's as white as a sheet.

Emma got down quickly from the trap and approached the house with trepidation. She walked through the bare, cold, stony kitchen to where Alderman sat among several cushions in a black, high-backed armchair in the living-room. It was true, his face looked ashen and sunk, though with a pallor not exactly white - more of a yellowish, marbled grey, clouded by his unshaven whiskers.

- Daddy! she exclaimed, going over to him.
- I'm so glad you've come, lass, Alderman said.

There was more than a hint of pathos in his voice, something, indeed, quite different. It was as if the Angel of Death had passed and whispered its message into his ear. Emma felt a flood of compassion for him; she loved him, indeed, as she hadn't since a child. She kissed him fondly and knelt beside him, talking to him softly, though he could hardly speak himself. She chatted glibly about her life at Matlock, her teaching practice, the other girls, the spring. It helped hold back the tears inside, which she had kept dammed up these many years, living, as the young will, from her self-sealed drive. She began - and it happened instantaneously - to realize how narrow her affections had been. Alderman, her dear dad, had been badly hurt. Now she was older and had talked with Tristan, she knew the origin and cause of it. No wonder, after that holocaust, he had taken refuge in the pale, pedestrian Marion.

100

And with the feeling came the realization that this Compassion was wider than herself. It wasn't just an emotional sympathy, which contained within itself its opposite, antipathy. No, it included an element of Understanding; it included, for the moment, at least, the whole world. It seemed to glow around her like a Presence. She could distinguish now between 'being alone', in the sense of knowing purely and simply for oneself, and one's 'modus vivendi' in the world. Hitherto she had confused them and her vestal aloofness had been, partly, at least, the consequence of this. What one saw for oneself was, in no way, shape or form, a possession which set one above the rest. On the contrary, it stirred up, it shook one to the root, igniting and enlivening every response, till it embraced, comprehended, illuminated to a fault every last aspect of Man's Glory and Fall. This was the Awakened State of Being. This she imbibed as she talked to Alderman, and when Marion came in it was there all around.

- How are you, M ...? she began, not sure whether to call her 'Marion' now.
- I'm as well as can be expected, said Marion.

And she fussed about busily, righting Alderman's cushions, giving the impression, as she always did, that there was much more to do than a body could stand. Emma thought briefly, bizarrely, of Martha.
- I've got your old room ready for you, she went on.
- O, thank you, said Emma. I ...

But Marion had already whisked by the chair and gone into the front-parlour, a duster in her hand.
- No Minnie and Martha now, whispered Alderman.

And they giggled together like two conspirators.


The late-April days were sunny and bright, and Emma spent much of her time outdoors, rediscovering her old, secret haunts, feeling again the pull of the Moor. She attempted to effect a reconciliation with Marion, helping her with housework and the preparation of meals, though she was never quite sure whether she was being a help or a hindrance, so rigidly did Marion stick to her routines. In the end she flitted inconsequentially around and spent many hours just sitting with Alderman.

For him the end was very near; he had passed into a kind of Twilight Zone. He looked aethereal, almost transparent. Every day the flesh fell off him, so that he no longer seemed to inhabit his clothes but to have had them draped over him for the nonce. He was not, however, bitter or cantankerous and, when, ultimately, he was confined to his bed, it was more by way of a natural progression.

Then Death lay down with Life in him, and the two Currents flowed on, side by side: the Water of Death and the Blood of Life, these two

101

streams intent, intermingled, strong. Emma, at his bedside, held one pale hand, the Angel of Death, the Dark Watchman, the other. And imperceptibly he drifted down, loosed more and more his hold on Life, entering the Shadow of the Other World.

And, perhaps because of this Initiation, this fresh intensification and new birth, he reverted in his mind to the time with Jessie, when life had been rich, overflowing at the brim. 'Jess!' he would sometimes call out in his sleep, but only, oddly, when Emma was there. It was as if the cycle had been turned back, the magic, mystic Circle closed, enfolding the three of them in its embrace. The $/\_\backslash$, which prefigures four--sided Completion, stood eternally on the earth, its apex pointing to the pivotal sky, part, no doubt, of the Sacrament, that Secret Wedding of body, heart and mind, which takes place in the so-called 'Tombs of the Pharaohs'. It was here among them as the Triadic Mystery, the first progressive mathematical Unfoldment, the deep-urged Bonding of mother-father-child. It was the statement of them and of all living creatures, the endemic quality of Green Life itself.

Emma and he were enfolded in it; they reverted to it, as a body comes to rest. Of necessity, Marion found herself excluded, which was perhaps as well - she had never been there. She had, 'somme toute', been a faithful wife, who had impinged very little on the depth of Alderman. And it wasn't now, while he was wasting and dying, that she was about to undergo a renaissance.

The Tunnel of Re-emergence that Alderman had entered faced Emma with a new dilemma: Should she, or should she not, in his transitional state, tell him that Tristan was still alive? If she did, she would be running the risk of souring, perhaps irreparably, the good man's last days, which at present were serene. If she didn't, she would have to live with a lie, because his false impression would still be intact. It was easier, of course, to save him the pain, to simply say nothing, to let it all go.

This line of argument, however, was short-lived. When Emma saw that Alderman was going, she was seized by a panic metaphysical and real: she could not let the truth go by, distantly watched, like a passing train. She, who had been a Priestess from the start, whose fealty to Truth was the well-spring of her being, how could she, on account of the upset it might cause, refuse its present Call to be known? She owed it to Alderman, and to him most of all, whatever the story of Tristan might have been, to tell him that his son was still alive. If it was too late now for a reconciliation, he would still know the truth; he would carry it to his grave.

She told him on the afternoon he died. She went into the front-parlour, where his bed had been made up, to make sure he was comfortable and to rearrange his pillows. He seemed very quiet, very untroubled, very calm. It was, she thought, the ideal moment.

- Daddy, there's something you ought to know.

He looked at her with his Dakin's dark eyes, and his eyes seemed to say what his tongue couldn't speak.

- Tristan, daddy, your son Tristan - he's alive. I met him some time ago, but I didn't want to tell you. He wrote to me: he wanted to see me. He would have liked to see you, too, but . . .

She paused. Alderman was looking straight ahead. His jaw had gone set but his eyes hadn't changed; they still had a lambent, almost laughing light.

- . . . he knew it was impossible. Daddy, he wasn't killed in the War. He, well, he escaped, but no-one knew till later. He knew he couldn't come back to Brewston, so he went away - he's been living in Scotland. Daddy, he loved you, I know he did, and it almost broke his heart to go away. He couldn't forget it for years, he said. He never married - you should know that: there wasn't anyone, he said. He became . . . well, he became a kind of monk. But he isn't unhappy - you should know that, too. Daddy, he told me all about Jessie and why he had to go away. He said he almost died for love of her, as, he thought, she died for him. He said that after that there was no-one, that probably there could never be. He said his love was in Heaven now. Daddy, I beg of you to forgive him; forgive him now, before you go. It doesn't matter that he isn't here: he will understand and he will know. Wherever he goes to, he will know - and it will make a tremendous difference to him. Daddy, something about him is unsettled, as if he'd never got over leaving home. He's become a wanderer, and it bothers me. I fear that, in spite of his seeking and searching, he's never going to be at peace. There's no home for him in this world, he says.

Alderman was straining to speak.

- How . . .?

- No, daddy, please don't try to talk. I'm trying to tell you what all this means - for you, for Tristan, for Marion, for me. It's the last chance we'll have to get it all right.

Alderman looked and Alderman smiled, and he held out his marbled, blue hand to Emma. She fell on it, kissing it fervidly.

When she looked up and Marion came in, it was as if, since all Eternity, the Synchronicity of the Moment had been planned. The mirror held up to Alderman's mouth showed not the faintest trace of breath, and while Marion drew the sheet up over his head, Emma went to the window and closed the curtains.

The funeral was fixed for three days later, time for the whole Dakin clan to gather. Emma sent a telegram to Edinburgh, with the bare bones

103

of details, but there was no reply. The whole event went ahead as planned. Alderman's brothers and Cecil, his second son, carried the coffin from the house to the yard, where they placed it on a farm-cart, drawn by horses, for the one-and-a-half mile ride to Elmsworth Church. Marion, as Chief Mourner, walked first, alone, while Emma was absorbed, intentionally, in a gaggle of cousins, brothers' wives and other kin. The Vicar of Elmsworth would officiate.

Emma couldn't help thinking of Tristan and his description of Jessie's funeral. She looked up at the long bank above the village and saw him in her mind's eye, a witness again. He had no words, just a silent gaze, featureless and figured, like a clock's. He was standing in the hours of the passage of Time, waiting, marking, inscrutable, fast. He was totally immobile, distanced, shorn, as if he had no connection with it all. The mourners went by in a satin Dream; the black veils were down, the black toppers jumbling. They dipped down by the end of the lane by 'The Dale' and entered the churchyard at the low lych-gate. The soil had been brushed like brown hair from the grave, and the rectangular cavity, some clay among the limestone, lay open and gaping like a mouth.

- The Lord giveth and the Lord taketh away; blessed be the name of the Lord, intoned the vicar.

The mourners shuffled forward and assembled round the grave, and the coffin, with a hefty slackening of straps, was slowly lowered down into it. The red faces of the bearers, hot and flushed from the day, made a blur against the gathered black. The vicar, stooping and casting thrice, sprinkled soil on the coffin lid.

- Earth to earth, ashes to ashes, dust to dust. Inasmuch as it hath pleased Almighty God . . .

He proceeded with the funeral oration, thanking God for the life of Alderman. He had been a good man, he said, faithful and hard-working, tilling the soil like his fathers before him. And now he was gone to his Eternal Rest. Amen.

If Tristan had been there, the Observer-on-the-bank, as he had been fifteen years before, then he would have noticed, as did Emma and Marion, that Alderman had chosen as his little plot of earth a grave-space immediately adjacent to Jessie's. And he might have reflected, Time foreshortened, looking on, that here was the place where he, too, should lie, if the loves of the earth have their Place among the Blest.

But it wasn't so: that Message had gone.


The file of mourners left the grave and proceeded, following custom, to 'The Dale'. Gradually the solemnity went out of the occasion, as spadefuls of fresh earth, singly, indifferently, were flung down onto the sanctified box. It was over. Conversation reverted to prices and yields, what cattle had been fetching at the market last Monday. The faint elevation the Death-tone brings, the Presence of the Angel, was quickly dispersed.

Only Emma could feel it still, out on her own, as she was again. She had no basis for communication. The world of the family, with its set preoccupations (baby's new tooth, the dog's diarrhoea) somehow left her outside its orbit, and its complex stream of quirky injunctions - 'well, you really *must* do that, dear' - came to her like a coded scrawl, whose meaning she could decipher but whose message she didn't want. In this sense she could not be 'of the women'. And the men, apart from the odd tangent to sport, spoke only of their acreage and bovine new birth. Marion was already back in it all, budging along with a shovel in her hand, farm-boots on, half-an-inch deep in mud. The Funnel had closed in; Gravity had won. Back to the land, the milking, the toil.

Thinking he had no son to farm Brewston - Cecil was already well established on his own -, Alderman had divided his estate between Emma, his daughter, and Marion, his wife. The farm, the buildings, the sloping fields were to be sold, according to the terms of the will, and the resultant capital split equally between them. They decided on a sale by auction, and a date a few days before Michaelmas was fixed. In the meantime Marion would have time to look around and find herself another place to live. This should not prove too difficult, since Brewston Farm, as everyone said, was 'worth a tidy sum'.

7

Emma disengaged herself from everything - from Brewston, from Alderman, from Tristan and Jessie. Yet she was drawn back once again, by the auction in September. Marion had already left. On the strength of the sale she had been able to get a mortgage on a new brick semi-detached in Bakewell, where she actually lived only a matter of months, being so unaccustomed to the town and its ways and so desirous to get back to the land that she moved in with an unmarried brother in Sheldon, who was happy enough to have her 'do' for him.

As predicted, the farm fetched 'a tidy sum' and gave both women the prospect of a sound financial future. For Emma it was quite a light on the horizon, as it meant she would not be forced to teach. She probably would, but not from necessity. She thought of Tristan and his wandering life, and how it might help him to have some security at last. She wrote to him soon after the funeral, at his latest address in Edinburgh, but though she wrote PLEASE FORWARD on the envelope, the letter was returned to her unopened. She tried again in the autumn, after the auction.

My dear Tristan,

I am writing this second letter to you 'more in hope than anticipation', as they say. When you didn't reply to my telegram and my letter of May was returned to me unopened, I concluded you must have taken off somewhere, possibly to your Island - though someone should have known that. I'd better recap. a bit what I wrote before, just in case you're back in Edinburgh.

Alderman was buried on 5 May; it was a beautiful day, with everything out. The whole extant family followed his body to Elmsworth. I thought of you often during the ceremony, partly because I imagined you there, just as you had been when mother was buried, partly because I felt you belonged there, that in some sense you should have been there - not that it's your fault that you weren't. There, because it was the end of Brewston, of everything that has had meaning in your life, so far as family, passion and connectedness are concerned.

On the day he died I told daddy about you, though by then he was quite unable to speak. I told him you'd 'escaped' from the War and had been living in Scotland as a kind of monk (I had to put it that way, to help him understand). I also told him I knew about mother and you, and I begged him to forgive you, which he showed me he did. All that is past and buried now; you can go on now - and I feel it's important - without the weight of his disapproval. I told him you loved him and I think he loved you - in spite of everything, the hurt and the years. He was buried at Elmsworth in God's Little Acre, in a grave next to mother's, removed from the rest.

You should have been there, because you *belonged*; you were part of the passion and substance of Brewston - more than I was, I feel, in the end. Something of you never left, and that is why you are a wanderer still, in spite of the Brothers - and I know they are good. You are a wanderer on the face of the earth. Your restlessness grieves me and, though I may seem to have cut you off, I did it for other reasons, which you know. At heart I am a Dakin, as you are, with a Dakin's passion and love of Truth. We must cleave to that, wherever we may go.

It is a strange, unfathomed, passionate, tragic tale, and someone some day should write it down. I doubt if it could be me, though, at least not yet. It's all too close and present at the moment - like having one's nose pressed hard against the window.

By the terms of the will the whole farm was sold and the proceeds divided between Marion and myself. It fetched a good price, so we are both quite lucky. Marion has moved down to Bakewell already, but apparently it doesn't suit her - I never thought it would. Tristan, I would like to share this money with you - if I can ever get hold of you! I think perhaps daddy would have wanted it, too; I'm sure you were reconciled in the end.

But you should know that Brewston is gone forever. The second day after the sale was made workmen arrived to start reshaping the place. The old cowshed at the corner of the yard is down: apparently they're going to make stables of it. Wood-cutters could be heard in Gladwin's Copse; for some reason, which I know not, they're cutting it all down. Soon there'll be nothing you'd recognize left.

I beg of you, therefore, never to return, or you'll wish you'd been buried with Alderman and Jessie. There is nothing, *nothing* of what you once knew. Even the ash-trees look different; so do the sycamores at the back, behind the house. They have turned overnight into someone else's property: they are legal, impersonal, part of something else. Nothing breathes now of the ancient, quiet Breath, which the Druids drew in the Circle on the Moor. It is all reduced now, flattened, broken up, part of this terrible, fast-driving world. With everything that is happening, in Germany and elsewhere, I feel we are in for some dreadful catastrophe. I only wish it hadn't struck here first!

From now on I am homeless, too, but that doesn't bother me overmuch; what bothers me is that Brewston will cease to strike the chords it once struck in our human hearts. From being the cradle of our lives and souls it will become what is for the passer-by: a cluster of buildings, grey, upon a hill. And what we knew in it of Love - the hearth, the home, the patient waiting fields, the sense of Being Here - will be crushed out like an irrelevance. Because the Vector has closed in; there is no room any more. Grieve or grieve not, but don't come back - EVER.

　　Your loving friend and fellow-traveller,
　　Emma

To this letter, also, she had no reply.

A Funnel in the Dark.

A Blank Wall.

A Finished World.

# VOLUME TWO: PARTHENON

## *BOOK FOUR: THE FIELDS OF PRAISE*

it was all
Shining, it was Adam and maiden,
The sky gathered again
And the sun grew round that very day.
So it must have been after the birth of the simple light
In the first, spinning place, the spellbound horses walking warm
Out of the whinnying green stable
On to the fields of praise.


- Dylan Thomas

# Then

Emma took a little time to come round: not that she had been particularly close to her father, but these last days of his had sealed them together in a sort of settled eternity. She came back only slowly to her Training College life, to its small but necessary regularities and duties. She sought within herself her own point of balance, that subtle but indispensable emptiness, around which all activity could revolve. And she began to dance again, alone for a while, till her dancing teacher's tour was over. Here, particularly, the emptiness was vital: there was too much, too quick otherwise; she would find herself pirouetting and falling about in a lust and folly of leaps and spasms. No, again No. Nothing. No.

1

Evelyn came back to the Midlands in late June, having filed away the whole episode with Emma and given what many of the critics acclaimed as the finest performances of her career. She had moved into and out of her own focus with a sureness of touch she had never known before. Was it Emma above her left shoulder, waiting? Was that the force which had drawn her on and out? Or was it the awakening of her own intuitive body, which seemed to tell her at every step and breath exactly what it was she must and mustn't do? For surely something new had happened. There was always the irremediable factor, the unremitting hours of daily toil, but when she danced before an audience all effort fell away - as if her years of training and competence had been put there simply to bring her to this, this moment of single, surefooted flight, when the embodied Cosmos danced through her. She never had to think or calculate a movement: somehow it was already *there*, waiting, as it were, to be danced into, to be executed on the final stage. The passing-into-performance was the last step, the last-thread-and-tissue-made-real part of it. And how the audience responded and loved it, caught up themselves in the threading and making, watching this dark, lithe, lovely body weave its version of the endless Dance. The concert hall filled with tangible magic, as it does uniquely on those occasions when a genuine, flying solo artist puts forth and puts across the Reality as they have lived it, until it becomes, though uniquely their own, part of a shared woof-and-weft with the audience, they too responding from their soul's depth, till a common substance unites them all.

Such were Evelyn Rodd's performances, and she was charged with the sense of an upturn in her career. But she also suffered privately, in the way an artist inevitably suffers: sublime 'out there', on the glittering stage, she came to herself feeling spent and alone, dissatisfied and quivering in her relationship with Emma, unable to turn to anyone else. This arrest was new and painful to her: she realised a new calling was upon her, something to which she must urgently respond. The change, however, was difficult, involving, as it did, a realignment of her being. She fended off the fantasies, which came to her nightly. She turned about herself: she was unmade.

When the lessons with Emma began again, there was immediately an unresolved tension in the air, that sense of something begun but not concluded. Initially, she took a wide tack with the girl, rather proud of her recent successes, wondering in a detached, ironic way why she was bothering with her at all. Emma, for her part, was watching and waiting, in that way she had of observing everything - organically aloof, as it were - till she saw how insistent her teacher would be.

Evelyn was very tough on her, demanding the very best of her: the most rigorous, prolonged and arduous exercises, all of which she had to perform on the instant. In fact, she went back to the beginning with her, treating her as a total novice and almost as someone she hardly knew.

And this regression became a new testing-ground, where the famous Evelyn of the hard-and-fast Rule put her pupil through her paces, aloofness and all. She wanted to see if she would break; she wanted her blubbering and pleading on the floor. Strengthened by success, she wore her armour thick: her intention was rigid, her voice imperious.

Darkly she worked her more and more. Then she began to realise the girl wouldn't break, because she wouldn't resist her, she wouldn't fight back. Indeed, she would do more than was asked of her: she would dance herself to a standstill, there and then. The Ideal was still alive in her, and in that weft and swoop they were conjoined. They were pinned to something beyond themselves: the common, ancient avenue, the entrance to the Fields.

But the Doom was on them, and they had to act. Evelyn, seeing Emma dance on, felt her armour crack, her nakedness return. Tenderness welled up and flooded her belly: her failure to break her was the task assumed, the unopened moment she had been waiting for, when her vulnerability came alive and she was ready once again to move to the Edge.

- That was very good, she said at last.
- Was it? said Emma, flushed and light.
- Will you come to 'Trentside' again with me?
- I'm not sure . . . When?
- This weekend. Why not?

It was as if the whole intervening space-time had been swallowed up in that swift concurrence.

2

There was, however, inevitably, a different air about it this time; the 'lambs in spring' were no more. There had been a stand-off, a slip of conjunction, and what showed up on the screen of their mind was the disparity of ages, maturity, experience. Also, as both of them saw for themselves, there was no way forward on this basis: there had to be some timeless element, some figure invisible like a monogram, in which they could find their two signatures writ. Otherwise, if they simply fell back, it would be awful; they would wander uncreated in Time's leaden Field.

They both had some instinct that this was wrong, but the crossing of the Bridge was what they feared most. There was hiatus now, there was discrepancy; there was a very real feeling that it all might come to naught. Emma continued to see Evelyn as her teacher, in spite of their almost-intimacy, and Evelyn could still, as she had last time at

'Trentside', think of Emma as a prudish virgin, whose sense of morality was based on recoil, rather than compassion or understanding.

All these impressions and counter-impressions, already dense as summer flies, flitted about them, irritating, teasing, as they sat on the verandah in the warm evening air. It was, in a sense, like Part One Revisited, and neither of them knew how to give it the push. Eventually, Emma, more forthright, less afraid, and finding the tension intolerable, suggested Evelyn get rid of the House of Lesbos: it had become a barrier between them, she said. This stung Evelyn to the quick. It was a judgement too swift, too final, too severe, and to throw it off, to come clean with herself, she let loose on Emma - who could blame her, after all? - the unbridled stream of her life's agony.

- Who do you think you are, you little tease? I invite you here, I give you everything, then Miss Noli-me-tangere isn't happy; she wants me purer than I am. Well, let me tell you this: I *am* what I am. Don't look for me to be any different. I've built all this from my own blood and guts, from hurts, loves and anguish you've never even *dreamt* about. So don't come here telling me how I should behave! Your ivory tower's not so bloody perfect, either - in fact, it seems more like a mausoleum to me. You can sit in it and rot, if that's what you want. But you won't find *me* there holding your hand. My days of hand-holding are long, long gone. In other words, take me as I am - or leave!

This barrage of words set Emma back: she recoiled from it and was about to go. Then, she did something for which, later on, she could find no explanation in reason: she walked over to Evelyn, who was still sitting in her chair, and with a movement, warranted or not, straight, strong, she slapped her hard across the face. Evelyn shot up with a flurry of fists, trying to tug at her loose auburn curls. Emma stepped back and caught her as she came, simply parrying her blows at first, sensing the desperation behind them. Then she moved in when the surge was spent and, younger and stronger, forced Evelyn to the floor. They wrestled and struggled there for some time, Evelyn flailing, striking, violent - for this very reason more off-key - Emma poised and self-contained, holding her for minutes long to the ground. Evelyn, however, struggled free and threw herself with fury at Emma, punching and scratching in a frenzied assault, determined she would bring the girl down. Couldn't she do just that with anybody, hadn't she proved it many times?

She got her hand round Emma's throat and, as the girl, voluptuously, began to cede, she felt her own blood mounting and pounding. Emma was yielding to her at last, to the strong, fierce force of her lithe desire, which flipped like a whip-lash over her. Emma sensed the change in her and responded, not with a blow to the head, but with a deep-caress which turned Evelyn about and brought tears of blessedness brimming to her eyes. Deep down she was fractured, as Emma was not, and in the girl's instinctive touch she felt the resurgence of a rich possibility: a healing at the source, a heart made whole. Her imperiousness melted to a stroppable thong and with it, slowly, like a licking flame, she caressed the young woman from head to toe; she drew forth from her the milk of her pores, till every pore unclasped, lay open, the breath and the life flowing in and out. With her tongue and her finger-tips aiد her breath she opened up the domain of her body, which softened from its virginal fastness, releasing a million glad soldiers from the fort.

Emma's body expanded and heaved like the ocean, as Evelyn took each part of her in turn, slowly, deliciously bringing her on, till she lost all sense of who, what, where. She wanted to cry out but that was already too conscious, too much part of the brittle spume of things. No, she waited; she heaved and swelled. It was her blood which, awakened and coursing with pulse, ran in her richly and made her quiet. Evelyn held her, her own blood moving, tenderness and passion flooding to her eyes. She was feeling the girl come alive in her hands, the unplumbed reaches of her being respond to her touch like coral in the sea. There were worlds to be touched now, opened and explored, infinite depths beneath the hard-glass surface. Evelyn's touch was ubiquitous: it danced on Emma in little tongues of flame. It was not a matter of parts any more, but of her whole body-being become sexual, its texture melted to smoothness and light, its avenues open, its portals strong. And it was only the culmination of the dance that the lithe dance-teacher gave her more, tipped with her tongue the little flesh (which, ever after that in their lovers' language, they called conciliatorily the Kiss of Lesbos) and every last shard of surface broke, the dark voluminous ocean broke and its waves came running, frothing, seething; they ran to a throated cry across the shore. In that moment also, when the sky heaved, when the horizon of the person crashed into the sea, a line broke somewhere, a stupid umbilicus, and Emma Dakin was born: a woman with a woman.

They lay for a long time interlaced, the hair at Emma's temples moist and pearled; Evelyn lay quietly with her, coiled. Then Emma, the good student, for whom work was play, began to turn the tables on her. She touched her choicely, chastely, everywhere, secretive and soft but impelled somehow by the now-aroused flame of her own carnal knowledge. She wanted Evelyn, as she had wanted her. But the manner of her wooing was different: it was tentative, distanced, humorous even.

She touched her at fifty places at once, with her eyes, even, drawing Evelyn forth, which gave her short, sharp, hot little spasms. If Emma was the ocean, Evelyn was the river, swift and dark and swirling like the Trent, with many darting rivulets, slow meanders, deep-locked light and surface ripples. She was swift and urgent in her response, unlike Emma, who needed to be worked. She came to a point and she came there quickly, tempestuous and fluid and aching-to-be-loved. Emma was tender and slow with her, letting her enjoy and enjoying with her every cellule of pleasure her body could afford. For, even here, there was desperation, a compulsive urge to cash in while it lasted. Emma, the good teacher, made her bide her time, was slow, even thoughtful and distant with her. She had that lost gift, sexual innocence, and she allowed it to hover like a guardian angel over all their play and counter-play. So Evelyn lapsed from her fraught stage-self into this soft and lambent flame, in which she was licked up from the base in a slow-fire, step-by-step transformation, her whole body shedding its nervous cage, becoming soft, transmuted, alive with light.

Emma learned the art from the heart: that is, her promptings were intuitive and spontaneous. She just *knew* what to do in response and in command, so that Evelyn's body became her Field, the acres of her sowing, the drop of her soul. She brought her on quickly, then ebbed and retired, allowing the pale blue aura of the Heart to move in her and show her what to do. Evelyn's body coiled like a snake's and was quintessentially coil, writhe, phallic slither. Anciently, it emerged from the earth, its muscles informed with the secret wisdom of the earth; it turned upon itself and was susceptible to touch, taking each of the touches it received in turn, transmuting them into belly-born movements, the concatenation of which was the Dance. Quick, lithe, unforeseeable - these were the messages, flickering, evanescent, which arose from the framed, formed body of the woman. For Emma had found the grain in her, the hidden, quicksilver juice of her, to which, at its bidding, she could respond, triggering somehow, at depth and in flow, a chakra-play of colours and nodes, which made identity entirely something else. Not that they were merged - that was folly, an indulgence - but Emma, from her still, strong point of poise, was gradually drawing the other woman down, till her body, her one true professional possession, became deep like the Trent and swirling like its drift. That is, it became for her, not a possession, not any kind of ivory-stage merchandise, but a form of the ever-changing, ever-moving Shakti, the well-within-itself, the Inexhaustible. Even the drive for her own pleasure vanished - or, rather, it was superseded by a thousand creamy orgasms, each one original, its hue and texture new. Unbeknownst, she had entered the World of Tantra, the place where sensation arises from its source, where the body itself can be transmuted and preserved. And it played in her like a rainbow-world, its droplets moving, iridescent, shining; it drove on, arching, bending, thralling: it took her down to her secret source.

Thus they abided, interfused, with every last ploy of delight engaged. There was never a deliberate search for novelty, but in the turning of a

113

nail, painted or plain, in the touching of an ear a new flame was fanned, which brought on a further and finer conflagration. They passed through all the gates of the temple - with their teeth, with their tongues, with their occasional devices - laughing and crying and scattering alms, till the god in them reigned in his secret place and was master and guide of all their play. The god of fire, Agni, rose and was potent; he glowed in them to utter candescence, transmuting their liquid, energized bodies into a form and feature of himself. He awakened in them every cell, till every last cell was working, alive.

It seemed, suddenly, that anything was possible. They did, as women will, wear each other's clothes, but now they might, or so it seemed, reach out heart-to-heart and be mutually transformed into deeper, richer versions of themselves. The body was not the end of it all: indeed, it was just the beginning, not the end. From it into reaches wide flowed the potencies of Time resolved: the endless mercurial Movement released, the Fields of Praise into which they had passed. They did not, nor could they ever know how, save, perhaps, that they held nothing back, were utterly present to one another. NOW hung about them like a talisman - or they wore it in beads around their naked necks.

Neither of them wanted to leave 'Trentside' and face the comedown of the day-to-day. They lingered until the very last moment, knowing quietly, without agitation, that such passages of perfection are rare in human life. Finally - it was into the afternoon - they caught the Monday train to Derby, where Emma would make her connection to Matlock.
- Derby, Derby: this is Derby! All passengers kindly leave the train.
Emma and Evelyn disembarked and stood, each with a suitcase in her hand, on the platform. If that station announcer, now voiceless and void, had instead been employed to look at people, he would have seen them standing in frozen time, lost in each other, as the indifferent world went by. Swiftly, from nowhere, the cosmopolitan Miss Rodd pulled out a pair of sun-glasses, while Miss Emma Dakin, the maskless, the country girl, just let the tears roll down her face.
- I've never . . . , she began.
- Nor have I, said Evelyn.
- Shall we . . . ?
- Many, many times, my darling.
They embraced on the platform.
- Till Wednesday, she said.
Emma stood there, rooted to the spot.

After a while, without conscious volition, she found herself moving with the crowd. It was about the time of the Jarrow Marches, and the newspapers and billboards were full of it. Emma bought herself a paper, partly to keep herself up-to-date and partly to form a screen 'à l'anglaise'. She was, in fact, so full and rich, so held by the wealth and the weight of the weekend, that her attempts at reading were desultory, at best. In no time at all the print swayed and swam, and she abandoned herself to a reverie, in which coloured emotions succeeded one by one the lifeless icons which lay on the page. She opened up gold and burning from her belly, and the grey, drab world of platforms and waiting fell into it like so much urban refuse. In tears still she sat there, burnished like an ingot, sublime, transposed beyond Time's trammel, Death's waste, while the 4:45 was shunted in, adjacent to the platform, her bench of wood and iron.

3

The journey to Matlock was neither long nor eventful, and she arrived back at college virtually unseen. She hadn't missed much, her friends told her - and what had *her* weekend been like?, they might have asked. But they didn't; they faltered; they *couldn't* really ask: Emma's downcast eyes and serious expression seemed to halt the enquiry halfway. She was altered; she was different - that much was palpable. What *was* it about her that gave them pause?

For herself, she remained quiet and abstracted, mixing only at the superficial level, keeping the reality of herself intact. She had undergone an initiation, a passage of deep waters, which had left her mute. The other girls, it seemed to her, were bobbing about on the surface of life, held up and sustained but not really immersed, not actually in touch with its deeper currents. Once one had 'been there' - for so she thought of it - ordinary day-to-day life itself became different. One didn't expect so much of it. It had its own pace, norms, rhythms, necessities: one shouldn't try to exceed or distend them. Thus, she remained, gathered to herself, like one who has seen the inner shape of things.

She shared the secret of the Dance with Evelyn. Their sessions together proceeded as normal, but they shared a sense of where they had been, in that utter nakedness of body and soul, whose seal and signature was the Fields. The whole bodywork now turned into praise, when Evelyn suggested for the first time that they choreograph and perform a set together. It would be, she said, their gift to the world. They could work on it at Trentside, as well as Derby, and during the summer - she was free, wasn't she? - they could live together on Myconos.

- You've got it all worked out, I see, said Emma.
- You mean . . . ? said Evelyn, suddenly unsure.
- I mean, I'd love to, Emma said.

Evelyn would make the travel arrangements, which included the Golden Arrow (London to Paris) and the three-night train journey from Paris to

115

Athens. She offered, feeling oddly embarrassed, to foot the whole bill for the two of them, but Emma was agreeable only to a loan, assuring Evelyn that she did have the money, that it depended solely on her getting probate on her father's will: she would get it any time. Departure date was fixed for the first of July.

Emma sped through the rest of the term, ending up in the top bracket of students but, because of the time she had devoted to dance, not quite as high as she might have been. She looked on her year as meteoric: the star in her had reached its zenith, but also she had been charged and molten, burning, touching and finding the earth. She didn't even know if she would go back to Matlock. But principally, and always, she looked forward to the summer.

Very soon the end of term came and, after a quick change-round visit to Brewston, she was back on the train again, heading south. 'South' always signified expansion, adventure, 'north' homecoming and austerity. She had made herself a pair of white slacks for the occasion, rather like the ones seen at Wimbledon, worn by Jean Borotra, Fred Perry and the like. With them she wore a pair of open shoes, rather schoolgirl-like, with a strap and button-clasp, a stripy blouse of muslin stuff and a broad-brimmed boater, from which streamed a red silk band. She looked a picture, she really did, and whenever the train pulled in at a station every head turned to look at her.

Since her meeting with Tristan she had not been to London, and the tumult of it fascinated her. What a hurrying and scurrying of people was there! She followed the signs marked 'Underground' and disappeared inside the Giant Mole. The place was heaving, fast and faceless, but the Tube got you there; it was a marvel of its kind. With her bag across her shoulder she surfaced at Victoria, a full hour and twenty minutes before the train was due to leave. She went to a stand and had a coffee and just looked. So many lives independently entwined, networked like the railways on indiscernible tracks! It was in itself a skeletal cosmos, a place of transition, a forked thrust of ways. Emma was somewhere suspended in it, initiate but inchoate, awaiting the return.

Evelyn arrived exactly on time, as she had an uncanny knack of doing ('part of her pertinence,' Emma mused). Dressed, as usual, immaculately, she wore a black cotton travelling-suit, slim-fitting, with a mauve chiffon scarf about her throat. In her hand she carried a black leather hold-all, which fastened across the top and had gold beading round its edges. She was wearing lush lipstick and just a hint of mascara. Her eyes positively shone with happiness, when she saw Emma waiting at the end of the platform.

- Am I late? she said.

- Not you, said Emma.

The two of them, their fingers interlaced, were at once in a conspiratorial enclave. They were outsiders already, beyond the pale, condemned by the watchdogs, the prurient, the plain dull. They were out on a limb, where all lovers belong, in their dreaming and pushing for the next, strong place. And where should they go to first but to Paris, city and matrix of the gifted-unwanted, realiser of lambent love-dreams?

They had a few hours to wait to make their connection; they took a Metro to the Louvre and spent the time in the museum. They were standing before the Venus de Milo.
- What do you think of her? Evelyn asked.
- She's almost more perfect like that, said Emma.
The armless figure stood before them, gently curving and gently swathed, the face, in keeping, detached, serene. What would now be called 'expression' was missing, because representation was only the surface and the movement outward only the half. The core of the thing and its indwelling purpose was the half-lidded, inward look of the eyes, which bespoke a world of Form within, out of which the body itself emerged. This intangible, self-disclosing Reality was the mystery at the heart of Greek art itself, and from it were spun out all the separate works: strong, striding Poseidon, the Young Charioteer and, here and now, the Venus de Milo. In one sense they were not human bodies at all: they were the living embodiment of Beauty, of Truth.
- That's what we must find, said Evelyn, that point of tension between inner and outer.
- Need we talk about it? Emma said, chastely.
They moved on and through the endless rooms of art-works. In effect, it was all preparatory, and when at five o'clock they boarded their train it was as if the Louvre had been, not just a fill-in, but an intended adumbration of what was to come: the celebration of life through art.

## 4

They didn't go to the island straight away but decided, instead, on a stopover in Athens, where they wanted above all to visit the Acropolis. The plug of rock rose up from the city and, in those pre-WWII days, when pollution was something scarce mentionable, the Parthenon had no need of protection but stood open, erect and clean to the skies. Sheer and pure, straight-edged like a virgin, it seemed truly the goddess giving birth to herself -not in any single human form, but as the temple receptacle of the Mother, that universal Person and Force, whose name is legion and whose place was here. Here she had emerged on the sacred hill as the self-begetting Aphrodite, goddess and product of her own seed, the moon, as they stood there, above her left shoulder, the small, abrupt traffic quickening below. And, truly, She was beautiful to behold: the sheerness of her columns was only the edge, the definition of the sacred precinct.

The two of them walked on; they were enfolded now, drawn into the inner being of the temple. It was a place of passage, obviously, a place of undying dedication. What Goethe calls the Eternal Feminine, that portal of beauty between the worlds, was here brought alive, made palpable and real. It wrapped about them like living flame, like the pale blue heart-light that spread beneath the moon. For it was, somehow, not abstracted, not aloof, not in any way distant from what they were now. On the contrary, it drew them, figuring, into that other Feature, which is what they were. For they were not now separate, disparate, aloof; they were woven in as a single tissue, as bond and form of a single truth: the Third Person, their signature, their seal. And without undue parley, together and apart, they made a vow with one another: that they would bring alive their own goddess-body, the slender Mystery waiting there; they would incarnate the blue-flamed Feminine, love it up to incandescence in the solid form of dance.

Next day they embarked for Myconos, at that time a barely frequented island, which lies several hours' boat ride away in the Cyclades. In mid-afternoon they stopped at Siros, where cargo was off-loaded and they bought loukoum. They were pulling into Myconos' half-moon harbour at about the time the real half-moon, standing out across the backdrop of the densely dark sky, was casting its light-line across the warm Sea's waters. The whitewashed walls of the huddled town gleamed in a kind of hoary luminescence, as if they were, dimly, themselves a light source. All angularities and gaps were smoothed over, just as, under snow, disparities disappear. It was like the Uncarved Block itself, that inward, utterly untouched No-thing, around which and from which all moves and is made.

As the jetty was made for light craft only, they had to transfer to a smaller boat, which bobbed about on the moonlit waves. They came easily to a little landing-stage, and it was no trouble at all to them, bag and baggage, to find cheap, clean accommodation in the town: there was a trickle of travellers even then.

- We'll move into the house tomorrow, said Evelyn, with a gesture to the largish converted property she had managed to rent through theatre friends.

The house stood back from the immediate bay and was reached by taxi via a circuitous, rough road, which climbed from the shoreline like a serpent uncoiling. At one of its bends the taxi shot off and forged a way between dry stone walls, overhung by cactus, prickly pear, dark olives. They came to a halt by the marble steps of what Emma could not fail to call a 'palace', so much did it accord in her mind and mind's eye with what she had seen and read of in books. Behind the peristyle was an atrium, over which a sprung wooden floor had been laid and which Evelyn addressed with a simple word, 'Voilà!' And, indeed, it was the perfect Open Space, open to sky, air, whispering breezes. Time's redolence congealed there and was contained; packed Memory ran in and was released through the Roof.

Emma came to it naturally; it drew her to it, as a mother her child. Evelyn, for all her experience, was more reluctant, more hesitant: when faced with the Uncarved Block itself, something inside her refused to move. Then she remembered the taxi-man. After paying him his fare, she came back inside and they stood together without a word. The sun plumbed down almost vertically, seeking out every last corner of the ground. The sun, almost vertical, ran in them, tilting to the meridian now, as they caught each other; the sea's mouths came alive, its salty, smooth acres came alive. They were pressing down to the bottomless sea, pulling up from each other the lost, buried treasure, as the sun pressed golden on the mouths of the sea, turning them over, their tongues lapping down. They were into and of each other now; they were back to the Place, which was no-place at all, but a source and well-spring of new life and growth. In that mute complicity light came in; it plundered and raised them to its own source. It pushed them to the depth of their own Dance, the Sea in its belly rocking and dancing, as the sea, come clean now, sparkled in the sun.

Thus, their New Time together began. They wove, not yet for the world to see, a tapestry of movements, incarnate and real, stuff whose basis was no-time, no-space. The piece was called 'Parthenogenesis'. They worked on it regularly, every day, and, strange to relate, as the title implied, it became less and less of a duet and more of a platform of possibilities, from which each of them separately could launch into life. They provided for each other a place of repose, to which each singly could always return and which gave her the courage to fly high and wide. Life and performance were germane to one another, so that it was difficult to tell - even in the form itself - where one ended and the other began. Evelyn, of course, had the greater range, the endemic capacity to come from 'somewhere else', which one perceptive critic had called her 'night side'. Emma, however, had a native strength, a sense of form and balanced control, which to all intents and purposes was classical.

One morning, some time later, they took a boat-ride to Delos, embarking at the little landing-stage and crossing the waters in an hour or so. Deserted Delos is the birthplace of Apollo, whence he ascended diurnally, establishing the famous cult at Delphi, where the python-priestess delivered the oracle, then lived on stony Parnassos with the Muses.

It was the morning of Apollo, that bright summer morning, with the sunlight dancing white on the waves; it was a morning of promise, youth, beauty and flight. They soon were across and had disembarked on the spare, white shingle of the shore. The museum, that temple of vanished gods, stood open and waiting up the ramp of a walk. They strayed among cases of artefacts, archaeologists' trove from the very first times: two-sided stones, clasps, bracelets, dull beads. Then they went outside to the Avenue of the Lions.

The sun was high and garish now, the early morning freshness dried and gone. Slalom-like, they wandered in-and-out the crumbled forms, wondering how long they had stood and blistered there, monuments of glories now forgotten, long sped. Perhaps they stemmed from the Leonine Age, when the human spirit itself was regal, when people were leonine and had the Roar. And like the human spirit they were dissolving: blistered, eroded and worn out by Time. There was a desert and deserted air about them, as if they were silently mourning the past, the time when Apollo himself was Adam, breeding new men on an untouched earth. And perhaps the time was coming again, when men, from their filth and corruption, would rise, would each individually, inwardly rise, become what they were: their own sun-god.

Neither Evelyn nor Emma banked on it. They had no connection with the political world, which, inexorably, from this time on, seemed to be absorbing everything. It was part of the marching madness of Man, his abdication of intrinsic worth. And, as if in confirmation of the fact, on 29 January, 1933, the mediumnistc Adolf Hitler was elected Reichskanzler of Germany. The world was entering the Age of the Shadow.

But for the time being, at least, there were no shadows. However one might reflect on Time, the inevitable bearing-of-all-things-away, today was the Sun from beginning to end. Emma had walked into her birthplace-by-right, the Ground from which the god had flown. She stood there, blest like the god himself, slim and regal among the lions, while Evelyn, transfixed, took photo after photo with what at that time was the latest box camera. Freud would have called it sublimation - and, indeed, what art and culture is not? - as she posed her in one place or another, trying to recapture, not only form and figure, but the grainy luminescence of her own desire. Light streamed in, that light which *is* Greece, filling the eyes to the uttermost brim. Light entered the box of the 'camera oscura', where on dark film it captured for keeping the image of an Emma rooted, secure, standing stately and god-like with the grainy lions, her hair in a loose, blonding mane, her arms bare.

In the heat they both wore head-scarves for the sun, as, among the hover and flit of dragonflies, they leaned against a well wall, Evelyn smoking. Its stone picked up the stone of the lions, and their bodies in the hot sun fused with it. The brain, now shorn of normal function, resumed its primordial task of cooling, and they knew in that moment of stilling and cooling a tenth-of-a-second of pure Indwelling, when they were no longer 'they' (normal function) but simply nodes or forms of Being *exactly* equal to the water and the stone. The flitting and darting of the mind died down, and in its stead there came to flower, like a lotus opening from darkwater's depths, a fully expanded mode of apprehension, breathing, receiving, leaving nothing out. Thoughts were the flies which settled on things, stuck to them, shat them about everywhere: they were crude, even filthy, approximations. This, however, was another mode, an undirected, unforced Way, a track of Unknowing which travelled itself. Somehow, it felt like entering a tunnel, but the tunnel was not one of darkness, but of light. It went on and on, illuminating, guiding; there were no meanderings, no turnings, no end. To this, ultimately, the world was related; the world, indeed, was nothing but this: this Light which streamed from beyond Time and Space, penetrating every nerve and cell. We *were* apollonic, beings of Light, just as water and stone were Light. They were shot through, as we were, and they were of us. There was no existence outside of this. Then, in a moment, the Moment was gone: normal function reasserted itself, with all its groping, dullness and pain. Evelyn stubbed out her cigarette; they walked off.

But somehow its potency remained with them, like an echo or an afterthought. It was the underpin to their consciousness, the fine, final flower, containing them and all. Around them, as the boat cut its sturdy way to Myconos, was a play and constant popping-up of dolphins,. And when a harpoon-artist, all straps and barbs, missed his aim and fell into the sea, it called, indeed, for what actually did happen: one of the great, forgiving creatures carried him back on his back to the boat. Thus, the Light, with its lightness, ruled the Day.

The evening, by contrast, was red and heavy, the sun spilling its blood into the 'wine-dark' waves. It was gathering all to a storm, Homeric. They had come to a ledge above the sea, for all the world like a temple plinth. The cooler evening air was raising a scent among the dry sage and rosemary bushes; the evening spiders were already at work. They looked westwards out from their temple-ledge, along the wealth of the sea-god's realm, just as Poseidon's votaries might have done, for whom the world ended at the Straits of Gibraltar. What lay beyond the country of the living, beyond earth's tillage, deep sea's ebb and swell? Out beyond the Edge lay exactly nothing, that final Nothing and craterous pit, into which the Dream-country of Atlantis had sunk. What lay beyond the sun and its setting no-one knew - at least, not by any construct of the mind. This was our world, this Sea and Fields, this daily passage from Delos to Dark. Outside it, creeping, ubiquitous, was the Void, and to that Void all must come in their time. It was as inalienable as the body's drift into death, this deepening, darkening voyage of the soul. One was engaged in it, whether one chose to be or not: to take it on consciously was the only thing. It lay in one, also, however distantly, this throbbing, persistent call to go beyond. It was like some lost Aramaic of the soul, which at the hour of death one might suddenly recall. But actually it was speaking all the time, joining its single, wee, one note to that vast, universal Sound of sounds, from which, in essence, it was no different at all. They turned to each other, warming, darkening; they held each other in a locked embrace.

The Void was no abstraction of their minds: it was the psychological truth of the times. The unassimilable death of God had left lost Man without a hold. He turned to ideologies more and more, to theories which promised millennial bliss. What did it matter that millions died, that the Oven and the Camps swallowed human lives whole? To establish the Kingdom on earth was the aim. Too bad for those who got in the way! It was coming, it was brewing, like blood across the sea.

What was the answer, then as now? Was it to retreat to some hermetic place-of-bliss, come self-sealed corner of hedonism, prayer, from which the world as politics was excluded? Or was there actually some way *through*? Emma and Evelyn felt there was: some original avenue, broad, joyous and furthering, but from which nothing, absolutely nothing, was excluded. How they might establish it they were not really sure, but they thought they had a track to it.

There was, what's more, a hesitancy about them, a desire not to break what they had built up together. For the world, fast-moving, was in flux and turmoil: the Shadow was spreading everywhere. Nothing marked the transition more clearly than the death of D.H. Lawrence in 1930. An age of liberation was being submerged in a welter of jack-boots, false loyalties, dreams. In fact, the ancient battle was on again, between the Forces of Darkness and the Forces of Light. People were little again, they *would* be little: they had given themselves over to Central Power, the State. Godless and gruesome, it would grind them to pulp.

Emma and Evelyn just ran, blood to blood, knowing the Edge was always there. 'Everything changes,' Evelyn said, but not with any sense of serene detachment. She felt her essays in flight and poise were moments snatched from the ever-present Chaos, to which she, like all other creatures, must return. As soon as there was Order there was Entropy, and even now, in their balanced bliss, in their coming and sitting and being together, the fatal winding-down was at work. Struggle as she might - it struck her like a blow - the overweening forces of Nature were against her; and not just against her, Evelyn Rodd: it was written as Thermodynamic Law, this motor-degeneracy of the entire Creation, its inevitable down-drag, dissolution and death. Ironically, it, too, was a cosmic force, and she was subject to it as she was to Gravity. It didn't much matter how and when it came: death had the last word, that much was sure. The Open Space, the Place of Possibilities, began to seem a Death-trap to her.

6

Feeling thus, and unable to contain it, she took to going out alone. At first, she simply went for long walks, as if the balmy evening air could do for her what she couldn't do herself. Every house on the island had its own small shrine, with a whitewashed cupola and, like as not, a wick-of-oil burning before an icon. Evelyn might stop briefly there; she might, as she stopped, turn, offer up a prayer for the seething in her body and brain to cease. 'The ants have come,' she said to herself.

She fought the depression with every nerve. Emma, being younger, was at a loss what to do, but she looked and waited for her patiently and, choose what time she chose to appear, never resorted to whingeing or nagging. At the set, now quite long, they were putting together they worked as often and as rigorously as ever, and at times, in the dance, the full flame was there. But from their intimate life it was ebbing, it was going: the Shadow was soaking up the Light.

'Is this how it is, inevitably?' thought Emma, but she never managed to bring it up. Evelyn, meanwhile, became more nocturnal. She roamed the rocky interior of the island, guided only by the moon ('my familiar,' she said) and sometimes getting drunk in bars. Then, on a pretext, she went to Athens, ostensibly in connection with the theatre, but actually, as she put it, 'to have time alone' and to tune in again to city life.

Action and distraction, attractive as they were, did nothing, however, to dam up the seepage: sops, swabs, whatever, the water oozed on. What was it that lacked and was going from her? It wasn't youth, litheness, performance or success; perhaps it was nothing ascribable. And yet it was as real as screeching Syndagma, real as the trolley-buses going by.

It lay somewhere in the unspeakable, unspoken-of Zone, that vast underwater nine-tenths of the Iceberg.

She kept dropping down, in the form of conjecture, slender lines of retrieval to it, but still it remained there, solid, congealed, an immovable body of black, blocked ice. How come her passion for Emma hadn't altered it? For surely, if human love existed, this was it. The girl was handsome, beautiful, aflame, capable of anything one might ask of her. She dipped down easily into the Well and brought up freshness every time, flowers and waters of rainbow wealth. One could stand on the lip of the world with her, looking out westwards over the Straits. In her company all seemed ease and potential: fraughtness went; she had the gift of taking the nerve-ends out of things.

And yet, unfailingly, increasingly now, the nerve-ends were there with sudden dread. How come, and from where? She had no answers. She was looking out past the blood-dripping sun, past the Straits of the Mind, to where the Zero lay. And the Zero is always a lonely affair: solo, endemic, unaccompaniable. It is the Moment of Dread in the human psyche, around which Life and our little lives move - pivotal, axial, every bit like the earth, from which one might at any time fall. Yes, the Greeks had got it right: this flat trajectory and land-locked Sea were the proper habitat for Man. Beyond was the bottomless Void of himself, through which only a god could pass with impunity. Now, somehow, she had slipped beyond the Straits, she was outside the settled circle of existence. And perhaps her passion for Emma was the cause. The very thing that had led her on - the purity and poise of that lovely girl - had now thrown her up on this unimagined Shore, where there was neither line nor limit nor rest. Could she take it? That was the question.

She racked and roamed around the city, making one or two business calls, visiting museums, selecting fish to eat in restaurants. But all the time the seethe was on; at no single moment could she really be still. She went to see a doctor, but he only counselled rest, and rest was the last thing she was capable of. In the suffocating nights she lay alone abed, thinking wistfully of Emma and the island, sucking up the odours of Omonia Square. For all that, however, she was loath to leave; something in her samsaric cycle made her stay. She belonged to the city, actually - to its cut-and-dash, sharp mind, quick deals. It was part of her, like the theatre and the stage.

These were just thought-shards, nevertheless, like sticks in a torrent, gone as soon as born. The ants were all over, especially at night, with the sweat, even nude, breaking out at her neck. Nothing doing here: no rest. She took to walking the streets at night, careful to avoid the less salubrious areas, looking for adventure all the same. For a few nights she frequented 'Le Paris', an artists' café off Omonia, but she quickly tired of the precious talk. She wanted something sheerly physical, something to which her body could relate.

She took a taxi to Piraeus, to the odd, bleak, oily, transitional port, where she would meet - she couldn't fail, could she? - her Rock of Ages, her strong, steel man. As if preordained, he was waiting at the dockside: Emil Alexis, just arrived in port. He fitted her description exactly. She wanted to lose herself in him.

The waterfront was dewy from the night and the odd, nocturnal spume off the sea. He was standing there in transposed time, saying, 'Hi! How are you?' and she was moving close. It was strange, how she heard herself saying, 'Fine,' then going into several bars with him, where she was eyed up and down like a fresh catch of fish. Strange, how they were teased out into the night, into its soft, amorphous, dreamy ambience, how they seemed to merge in with the large, moored boats, wedded, in a way, to their greater strength. They walked, arms linked, along the waterfront, he beginning to tell her things about himself: that he had just come in from New York, for instance, where a number of his family had emigrated. They were still Greeks, however, he said ('once a Greek . . .'). Evelyn said simply that she was a dancer: he wouldn't know who she was, of course. That way she could put her stage-presence behind her, reassume the facelessness which most of us share. It was a bliss and boon to be thus no-one, to be again just one of the multitude. Perhaps, she mused, it was that that was wrong: she was too exposed, too much in demand; there wasn't a single corner she could hide. She was, as much as anything, a victim of the age, for people, like the age, were being turned inside out. She was looking for refuge, like a child.

She found no refuge with Emil Alexis, when, through a bleary, fetid dawn, the black taxi brought them back to her room. The long, strong, never-ending penetration, the awesome intercourse, the loss-of-night-and-mind didn't happen as she wanted it to. Instead, a sudden spillage, a damp patch, quick waste: it was all over and done with, and he lay spent beside her. She felt the folly and the drain of it. Hadn't she been through all this before, in countless hotel bedrooms in New York? What made her such a fool that she back-tracked thus, attempting to play god and make up for herself a hunk of flesh-and-blood who would assuage her drought?

As time and tide went by, it got worse. For her dream-man turned out to be, not a rock, but a mother-ruined pervert with a lot to cough up. He was after her (his 'cute little whore') in the flesh, raging and raving and lashing to a lather, and it was down to her agility, her deftness, her sheer 'savvy', that, instead of being beaten black and blue, she teased him into making love again. It was, nonetheless, a fraught affair, his anger and bitterness pumping through, like a wrath and a punishment inflicted on her. It was her carnal body acting, insentient, that slowly, dispersingly, took him down, so that when he came he was grinning like a baby. She might have been a million miles away.

 She told him (it was half-true) that she had an appointment and made a show of pressing a button on the wall, saying it was room-service (not even half-true). There must have been some quirk of moral training in the man, which made him feel he shouldn't be there: he dressed rapidly and made for the door. When he had gone, Evelyn fell back on the bed and half-laughed, half-cried herself into a sleep. Waking at noon and feeling for her watch, she found beneath her pillow a wad of greenbacks, all laundered and clean, as if minted that day.

 - How like a man! she said to herself. How finally and totally humiliating!

 She took out her lighter and burned the notes one by one, watching them drift through the open window, to join the scraps and refuse in the sealed shaft below. Each one was like the fragment of a burned, bad dream.

Although it was broad daylight, she dressed as for the night, in a sleeveless black blouse and slim-fitting black slacks. From her shoulder, on long thongs, hung a black leather bag, into which she had stuffed a wad of notes, a handkerchief, her make-up and a small hand-mirror. She stepped out into the hot, glowing street.

 It was oven-like and unbreathable there. She didn't know where to go or what to do. Clinging to an atom of flotsam from the past, she hailed a taxi and drove to the Acropolis. Here, also, there was no relief, as the sun beat down like a drunken drum, blearing, queering, smearing everything, and she climbed the ramp to the Parthenon. Sheer, white, sharp, unassimilable, it glared before her, hurting her eyes. Where was the Goddess now? Dead - or fled? She could find no trace of her anywhere, nor of the magical atmosphere she had been in with Emma, which she, perhaps, had helped to create. It had all slipped out and away from her. She cast about herself for clues, for a simple couple holding hands, admiring it, perhaps, as their own petrified Venus. But even something as tangential as this - a nonsense, really - had no effect. The vast Undercurrent, the Heave moved on.

 Somehow, she had come, and then not come, to This. She had heard the Secret Sound in the Shrine. It was there, immutable, hidden, discreet: the very hearing of it was a benediction. And Evelyn knew it in her heart of hearts - that's why she had come - but she was severed and lame. Perhaps it was only because of Emma that the whole experience had come alive. That was beauty, after all: to be united with the secret source, not merely with the person or the artefact. That's what she had felt when she had been here before. Emma, however, had been the polished mirror, in which she was able to see things as they are: pure, pellucid, free of dust and dirt.

She decided she must get back to the island; she had been a fool to stay away so long. She mused, in the taxi back to her hotel, that now she might feel better, the decision made. But the Furies were there still, pursuing her - in her bath, in her bed, in her fitful siesta. It was like thorns or hot needles sticking in her skin, relentlessly, like some Chinese torture. Moreover, someone was drilling downstairs, and the composite effect, with the window-frame rattling, was of a House of Torment, where nothing was still.

Pills and hope were useless: she was adrift. Like Kafka's machine, her Harrow went inward, working its sharp points into her flesh. And, as the pain intensified, she began, in an auto-destructive way, to find methods and means to make it even more, to affirm it quirkily to herself, to ensure she all knew how bad she was. There was no escaping from it now.

She decided to leave that very night, but actually it was three nights before she did. She spent her time loafing and smoking in her room, leaving it only to purchase cigarettes and to eat expediently in the restaurant below. She wrestled with Nothing but found no way through. 'It's all up to me,' she said, 'and I can't do it.' The Shadow was lengthening bit by bit.

7

We live in an Age of Uncertainty. The Olympian Observer, that creation of the Greeks, the further creation of Renaissance Man, is really just a fiction, after all. The observer impinges on the thing observed. This means that nothing we do is neutral: it has some effect, however small, elsewhere. We have entered a new phase of Possibility.

This is not so easy as it may seem. We have been brought up and live by Certainties - if not those of the Old Testament, then those of the nineteenth century law-makers: Freud, Marx, Darwin, whose theories ensured that god, fled or dead, was kept out of it. For one thing, it opens up the Sea of Angst, that grey and fluid Field of Vacillation, that mute imponderable: Who am I? If I am not the Olympian Observer looking on, untouched, unscathed by what I see; if I am irremediably here and now, imploded in space-time and not apart, then everything, equally, impinges on me. What happens *out there* is *in here* also.

It is one thing, dear reader, for thee and me to ponder the matter intellectually in our room; it is quite another to have it in one's guts, aching and pressing for a response. Evelyn was in the latter case; she had to get herself up off the floor, before the Floor itself opened up and she disappeared down it, identity and all. She might chew it over with Kierkegaard or, impossibly, of course, with her latest lustling, she still had, she, to break through, to come real. It was a task unaskable, mad, unreal! There she was, blistering, toeing the Line.

Eventually, she got herself down to Piraeus in time for the afternoon boat to Myconos. Physically, at least, it was plain sailing after that. Her mind flashed back to her travelling with Emma, but the first-time newness had gone out of it. She walked the deck, smoking, looking out, went below, felt stifled, came back up again, sat down. The sun was an agitation to her brain and, even with a headscarf on, it hurt. She tried a few practice dance steps to herself, but these, too, had lost their awakening effect. Finally, she went off into a doze, from which she emerged woozy and infirm, with a sickening headache and a foul-tasting mouth. She gargled with sea-water to swill it out.

Towards the end of the brief voyage a wind got up, common enough in those Islands in summer. The boat pitched and tossed, and the small, tough crew ran around the deck with buckets and bags, helping the hapless to puke straight, at least, or over the side if they were near enough. In that mess and slother of sea-water and spew they became quite markedly different: they were in charge now, important, with a job to do. They shouted to each other, like people in the know. And all the time the water got blacker; the sky got blacker, meeting it: the horizon had melted long ago. A few desultory stars were overhauled by clouds. They would soon be drowned, all of them, if they weren't lucky.

Then Evelyn saw something, like the eye of a Black Hole, and it was travelling across the water towards her. It had a presence to it like that of a person, and it moved and glowed with an aura of light. Had it come to pick her up from her morass, where she lay, vile and green, on the boat's bare boards? Had she come to the end of her nullity at last? It passed across her like a warming hand.

She could not have said who or what it was, whether it was human - it seemed to be at one point - or just the movement of the gathering of the Light from a point far-distant into herself. For it seemed to gather her into itself, to assume for the moment her body's wrack and pain, the unspeakable anguish of her soul's dead drift: to relieve her, like the hand of Mercy itself, of all her fraught, earthly frequentation. It was a glimpse, perhaps, only, snatched from the Void, brought about by the Void's intensity and a Response from somewhere, mitigating it. She lay like a child in loving arms.

Such was the human aspect of it. There was another, however, more impersonal. It had something to do with the Light itself, travelling back and forth from its single Eye-source. This entire Creation might pass through it, might disappear through its Origin, yet Light-in-itself would remain the same. It would travel always, imploding, expanding. The material world was just a fraction of it, an infinitesimal afterthought, and yet it was the focus of all energies and, therefore, the place for becoming real, the locus of actualization, of perfection. And Light it was which danced in us, which danced in the darkness of the thickening storm. Light sustained and bore everything up, giving it back its true, inherent nature, restoring to it the vision of itself.

Evelyn was solid, in and of it now: she was transmuted by the travelling Light. It came towards her and it entered her eyes, so that in her eyes, in the sockets of her eyes, was only the play of the Light, nothing more. Her consciousness had gone out into the Light, had become an atom and aspect of it, travelling for ever through a world reversed. For she saw now as she saw, not as she *thought* she saw - without the brain's least manipulation. She, the beholder, *was* that Light: she was not a bystander; she never had been. Whatever she was, her least mineral essence, was wedded in with the travelling Light, belonged to it, arose from it, had no separate existence. The world and every living thing was it.

She was, suddenly, part of a New Dispensation, of a Groundswell of movement in the Universe itself. Something had happened; an *event* had taken place, which mean that the world was no longer what it was. It was, yes, ostensibly, the plain, same world: Gravity was still in place, and all the laws. But there was, distinctly, a different movement to it: something had changed - not on the surface, not at the manipulable, human level - but very deeply, in the bowels of Being, which meant that Life itself was not the same. It may *look* the same, but its substance had altered. This was the Intelligence of the Light.

It came to Evelyn, not as dull thought, nor as any miserable ratiocinatation, but as direct perception of the Undying Field. It was forever constant and forever in flux: it lived into and out of itself, without loss. It superseded the mechanical law: that of dying, of heat loss, of Entropy. It belonged to a different order of things, where Being gave birth to itself like a child, and therefore was sempiternally new, fresh, unsullied by Thought or Time. It was the moment before the reversal of the image, before the brain got to it and tried to put it right. In this moment, as the Child, she saw and *was* all.

Then, as suddenly, the moment was gone: she was back in the world of the Blank, the Dark. Meanwhile, the storm had subsided somewhat. Crew and passengers still dashed about in what seemed to her now an unnecessary frenzy. Had they not noticed the weather's shift? That was it, really: one got into a mode, a 'persona', a way of doing things; then, after that, one just followed its track, and the subtle changes all around passed one by. It was happening now, it was happening to her. Could she respond better now, more agilely?

The storm was passing off to starboard and was rumbling, blue-black, over the sea. It echoed in her, drumming, reminding; she righted herself against it, so to speak. For she was herself now back in Time, to its version and image, its face and plod. The splendour of the Unified Field had gone. She wanted to recapture it, to make it stuff and stem of her being, but, like a taunt, it eluded her. There were only the ashes of it now.

Ashes to ashes, dust to dust. What, in the configuration of the dance, could give them the Spiral they were looking for? Evelyn recommitted herself, trying to put the emphasis there, shying away at first from intimacy with Emma. Emma, for her part, shrank from Evelyn, not asking questions but, as a defence, retreating more and more into herself. After all, she had been abandoned and had had to make shift as best she could. Then Evelyn tried to tease her out - with presents, cajoleries, 'femme fatale' seductions: candle-lit dinners, little hugs on the hoof - but Emma could not come round so quickly. She had taken a knock and it would take her time to assimilate, come true with and take the sting out of these quixotic adventures and sorties of Evelyn's. She picked her way along their trail, carefully discarding what was mere escapism, holding to a line with the unpredictable dark lady, knowing deep-down there was a thread somewhere of 100% integrity. She felt she had to *hold* her, somehow, lest the meteor in her crash and burn out.

For herself she had lived quietly alone, going to choice, unfrequented beaches, where she could bathe and sun-bathe nude, undisturbed. The interior of the island was barely inhabited, and she wandered at will for miles in it. Sometimes a peasant, all blackness and wrinkles, would emerge from the cactus and scrub with a donkey, wearing a black felt hat on his head. Or he might, the same he or another, show up in the light-fierce square of a village. He would nod to Emma as he went by, in that ancient, earth-rocked way of his, and it made her feel a stranger there, with her northern lineaments and lineage.

She craved the warmth of the sun in her; she craved the stirring of the solar mind. It wasn't a human urge or emotion, but rather a mineral intensity, what subsists in the seethe of the heat in the ingot, when the whole body-mass is ignited from within. This worked in her, as she lay out on the rocks, their heat infusing her, melting her down. She lost the sense of separate substance and became, in the dazed stilling of her senses and mind, just part of the fusion of the mineral world: the sun's hot presence in the yielding rock. She gave herself up to pure, strong sensation, the sun entering her like a molten god. And it seemed, as she did so, her senses expanded; her brain slipped back many, many incarnations to the time when she had had reptilian nature and had lived unremittingly through the sun. It was a revelation to her - not just the fact, but the utter unforced simplicity of it.

For unfortunately - it was a fact we all shared - our lives had become so complicated! And it affected us at every level: mental, emotional, physical even. We never went through to the end with anything: there was a residue, a blockage of filtered impressions, which meant that every experience stopped short. As the silt-up set in, memory started gristing, making a mental construct of perfection, which was utterly at odds with the actual real. So it went on indefinitely, till the psyche was overburdened with its churnings and thinkings, submerged beneath the weight of its unfulfilled desires. If, however, as she was now, one could be one thing purely *right through to the end,* then the net, the web of illusion might cease; one might be let down, the experience assumed, on the Bedrock of Being, all filters cleansed. Then the sun in the sky was one's own solar being: it was the chanting of angels from place to place. There was then no dross, no residue, no karma, but all was instantaneously what-it-is, and distinctions of mind-matter, flesh-spirit, good-bad were superseded suddenly by an ever-exploding, -imploding Field, where all residual categories of thought could be seen for what they were: way-markers.

She realised this as living truth, not as something gained, accrued. She took the truth of it into herself, as the sun in her belly worked, fecund and warm. It nourished her like the sun itself, which illumines with light and irrigates with warmth. She became, thus, herself a solar node, her plexus strong, arterial, made - not in the sense of up-there domination, but very much down-here, sealed in at the conjunction, serene and festive at the place of Crossed Light.

Emma held her own with Evelyn, knowing it was only in this parity of strength that anything of value could come about. Sometimes she even forced the pace, to make sure the other knew of her strength. Otherwise, she realised, Evelyn would squander, would, in her stagey, meretricious way, pull them both down into her own morass, to emerge again later, solo and triumphant. No, that was neither right nor fair. She would have to hold her at every step.

The dancework was the perfect correlative: in it, inevitably paired, they came at one another constantly. They drew coloured scarves around each other's necks; they arched and pushed like a double rainbow. No nuance here of teacher and taught, but a self-discovery mutual and constant: the Moving, the Abiding; the coloured light, the white.

Within it Emma pushed for her own, the innate expression of her leonine being. Evelyn was forced to recognize it, to give space to her strength, as it unfolded, uncoiled. She could, then, in herself find the opposite Spiral - not the spinning-out, the evolutionary, but the inward-of-Grace, ascendant, purgatorial, the involutionary Spiral of the Heart. This, of which she had so much need, she found with Emma as they choreographed together, freeing herself from the rainbow colours, from their need and greed, like a dervish on the turn. It was true, as she mounted, the Heart was there: it awaited her in the Open Space. She entered it on the tip-toes of herself, all experience flushed out: she entered the One.

Even this, however, was momentary. There was a constant drive for drama about her; she had taken it into her body, like a drug. It sat there inside her, seething and stirring, making her move along its own set lines. When she wasn't ecstatic she was almost always bored, as if the sheer weight of her current incarnation was such she couldn't countenance the Fall, universal and ineluctable though it was. One can't strive *all* the time - it's humanly impossible - and yet she needed, unforcedly and always, the flick-up of the Spiral, the movement to the Heart.

The problem was, having known it a little, to have fallen back into the desert, broken world. There seemed to be no remedy, after all. It was the human condition, wasn't it? Seen this way, all striving was useless: there could be no breakthrough of a permanent kind. For no sooner had one mounted and aspired than one fell back, further and swifter and deeper than before - as if the very movement of mounting and aspiring had laid the trace and dug the pit, into which one would inevitably fall.

It was a problem she wrestled with night and day. She was in the Scrapyard most of the time, among broken cars, torn wheels, spilt oil. She walked in a soak of suppurating fumes, in the noisy toxicity of her own cog-brain. She had managed, if she were lucky, most days by five to navigate herself through the standing black water, past entrails of engines, the exposure of filth, to a place just out of it, from which she could observe. The whole scene, then, in the softening pink light, lost some of its angularity and menace. They wouldn't get her today, at least.

Even rationally, however, this was just a postponement. In the hard shards of morning the drive was on again, and Evelyn was faced with the fraught imperative of meeting her day without going under. Nothing sang in her soul for joy: there were only dead ashes, wet from the rain. She had to stir them, somehow, from her blood, till some sort of spark could be found in them. Only then could she rise again.

8

By now September was mellowing out, and Emma's return to England was imminent. This, too, seemed to work in Evelyn like a shock: it was as if she were losing her pivotal node. She could keep the house for as long as she liked, which, from an Olympian point of view, was not so advantageous as it might have seemed: it gave her, if anything, too much choice. But she had no official engagements till December, and on the face of it she was well set up.

The Current of Death is part of Life, although we persistently ignore the fact. This current moves in us all the time, with its wealth of dark waters, its fecundating Unknown. We shy, we fly away from it: it passes by us in its terrible Hearse. And yet, truly, deeply the healing lies there - not in the fraught, fractured, brittle Landworld. We need to dive into that Sea.

Evelyn, dimly, was aware of this and, truth to tell, it was out there for her, displayed before her in the Greek seascape. There was a line, as if ruled, between sea and sky, separating the worlds from one another. It was fine and strong and unequivocal, cohering like a cord in the very horizon. Because of the intensity of the light, Death's body also moved with a swell; it was the matching belly of the waters, heaving. It had equal poise and purpose with the light.

She sensed it somewhere, subliminally, and it had perhaps some effect-at-a-distance. If only she had been conscious of it! But she knew it only as a seethe of wires, a burning, black and ubiquitous, of ends. She felt everything going away from her, her life like a train in the night going by. It was brief, it was ephemeral; it was coming to its end. She felt it in her belly, in her lone womb even, where no seed had ever grown to fruition. For she had sacrificed everything to being a stage-star. And now the whole Underbelly of Existence, the Sea, which is more than the Land, had come back on her: it had recoiled against her, to remind her of itself. Or, rather, it wanted Evelyn for itself, to make and shape her to a different mould, one on which she would assume Death's body, feel her aetiolation fall away, limp.

Did she have the courage, standing there, with the Open Space stretching up all around her, with Emma, the Angel of Hearth and Home? If she did, she would stay on, on Myconos alone, face what she had to face, go through it or go down. If not - and this, in terms of the Field, was just one other thought-mode, an alternative - she would have to go back to England with Emma and trust to the relationship to pull her through. Something in her recoiled from this. And so like the rest of us, who do not see the Whole, she set her store by what she saw - what the gods in their wisdom, in their stand-off with mankind, might have called an heroic engagement with Life. Like the rocks against which the ceaseless waves ran, it became in the coming months her testing-ground, her nemesis.

For Emma, also, it was a touch-and-go affair; in her life, too, there was no place of pause. She was one of those people who want others to be happy and who suffer immensely because they are not. It might be a long way away, it might be near - her response was never to run around and try to change the material environment: rather, she sought to weave and work within a new living tissue with which to meet the dearth. Thus, she tended to be rather passive: to wait for others and respond to their initiatives. With her partner changing her mind all the time, she found her resources taxed to the full. She was much too fine, too aristocratic a person to impose herself and deny Evelyn her freedom, but she would have liked her to come back all the same. Evelyn sensed this and wanted it, too, but her 'daimon' was restless, volatile, unsure.

Her vacillations were not contingent but part of some pulp-heart mould of things, an incipient, terrible tearing of veils, from which every nerve in one's body must shrink. It was the utter *otherness* of the event, the deep-sea frequency of which she was afraid. Like Death itself it had volumes of water, was vacantly potent, absent with strength. It could impinge on one at any time. Life as we knew it was bubbling and swirling, but confined to the upper reaches only. This Drift, by contrast, was vast, untrammelled: it had its own dark, deep, silent movement. To enter it was to lose oneself, to be broken open by the Frequency. And surely, at first, she had been happy enough, in those first strong moments of love-making with Emma, to lose herself, to enter the Stream. But now, somehow, it had come to her uniquely, as her own life's focus and point of passage. Emma was just the witness now.

What united the two of them at the root was a mutual commitment to total freedom: neither would stand in the other's way, whatever the immediate consequences to herself. Such people are rare and, rarer still, is the capacity to live with total freedom. Emma seemed to possess it from the start, as if many turns of the Wheel had gone by. Evelyn was inchoate, waiting, dark, plunged without warning into a Mystery, which overturned all her previous parameters.

First, she decided she would go back with Emma, then, with all her bags packed, that she would not. It meant suspending their dancework together and perhaps, eventually, abandoning the piece, but even this was not sufficient reason. It was useless, she felt with an agony, to try to work from the contingent inwards, regulating oneself by the pragmatic fact: a deeper, consuming need burned in her, which no amount of adjustment could assuage. No, she had to be alone with herself, to face the fact and the truth of herself. Then only, perhaps, could she become what she was and realize herself as a free human being.

9

Emma didn't want her to see her off, as she boarded the small skiff in the half-moon harbour, which would take her to the boat which would take her to Piraeus. She had her mind already set to the North, to homecoming and austerity, Brewston and Matlock. These months and weeks had seen her through to a poise of perfection which was completely womanly, and on the marble steps of the Open Space, a bag across her shoulder, her auburn hair aglow, she seemed to embody, to bring alive again the running-light Secret of the ancient Greek world: a body made perfect by its quickened living truth.

Evelyn retreated from her apollonic splendour, evoking the strong caresses of yore and collapsing into a three-day lethargy, in which she drank rough red wine and smoked herself hoarse. Rising on the fourth day, her star was ascendant, and, defying all laws of yoga and health, she danced uninterruptedly for hours, finding again that fine intoxication - what the hell had been wrong? - which audiences craved.

She was sane enough, however, to want to find the Key and this she sought among the straggle of foreigners who came to the island, some of whom stayed. Among them was an ageing Dutchman, called Coelman, who had lived in Indonesia for most of his life and carried a Lord Jim, 'one-of-us' air about him. He rarely spoke about himself but managed to convey, as some people will, the strong impression that he knew more than he said. One evening, among the ouzo, calamares and black olives, those staples of twilight on sunblest quaysides, she found the temerity to prime him on a topic, about which she knew nothing but felt sure that he, having spent so much time in the 'mysterious East', must - and he did, didn't he? Meditation.

For he was one of those odd-balls Life throws up and who find their way to Mediterranean islands. Seeming to subsist by mysterious means, they comb beaches, sell pictures, do dope, find each other and commit themselves - this they all have in common - to a way of life beyond the grey, bourgeois pale. 'Mr.' Coelman, as Evelyn called him, had been in his youth a heroin addict in Paris. Realizing he was on a killer course, he had taken to his heels and made for the East Indies, where, ostensibly married - he was unforthcoming on the point -, he had made a living as an unofficial doctor from the tea-plantation which served him as a base. Now, for some reason, he was back in Europe, but still with one foot in the East and a certain nostalgia, which he didn't hide, for its warmer, gentler way of life.

Evelyn invited him to dinner one evening and gave him the kind of meal she knew he would enjoy - candlelight, two wines, moussaka in plenty - fully expecting, in addition to this, to pay the price for her occult initiation. She needn't have bothered: he was a gentleman through and through, one of the Old School, the *very* Old School, who put

135

women on a pedestal and worship them there. He went into rhapsodies over Emma, whom he had seen, he said ('the old voyeur!' thought Evelyn) pirouetting and cutting a swath through the house and whose name he had changed to Terpsichore for the nonce.

- A little more coffee, Mr. Coelman? said Evelyn.

- Thank you, he said, as he lit a cigarette and inserted it into an ebony cigarette-holder.

He sat there, bluely smoking and extolling, while Evelyn, now quite sure it wasn't *her* he wanted, exited and changed into something less seductive. 'Such fondlers of feelings!' she thought to herself, with more than a touch of irony.

But when it came to the topic in hand, meditation, he was much more rational and down-to-earth. He said, in fact, that he didn't know much and she had better not make an authority of him. All that he could suggest, to begin with, was that she sit, relaxed, before a lighted candle and concentrate on the candle's flame. She should exclude all thoughts but the thought of the flame, then finally the thought of the flame itself, so that all that remained was pure visual perception, with no admixture of thought whatever. Then something quite different might come about.

He suggested, also, that every morning she sit quietly by herself and consider her day: its necessities, her plans, her possible encounters; then, in the evening, that she reflect upon it, drawing some kind of match between the thinking and the deed. In this she might find, as she became more aware, that the gap between intention and actuality narrowed: it became a kind of Thermopylae, a point of passage to the Unified Field.

# BOOK FIVE: THE DARK LADY

We may be brothers after all.

We shall see.

One thing we know, which the white man may one day discover - our God is the same God.

You may think now that you own Him as you wish to own our land; but you cannot. He is the God of man, and his compassion is equal for the red man and the white.

This earth is precious to Him, and to harm the earth is to heap contempt on its Creator.

The whites too shall pass; perhaps sooner than all other tribes. Contaminate your bed, and you will one night suffocate in your own waste.

But in your perishing you will shine brightly, fired by the strength of the God who brought you to this land and for some special purpose gave you dominion over this land and over the red man.

That destiny is a mystery to us, for we do not understand when the buffalo are all slaughtered, the wild horses are tamed, the secret corners of the forest heavy with the scent of many men, and the view of the ripe hills blotted by talking wires.

Where is the thicket? Gone.

Where is the eagle? Gone.

The end of the living and the beginning of survival.

- Chief Seattle, 1854

# Then Again

Tristan did not receive Emma's letters for the simple reason that he wasn't there. Even the Western Isles he had left, in a journey and direction similar to Emma's but in a different context, with a different aim. 'In the beginning was the Word' had become his text and St. John the Divine his inner Guide. To prepare himself, as he put it, for 'the Event', he had consequently betaken himself via Athens-Piraeus to the Island of Patmos.

And there, holed up, simplified, made spare, he sought the lost rhythms of Vertical Strength, which every Hero since time began has known he had to find, climb, fathom. No question now of making his quietus: a whole New World was opening up. Not dying at Pen' march but living on Patmos, he walked, he sat, he pondered, he studied those glyphs and runes engraved on rock, which are at once Standing Stone and Revelation. Like most of us, though, in those early days, he still looked out and along at life: he had not yet caught its indwelling spirit; he wasn't yet able to sit and spin. Gradually, however, it dawned on him that, if he could sit and simply *be*, then the whole of time past would meet in him, *did* meet in him, as he actually was. For along the Vertical Axis of Life all things were eternally present to themselves: they passed through the Zero, if one could only sit and be. In this rhythm, which was not that of Time and Waste, things interwove in an endless Play; they were new-born and forever passing-in-and-out. They cohered and were in tune with the Horizontal Grid, with its lethargy, loneliness, infernal drag. They took each feature and morsel, nothing split; then they turned it all minutely about the Vertical - and lo! it was no longer at all what it was: it had a quite different imprint and resonance, one which related to Being-in-itself. Thus grounded, assured, it was free, it was light: it embodied deep-truth and knew and *was* itself. Thus, uninterruptedly weaving and moving, all faces and places were synchronistically *there*: they were there in the sense that they had gone through the Spiral, had picked themselves up off the Floor, so to speak. And their faces, not turned to death, desolation, the inevitable push and plod of Time, were now, in their transposed state, *new* faces, born and turned minutely to the Light. It was actually - he realised at that moment - the most imperceptible, the tiniest of shifts. And yet, like the smallest of flames in the hearth, the weeest that ever was - you almost missed it - it held the clue to everything: to Time assumed, Death transcended, Life's Tree. It was a totally different vision of things, where Eternity flowed into and out of itself and where, in that light, which is the true Light, things *are.*

Tristan gathered himself at the Zero point, looking up, as it were, into the Tree. And when he did so, his Ladder opened, with all its fine poise, holds, gradations, steps. The divine intention was, then, not a bliss-out but a historical record, albeit a visionary one, of what happened once in that fabled time-place.

The Findings of Archaeon are by now familiar to all but the lukewarmest of Atlantologists. But in the weeks, months and years leading up to that conflagration which was at first World War II and then, simply, 'the War', little was known of those revelations, wrought in blood and set down in fits-and-starts, which constitute the essence of the Findings. Walking along a carpeted corridor to a small room marked discreetly A101, then taking out the documents from a folder labelled PRIVATE, it is hard to imagine, in the library's glass quiet, the sheer surge of adrenaline which went into their writing. The record, nevertheless, stands thus.

- April, 193...

I came out here on an impulse, really - to this long, spare island near the Turkish coast. It might be the island of Shakespeare's 'Tempest' or, indeed, any place whose primary purpose is the focusing of the energies of Darkness and Light. This takes on a form almost physical here and is in no way any longer an abstraction. In our northern mists we tend to lose sight, not only of what it means to live, but also of what stands behind our life: I mean, the Backdrop - or the substratum, if you wish. In our struggle to survive and dominate conditions we live, inevitably, at two or there removes from what our Elders and aboriginal Betters would have called the Dream Time, the Land of That-which-is.

Physically and metaphysically, this plunges us in darkness most of the time. I am now concerned to emerge from that darkness, to live and write in such a way that no trace of experience shall be lost, but garnered, fostered, distilled to pure essence.

- April, 193...

The long-awaited Dreamwork has begun. I found myself in an open, sunlit space between two walls, which seemed to converge. They converged behind me, and I stood in the space. It gave me the feeling, veridical from the start, that I was in a place in a civilisation, the like of which one wouldn't find today. The walls were made of a sort of black marble, and at two-thirds height was a deep orange stripe, bordered top and bottom by white. Though the walls converged, they never met.

As one stands in a dream, expectant, firm, it was as if I were the first person on stage (Act One, Scene One) and all the rest to come. A dribble of extras filtered on, emerging from the funnel of wall behind, and disappeared front-stage without a word. They were uniformly dressed in black. There was no shade anywhere between the walls, and the sun spread among them like liquefied gold.

Then I realized it was nothing arbitrary at all, but a deliberate, though loosely connected, procession. Behind a small college or band of Initiates there followed, between two bearers, the High Priestess herself. She was dressed, like the others, all in black, except that the tissue of her clothing was finer. Over her shoulders, loosely draped, hung the cloth-of-gold garment that signified her Office. A head-piece, whose ribbed and regal bands alternated from turquoise to gold, covered half her head, with its jet-black hair. She walked in a stately, half-hovering way, her eyes invisible except for their dark lashes, her gaze turned inward upon herself. She could have been carried - that much was obvious - but, for one reason or another, had preferred to walk. Her bearers carried rods in their hands, much like the lictors of Roman times. They were extremely conscious of the honour of their position and walked at all times a studied half-pace behind her.

I knew without any further indication that she was the Priestess of the Sun - it was as if she wore the sun on her dress. A great Sun, red and round, was her being, and to it, to the dome of her solar plexus, the sun actual came flooding, irrigating, warm. To stand within her Field, which, as she passed, I briefly did, was to experience the Sun as indwelling body, as flush and flux and infusion of warmth. I looked intently for her eyes, but her eyes were downcast, her gaze inturned. She walked on, and her entourage closed about her.

I felt in no way shut out from her presence, as I carried the warmth of her presence in me. It was, simultaneously and completely, my own body-being at that point, the solar conjunction of world-within-world, where distinctions of subject and object disappear. Dramatically, like the sun itself, I became in myself the sun's own seasons: bud, blossom, flower, deciduous red leaf.

2

The City of fabled Atlantis is hermetic, held in by three concentric walls and accessible only by canal from the sea. In the centre of the island on which it stands, turreted in gold and lined with silver and orichalcum, the Palace of Poseidon greets the sun in a welter of atoms and burnished light. Radiating outwards, the reflected light plays on the surface of the sea-between-the-walls, the same sea also receiving the light, plucking it, burning, into itself. The two canals form the vertical axis of a Cross, at the centre of which is the City itself. Beyond the City with its triple wall a fertile plain stretches for miles, surrounded eventually by a huge dike, which is more than a thousand miles in length. Then begin the mountains towards the north.

- May, 193...

I enter the Spirit and look upwards at the stars. Night's star-beauty comes to me - rich, revealing, disclosing itself. It is the dark-blue night-body of the goddess Nut, and she fills the heavens from end to end. Her body is night's mantle, the covering of the earth, and the stars are like little incisions in it.

I am conscious of belonging here, in this space of spinning constellations, where Night is all-powerful and Day a mere fragment. Creation is overwhelmingly reversed: no longer focused on this little

140

earth-plane, it is a vast and throbbing metaphor for something entirely beyond itself, for which the word 'creation' is already inadequate. I simply have to sit here and receive it, as it comes down to me, milked from the stars.

And then, her body is potent like the night; we turn through a gyre on the hard, marble roof. It as if we had lost connection with the earth and were somewhere intermediate - neither heaven nor earth. It is like the return to some original Place, a locus and focus of Energy, which *was* before this Creation began and which *is*, in the sense that all things inhere there. In this Place, somehow, Day and Night cohere: they push to a point beyond themselves. It is the point where Day and Night disappear, where, rather, they merge into what gives rise to both. At this point, also, arises the Tree: the effortless, the beautiful, the true Tree of Life.

- May, 193...

It's part of my diffidence, I suppose, to imagine that priestesses don't have names. Not being of the priestly caste myself, I make of others more than they are, elevate them to a position beyond my own, where normal criteria don't apply. I am just a poor country boy, after all, and she is Agwen, Priestess of the Sun. I am not allowed to tread where she treads. And she goes by me daily between the black walls, her swath of a retinue following her. She doesn't stop and she doesn't speak. There is no resemblance between us then.

Many a time I have watched her go by - in fact, it has become almost a ritual itself - with a follower bearing a lamb on his shoulder, or a slender goat as sacrifice. She embodies at that moment all the dignity of her Calling, her fine body bent to the tilling of her Art. She couldn't at that moment speak to anybody, even fractionally acknowledge their existence. The sun drums into the outstretched walls, which open like arms to release, to receive. And she is held by them, as in the living Moment; she has become the Channel, the pristine Priestess.

She draws her retinue of Initiates to the altar, where the sacrificial beast is slain, its death a foreboding of their own death-in-life. For they are being prepared daily, step by step, for a world-beyond-the-visible they know they should inherit. It is sketchy to most of them - that much I know. They do not appreciate what it's all about. To them the Table is just an altar, the beasts' blood a leaking and a pouring out. They haven't quite caught the sharp incision, the going-through-the-passage, the momentous Now. And yet our City is built upon it, around this very tangible transcendence: it is built at the Place where the Axes meet.

But who amongst us knows this now, when even the priestly Initiates are blank? It is something we can hardly speak about. Our lives have

141

been taken away from us - or, rather, the subtle spirit has. We have acquired the sense of all-power-to-ourselves; we have become bosses, instead of brothers, to the land. We have perverted the Mystery of the Sun, which has been our cult since Time began. Instead of living from its dark-edged, deep-feeding Potency, we revel in nuclear fission and fusion, the light 'out there', brittle knowledge, nerve-gas. These can never make men whole. It all depends, as depend it does, on that seed of truth which is our one real possession, the little living flame, without which all is vile.

Here it was meant to breathe and thrive, in this glorious City, where the gold burns black. But it is dwindling, diminishing, thinning here, too; it is weakening daily in the face of greed and drive. Now, on a vast scale, the Engines have moved in, plundering, wrecking, digging to extinction. I see on the hills where my family came from the forests burning, the soil turned to dust. Contemplating all this, I feel powerless to act, and I turn for strength, for inwardness, for beauty to Agwen, the Priestess, the Body of the Sun.

I live in the in-between world with her; she initiates me slowly, turn by turn. Around her, like a halo, glows the haze of the sun, the sun-at-midnight which she incarnates. For hers is the Mystery of Day-in-Night. The stars are myriad about her head, and I draw them to me, like milk, through her. They are Night's sustenance, deep-drawn, warm. To be able to hold her is my poise, my subtle equation with day-night's cusp. She is open and warm like the spreading night, but it is not a warmth of comfort, of ease: rather, she is calling me out and down, to a place within myself, to my own body's root. It is this calling to each other which is making love, the body obeying its subtle, dark voice. It is this, the night spinning, replenishing itself from some secret, infinite, fathomless source.

And this we enter into now, through progressions, escalations of the Music of the Night. It is dawning, awakening, urging to be born, like the sun itself from behind dense clouds. Agwen's whole body is arqued like a bow, her head dipped right back, her shoulder-blades to the marble. She is softening the marble, making hard the streaming night. Fixity and flux meet each other, interchange. Rather than persons, we are figures and forms, moving darkly, swiftly, brightly in and out of what we are. For we are not just persons, actually: we also embody, incarnate, *enact* (whenever we have the gift for it) the exact Geometry which underlies the world.

We have come into That, we have entered in, and it is singing and dancing around us like a choir. The glorious, gold-bursting, nocturnal sun spins in upon itself through the navel of night, to emerge as a triangle, jet-black, downward-pointing, from the solar plexus to the base of the spine. The effect of it is electric and direct: I lose all sense of human identity, so focused, dark, insistent, edged is the pressure of this solid, emergent form. It has nothing of the vapid, the inchoate, the unsure, but it carves me out to a new body-being, a pulse and presence of its own deep-strength. With it - I can feel it - I am being refashioned, shaped afresh from different stuff: not perishable water-and-clay this time, but the crystalline veracity of the cosmic dark Diamond, the other half of which, light and upward-apexed, is rooted in the Heart and pierces to the Sky. Through it, in liquid distillations, I absorb and record the filtrations of the Word, like an alchemist whose base metal has turned to gold.

It is the point where the Fourth Dimension opens up. In it the body, one's feelings, one's thoughts are all contained as within a Vessel. It has become the Tract, the Force of the Unknown, and it bodies us forth across the Ocean of the Night, the stars dipping down to us, essents of us. They mirror the Diamond which is our own real Being, what we really *are* when the mist is cast away. And, palpably, it comes to me through Agwen, for she has made the marriage in herself, gathered to her focus and axis of being the dual natures of the Darkness and the Light. From there, her sun-centre and place of poise, she has drawn me into the Mystery, that hidden acre where the two natures meet and dispersion and conflict become equipoise and stand. It is the place of *I am*, substantial, made real, standing, as it were, erect within itself. It is the true Place imperishable, the Cave of the Heart. There all existence comes to rest; it enters into its single Home.

I was married to Agwen, with the whole College present, and given the name of Archaeon. It was an elevation of status I hadn't bargained for, but it anchored me firmly in myself. It was as if, until then, I had been insubstantial, merely a token presence on the earth. I had been called, moreover, I-don't-know-what, but now I was Archaeon; it fitted like a glove. It was as of I had always been Archaeon really, and the naming had just confirmed the fact. Hitherto I had been dreaming: now I was myself.

3

Civilizations founder, as individuals do, because they do not remain true to themselves. The Atlanteans, with their prodigious capacities, were no exception to this trend. In fact, they sought out with great inventiveness every form of mutual indulgence, exchanging and possessing one another's bodies with a rapidity unknown to the more earthbound. They were astral magicians, these people, no doubt. In a trice they could cast themselves in someone else's mould and be instantaneously where he/she had been. It wasn't a matter of infiltration, either, but of a total, lock-stock-and-barrel takeover, with a sex-, age-, personality-switch, and naturally it happened mainly at night. 'Glam-travel', as it came to be known, was at first an essay in experimentation, a genuine if rather reckless attempt to transcend the body and its pedestrian norms, which degenerated rapidly into Free Market Exchange, with speculators and brokers selling bodies like bonds.

Then there was fundamentalism. It wasn't enough to be male or female any more: one had to have one's share of both. This spawned in the name of 'reptilian reversal' (many centuries before Darwin dreamed up Evolution) a whole host of masks, disguises, velvet furniture, the sole purpose of which was to bring about the androgyne. For, of course, it is one of the characteristics of Man, never to be able to let it go at that: we always seem to need what we haven't got. 'Getting it both ways' became so desirable that if one hadn't or didn't one was looked on as bizarre, some actual kind of aberration. There was a tilt in Time's circle; the Prophets went unheard.

It was part of a downtrend as actual as Gravity, a plunge of morale that left everyone weak. It was as if this civilization, from the first, had been engaged in the sisyphean task of rolling its rock to the top of the hill, only to see it roll back down again. Now they were finished; they had had enough. Even glam-travel was just a distraction: what had really happened was a loss of inspiration, a seepage of strength, an ageing of the will. It was an entropic failure, as rife in cultures as it is in each one of us 'qua' human being. The Findings of Archaeon describe it thus:

- July, 193...

Nothing in the mood betrays the secret sense: it continues, smooth and flowing as water. But the undercurrents, as always, are there; I cannot stop or alter them.

Agwen and I discuss all this. She feels, I think, that the present crisis is inevitable, that the final catastrophe is never far off. Things have gone too far, she says, for even the best of us to redeem them. There is even a kind of quirky pleasure in lying back and being borne away. Most people are supporting and colluding in this - as much by their silence as by anything they say - and the whole appalling drift of our culture is to further aetiolation, breakdown, abuse. It is like some rampant soul-disease, the cause of which is loss of bearing, loss of Light. I don't know how I apprehend this, either - I just feel it in my blood and bones.

The disease is getting to me, also; it isn't as if I were exempt. I even have premonitions of the End - rifts, craters, meteors, nuclear explosions - I've seen them all in the space called mind. It is part of our dreadful absorption in Nullity, the final triumph of Purposelessness, when the rock, rolled down now, lies still for good. What, then, is all our struggle and striving, our wild aspiration to go beyond? It is part of the Dark Flux, stateless, faceless. We have no claim to any of it.

I try, in response, to focus the twin forces, to become myself day-night's consummation, but what works between us doesn't work in me. I somehow need her dark, arching body: the breath, the warmth, the strength of her. Without her it's a desert and I a broken man, having come thus far, the possibility awakened, yet stopped, stymied, waiting, my lucid glass in shards. For the dark-light split won't go away: it belongs to me, ontologically. It's as if the two triangles born in me, the black and the white, were pulling apart, while what I need to do is to weld them, marry them. It's as if they both had separate lives and wanted to lead them, independently. The split is a breach, a divorce, a treachery.
Intermittently, moreover, there is peace, but sooner or later it breaks down again. I can't live 'up there' with Agwen *all* the time and, increasingly, she expects me to move alone. I would if I could, of course - who wouldn't? - but without her live, inspirational presence I feel beleaguered and pressed, a refugee among the ruins. I wonder at such times if my premonition of disaster is not just the projection of my own subjective state. But the mirror of the present is truer than that.
Out there, on the plains, there was a fire recently. It flared up in the night and seemed a million miles across. At one point there were fears for the City itself, but fortunately its walls and waters are proof against incendiary, as well as military, attack. I climbed up onto the roof of the Temple, from where the Interior opens to the view. It was blazing as if it would never stop, engulfing wheat- and maize-fields, great forests of trees: all one could see was a wall of red, inflamed and advancing, pushing up black wrath.
I called to Agwen, but she wasn't there. At times of crisis the whole Sanctuary Clan gathers together, prays and 'sees', with the intention centred, honoured, clear, of discovering the source of what is going wrong. On this occasion they sat for hours, looking through the 'pyramid prism', a kind of window on infinity, all angled edges and tetrahedron base, about the size of a largish diamond. They use it as a focus of concentration - for many things are visual, after all - as well as a means for penetrating the hidden causes of a shift gone wrong. Something, which I have never quite fathomed, reveals itself to them at these sittings ('something appears in the window,' so they say) and, more often than not, it turns out to be right. I'm no judge of these matters, of course; I'm just a layman.
At any event, in this particular instance, it was definitely demonic forces at work, taking advantage, as they always do, of the slipshod, the careless, the self-engrossed, the plain dull. A group of workers from the

outlying regions, feeling there was nothing they wanted more (the seminal intention is very important) had lit a fire to clear up some brushwood, then left it to burn itself out and gone home. Nothing much to it, on the face of it. But that's how the Plunderers work, so it seems: they get in behind the slightest indiscretion, through the most minimal gap in the hedge they can find. Then they scatter, explode, turn the temperature up and, in general, frolic, foment, glee in the sempiternal fallibility of mankind. They could see them, Agwen said, through their magic prism, dancing and prancing, making havoc, having fun.

Why does it need some external calamity to show us we are on a disaster course? Where is the quick seed, latent within? Originally, so the story goes, the Atlanteans possessed the dual nature whole: that is, we had an intercourse between heaven and earth, which was not thought-controlled or approximative: it didn't live by imitation, version. Instead, it lived by rhythm, plasticity in a wonderworld of opening and figuring-forth, which was not the consequence of act-on logic. It had more in common with evolution-as-transformation, as pupal growth into butterfly. There was an upsurge in the Heart, a vast pouring out and an indwelling, the suddenness and brilliance of bright wings in summer light. It was *active*, intuitive, primeval almost, arising from some rich, deep source within-without, when the music of the skies and of the earth was unbroken. We celebrated then our *inherence* in the world.

This was also the time of our monuments and henges. For we had the power then, which since we have lost, to move matter around by sympathetic means. The stone for the Temple here, for instance, was brought from a place beyond the Northern Heights. It was not just a question of sweat and toil. Then we had the Knowledge to know things as they *are,* as they are in themselves *of their own volition.* But this certainly surpasses my meagre intelligence.

As I was saying, the Original People didn't think first and then act later: they knew themselves as essents, not agents. Before they got involved in any activity, they would gather and sit in a circle, just *be.* Then, when they were clear - not single or with each other, but together as one, as one body-mind - they spun out the threads of the action itself, which Creation knows as the textured Self. Their thinking was, thus, of a different order, proceeding, not from fragmentation, the pot-shot approximations of the brain, but from direct, unfiltered, unpolluted perception of the Ground of Being, on which we stand. This standing, which is *under*standing, they had, and from it, as from a cave in the mountains, flowed the river of action, unbroken, whole. They held to the moment before the Fall, when language and metaphor still inhered, when to speak was to live in the marrow of Life, to know no separation, no doubt. We refer to it now as the Diamond-Rainbow Time, the Time

146

when Man knew all Creation as his Brother; we call it the Rock and River Time, the Time before the Loss, the Great Time, the One.

By contrast, what a mess we are making of it now! The streets of our City have become unsafe: no child or elderly person can walk there. The reverential base has gone and, with it, the sense of the sacredness of Life. Gangs roam and plunder, ugliness abounds. From the open spaces, the never-ending fields we have come into the false world of cut-throat Enterprise. We act at some hideous, abstract distance from the basis of our life, its physical base. And because of this we are bereft: we are losing the nurture of our Mother, the Earth, from whom we are estranged, whom we have raped, pillaged, plundered. She is weary, the Earth; she must be sick of us - with our bombs, with our missiles, with our sempiternal strife - it seems to have been going on so long. My whole body aches with the sickening sense of a world disintegrating, about to collapse . . . 'It is enough,' she seems to say.

4

Somewhere along the Way I met Bella, the old sage lady with the knowing smile. She looked at me, frankly, as though I were a child, some sputtering infant with more spit than sense. She beckoned to me to come and sit by her, asked me how long I'd been here, etc. I told her briefly of my heritage, my life in the mountains among woodcutter-folk. What did I make of the City, then, its fierce, reduced streets, its deadlier-than-thou?

I could not answer, which was answer enough.

- And in there? she said, pointing at my belly.
- In there I'm frankly falling apart.
- I can see that. Why is it?
- I don't know.

She took my pained head between her two hands, soothing the ache at my temples away, then she drew back from me and looked me in the eyes. It was one of those looks, searching and sustained, which seem to go on for a million years or, rather, to exist outside Time altogether. Unlike most of us, she had blue eyes - not the blue of the darkening Ocean, but a turquoise blue, serene, deep-gazing. It was like looking into a limpid pool.

There are many of us, aren't there?, inside the skin, fat men and thin men jostling about. We are not a unity at all, but a contorted amalgam, a twist of selves, each one vying with the other for distinction. They slither around like monsters in a swamp, and rarely has any of them got a clean edge. Here, with Bella before me, it was different. Each one appeared in sequence, in Time, and so far as I remember it went like this.

147

First came the strutting, vocal self, the me-on-the-platform, the peacock-in-the-ark; then, as his opposite, the self-effacing sort, who would rather - much rather - shuffle round a library, feeding on other people's thoughts. I was, alternately, a shining lover, with a bellyful of bluebells and her-of-golden-skin, and a drab-and-dreary, macintoshed creep, waiting in the shadows as the girls went by. All this I was and much, much more. I went to the end of everything. Whatever I thought or imagined became real, took on substance and contoured form, so that it was impossible to say what *was* real, in fact, our reality being, in some sense, a construct, a tangent to the Circle, a waiting at the Door.

Image succeeded to flowing image, and there was no point of pause in the stream of it. My selves paired off like couples promenading; they married and argued, as couples will. Referees, umpires, a whole retinue of aides came into being, each with his bit. Each one wanted to rule the roost. But, as soon as he gained the ascendancy, became in this mini-society of mine the lord-of-the-manor, the top-dog, the Chief, immediately he splintered inside himself, became his opposite, the foe-unto-himself. He had made, so it seemed, the fundamental error of putting his weight down on a false ground, because it had presented itself as real. And it went on everlastingly, would so go on till Time itself stopped. There was no redemption or help for it. It was as inevitable and axiomatic as ABC.

I watched this current pass and repass through me, as some people at death are said to see their lives, in a never-ending, coloured stream. No question of judging or controlling now, for that person (the judge or controller) was seen as a figure-of-the-stream, nothing more, nothing less. He had no dominion - none of them did. And yet the welter of experience, which was mine, which was *me*, was not chaotic, random or arbitrary: it had an inner cohesion of its own, not brought about, imposed by any of my 'selves'. There was a living filament of Grace to it, a thread, as it were, a coded Core. Although I was everywhere in my life, I was always and only at One Place, gathered to my Self, the Flame of I - I.

I began, from now on, to see myself as part and parcel of the larger Creation, as each one of us *is* the history of the earth. I followed along the track of Time, through all my human births first of all, then back and down to Primal Matter: the savannah, the forest, the hot swamp, the sea. In all my peregrinations and lives - as bear, bird, reptile, mollusc, amoeba - I found a hint, a trace element of that Imprint, that forging of the link of self. And it was there, somehow, to be gone beyond; even in the dark, strong tree it was there. It was there in the budding and blossoming-forth, in the clear mathematics of the fern as it uncurls. Order was there, from the beginning and before. Order was the radiance of Bella's blue eyes.

I stayed for a long time, looking at her, at the magnificent telling of her native blue eyes. All experience came down to this: Light *was* in the beginning and it was working now. It was the subtle substratum, the Jewel at the Core. And what passed between us was light itself, informing, linking, making one and whole. It was the same, the very same, in bird, beast and tree, for they, too, opened unfathomably. It was all a Play - I saw it in her eyes, I felt it in the roots of my incarnation - of Intelligence weaving through structure and cell, invisible, durable, constant as light. From it as essence spun out the stars, the wide galaxies and the aching earth; similarly, it was present in every tiny thing: it was minute, even, even imperceptible. Only the Heart knew it, when thinking was still. This I gathered to myself with Bella, knelt before her, quietly left.

I was in my vertical-veridical body, where everything comes and goes at once. It stands to our linear view of things as the other co-ordinate, the synchronistic, the combining factor that plots the Point. It is, in a sense, the trap sprung on Gravity, the opening up-and-down, the penetrative. And in it, through it only, we can get the balance right; otherwise, we live on bread alone. To the Zero, then, I had come finally, to a crossing of the Ways on the Temple-top. I saw everything as happening instantaneously NOW, and in that Now the whole future was contained.

- August, 193...


There has been a rise in temperature. Obviously Bella expects more from me. We walked out yesterday on one of the dikes, which separate the concentric circles of sea. She asked me if I had 'moved' since last time and what I had made of my inner revelations. I was somewhat nonplussed: I realised I had done nothing; I had sat on my gains, like the ungrateful servant. I had been swimming and floating in my own truth-dreams, with very little to show for it. The lightning conductor hadn't reached the earth.

- You must learn to prepare yourself, she said abruptly.

- In what way? I asked.

- Not 'what way' - just listen! Seismic convulsions are seizing our land, from the Northern Heights and way beyond. It's part of a vaster turmoil, preordained. In a sense, we've brought it on ourselves, by not listening to our Prophets, treating Mother Earth like dirt. No-one can act with impunity: there's bound to be an effect somewhere. This you know, of course, but you have to *live* it.

'Technologically, we have gone very far - particularly in the last few decades. We have outstripped ourselves in capacity. But for every gain there has been a loss, an inward atrophy, a dying of the heart. We have become brains on stalks and our lives are little, mean. We plunder and experiment everywhere, attempting, usually behind locked doors, to alter the course of Nature to our style. But Nature is mighty; she is terrible, awesome: our wanton enterprises will backfire on us. In fact, they are already doing so.

'Take the logging of the mountains, for instance. We were told long ago that it would have consequences for the plain, particularly if pursued in the wholesale manner to which we have now become inured. Absolutely no doubt about it. But what did they do? They went ahead anyway. The Interests were at it, and Interest is all. In consequence, the fringes of the plain are drying up: they're arid and useless without the rain. The farmers are being forced to join the loggers, or face the prospect of immediate starvation - they who for centuries have tilled that land, lived on it, nurtured it, made it grow! It's a crying shame, and the land is crying out.

'It is the same everywhere, where They have moved in. The Faceless Machine has taken us for a ride. We don't seem to recognize the sheer danger of it, this abdication of our humanness; we don't seem to see that in handing ourselves over we make ourselves mean, small, impotent. An ineluctable retributive logic follows: we are ground under by the very machines we invented.

*They* predominate, *they* take control, and we get the scraps, which is what we deserve. The loss of ontological presence, our loss of *Being* is the real tragedy. And it's solemn solace, after all, to think that a few of us could get away. Some of us can travel, while others cannot, and there are other places, to west and east. It's small consolation, as I say. If only we could *change*, change radically now.'


Bella looked at me silently, allowing her words to percolate. There was such a symmetry between her being and her speaking that no hiatus occurred when she stopped.

- You see, she continued, all this is preordained; it's part of a larger orchestration of things. Man, at the deepest level, craves wisdom, which alone can show him what he truly is. Wisdom is the cradle of civilizations - not just climate, warm rivers, bridge- and crossing-points. Ease of living is one element only, a dangerous one when the other isn't there. I am telling you this because the danger is apparent, because we are falling into the Abyss.

'Wisdom isn't there for the taking, you see: it's something you have to seek and find. It isn't a province accessible to all; in fact, traditionally, it was reserved for the few. And of those few who seek very few find; the majority get lost somewhere along the way. A self-substantiating person is rare, one who lives by his own candle-flame. Most people are dependents of one kind or another. Even that is not so disastrous, if the

150

overall level of awareness is high. But today, as you know, we have reached the nadir.

'Atlantis has existed since time out of mind as the earthly repository of the eternal wisdom. The Ancients knew this and handed it down from generation to generation. But, then, they had the balance right - the balance between knowledge and wisdom, that is. When things fall apart that is what goes: it begins with imbalance, actually. Knowledge, after all, is a danger on its own. That's why I asked you about yourself: the split begins there, in all of us.

'Though one shouldn't romanticize, of course, the Ancients *did* seem to have the balance right - one has only to look at our folk-art to see it. There was a sense of cohesion, playfulness, joy: those blue dipping swallows, brown naked fishermen, garlanded bulls with the gymnasts leaping over them. Naturally, in the hands of the craftsman it was unconscious, but in the hands of the priest it told a different tale. For him those pictures were magic, they were runic: they were the ciphers of an intermediary world. Rather, to put it more clearly, they were *messages*, the coding of Being in open form. Through them he touched on the Numinous - or they *were* the Numinous come to him. For life is obviously very different, when what you see is what you are. Today - and that is part of our misery - we see and are only objects: we have reified ourselves, turned ourselves into commodities, *things*. We have lost the sense that the fisherman, the swallow, the garlanded bull is our brother; we are he. Because the Underived is fine and escapes the gropings of the mechanical mind, we have ceased to give it any credence at all. It is, for us now, a whim, an excrescence, and we do not realize how our gross ignorance is pushing it further away all the time. We think more and more in terms of externals, and this makes us heavy, lumbering, dull. We are in very great danger - this I must stress - because the outer capacity has outstripped the inner meaning and we do not see where it all ends up: in violence, mental agony, crime on the streets.

'We have, somehow, to go on and go back: back to the time when the artist and the priest were brother-seers, bringing through the Real; on to a time when each one of us becomes his own artist, his own chalice-priest, when he is able to offer the Cup to himself, turn water into wine, come through and come alive. These are moments in the dispensation of Time, the opportunity of which must not be lost. The Calling is upon us now, as crime stalks the streets, mental agony increases and human degeneracy is the visible norm. We have no choice, when you think about it.'

- What do you think I can do? I asked.
- Don't ask that question, just get on!

A sigh escaped from her, a deep, heaving sigh. Visibly, she had come to the end.

We were back in the Temple precincts now, in that quiet, dark place at the City's heart. I took my leave of Bella there, by the winding staircase which leads to her room. It is always very quiet and very dark there, like the place into which she herself had now withdrawn. It was like a resonance of rich, deep music, spreading with the failing and the falling of the light. And it was into That that she had now retired, climbing the staircase like an uncrowned queen.

A mood of sheer panic washed over me, as I realised the truth of what she had been saying and the utter necessity that I act. But *how* to act; that was the question. I was so unmade still, such a country boy at heart. I knew not, neither could I spin. The doubts and misgivings which overcame me then were such, certainly, as all seekers feel, but that counted for nothing as I, lone I, sempiternally single I, left the dark temple-place beneath Bella's stair and accosted the stridency of the street's blaring light.

5

There seems to be a hook-up at this point: an outer-inner, Tristan-Archaeon correspondence. We are back in the comparative present of Patmos. 'There seems to be a rent in the Dreamwork,' writes Tristan and, while there is speculation as to why this was so, it is of no real interest to the serious past-life scholar. He has his job to do, like anybody else, and why, really, should he be held up by the failure of the time-traveller (a dreamworker, at that) to put pen to paper consistently - unless, of course (which is even worse), it's the fault of that infuriating breed of incompetents, archivists, who can't keep track. But there you are: it's an imperfect world.

Tristan was back with St. John and his Beasts, and the likelihood is, he had lost track himself. Channelling is exhausting, as well as exhilarating, as anyone who has 'been there' knows. He needed to withdraw from the vertical fray, get back into his body, ease out, relax. He craved the horizontal, in a word.

It came to him in hot waves of lust, the piling-up and swarming of images. It wasn't physical desire, that immediate thing he once had known, but a cerebral mish-mash, a tabloid excitation. It was no good to him, no good to man nor beast, and yet it visited him day and night. Yes, he had come to a bitter point, a fatal and necessary point of integration. Since Jessie there had really been no-one in his life, and he had sought his redemption in flight, in upthrust: he had wanted always to go

152

beyond. Now the earth, the nude earth of Patmos, was calling him back to his nether self.

He didn't know what to do about it; his energies were everywhere, uncontained. The women of his mind were insolent, blond, half-clad, masturbatory: nothing about them was grounded or real. Then the Dark Lady came to him; she rose up, more, from the root of him. Curiously, she seemed to be part of him, as if she existed somewhere inside him, waiting for him to call her forth. Unlike the frothy females of his thoughts, she might also be a real-life person. It was an adumbration, actually.

And such, gentle reader, is the fate of angelheads: they have to find a place on the ground.

6

Hence, to Piraeus Tristan made his way, with some vague apprehension that 'she' might be there. But actually what happened was very strange. On board he made the acquaintance of an American, who told him in the familiar speech of that time that he was going to the Other Edge. Without bothering to pin down or redefine the term, Tristan asked him what the going was like.

- Plenty o' night-ladies, he replied. Pretty good.

And there the conversation ended. But during the night-journey from Patmos to Piraeus, Tristan fell into a very deep sleep. He dreamed he was walking in mucous-dawn Piraeus, with a faint mist hovering and the swirling waters deep. He was carrying a guitar slung over his shoulder, and he had the smooth-shaven, crew-cut look of the American. As he walked down the ramp and onto the quay he noticed in the bleary morning light a sign above a bar, flashing 'End of Atlantis'.

Wasn't it the most natural thing in the world, to be alive and well and in the body of the American? Surely it was, since his tread was so sure, his body erect, penis like a periscope. Certainly he knew where he was going this time!

She was there on the quayside, as if summoned forth, as if she had grown from the root of him. She stood in the opening of the morning world, black leather coat open, head held back.

- Expire with me, she said with a smile.

- Expire?

- Desire.

And she held him very close. He heaved with her body like the swelling sea.

- You must have come a long way, she said.

- From Patmos, said Tristan's American voice.

153

- I thought so; I've been waiting for you most of the night.
- You have an English accent. Who are you?
- People call me the Dancing Dark Lady. I was born of Oceana and Poseidon, my sire.
A cab drew by, sleek, black, predestined and drove them to their appointed place.
- This way, said the lady. Kindly pay the driver.
She led him through a maze of dark passageways, up coiling stairs, to a small, prepared room. All that was in it was an open bed, white.
- This is my love-cave, she whispered in his ear. This is the place where all lovers meet.
She pointed to a spot in the middle of the ceiling.
- They'll all be watching us from up there.
- What's your name, babe? came the voice again.
- Do you mean to say you really don't know? I'm the one who was waiting for you, the one you've been looking for all your life.
- I know - you're Isolde.
- Of course I am! I'm all women who take men from the sea.

Who knows - and in what meridian, continuum - they may have known each other before? The fact is, there was no hiatus between them, not a millionth of an inch of unfound ground. It was, in that tippling, open place a veridical-vertical Night Journey, a dropping down. For it went from the bottom of the throbbing Sea to the Sky's sheer peak, bursting through the Void.

Desire had imploded through itself, had become, itself, not a means to an end, but a language, an element, an unfoldment from the Root. Because they had sealed the Circle, so to speak, had let it fuse without spilling a drop, they had passed from the acres of Time outspread, the fraught and narrowing Gate, the fast fuck, to a Land whose diameter dipped down and away, whose radius was infinite, its Fields wide and waiting. They had entered the world which waits just behind this one and prepares our entry and our going out. He felt it in the upthrust of his dream-body, in the called and immediate response of hers. It was a giving-birth and a dying-away, a rocked and seasoned moving of the waters, the breaking of a tightness which all humankind knows.

It was a Music instantaneous and mathematical, a carefully laid out, preordained score. They *heard* it, somehow, first; their bodies heard it: they drank it down into every cell. It was then, not them, but that Music moving through them: it was the Order of Perfection making itself heard. Released at last from 'meat-ball madness', the perennial, ultimately intolerable sense of Life's confinement inside the skull, they were free to come out, to look around, to pass through: they were free, at last, to be themselves. They had inherited, walked into the Fertile Fields.

The dumbness and numbness of living were over. This dense, compact, ensnared space-ball of ours (which the majority of people call the 'real world') had here cracked open and from its core had arisen, not blueprints, definitions *newsprint*, but the most beautiful, most natural, flowering Tree, roots in deep-earth, heart in the middle, branches reaching to the sky.

This was as real as any 'real world': in fact, by its im-and explosion, *more* real. It was what subliminally, fluidly, permanently supported this world, with its fragmentary impressions. It was the substratum, actually. And, as such, it subsisted when thought and sense were quiet; it was free to flower when they were quiet. For in that quietness the 'real world' itself underwent a transformation: it was no longer an amalgam of fractured feelings, moods, reflections, masks & revelations, but rather, the essence of the Mirror itself, its durable substance giving back the Light. It had that quality of something solid, which cannot be put aside by thought. At the same time it was growing organically, with immense strength and power, inalienably, from its root. It was, thus, not a world of dead objects, a fixed and finite spinning ball, but an infinitely extending living Dimension, a fluid Continuum, a World-within-world.

And they knew it by direct inherence, without any intermediary of thought. They could not for a moment have operated on it, for, living and breathing, they *were* That. The graceful curve of the lady's neck, her belly moving like a deep guitar - all this fell back, fell like daisies to the ground, from the garlanded present of Child's Play upon the Field. It was That which turned and moved, in fact, That's passage through the eye and the gyre of the Now. They were merely its existents, its agents, Field's figures.

Day slipped into night, and night became day. They lived at the celebratory Edge, where metamorphosis is term, clue, essence. There day met night along the seam, was sealed and firmed, sewn in with it. There was no future to it, actually, just the living, ever-fecund present, the place where time and eternity touch. And that in itself was place enough - the place and presence of the pyramidal Heart. The two became one there: they had never been apart.


The dream-continuum was coming to an end. Tristan heard a tapping at his lady's chamber wall and awoke to find himself arrived in port, with dock-hands shouting into the dawn and the ship itself knocking against a row of used tyres. Cargo was being discharged on the quay, in that wash of sea air and oil-slicked sea which seems to inhabit every port. Time to get up now, assume another day; clean out the mouth, wash the body, Time's pawn.

He looked on deck for the American, then vaguely again at the bottom of the ramp. Somehow, he felt, they must be allied, since he had co-opted the other man's body. But, no; there was no-one: he was quickly away. Unlike Tristan, who took time to come round, he must have been off the boat in a trice and be already somewhere off Omonia Square, in his own living flesh, with a lady of Athens, Obviously, he couldn't wait.

Tristan wondered if he should follow suit, then realized how fraught and foolish that would be: he was still in the ambience of the Dancing Dark Lady. He took a reflective breakfast in town, thinking that in place of paid intercourse he would, instead, go cultural. The vertical reality still burned in him, darkly luminescent, fecund, warm. He would go to the Acropolis, he thought.

Accordingly, he took a cab to the foot of the Hill and, walking up past the fruit-sellers' stalls, he came to the spot where, only two months before, Emma and Evelyn had stood together. He appraised that point, which is the Point of Entry, the columns with their sharp Dread rising before him. He wanted to enter into that Space, to be absolved and irradiated by its Light. He had come as a votary to the Parthenon. But the temple itself was cool; it was aloof: it held itself intact, like a virgin. He walked around it several times, performing the ritual circumambulation, praying inwardly, looking for a sign. But no sign came to him as he walked and as he paused. She herself was sheer, stony, mute. Whenever he stopped She seemed to say: 'What are you waiting for? Get on!' And so he continued his circumambulations, looking all the time for an utterance. He longed to say, of course, 'for you', but the words seemed foolish and froze on his lips. He couldn't get Her on his terms. 'What is it You want?' he asked Her in his heart, and swiftly and inevitably came the answer: 'Nothing.'

He realised the point of dialogue had shifted: instead of asking questions of *Her*, he had been addressing them to himself. He realized the Nothing *was* himself and that all outer questions were mere tricks, evasions. It had been part of his immaturity to go walking round the Parthenon, mumbling to himself. Where in all the world *was* there another to address? It was part of some spurious refining process that left one high and dry, crystalline, in a sort of mausoleum, the sap-of-life shut off. It was an aetiolation beyond his proper point.

Curiously, then, he turned within himself; he took a step down from his strained sublimation. He had been on a false track, obviously, but one which, to his Sunday-school mind, had presented itself as 'the thing to do', 'the place to be', or some other such nonsense. Stepping off the plinth, he came back to himself; forsaking the role of suppliant and votary, he became again - and it was right, it was good - just another traveller looking at a monument. For, while it was good to be a brother and a priest, it was no guarantee of inward worth - indeed, one might miss the point completely. Whatever one's direction, Life must be strengthened; there was no way forward otherwise.

He continued to look for the living lady, the flesh-and-blood woman who would take him through the Gate. Depression or no, she *had* to be there. Leaving the Parthenon, he walked down into the town.

7

Next day he took a trip to Delphi, catching an early morning conveyance from a bleary bus-stand off-centre from town and arriving in Delphi some three hours later. The day warmed gradually as they drove, and at a certain point they passed the spot where unwitting Oedipus had slain his father. Tristan, in a time warp, was back at Crowdecote, pushing up the steep hill with his brother Cecil; their father was glaring down at them. He had betrayed his father - his father lay dead - and his punishment was to wander the earth, unable for ever to find peace, to find rest. 'I'm trying,' he thought, 'I am expiating.' The bus, in a blue sweep, passed ancient Thebes in another time-space now, a modern world - absolved, or so it thought, from guilt and retribution - its walls thick, crumbling, mellow in the light. Soon they were climbing partway up Parnassos, swinging across the fabled hill, till, through a welter of sheep and goats, bright trinket vendors and shops agape, they pushed into Delphi and got off the bus.

It was to this site, sitting athwart Parnassos, that Apollo came from his birthplace on Delos. It was the site of the marriage of Heaven and Earth, the Golden Eagle of the Sun swooping down - hale, vigorous, triumphant, spread - to take the Serpent of the Earth to his breast, She whose body has the Music of the Earth, He whose wings reached up and out. That marriage-bed was a Temple in itself, and a temple was raised in honour of it. From it the Children of Insight were born, who come whole, pure and tumbling into this world and who tell it exactly the way it is. The python-priestess acted as midwife, dedicating her whole life to the task and delivering - on demand, or so it seemed - the exact right child to the anxious enquirer. Many sent their petitions to Delphi; no-one was ever refused or turned away. For we know it, don't we?, actually: we live in a hit-and-miss, muddled-thinking world, where the best we can do is approximate. We need the Marriage of the Eagle and the Snake; we need it in-and-for ourselves; we need it now.

Tristan drifted down to the temple arena, where three several pillars support a lintel. There he sat on the circular plinth, looking down to the valley with its million olive-trees. They received, imbibed and held the sun, and he ate some fruit and yoghurt where he sat. 'No goddess coming today,' he thought. 'No goddesses anywhere any more.' And, as if by way of consolation, he took from his pack a borrowed 'Guide bleu' and buried himself in the details of the site.

157

It was, however, just a palliative: it gave him information, nothing more. He wandered, ill-at-ease, all over the site, seeking in the broken steps of the stadium some echo of the Charged Time, now long gone. It was a fallen world he was walking in, a world of cracked stone, dust, despair: it was a world from which the gods had fled. 'Even the dryads are silent,' he thought, looking down at the crown of the million olive-trees. 'It's no wonder, either: we have driven them out.'

What impressed him most in the small museum was the bronze, erect statue of the Young Charioteer. The silence which lay at the heart of it spoke to some centre in Tristan, stilling him. He entered a moment of pure repose. For this was, of course, no bronze, erect mortal, no fragmentary figure snatched from Time, but a casting into human form of what stands behind it, the human Idea. As such, it was perfect, impeccable, complete: its serenity came from that essence assumed. It shone forth, then, unbrokenly from the blackstone pupil within the white eye, ran into the hands from the light-clad shoulders, was eloquent and poised in the smooth-curled head.

Tristan wanted to reach out and touch him, so much did that very essence of his summon forth in the observer his own humanness. No creature, this, of bleak transcendence, no weeping figure before the Cross, but a living, delivered, first-born, flaming node of the One Fire running and smelting all. That was where they met, in *that* Fire: in that consummation observer *was* observed. Linked to some rhythm indescribable, the signature of which one comes upon or not, they stood there, both, on the floor of the museum, the mortal man of flesh and the imperishable Boy. And it was that which rose in one, after all; it was *that* which was the cornerstone of Art: this capacity to rise erect and serene, to look straight ahead, to grasp the reins. Tristan felt it in him like an infusion, a gift of strength from the standing Boy. He had it in him, he knew he had. What he needed now was to trust it more.

Outside suddenly, the sun was hot. He bought black-and-white photos and went to catch the bus.

Then one evening, under the arcades near Syndagme, he thought he caught a glimpse of the Dancing Dark Lady, but as he approached she as quickly disappeared. 'No' but a fantasy,' he said to himself. But then, as he was setting off back to Patmos, leaning on the rail and watching the quay, there she was again in a dark café doorway, which, when he looked hard, really stared, drew her into and through itself. 'I must be hallucinating,' he thought, and gave himself a literal pinch. The place was still there, all right, large as life, but *she* had completely disappeared. What was the meaning of his seeing her - if indeed, it had any meaning at all? Was it a false hope, a fond illusion? Or was it a visit from another plane, a hint of things to come, an adumbration? There was no time to investigate: the boat for Patmos was leaving right away.

Tristan felt suspended, unsure. He was adrift again; the Sea's motion held him.

On the way out they passed a spit of land, on which a temple to Poseidon stood. There, a fellow-passenger told him, club-footed Byron had scrawled his name - old Byron, who was still a legend in Greece, first and foremost of graffiti artists. He had left his mark on History. But what did that mean: to leave one's mark? What mark would he, Tristan, ever leave?

He thought of Prometheus, out on his rock, the Eagle picking his liver by day. It was like that, actually; he was like that: he had stolen the fire of his father's bed, and his punishment was to be chained to the rock, to bare existence, to know no relief. He was getting, and would get, the Visit every day. Wherever his flights and elevation took him, there was always the Bedrock, to which he must descend. There it was, the rocky promontory, the bleak, nude place, on which the ruined temple stood.

History was like that, actually: it had been built up like the silting of a river. Huts, cities, temples, monuments and meanings - they were all in there somewhere, if one threw down a line. It depended how deep one wanted to go. If one really believed, like Schliemann, in historicity, one could have a good dig and pull up Troy. Nonetheless, basically (because that, too, was a ruin), the eye travelled over an unpeopled land, a place on its way to final Reduction, islanded, isolate, whose first breath was its last. Tristan was sitting in History.

8

The boat to Patmos moved inexorably on, carrying Tristan away from these reflections, and in no time at all he was back in the Dream. His words are recorded, seriously archived, under the title: 'The Last Writings of Archaeon'.

- September, 193...

Bella's blessing has been doing its work: she is showing me, little by little, what I must do. There are various connections a person must make before he/she can really serve the Work. And it seems to be a tone-truth - in fact, she has confirmed it - that, until these connections have been made, all our attempts to restructure are vanity. We cannot do it on our own. Patience, always patience, she says.

It is hard, however, to fix one's attention on the Navel of Change with chaos all around. How can one, in all honesty, shut oneself off from the situation-as-is and give oneself over to 'inner work'? It is we who have brought about the snarl-up, after all. Shouldn't we, then, be the ones to undo it? Sitting quietly, doing nothing - is that *really* the way to help?

What is happening all around is drastic, dire. The pressure on the priesthood is mounting all the time. They alone now feel responsible, while the whole race of politicians is corrupt to a man. No office is gained nor position secured without some kind of graft or bribe; no-one can stand against the game. An atmosphere of moral torpor has set in, where instant gratification rules and the soft 'Why not?' has removed the Edge of 'Why?' Society has lost its endemic Root, its organ of Grace, its very own Field, and it lives now only on foreign food, Market directives, convenience crap. It is vanishing up its own slipstream.

Agwen has moved away from me, so concerned has she become with the current crisis. We continue to see each other, of course, but the meat and meaning has gone out of it. Crisis or not, I tell her, people are still real; why can't we simply hold on to that? But she tells me, by way of answer, that I don't understand: the priestly function is to live from within, to feel deep inside one the reality of things, then move from there, all people included. It's a different emphasis, naturally, and it lands one in quite a different place.

It puts me in a quandary, though. I fear she may have got it all wrong. For how can that which claims to be inclusive impose restrictions on itself? Or is it just another of those quaint devices that turn people into narrow, tortured things? Being a country boy myself, I stand somewhat outside the Structure, and the view from where I stand is mixed, to say the least. I see this narrow focus as a dangerous thing, a shrivelled response to the searing world at large. The world is burning, obviously, but is it the right answer, to focus, to exclude? Agwen says the Way is sheer and, therefore, all else must be laid aside. But that is one of the difficulties, surely: that by cutting, excluding, paring everything down, one kills the vitality needed for action and reduces the world to a small, hard ball. This we cannot and should never do.

Agwen's gravity, however, is never in doubt, though she holds herself aloof, above, between. It's as if she were moving, not just away from me, but from the whole matter of relationship 'per se', beginning to home in more and more on her soul's intentions and her body's end. She is searching, she says, for the Ground of Being; there is no time or energy for anything else. I can see what she means (the situation *is* bad), but I'm not at all sure it works that way. Surely it's better to move forward as one, with all one possesses - a total movement, so to speak - even if it does, or might, take longer. I don't know, however, I really don't.

- October, 193...

The situation is worsening rapidly, and Agwen is talking of self-immolation. She calls it 'sacrifice', of course. She says it may be the only way, that everything else has been tried and failed.

The Continent at large is in turmoil: there is constant strife on the Hills and in the Regions. The March of the Interests goes on unimpeded, and anyone who stands in their way gets butchered. Simple farmers are driven from their homes, which are then razed to the ground and their land possessed. They have no recourse, no Court of Appeal: out there, the legal machinery has collapsed.

Things are no better in the City, either, though this was a haven among havens once. Now people are afraid to walk the streets at night; old people are afraid, the young violent, adrift. And the Temple precincts, to which anyone could repair, are no longer safe, not even for priests. Yesterday, even, someone was stabbed; there are rapes and murders in broad daylight. Together with the slaughter of the Marginals, it all seems part of some floodlit nightmare.

When the One Thing goes, all the rest is forfeit, and that is what is happening to us. Even our beloved Earth, sick of blood, is opening up chasms, claiming her own. Last week in the west, many miles from here, a volcano erupted, destroying a town. All its buildings were swept away or buried; people were incinerated where they stood. At the same time, so they say, flaming asteroids landed, pummelling the Island, and some of it sank. Those in the know used their mind-screens to observe it; those, like myself, more pedestrian, got to know about it second-hand. It's part of the accumulating ruination.

The Equation of Heaven and Earth is mighty, what passes between them an ancient, strong story. It's as if there were a Ladder somewhere, an ascending-descending, surefooted Link. By this, and on this, we have lived all these years. I also have it in my body and blood, like the frets of some ancestral instrument: I am a Channeller of Music, nothing more. I could run up and down that Ladder once, as if Heaven and Earth were just next door, all intervening space and distance gone. The immediate Scale rang a bell in me.

Now, as the outsider poet-priest, I have become aware of the deafening Void, the vacuous Din, the agitated Zero, the sickening Snot-element in which we all live. It is, at one and the same time, glaring and amorphous, blinding, paining, insubstantial - like living on coloured cotton-wool. It is what we have come to, finally. Having lost the one essential Connection, we cast about for an alternative, the whole fraught world of experiences. But these are fleeting, surrogates at best, part of the tissue of the mayic Unreal. That is how we are caught at present: on the antithetical, downward Spiral, the one which feeds on Delusion, on Desire. And, once we are on it, who cares to get off?

This is where ritual sacrifice comes in - as the ancient, necessary antidote to the festering, self-fostering, vicious crime-mind. Once everybody believed in it; now only the priesthood keeps the faith. They say that, without it - and I sympathise -, Man always takes the wrong, left Path; his proclivities are such he will always go down. There is something required of us constantly, the which not giving we bleak out, we grow pale; we wallow in mediocrity. It is the final nadir of humanness, the bow gone slack, the heart dried and hollow.

Some of the priesthood advocate non-action, feeling the Void is a place of transition and trusting in what they call 'natural goodness'. Others, like Agwen, are dead against this: they feel what is happening is *so* bad that only the best is good enough, i.e., in this case, the most extreme. They are all for up-and-doing, and the College is split. I have sympathy for both sides, I must say: I feel, with Agwen, the urgency; on the other hand, I'm not at all sure that self-sacrifice is the proper response. She will certainly go to her death for this, but what will it amount to in the long run? All I can do is look, observe. But, as often happens when things are bad, anything one does seems to make it worse.

- November, 193...

We came out onto our high place again, the place above the marble edge, where we knew the Space of Fire, the luciferic spot. We were again ourselves with one another, as if all the intervening time-past had been just a dreadful desert waste. All the same, I felt Agwen becoming remote, as though her inalienable destiny were being worked out, even as we lay there. It was no longer a festival of coming joy, with lights, candles, greetings-cards, new life for old, but a momentary pause, an echo of the Sound, in the long, slow march of inexorable Fate. For this reason, I think, I have never been so aware of the actual *presence* of pain in pleasure. I didn't have to wait for the kickback this time: I knew it as instantaneous measure.

Things and people fall apart, and when they do the slide is unstoppable. One can try here and there to sling in a brick, but when the whole Bastion is coming down, then what is the use of one's trying? Tell me. So it is with Agwen and me: she is going to her fate and I to mine. The rocket in orbit, of which we were, is being pulled back with steel-hot friction into the gravitational field of the earth, there to explode and disintegrate in the maw of the monster, Necessity. From now on things take their inevitable course.

- December, 193...

162

As I have seen her, so she goes by, draped in black, with the barred turquoise head-piece. I see her now as she has always been, the burning vestal, the Immaculate Dark Lady. She is going to the place from which none return.

In front of her walk her ritual rod-bearers, then, in a column on either side, the single files of her officiants, they too dressed in black, with downcast eyes. Behind her, because this is drastic death, walk a drummer and a piper with wailing sound. Withal, there is an air of solemn celebration - as if she were the Chosen Bride and this the walk to the Altar of Consummation. This, I know, is the way she understands it: not as a misery to be endured, but as a rich, hymen-ripping Burst of Joy.

Nonetheless, her heart must be pounding, as mine is pounding, watching her go by. She must know we were *here* once and now she is *there*: the terrible, objective fact of it. The drum is giving out little taps, then rolls of raps, with a fast crescendo. The piper has lost himself in his playing; his sound wails and spreads, pervading, entering. It's as if he wanted us all to know that nothing in this world is gratuitous.

From the Temple Door the High Priest emerges and stands above Agwen, the priestess on the steps. He is holding the sacrificial knife in his hand. She has to move up to him, kneel before him and kiss the blade on both flat surfaces; then she must also kiss the blade's edge. Only if there is no tremor of fear, no trembling, no anxiety, no spilling of blood can she rise and enter as the true sacrifice. She must have no personal feeling left, but be utterly free of the sense of 'I' and, thus, made ready to be perfect in her death. All these are tests which the High Priest applies, failure in which incurs the deepest shame and leaves ritual suicide as the only option.

Agwen advances and catches up her cloak: she must not trip or stumble now. A small crowd has gathered, fallen silent, as she walks above them up the marble steps and kneels on the top step before the High Priest. Seemingly the hard edge of joy is hers, because she takes the blade between her teeth and holds it, suspended, in her mouth, playfully. The Priest bends forward takes the knife, raises her, and they pass, she first, he following, arms outstretched, across the level above the steps, between the pillars of the portico and into the mouth of the dark Temple Door. She is going, triumphant, to the vast Unknown.

We watch her go into the lifelong Temple, the place to which she has dedicated her life; we see the dark doors close to behind her. Banished from our sight, her Journey has begun. The High Priest, with a sweep and a brandishing of his knife, has followed her in; the sacrifice is now. A few minutes later he re-emerges, with the blood-fuming knife raised, dripping, in his hand. The crowd, held in thrall by the majestic death-marriage, falls as one body, forehead to the ground. We are mute in awe before the spectacle. Then the High Priest, his face turned to heaven,

163

thanks the gods for their acceptance of the sacrifice and prays that, by this spilling of blood, the Earth may be redeemed from Man's monstrous wrongdoing.

The thrill of Death passes through the people, and they are momentarily cast out of themselves; they are momentarily opened themselves, as the Door is opened by the Angel of Death. They have been delivered onto a different Ground, one whose Walls go out and away, and they have lost their puny preoccupations in the face of the dark Edge of Agwen's gift. 'She died for us' sounds sentimental, and yet the emotional charge is there. It gives us a plumb-line into the Continuum, the darkly swirling underwater World, the world, perhaps, from which we emerged and into which we are sure to be dissolved. It re-establishes Primal Unity, the world beneath, the world *before*; it delivers us back to the dark, abiding Flux.

- Theton, 12 Ziz...

Time is bearing down on us, reducing to ruins the fraught period of peace. With Agwen's sacrifice complete, there came a dilation of the energies, as if the public at large were waiting, watching to see how the situation might develop, which is now referred to as a Matter of State. This was quite frankly a misnomer, at best. For it is surely one of the curses of our time that the State takes over everything, leaving us feckless, sapless, bereft. We looked, but did not see, the Rose of Agwen's death. She was trying to show us all something true, to give us a charge, a pulse of awareness that would carry us past the current crisis and see us through to an untouched Ground.

We flunked it, I regret to say. Whatever we had in the wake of her death, whatever half-digested morsel, was soon lost and buried in the common press. The Ethic of the State, like the work ethic, implies, not rigour, but massive Control. This is our substitute for Grace. We could not live with Emptiness, the vast antechamber to death's Unknown - perhaps we could not take the angst - and, because of this, we filled the Void with plans, diversions, piling technologies. Anything but face the truth of what we are, anything to avoid the being of Nothing! Thus, a beautiful Dream is spoilt, the Vision goes begging, the plug's pulled out. The loss of that finer attunement means that we shrink and grow down to the level of meat-mind. Thereafter there is only strife. The onlookers saw the Pole was cracking. If we couldn't do it, who could?, they must have thought. I, Archaeon, who was privy and a witness to these things, have written them down for those who come after.

First, the Temple was struck by lightning, causing a conflagration in the Sanctum. Then an earthquake shook the outer walls and part of the East

Gate, the Gopuram, came down. That was only the beginning, of course, a sure sign to all that something was wrong. The blood-sacrifice had not been enough - or, rather, it had only served to delay the by now all-pervasive, creeping sense that our central Unity had been destroyed. There was no place left to which one could repair.

Following the destruction of the Temple, things quickly went from bad to worse, though some may argue that the Temple was an irrelevance: it would have happened anyway. The destruction passed to the City itself, where vandals, vicious, thuggish, armed prowled the streets day-and-night and murdered at will. Nobody was safe at any time, and it was literally suicide to go out after dark. As ours is a society based on trust, which has lived unpoliced for centuries, we had no means for dealing with this downturn, this violence. The negative Spiral was working its way. It gathered like wildfire and spread through the City, so that the ordinary, decent man-in-the-street turned his head the other way and became spineless, demoralised. The New Barbarism came in like a cult.

The Forces of Darkness spread rapidly, eating up the farmland, burning down the forests. To meet them in one place - and it was difficult, difficult to track them down - was to see them re-emerge with tenfold vigour in quite another: they were everywhere. Such resistance as there was was individual and, though this produced a few temporary heroes, the overwhelming Tide dragged them under, drowned them too.

Finally, the convulsions of which Bella had spoken, the seismic, the meteoric, struck our land. It wasn't one earthquake, collision or explosion but a successive welter of angry events, which perfectly mirrored the inner chaos of the times. Fire rained down, pavements were torn up and lost people, going from place to place, were cut in two or burnt alive. It was as if the regular Earth were off its axis, atoms scattering randomly, and hence made naked, vulnerable, exposed, a receptacle and a housing for every piece of cosmic junk. Asteroids and comets, colliding in mid-air, gathered their fulsome, fatal strength to bore down hotly into the earth, opening up craters where none had been - in the middle, for instance, of the fertile Central Plain. There was an unprecedented succession of these, each one louder and deadlier than the last, till all that remained was one huge black gash, down which - tottering, screaming, falling - houses and inhabitants were poured like corpses. And still, relentlessly, the Wrath of Heaven struck.

Then came the answer from the Earth. A volcano in the north, which had lain dormant for centuries, erupted violently with no prior warning. The flow of molten lava immolated towns. When it ceased the towns were fixed, the people carbonized, stuck in stills where they stood. The horrors and terrors came thick and fast. Men, women and children were melted down to zero by sudden sunblast, which no-one could explain. Then, in the night, vast meteors fell, crashing, breaking, destroying for good the long acres of land we had thought of as permanent: 'Atlantis for ever' - or so we had thought.

Into this geomoral, ecological Morass came no Redeemer to put things right: we were all inheriting our own Nullity. Each man focused on his own dead Zero, through which he was sucked, as through a Black Hole. A negative Constellation followed, a simmering and seething which left him no rest. There was a buzz in the air, as of a Plague of Insects. They settled on everyone. Madness was rife.

In the end it became obvious that the Continent was going. The break--up began in the north and was swift. Incessant bombardments by celestial bodies, volcanoes, earthquakes and inexplicable explosions - these combined to make Mother Earth despair of her Children and their tenancy. Towns, cities, villages, all went at once, engulfing the rest of the population. The last of the Temple-line, the Initiates, stand ready to leave by their own secret means. Bella's not going - she says, for her it's too late - but the others are talking of enfolding the Essence and making it live again somewhere else. There's hope still, I suppose, and a prospect in that. For myself, I'm just waiting for the Maw to open, to be swallowed, drunk down to the bottom of the Pit. For myself I see no hope at all: my psychic shortfall is too great.

## BOOK SIX: BLACK SAILS, WHITE

Le poète est semblable au Prince des nuées,
Qui hante la tempête et se rit de l'Archer;
Exilé sur le sol au milieu des huées,
Ses ailes de géant l'empêchent de marcher.


Baudelaire


# Finally

'Incandescently it glows, there before me in the dark, receding room. It tapers to a point, a fine film of disappearance; the darkness around it seems to quiver. It is not like an ingot, solid and single, but deeply from its base it rises like a rose, around which again, climbing and slimming, the edge of the flame bears in to the tip.

'He told me to fix my concentration there, to push out every vagrant impression and be just singly, visually *here*. I'm not sure how long I can keep it up, though: it seems to be a mental exercise, at best. My thoughts go dipping into the night and my lonely, aching body waits. Why on earth did I let Emma go, when she was so wholly, singly and simply mine? Who knows what she may be up to now - I never even thought of it!

'I have to admit, however, if I'm honest, that her beauty and innocence were just too much. She could draw me out and on as no-one else could, and yet she remained immutably alone. I wanted to attack that aloneness-in-the-world, that sense she always had of being out of things. But she resisted it, without resisting me, so I went back again to my old turbulence. Such are my nocturnal ramblings, as I look at the flame and the flame burns in me . . . Tomorrow, perhaps, I shall set out again.

'Today I have danced for the first time in days. Curiously, it was wonderful - like being back again in the days of my youth, when I was a girlish novice, before Martha even. Subjectively, I have to build back, to go through the solid wastes of myself, those blocks and passages of downright dirt, unblinkingly, without a light. Yet can I? I sit here, so-called 'meditating', while the webbed withered skin of the past moves in; it throws its tentacles around me like a sea-monster, almost before I have time to say: 'Off!' I say it anyway, of course, but only as a gesture. I wish Emma were here.

'But that's enough - away with reminiscence! I have to face myself as I am: the past, the turbulence, the weight of myself. I have to go through something on my own. This much, at least, I have learnt from her. Once she was my student, a willing, waiting waif; now it is I who am the inchoate one, plunged by her - God knows how! - into this maelstrom of melting possibilities, all safe anchorage come adrift. Somehow she has turned the tables on me, and unfortunately I feel 'it's for my own good.' I hug her to me tight. O, God, where art thou now?

'My mother was a whore in little old Leicester, where she picked up her clients in Spinney Hill Park and brought them back to our Highfields home: soldiers, sailors, aliens from everywhere - anybody, in fact, who could pay on the line. Most of them did, surprisingly, though now and again she might have trouble with a drunk. She had once been the favourite of an aristocrat, who kept her in a manner to which she had been totally unaccustomed - the finest suites in the best hotels, ball-gowns, hot baths, sumptuous dinners -, till age began to tell and he tired of her. She told me how, in her younger day, she had been a soloist in a Closed Club in Paris; all the crowned heads of Europe had come to see her dance. She was a fool to herself, more than anything else, trying, with the help of some dreadful peroxide, to make out to the world she was still a blonde. Paradoxically, she was quite a good mother, and I was always sent neat, washed and tidy to school (odd, isn't it, how we live in bits?) I got the hell out as soon as I could.

'It was only later, when I was living in New York and beginning to make a name for myself, that I realized history was repeating itself. Without looking up or thinking to take notice, I was following willy-nilly in mother's footsteps: men were also my merchandise, dispensable means to success, survival's goal. I saw with a shock that I had never really *had* one: they had all passed through me like trains in the night.

'And so I sit at the base of the candle, my heart's Rose open, incandescent, hurt. Simply to love is not enough; there has to be some healing, too. I was 'en route' for this with Emma, but - shit! - I couldn't hold on long enough. Won't somebody come to me through the night and take my secret sorrow away? No, of course they won't; how could they at all? I have to do it by myself.

'It's no use my dwelling on the past like this: I have to be up-and-doing, here-and-now. It's just that, when I step into the Open Space, there she is again, my familiar, my friend. Her lovely body curls around mine, and I bury myself in her breasts, her loins; then I, too, emerge victorious. She has given me the inward grace and strength, as I gave her the practised dancer's touch. We were such a body-as-one, we were! Still I can feel her, within me and around.

'I must have drifted off somehow. The candle is sputtering, guttering out: time to go to bed, to sleep. What did I do today? I danced. The curtain is rising on Africa, and I am wading into the waiting Sahara. Hot sand flushes over my feet; I could bury myself in it, up to the neck. They say the desert is dead, but it isn't: it's full of the freshest, greenest spring-life. I can show it to you, if you will only follow me . . .

At the Intersection stands the Man.

'We glide through the waters of the blue Aegean, stopping off occasionally at an intermediary island, where the sea grows turquoise by the rocky coast. Lesbos is one of the farthest-flung islands, almost a stop-off to the Turkish ports. It had assumed a different ambience now, brought down somehow to the modern pitch. Nonetheless, I'm told, resonances remain, echoes among the stridencies, of a time when Poetry was meat and drink, when the Moment was culled by bacchic Women in spontaneous diction to lute and lyre. Just such a pirouetting Poetess am I.

'I walk onto the island as I walk into my fate, that tapestry woven for me from all time. Although it's late afternoon, the sun is still hot; it scorches into the towering cliffs. They stand independently, almost, of the coast, as if they had been plonked there inadvertently - so much so that I look again, to convince myself I haven't dreamt them up. No, they are real, substantial, sheer.

'The taximan is the double of the one on Myconos: small, dark, stocky, with a lingering look. I let his look pass over me, knowing that with the slightest flicker of an eyelid I could ignite the flame of his simmering sensuality. But I haven't come here to repeat myself: I have, as it were, a fresh job to do.

'I'm dropped off at a small hotel, abutting the narrow, fertile coastal strip. Time is, Time was; this is it, as it was meant. I sit out on the veranda with my coffee and cigarette, looking at the rich, red soil, the olive-grove, while I wait for the woman to heat water for a bath. I could always bathe in the sea, meanwhile, but I'm happy for now just to watch it lap and seethe. It breaks evenly on the sand like a well-trimmed lace frill, which one would like to catch up and cast about one like a cloak. It would cover my failing, frail nudity.

'Waiting, that's what I'm doing: waiting. When you think about it, everybody's waiting - for a bus, to see the dentist, to find true love, for death. It's something like the stages or ages of Man: each one

169

evaporates, distils into the next. I, however, am waiting consciously; it's more than a gap, it's a deed in itself. Time is passing through me like a thread.

## 1

In one of those Acts of Synchronicity, the workings of which are normally hidden in the Weaving, Tristan, our Tristan, was pulling out of Patmos and also making his way across the sea to Lesbos. Shaken and perturbed by his cataclysmic visions, he was looking, as they say, for 'a breath of fresh air'. He fastened on Lesbos because it was near and because it had everything to do with women, the one strong topic he couldn't get his mind off. It was a whim, of course, a chance arm of Fate, but who, by taking thought, can come closer than he?

He felt the island drawing him in, as he entered the harbour waters and the boat docked. He had been vague, distraught, adrift on the voyage but, once landed, he was here-and-now. The taximan who had taken care of Evelyn was also the one who picked up Tristan and ferried him the few rough miles to a hotel - not the same as Evelyn's, to be sure, but a cheaper one, closer to the town. There he would have access to the local 'taverna', frequented exclusively by men and where he could eat and drink at local rates.

There was little tourism in those days and, what with war in the air, less than usual. Nevertheless, at a nominal charge, a rickety bus ran visitors round the island. Imagine, then, a bright morning in October, the sky still blue but a freshness in the air, and two people who, from this Mediterranean perspective, derived more or less from the same source, getting on at different points and meeting up with one another. Imagine, further, the conversation they had and the look of astonishment on both their faces, when they realized they had someone in common: Emma. It was about the time when she was back in England and the auction at Brewston was going through, and for some reason the urgency and finality of this operated on them like action-at-a-distance. Her presence, in fact, was everywhere about them, establishing itself as an objective referent, so that they tended to speak through her, although she wasn't there, like foreigners through an interpreter.

The bus rolled on along the coast road, and they sat immersed in their mutual disclosures. Someone was trying to act as guide, hopping from Greek to rudimentary English and making much, in a nudge-nudge vein, of the Lesbos-lesbian connection. At a certain point, just along from the port, they all got out: it was Sappho's Rock. From here, said the guide, the poet Sappho had thrown herself, because she couldn't live. She had composed, sung to music, made the sea and air sing. And even now, if one listened carefully to the soughing of the waves in the zawn below, wasn't it just like that final swansong - some such hyperbole - couldn't it be heard? But who, in the indifferent crowd that day, cared about Sappho? Who listened at all?

Evelyn and Tristan walked towards the edge, from which a view of the sea could be had. The sun shone into it, pealing its waters, throwing up shards of hard, bright light. 'It's bearing me down and away,' thought Evelyn, as she teetered, clutching at Tristan's arm. The sea became filmy, with javelins of light, and it seemed to her it was the last substratum, the Ground of Death, to which all must fall. 'Hold me,' she said, as she fainted sideways, a startled Tristan breaking her fall.

'To helio, to helio,' was passed around in whispers, and certainly the sun had grown hotter with the day. But it wasn't the sun - that much Tristan knew - or it wasn't the sun exclusively: the sun was just a reason-for-the-nonce, a net cast out to capture the event, as we all want to capture and encapsulate everything. No, there was something deeper-down, an urge and impulse fraught with destruction, in which sea, sun and verticality had combined to make that spot a bare-soul place, a tract of icarean fatality. Yes, she might fly - didn't she say she was a dancer? - but, for her flying, who paid the price? Who but the breaking artist herself, fined-out, tuned-up, too winged to endure?

- Full hund'ed metre, the guide said, down there.

Tristan peered at the rocks below, into and between which the sea flowed and frothed.

With a draught or two of some carbonated water Evelyn came back to herself again. Tristan was solicitous, holding back the crowd, shouting: 'Fresh air! Fresh air there! Aereas!' It did the trick: the crowd furled back, opening like a funnel, into which the breeze blew. This, together with the bubbling water, brought Evelyn to an upright sitting position; the blood, which had drained from her face, returned.

- I'm all-of-a-piece again now, I think, she said.

Tristan took the wise precaution of screening off Evelyn's view to seaward, as the two of them, she on his arm, made their way back to the waiting bus. The rest of the trip had a past-tense feel, as if the drama were already spent, and during the course of it Evelyn was bland, allowing her dark hair to fall across her face, burying herself in clouds of smoke. She simply had to shut off for a while.

It wasn't until the evening, in fact, among the ouzo, olives and calamares by the port, that she began to feel herself again - as if, until then, the blood in her veins hadn't quite reached the extremities. She sat back in her chair and laughed at Tristan struggling with a recalcitrant piece of squid. Whenever he tried to pierce it with his fork, it shot off to the opposite side of his plate, sending up a flurry of juice and oil.

- Use your fingers, she said eventually.

171

Which, blushingly, he did, trying to appear nonchalant.

'Wine and moonlight did the rest': thus Evelyn put it to herself.

After dinner they walked along the pier, listening to the warm waves beating up the wall, held by the moon as their point of poise. Evelyn's body had come alive now; it was urgent now, like a flexed bow, waiting. She was calling to Tristan from her deep body-nought, from the Raft of Agony on which she was adrift and on which, temporarily, she felt at ease. He, for his part, alerted and bovine, was stumbling and clumsy beside her, but strong.

They passed out of sight of the small, winking town to behind an unillumined stone beacon, which once must have served as a warning to sailing-craft. Tristan was pent-up, wired with desire, but mightily unused, suffocating almost, as he fussed and fumbled through the buttons of his mind. Seeing/feeling this, Evelyn leaned back against the beacon and drew him to her, breaking the awkwardness. His body unsheathed itself on the instant, as the outer skin of stiffness was shed and he leaned down to her - she was smaller than he thought - and kissed her lightly, softly on the mouth. Some skin of stiffness also burst in her: she rejoined the mortal currents of herself, from which, shard-like, she had been estranged; they welled up in her - in her eyes, in her belly. She wanted him strong and solid inside her, but was it the time and was this the place?

For Tristan already there was no other: the night, the world, the whole universe had come homing in on the arrow of desire. Only the waves rocked gently in his ears and the town, behind the protecting beacon, was faintly aglow with neutral light. Evelyn's lips were parting and drawing, and the weight of their tongues was like whales in the sea. Indeed, the sea in themselves was heaving, going over and under like whales a-play. For the bleakness of the morning was being redeemed, being culled back, warm, in the fluid, moonlit night. There was nothing for it but to yield to the moment, to open up a path through the parting Red Sea.

Evelyn's body was like a coiled spring, as she threw her arms around his neck, her legs about his slim, nude waist and felt him enter her, strong as steel, his day-time personhood cast aside. He was silent, solid, motionless, working her serpentine body round him, as she rose and flickered, her tongue flicking out, her arms under his arms, hands back across his shoulders. He made only the slightest of fine, controlled movements and each one - an incipience, really - sent a pointed explosion through her frame. She was going on him like nothing on earth, praying to him to hold the flame, to keep his ramrod strength inside her. She let out a soft moan every time he moved, as if that moving itself were enough - no pushing, no direction, no climax required.

- Don't come! she said, impaling herself further, wrapping herself round the hot seedhead. Fastidiously, he bent her back against the wall, feeling for the angle of maximum penetration, losing nothing meanwhile of his tensile strength. Tears were streaming down her face, and she cried to the night as much as to him:
- Love me! Don't leave me! Don't ever stop!
Hearing this, her cry on the night, and feeling, more, her abandonment, her utter, naked vulnerability, Tristan plumbed down and summoned up more; he pushed to a point of self-obliteration, where moon, stars, sea, the still-warm stone were caught up, consummate, in his drive. He did not slacken but, shiva-silent, sent shocks and tremors from his body to hers, each of which was a star-detonation and brought down a libation, wave upon wave. She was crying to the night, to its drinking distant dome, from this Circle of Perfection to which she had been brought. Then from her heart a great sob burst, as if all the horde of her sorrow had been there, waiting for this moment to hear its own sound. 'Yes,' she was saying, 'Yes, O, yes,' as he worked himself up through the ceiling of the sky. He was in touch with every atom of her, from her lissom limbs to her soul's void's depth: there was nothing of her which was not here-now.

Thus she had always wanted it to be, through all those brutal, sterile encounters, the lost, blighted acres of the former time. She had wanted always to be out of herself, to be free of her self - if only for a moment. And her yes was the yes of forgotten time, a grab at the moment, the fleeting, the real. For the Ocean was giving way in her; it was drawing back, furled, through acres and aeons. Warm waters were washing, rushing to a seethe; they were breaking down every blunt parcel of land. That land was herself, was what she had known, the blank, infertile terrain of her days. It was her secret life which had to come alive, the quivering, silent, ungrown seed. It was desperate to grow; it *had* to grow. She felt herself coming mightily, from depths she had never suspected she had. It wasn't some quick, excitatory spasm, but it *was* the night and the sea-in-the-night; it was the stars in heaven, threaded through her womb. They were all crying; they were singing there, singing as Sappho sang while she leapt. Her face, upturned, smooth, radiant, ecstatic, was calling the stars down into her. And the sea was lapping, frothing, coming; it was beating like music into the wall. Then his strong body shuddered, his seedhead burst, and she folded into him: she was a woman with a man.

Later, in bed, she felt the years roll off her, like so many layers of dirty clothes. How strange and welcome-new it was, to lie thus naked, washed and cleansed. For some reason she thought of the black canal in Leicester, walking with her mother on cold Sunday afternoons. The

173

whole mind-picture of it was so vivid - the towpath, the moist chill air, the bowed people - that she shivered in her bed in spite of its warmth. How much in a life stayed indelible! How much, all the same, one needed to clean out!

2

After the double-drama of the day before Evelyn had thought to spend this one alone, and she was taking breakfast on the veranda of her hotel when up stumped Tristan, all windmill-waves and greetings. She realized with a shock that she didn't want to see him, and then his presence came to her - his strong blue eyes, his loose brown hair, his boyish mien and gangling gait - and she felt him inside her again, like a root.

- Why don't we go for a walk? he said.

She wanted him there and then, in her arms, but she heard herself saying:

- Later on. This afternoon.

And they did ramble later along the shoreline, to where the rich, fertile coastal strip runs out. Here there were rocks and little inlet beaches, the sea running into them, smoothing their sand. Evelyn, in one of those drops of time - like the lift going down to a lower floor - found herself back on the temple plinth, looking out to the Straits in a wash of sunlight. In fact, the sun was beginning to go down, oozing its colours into shoreline and sea. And they sat on the rocks, he just back from the sea, with the saltwater pearling and running off him.

Downwards they went in a tumbling embrace, over and under and over again. Evelyn felt his body, fresh and cool, as a thing pure and separate from herself. She didn't want his deep incursion, the formal, upright marriage-bed; she craved only, for the moment, his tree-separateness; it was like a deity to her. First she unknotted the towel round his waist, which fell back onto the sand beneath him; then she took him delicately between her lips. Utter, pure sensation gripped him, as the tips of her fingers caressed his thighs and her mouth held him upright, her tongue tucking round, and she drank the saltwater, every last drop, till he was hot and dry and bulbous and taut. She teased him now, drawing back, holding off, till, taking her face between his hands, he penetrated her to the very gills, the sea-suction in them doing the rest. She felt the insistent urge of his flesh, like a piston of power inside her mouth, and that very urgency became her own; she was pared down also to naked rock, stripped of personhood, everything, in this working and drawing of the surge of sap, its rising, issuing, blond sunburst.

She wasn't given to virginal qualms, to anything less than total sexuality. She wanted all of him, every last drop; she imbibed him

174

whole, strong, pushing, extreme. She wanted to land on a different Ground. It, nevertheless, was an art for her: how she pushed against his thighs with her hands, drawing him longer, stronger into her - she didn't want him willing away; she wanted the furnace hot all the time -, how she fell somehow upon a rhythm of his, which was like the call of his blood in her, and she worked him from the root to the speared purple tip. It was a rhythm like that of feet against the earth, the taut-skin drum the pulse in them, ancient, ritualistic, going through and going down, her eyes on the upstroke meeting his. His head fell back - he was starting to come: his thighs were ceding, the blood was racing there - and, in a long column, slowly at first, his come passed, gathered, rushed and then burst in a spray like salt seawater down her throat.

It was the end of all desire for her but, for Tristan, it set him on sensory alert. He was after her now in agitated earnest and, though they spent their nights apart, he was visited constantly by wafts of her - her swath of dark hair, his own trailing sensations - and scarcely got a wink of sleep. She, by contrast, was quite detached, when the things was over quite out of it: she remained an artist, even in love. It was a gall and torment to him, her detachment, especially when she told him - and was it true? - that she would not be 'available' for the next few days. He fretted and steamed inside his House.

3

Fate was moving them forward, anyway, weaving its Tissue of unseen Threads. They thought they would leave this sudden place and go to the ancient island of Crete. Tristan was aroused, hard, fiery, unsettled; he said they should go somewhere and 'get to know each other'. Evelyn was for it, in spite of the fact that they had only just met here; they were still only new. She wished, in her heart, she could have had an objection, something to staunch the shifting blood, which forever, so it seemed, went running from her. She wished she could have sat still for once.

Nevertheless, they went to Crete, passing, as one always must, by Piraeus. The twelve-hour voyage brought them in at dawn, with black-clad Cretans dancing in the hold, a handkerchief suspended between their hands. They docked at Iraklion and, after disembarking, took the bus along the coast to Mallia. Once in the town, they looked for a hotel and were directed to a place, not unlike Evelyn's on Lesbos, which stood out white against the red soil and had a right-angled balcony on one side. From there - their room opened onto it - the eye travelled out to the soft-furling sea above a grove of silver-green, gnarled olive-trees. They passed themselves off as a married couple and signed in.

175

And again they walked in the passional red evening to a dark consummation beneath the trees. Tristan was determined to hold sway over Evelyn, not to allow her sexual strength to squander him, because of his sensual passivity. There was still within him, in spite of his years, an unspent vein of narcissism, some wish to lapse back into himself, to be subject and object of his own desire. This, he realized, must die in him - or it must become his second Edge. Consequently, he made love to her in a careful, almost studied way, melting her out - she was eager, she was quick - into a strong derivative of himself. And curiously, perhaps, she took his shape, as a sexually flexible woman will, becoming in her coming fiery, firm, fast, as a bronze is cast by the hands of a master. Suddenly she was his adjunct, his wife, his horizon, his depth, his virtual subordinate.

But this was only for the nonce: again there burned in her, fierce and bright, the inalienable claim of total freedom. There were no lengths, really, to which she wouldn't go. They took each other at every turn, by every quickening impulse of the way. She became, her face also looked like, him; his mark and signature were on her brow. She wanted to mould herself entirely to him, to become his deep-familiar, his charge; she wanted him to enjoy her all the time. This very self-abasement was an agony of pleasure, an inner role-reversal which astonished even her: there was nothing, simply *nothing* she wouldn't do for him. And yet that part of her, which is aloof in everyone, looked on disconcerted and felt the jar.

They wandered round the ruined site of Mallia, one of the three great palaces of ancient Crete. There were hip-high walls and a groundplan of a sort but, beyond this structure and some suggestion of content - patched-up amphorae in a pit marked 'storehouse' -, there was little to evoke the grandeur of the past. Phaestos, however, was altogether different. They came to it by bus across the island's backbone, a spine of mountains running east-west. Set at a comfortable height in its landscape and held to the west by a conical hill, on the far side of which lies Agia Triada, the site lies open at three descending levels and once commanded access to the sea. Now it looks deserted like a rubbly plateau, holding its flat face up to the sky; it seems to be sleeping, suspended, undeciphered, like the incised Disk which was dug up here. It seems to be dreaming between heaven and earth.

Evelyn and Tristan found the connection: they were united, hand in hand, through time-past, in time-present. They were melted back and down through the priest-recesses, the secret places, the corners, the holes, from which the snake-goddess emerged belly-warm and transmitted the dark, living wisdom of the earth. It was lovely then, it was practical and perfect - no wars to speak of for 1500 years - and

176

daily life was its own celebration. They gathered it into their body and blood, for it was at that moment their own proper station, their lyric attunement and place of poise; it sang in them of the living past, its fragrance and lightness hovering there.

They moved on later to Agia Triada and the tomb with its open, eternal Eye. The soul of the dead king was being offered for weighing and, according to its heaviness - feather-light or not -, it would be released like a bird or bound back to earth. This weighing of the soul was a clean, prompt act, totally devoid of semitic torment, and the judgement, when it came, would be natural, scientific, following the curve of the Laws of Being.

- It's like something I've seen before, said Tristan.

But his remark went limp against the air.

Evelyn was not in his psychic space: she found it all too rarefied, remote. She wanted to press him close to her, to feel again the resistance of his body. In the taxi back to the island's north coast she looked at the scenery as if in a daze. It was all unreal, this outer world; it was all some natural or human concoction: what *was* real was the inner impulse, the drive to be united, the end of separateness. And how could mortal woman attain to this, except by and through the man she loved?

It was one of those taxis, common round the Med., which pick up passengers along the way and provide an 'ad hoc', point-to-point service. A Cretan got in and took the front seat, looking back and across at Evelyn and Tristan. He said something to the driver, who smiled complicitly. Indeed, an invisible curtain had fallen between the front seat and the back. There was an auric haze round Evelyn's body, as if unseen hands were smoothing it out, and her face had a radiance, streaming from within, which derived from nothing but that one single source. Her pleated skirt - an encumbrance, really - folded down between her thighs, while her breasts urged forward inside her blouse, saying to Tristan: 'Touch me, please.' Her whole body glowed with the lambent flame of a woman who feels herself loved all over, loved as if for the first time to the core. For a woman carries her love everywhere; at no point can she set it down. It will flame up at a touch or a glance, but permanently, in the limbs and loins, it builds itself into the tissue of her life. A man can put his love on the shelf, and that is one reason why heartache occurs.

Evelyn mused, as the taxi drove, on. She was in a settled stillness now, waiting for Tristan to come to her. Crossing the mountains, they descended to Hania, from where they caught a bus back to Mallia. It was early evening, that wine in the air, the land sun-warmed, eased-out from the day. They took a path back, along by the sea. For Evelyn, again, it was the Straits and the Edge, but this time she was contained this side: no more sites to visit, no falling; she felt safe. History she had emptied

177

out of herself, while Dance seemed more remote than the stars. She was locked into Tristan - her existence was his - and she swayed and was blithe, thinking this to herself. She swung round and kissed his open throat; she felt him coming alive to her. She was sure of herself: she would come and be clean, and he would come and be clean with her. The years and folds of pained, thwarted life would roll away for him, as they were beginning to for her. Yes, they would find - she would find through him - the Tree that stood in the midst of the Garden, the solid-knowledge Tree, not the fraught, forked, the baleful.

Thus, she built up the Dream-circle in herself, to which he would be the Avenue. He would go with her - surely, he must - for the dream was too beautiful, too all-embracing for him to stop here, just at the Gate. No, he would enter, as he was entering her now, reducing her to sacrificial ashes, from which the phoenix of new life would rise. It was a shedding of ruins and hurts transcendent, a sexual healing magnificent and dense. It was going down into and through the Zero, the final nought where the flower lies, and up she would come, rose-red and cured, bearing herself like a truth in the world. There was no end to it - it was like coming, only more so - it was total unfoldment and ecstasy. She heard herself cry out on the night, like a flutter of bats' wings strafing the darkness, and she felt Tristan everywhere going out, as if the matrix of her new being, her 'I', were releasing itself, breaking waters, giving birth. It *was* him still, strong, pulsing inside her, but at the same time it was the underarch of trees, the flying night-sky, the strong, fertile earth. It was a consummation between heaven and earth, as real as that place they had visited, Phaestos, as real as the junction of the neverending Now. It was there in their breath, in the scent of the olives, in the push of the gnarled tree up to the sky. And it was there, dipping down, going in and through them, as the node, the presence of the Eternal Now. There was no separation to anything, but everything was woven in with the rest: indeed, it *was* the rest, without distinction. They were coming; they were coming into their own.


- I think it must have been the olive-tree in Eden, said Evelyn, lying on her back. Her limbs stretched out like the limbs of the tree; they branched out, tactile, contiguous with the stars. The tree above her was more than itself, more than a mute, fixed, gnarled old *thing;* it was a Power, suddenly, festooned and born, climbing from earth to the sky's dark vault. Each branch ran out from the steady stock, curved its own way, ran out and ran back, inhering always, movement and fire; it doubled, fingered out, became fleshy and fine, erupting here and there in small spears of silver leaves. She, Evelyn, was united with this same earth; she was part of its rude, tough, bonded breed. She reached out a hand and touched the olive's bark.

Then he was finding her again; she was finding him in the substance of the Dream. It was as if they had sloughed off initial skin and were now ready, eased against the earth, to put on and perform the Mystery of Phaestos, the daily, unbroken Play of oneself. He seemed to her then a god new-born, as he hovered, bright and unsheathed, above her. The secret, thrilling Wisdom of the Earth was theirs for the taking; it was waiting like a Chalice: they had only to drink it into themselves. It was the potent Snake-cup, the bonding of the natures: the masculine, the feminine, heaven and earth.

She was there, quite certainly, that ancient goddess, lithe and nubile, seeded in the earth; she was coiling and rippling through Evelyn's body, pushing through the texture of her lambent skin. Her body exalted itself in its mounting, its tumultuous possession of itself, so that it was no longer strictly human, this motion, but an energy raised to the power two, a potency squared, a line, a force, something indwelling at the base of the spine, in the small of her back, where his fingers pressed. There was not the slightest trace of frenzy about them: they were as old and as ripe as the Mystery itself, into which they had stumbled and been initiated and for which there existed now no name.

Then, like a celebrant, he wanted to shout out, but she held her hand across his mouth. She wanted the mutest and quietest of comings, as befitted the solemnity of the Place they were in. She could feel herself lapping on and back, like a sea unfurling from its coastal fastness; she was slowly, ever-so-slowly coming, as if all the stars in heaven had conjoined and were filing down a funnel, while the dark sky heaved. There was no longer any personal emotion - that's why she had wanted to stop his shouts -, just the velvety subsidence of heaven into earth, the star-milk down the funnel, the sea unfurled. All her barriers were breaking down, all the stupid cardboard walls, and she was seeing with her soul the shapes of the Unbounded, just as a person, blinkers removed, sees for the first time the view all around. It was like walking, silver, silken and alone, along a pearled and streaming shore, where foot had never trod. The sea beat up to her, softly, incessantly, its foam seething into her every living pore. She was no longer upright Evelyn, incarnate, encased, sealed up, imprisoned here; she had left all that behind like shed snake-skin and was walking, primordial, on the naked, glowing earth. Heaven was wheeling and stars were coming down, touching and firing the sea in her. The sea rose and swelled through the acres of her belly, as the fire-night dipped and touched the tongue of the earth. The waters washed round the little, tipped tongue, and it was if her eyes were the eyes of the moon, pitted, and lidless like the eyes of the snake. She *became* at that moment the primordial Serpent, lapping its coils around the whole world. She *was* the guardian spirit of the world, thrust out of the Garden by the cupidity of Man. Far from being

179

the temptress, a low Slut, she was body and power of the Universal Mother, our earth-connectedness, our back-link. By cutting off her head and satanizing her, we had put ourselves into a conflictual brain-stew, from within which, inexorably, there was no release. Now we were waiting, all of us - and our life, perhaps, depended on it - for the massive rebirth of the ancient serpent-power, the belly-born spirit of semence and strength.

Evelyn felt this power in herself, this vast energy-potential of awakening to Life. What a misery and drudgery we had made of it, what a furtive sneaking-off into holy, dirty corners! How miraculous and new this pristine world was, the world that *is* when the skin has been shed. She felt it, lying there beneath the trees, on the clean, red earth, in the olives' breath; it was urgent in her like a growing child. She wanted only to give birth to it: to bring it, fine, naked and strong into the world.

Then she noticed Tristan asleep beside her, his head rocked back, mouth slightly ajar, and she became aware of herself on the instant as a single, separate entity, a person. She lit a cigarette and watched the blue smoke curl in lazy circles round his head. It was somehow rich like the perfumed night, and it kept the gnats and mosquitoes away. She felt herself buried deep within the night, as if night's body had closed round her and made its living body of herself. She *was* the eternally deep, dark one, the goddess of true-earth, the stratum black beneath; she was right at the pivot, the fold-point of the earth.

Tristan awoke also to the original Place, blinked, rubbed his eyes, asked Evelyn who she was, then laughed at himself for being such a fool. And yet it was not entirely folly: there *was* a kind of change in her, a move to a mode behind the appearances. And he, too, in the fluid lambency of night stretched out and beyond the mental scope, like the sky itself travelling, suddenly unconfined. They had gone back, both of them, to some lost Point before the Egg split and the yolk and white ran out; they had crossed the sad acres of trodden Time. They were hovering still in the Middle Ground, on the braided arena between two worlds, before the Exile was completely confirmed; they were still tangential to the Circle of Life. The Gate - they were at it - was strait and smooth, and yonside of it was the Place-which-never-tired, that locus and focus of energy, surpassing but containing gravity and matter, where once we might have dwelt, had we understood the Laws.

Their sojourn, however, was minimal: it was abruptly interrupted by a glaring bus, which rattled past them, all eyes and lights. They felt for their clothes, got dressed, moved about. And it was all to the good, because at that moment a local went by - boots, briskness and a fishing-rod - making his way to the waiting sea. Tristan and Evelyn, clothed beneath the trees, watched him approach the scarcely curving bay, drag a flat fishing-smack across the quiet sand and push it, clambering in, onto the water. They embraced one another and went back to their hotel. It was, however, a confinement to them: they felt shut in from the spreading sky. All strictures and derivatives are the product of Man's thought, and without our indoor foibles they are null and void. They felt it like a shock, a fall.

Some men were playing dominoes downstairs, among the clink of retsina glasses and that peculiar swirl of acrid smoke, which seems to inhabit and absorb the air. They glanced up briefly from grey, stubbly faces, with the measured look of people who see, but who do not disclose what it is they have seen. 'Those two' (so they had come to be known) were like creatures from another world, suddenly dropped or piloted into this one down a secret Vortex, a time-warp's Whorl. They stood there, Tristan grinning faintly, as if he were half-tempted to join in and have a game, Evelyn aloof, no overspill at all, her mind cut clean to the edges of her form. When they were back in their room she said:
- What made you stand there, grinning, down there?
- O, I don't know . . . just the game, I suppose.
- What makes you want things apart from me?
- Do you want things apart from me?
- You know I don't; that's why I ask.
Tristan fell into a troubled silence, as if she had struck across his sight. Everything had been flowing, continuous and smooth, without the least hint of a block or hiatus. And now, downcasting, gravity had struck - with that one whiplash stroke every woman keeps in store.

He was helpless like a boy again, feeling he had done wrong, but God knows how. He had no edge with which to meet her, nor did he seek to defend himself. He just sat there, still half hung about with the halcyon world from which they had returned: in his slow, contained way he could not understand how the switch had been so brutal and so swift. And that made their room even more of a contortion; it bore in on them like a Hall of Mirrors, throwing back versions of the fractured twain, their bodies no longer naked and mellifluous, but upright, conscious, covered 'you' and 'I'. They had the knowledge now, all right: it was there in the artificial light-bulb, humming, as much as in their own domed skulls. They knew themselves and each other as separate: the dread Rift-knowledge had come to them.

Evelyn picked up a magazine, then flung it down and walked out into the night. The stars were pelting their real light down and the moon was higher still above the sea. She stopped at the fringe of the slightly curving bay, feeling the breeze waft through her hair and wishing she had not, in her fury to get out, forgotten her shawl in the fraught bedroom. With difficulty she lit a cigarette, and she felt a rasp, a catch in her throat, as she inhaled the smoke in the dry salt breeze. It was, at once, an irritation and a solace to her, as she stood there vaguely, looking out to sea. She was finely wrought - that much was certain - but where moved the naked 'daimon' in her? It was an unquantifiable, frisky young thing; all she wanted was to let it run free. No-one should tame it or chain it down. No-one.

She was startled by the boatman, back from the sea, by his clear, firm 'Kali spera' to her, as she walked above him along the margin of the bay. She still felt stung by what she had perceived as Tristan's bar-room indifference to her. What was it about him that had hung about there, when all she wanted was to be alone with him? Or was it that, demanding total freedom for herself, she was less than obliging when it came to others? She had that in her, that much she knew. Still, there was more to it, wasn't there? Hadn't he been ready - they were all the same, men - to step down the level of his love for her to something mediocre, half-hearted, part-time? It was there in the germ, this indifference. And she, who was giving everything she had, hadn't she the right to *all* of him? It stuck in her throat, his turning away, and this feeling, this sharp urge grew in her till it took on the form of a pleasurable vengeance.

What she didn't realize was that Tristan had followed her, within a few minutes of her leaving the hotel. He was standing now at some distance behind her, waiting in the olive-grove for some movement of hers, which would make it clear where she had gone. Then he saw her drop down from the margin of the bay and walk swiftly towards the open fishing-smack. He seemed, in an instant, to be there, where she had been, but it was already too late: the boat was pushing out. She must be lying, supine, in the bottom; the boatman was gently plying the oars.

Tristan stood stock still, an observer fixed, as he had, now many years ago, when he had watched from the bank above Elmsworth Church, as Jessie's body was carried to its grave. It was a flashback all too searing and potent, a desperate downdrop through the closed ground of time. He wanted to cry out but his mouth was sealed, as if the torment were too hot and arid for words. Yes, it was she and they were going out; they were gently adrift in the dreadful moonlight. It would have been better, surely, to walk away, but he stood there looking, bonded to the scene. He watched the boatman lay the oars aside, then pull them into the slightly bobbing boat. He blazed with fury and impotence, while the boat rocked on, bobbing and oblivious, and the waves eternal came running to the shore. He wanted to stride out and get her there and then, but somehow he turned his mind aside; he went, instead, to walk in the grove.

The sky had bleared out - were there more lights on? - to an ubiquitous glare: there was no Inherence. All was barrenness, as it had been in the bedroom, the soft folds of night, like curtains of consciousness, having been torn aside, cut along the cleft, to expose the bare stage agony. And here it was - worse than sorrow, worse than death - this frightful Field of undying Pain, this floodlit arena with no place to hide. Tristan beat his head against a tree, till he felt the blood like sweat along his forehead; then he snatched off a branch and broke it in two. His body was a jangle of hot, naked wires, and he waited only for that boat to come in.

He caught sight of Evelyn coming from the shore, her dark head nodding against the background of the sea, and automatically his feet followed her. Then all his hurt and rage welled up, and he started to run to catch up with her. As if she knew it - she never looked back - Evelyn, too, began to run. They were still at some distance from the hotel and would have to pass through the olive-grove. Tristan knew this and cut a corner off, catching her and pinning her against a tree.

- Let go of me! she screamed. Have you gone mad?
- Where have you been?
- For a walk by the sea.
- Liar! You liar! You know where you've been.
- Why do you ask, then, if you already know?
- I'd like to hear it from your own lips.
- All right: I've been for a ride in a boat.

She said it with such a natural air that poor, hurt Tristan, so gullible was he, so ready to countenance what gave him slightest ease, almost believed she was innocent. And, indeed, it was apparent, utterly transparent that the whole episode was finished-with for her; she had rid herself of her snarling dark pain. Now there was nothing; he was pummelling the Void. Nonetheless, the thorn turned in him, burning and burying itself in his flesh. He was clearly in Doubleland, the sphere of ambiguity, seeing her so, unaffected, assumed, yet sensing simultaneously in his own trace-field the presence of an element intrusive and sharp. The arm went limp, which was mean to strike her down.

Something in her hated this, the arm gone limp, his failure at the Brink: he would never go to the ultimate pitch.

- Hit me if you want to, she said, looking down.

And, thus emboldened, he struck her twice. How much more, she thought, she would have loved and worshipped him, if he had hit her sooner-harder, without being told! But such things are hidden from moral men.

She took his blows without demur, batting her eyelids, abstracted, intact. He was longing to get at her lush, dark eyes, but she kept them averted, like a servant's. He wanted to get at what was *real* in her, but she had come back enfolded, complete-within-herself; there seemed to be no gap of need in her. Consequently, he bobbed and weaved around her, unsure of how to act, such a puppy-dog still!

183

She sensed this lack of sap in him and, moving forward, she caressed him boldly. His hands were firm about her waist; gradually, he was coming into his own. From now on there would be no retraction for him, no false starts, no mild undoings. Somehow, somewhere, at levels unspoken, she had given him 'carte blanche' to do as he pleased. And that, in the ensuing days and nights, was precisely what he did, in a frenzy of release. It was all too much, when he thought about it later, this outrageous self-outgoing, this unguided missile spent. The moralist in him was blenching all the time, afraid to let go of the timid fetters, the strings of control which kept him tied. Yet that was exactly what she was pushing him to. Was he bold, strong, man enough to pay the price?

She believed in him, deep down, that he was: he could, through the frank insurgence of his blood, break every cord that bound them to the world; he could set them down otherwhere, that he could! It was this she wanted on the curving earth: his bold, strong, firm, destructive stroke. It fainted in her for bliss of him, that he was thus masterful, impeccable, erect. She wanted to go out and down on him, lose herself utterly in and to him. Everything that flickered through his mind as desire she knew on the instant by a swift intuition; she anticipated every last foible of his, preparing herself as a priestess for her god. Her own body-being had no other purpose than as a vessel for his body's entry's work.

So they abided, lingam and lip, in a closed, dark sanctum, whose only name was theirs. He was freeing himself from the bald, bare Rock, the hideous day-nightmare to which he had been chained. He plundered her nightly, day and night; he drove into her all his hidden torment, the guileless guilt he had sucked up from the first. He held her poised, his martyr, his lover, pushed, teased and driven out of his mind. He fed her all the poison he had, the dreadful disease of his chained, exposed life, and she took it into herself in his semen, drawing him out from Original Pain. She was nothing but a channel for him - giving and taking, drinking his sweat - while he stormed and thrashed in his body and blood and was finally cast forth, melting, from the Rock.

She was like a mother for him, inwardly: on their light, white bed on that sun-streamed island she gave him the initiation of new birth. He saw himself tumbling through the stars, born here-and-now anew, freed of fraught history. He came down alive on a beautiful new earth, like the earth after rain or like a white sand beach, when the sea has receded and left it clean. She was, for him, the potent matrix, the womb within which he could grow again, pumping from her heart-source new blood into his. And she never noticed, because she didn't count the cost, that in all the burgeoning of the constant Garden she had given what the bee gives and cannot retract: among the sipping of nectar, the fall of pollen dust, the irretrievable sting of herself.

184

They hired bicycles and rode to the island's edge, to a place where cliffs fall steeply to the sea. Here, in a sea-seethe of caves and rocks, they found another kind of ecstasy: pristine, mineral, uncompromising, nude. Only the fierce, clear elements raged; the human dimension had been whittled down by centuries of sun, wind, relentless sea. No people lived here - it would have been impossible - and yet it was the perfect place for them. They took the rock up into their bodies, bore its imprint, drank the sun; they dived from a rock-ledge into the sea. The water at depth was smoky and cool, with tongue-tip coral in a bar beneath the ledge, and they made love in the water, scarcely moving in the swell. Evelyn, again, let everything go.

Her life fell into a focus of a sort. For hadn't she been seeking this, just this, in the Open Space with Emma and through all the time before? Hadn't she been after this nude Crosspoint? It had been waiting for her, surely , and this was it: this was the loss-and-gain she had craved, something, after all these years, like Mediterranean tidelessness. It gathered in her belly, where the light hardly reached; it moved up and through her incessantly. It *was* the plumb-line she had thrown to herself, among the dark waters the steady, straight, true. It was this she had been working for and wanted all the time.

Isn't being in love its own subject-object? We seldom consider, when we are in love, what residual, unresolved morsels of impulse are dragging, fermenting, through the other's psychic Web. We are, to ourselves, so completely satisfied that we even consider it an outrage against Love that the other might have promptings which are not within our Field. Eros, indeed, is a tetchy brat, vulnerable, highly strung, arrow to the fore. He wants and keeps us on edge all the time.

- You haven't kissed me all morning, said Evelyn, as the clock stood suddenly vertical at noon.

Tristan looked helpless and sheepish again.

- You don't know how deep a woman's love is; you don't know how much she gives of herself.

- I give myself, too, he said, tit-for-tat. But his words fell back: they had not the force of hers.

She had entered a Zone where she didn't want to be, one to which susceptible Eros gives access. Did Tristan love her as much as she loved him? That was the question, the unthinkable. Or was there something in him holding back, some vronskyesque sense of having somewhere else to be? Evelyn began to feel there was and hence, of course, to find evidence for it. While she lived only for and through him, he had a corner which was still his own, and though, in principle, she accepted this - wasn't total freedom everyone's right? - in practice she resented and fought against it. She got anxious if he was just two minutes late, imagining him already off and away. And didn't she detect, in that sheepish, sidelong look a falling-off of his direct desire? Was he beginning to develop another track? She must get him back on hers, at all costs.


After Phaestos, Knossos was a disappointment, in spite of Sir Arthur Evan's reconstruction: there were too many people, it was too near the town. The museum, with its treasure, was scant consolation - detached, encased pieces, the living spirit fled. They were looking at 'objets d'art', nothing more. The ancient, contextual richness was gone: all that remained was flat, reduced, reified. It wasn't going to be easy any more.

Taking advantage, perhaps, of the fact they were not alone, Tristan said, as they were on the bus to Mallia:

- I must go back to Patmos for a while.

Evelyn both heard him and didn't hear. She sat looking out of the window, aloof.

- Why do you want to go to Patmos? she said, when they were back in their hotel room.

- I've got one or two things to see to there - and one or two people I need to see.

- More than you need to see me, obviously.

- Different kind of need, he said, with uncharacteristic self-confidence. She smiled as he smiled and felt curiously reassured. Perhaps, after all, it was not so bad: if he went back to Patmos, she would go to Lesbos. They could meet up again later; it was all in the clear.

What decides it, in the end? It isn't the pitch of the stone down the well but the ultimate bottom, the deep-drop, the splash. The moments in-between are moments of waiting, the motion of gravity down the shaft. Feeling this, Evelyn sombred inside, the brightness of her mind become shard-like, sharp: her premonition was of a fall.

She took herself to task for her lack of independence, made out it was all all right, what was the bother? She played on Tristan's meek immaturity, his lack of real substance, his want of experience. She gave him, in consequence, so much terrain, so many sunlit angles and dark corners of herself, that he was, willed up from her secret source, with nothing left begging, surely all hers. She went to the last drop down that dark well, and they rose, aureoled, in the midnight sun.

So when they went off later to their separate islands, she in that pale green skirt of hers, which contoured her body better than it clothed it, bare arms bronzed now by the sun, it was almost like a well-timed, natural parting, with a minimal sense of 'mourir un peu'. She never watched departures, anyhow, she said; what was the point of such lingering? Nevertheless, she didn't turn away and take refuge in the warren of streets behind the harbour, but ordered a coffee in a waterfront café, from where she could see, from a slightly raised terrace, the steel ship cutting its way across the sea. She smoked a cigarette, reflective, firm; she would send him a card from the immediate bay.

Tristan, meanwhile, was out on deck, a passenger again on a voyage not-back-home. His mind went back to that day in Calais and the greyness, darkness falling, the first phase of his life. What had changed for him through this turn of the prism? What was he now, which he hadn't been then? He was a different man, it was tangible. Evelyn's touch was on him still; it nestled in his loins and made them stir, warm. Her passion had been a crusade for him. There was no denying where they had been, how magnificent, rich, strong, vital she had been! She had forced him onto the ground of himself. Now he held there, motionless, secure. There was something in him which sang for joy, like the deep blue, tideless Mediterranean. There was also something like a question-mark, the presage of a power yet to come.

187

Evelyn hung about the town, repelling all offers to have dinner and the rest; she hung in a state of fated suspense. She felt rich deep down, assumed and complete, and her darkness was like an aura about her. She looked around shops selling goat-skin rugs and vases; she bought a necklace in one of them, and a pair of matching earrings. They were turquoise and pendant, touching her neck, and her neck was smooth like a find-sand beach. The sun had grown into it, as it does into a tree, and it held there, beautiful, poised, olive, dark. She seemed, for the time being, to be perfectly intact.

It wasn't for some days, actually, that she began to emerge from the aura of 'that time'. The bedroom in Mallia was still replete, rosy and warm, as if it had drunk soft sunlight; there still was a presence, a nuance of him there. Then there came a moment when that presence waned, when she felt herself vulnerable again, cut down to size. In a way, it just happened overnight: the furniture was edged, the street wore a threat; the sun had become a glaring, hot eruption. She was solo again; she was separate.

- Don't become strident, she said to herself, conscious of her tendency to use up her stock.

- Don't let it all puther off down the drain.

And she cast about for things to do. She would, she thought, go back to Myconos, where she could dance in the Open Space; then she would carry on to Lesbos and there meet up with Tristan. That felt right.

Again she was on the night-boat to Piraeus. At first she thought of sleeping below, but the designated area was lit-up and nauseous. She went out on deck with her hired blanket and gazed at the quivering starlit night. There were, she reflected, several sheaths to it, several bodies and densities. In winter it seemed hard and sharp, pushing to a point like a Gothic cathedral; here, on the other hand, it was round, soft and swelling, and the stars shone through it as through rents in spread cloth. Nothing, not even the sun by day, spoke so eloquently to her of the difference between the Mediterranen landscape, its scant-treed horizons, the ever-outgoing play of the senses, and the huddled forests of the North, the bleak, sere grass, the Walls of Enclosure. Why, she wondered, had she been born in the North, when she was such a creature of the South? She looked around for a convenient spot - there was a foreign couple not far away - and stretched out on a bench to sleep. A voice was coming to her from the night, whipped up off the sea since before her birth: it was ancient, drumming, since before That Time, the time when she had been olive in the olive-grove; it was taking her back to where she had been . . .

She couldn't have said how long she had slept, but she was awake now all right: she had to be.

-- One peep, babe, and your dead - O.K.?

She felt the knife-blade against her throat and the weight of his body under the blanket. The foreign couple had disappeared, and apparently the generator had failed, for there was not a glimmer of light anywhere. Only the stars, ever-present, ever-distant, wheeled and stared from the indifferent sky. A cry for help gurgled dead in her throat, stifled by the dryness and contraction of fear. Her whole body stiffened: the knife was right there; she felt the warm ooze of blood on her neck.

-- See what I mean?, the voice said hoarsely.

He was tearing and forcing her, ripping her clothes, and she lay there blankly, paralyzed with fear. She staved off the hand which held the knife, but this only served to stimulate his drive, making it quicker, more intent. He was sweating, malodorous and clean-shaven, and she thought, in a flash, he might kill her as well. She couldn't even see his eyes. Then her body underwent a terrible spasm, as he forced his way through and into her. It was a swift, sharp agony of shards inside, the light-splints shooting up and into her, her womb made garish, bleared, barbed, flayed. She suffered and endured it, fearing the worst (would he also stick the knife in her?). It was even, momentarily, a relief when, instead, he writhed off her and as quickly disappeared. She lay, blank and broken, looking at the night.

She immediately thought of flying to Tristan and, just as immediately, dismissed the thought. Some fine-tuning in her wouldn't allow it, the dread down-grading, the killing of the Dream. Mustn't she, nonetheless, tell someone? The very prospect coiled in her; it gathered and raged like mutilation.

The light was coming, grey, on the horizon, ushering in the next bleary dawn. It was the moment of the junk-sick, the outcasts, the homeless, the lonely newly-pregnant throwing up in the sink. She would go and find the captain before they got to port. She rehearsed a few bald sentences, feeling only, in her uncertainty and grief, how small and ridiculous she was making herself. She steeled herself, all the same, to speak. Then she saw the captain coming down from the bridge, and all her antennae came alive. Such a face as his she had seen many times - round the corners of curtains, up back-stairs, in bars. 'Greasy, oily, smarmy bastard,' she said to herself as she passed him by. She couldn't have told him a single thing.

She felt his glaring, lecherous gaze bounce off her buttocks as she walked out of range. And, finding no place to sit anywhere, still too traumatized and frightened to stay alone, she clung to a four-square, protruding bar - one of a set on the wide funnel's side - and sank into the final refuge of tears. They poured down her face from her reddening eyes, and gulps of throat-rattles contorted her face. The irremediable agony was back, the selfsame, perhaps, as had assailed van Gogh when

189

he put the pistol to his heart: 'Misery will never end.' Evelyn's misery was rife and streaming, a gush of terrible salt and gall. She didn't even try to staunch it, so much did it rip out from her like bile. This was no theory of universal sorrow but a gut-wrenching pain in her violated womb. The knives were going at her still, cutting and tearing, pulling her apart. Was there no humiliation, no bitterness and pain too terrible for a woman to have to bear? She didn't think it, she just survived: synaptic firings, these, not thought-forms.

She decided to look for her assailant herself; she must be able to find him somewhere! But, like some blur of bulbs in the night, the string of events was garish, ill-defined, as the ship docked and the indifferent straggle of passengers walked down the ramp and onto the quay. Where *was* the malodorous, clean-shaven git? Why couldn't she pick out his accent now? Was that him there, just getting off? No, he was lost in a bunch of beards, belonging, so it seemed, to some male collective. Disguise! She hadn't thought of it. How easy even that was for a man! A woman spent her life getting made-up, dolled-up, but when it came to the crunch she was always exposed.

She held on to the handrail for support. Her childhood fear of the gap-between-steps rushed in on her now and made her feel faint. It was worse going down: one couldn't even run. At the bottom she felt bleared and almost collapsed, but some voice inside her told her she mustn't: she must stay upright and drag herself on. Taxis drew up at the end of the quay and one of them, conveniently, had its door open for her. As the driver was putting her bag in the boot - she was holding on to the silver back-door handle - a figure rushed by and thrust a note in her hand. Feeling too weak to do otherwise, she opened the door and fell onto the back-seat, clutching the note, which she crammed into a pocket. It wasn't till later, when she was in her room, an elegant, expensive room at The Acropolis, with the door double-locked and everyone shut out, that she unfolded it and read: 'So long, babe!' So that was it - the bastard had escaped! She collapsed on her bed and, this time, did pass out.

She came to as the evening was beginning to stir; the shops and stalls were opening again, the sun going down in the bloodshot west. There was a hint of it even through her shuttered window: suddenly the air was less oven-like and the breeze had a tremble, even an edge. It was as if an oasis had come to her, after her day- and nightmare of heat, light and pain. She decided to confirm it with a long, hot bath.

But the minions of Grace were slow in coming; she still ached slowly and dumbly from the assault. After her bath she took dinner in her room and looked out from her balcony at the bright city night. It was a wonderworld of gadgetry, cars, trams, mobility, teeming with noise and garish with light; it was the perfect foil and backdrop to her own stage life. Everywhere it had been, it was always the same: London, New York, Paris, Athens. The world had come down to this, finally - a throbbing, drilling, destructive Machine. In such environments governments sat, fortunes were made, history was sealed. Nor was there any escape from it. To live in the country, as the gentry had done, was now just a failing irrelevance: this is where the action was. For all that, Evelyn craved clean air, sea- and sun-washed spaces, leaps within the soul. She could and she would go back to Myconos.

She embraced the island vividly at first, as if her trauma had been forgotten, though it waited in her still like poison unspread. She moved quickly into the Open Space and, uncharacteristically oblivious of herself, danced daily though all the options of the Gyre. It was not, however, quite the same, and it wasn't simply the absence of Emma; it was, more, that in *her* there had been a subsidence, a scarcely perceptible falling-off. She knew it directly, inuitively, as a mother knows a child is not her own. She cast about in her mind for causes - the rape, the breaches in relationship - but with these, also, she was not satisfied. There was a factor 'x', not part of the equation, like the catalyst in a chemical experiment, and this, too, had made its contribution, had dropped its stone and let it sink. Though she performed everything just as before, with the same tight attention to line, form and detail, that unquantifiable special spark had gone, had quit her arena, flown off like a bird.
  She tried to work herself up to a pitch, to recapture the Centre, the poise of hold. She went for long invigorating walks, did regular exercise, took cold morning dips. None of it brought the magic back, nor did she ever experience again that fine, controlled ecstasy, which is the dancer's flame and goal. A sense of rupture began to seep through her, like stones falling out of a once-stout wall. And try as she might to put them back, the cohesive backlay had somehow gone. She found herself flailing, instead of moving free.

The worst despairs are the ones we control, those which mercilessly, day-in day-out, we hold down inside us, till we perish from their blight. Evelyn had always taken for granted that she would be able to reach that special Point, that Eye within, which everyone knows and with which audiences, momentarily freed, are able to see in their communion with the artist. Whatever the dross of her life had been, that special place had always been there, and always (well, almost) she had been able to find it. Now it had begun to fall from her, in an unforeseeable entropic slip. A spasm of panic shot through her, and immediately she sat on it: she contained it, fought back, was against all back-sliding; she did more, trained more, pushed herself harder. But all her efforts - though they seemed to bring her back, and the casual observer would have noticed no difference - were unable to induce the rigorous rapture, the fine-chiselled edge of what Evelyn, at the Parthenon, had defined to herself as the Bevel of Perfection. It had stood in those columns; it had *been* in her.

She was searching for it now in the Open Space and, out and away, among the stars at night. But no clear mellifluence came to her, no split-second, even, when the Temple stood. She was a struggling outcast like the rest, the vast majority, who barely live. The sorrow of it spread across her face, contorting her features, making them hard. That soft transfusion, which lovers know and the artist, alone, feels the ecstasy of, was now an absence: that blood drained out; the flesh of her cheeks caved cavernously in. She began to wither in her heart of hearts.

It boiled down to an existential collapse, a loss of Being drastic and dire. This, more than any of the events in her life, was the 'summum malum' which had overtaken her - or, rather, she had fallen into the Pit of it, which ran round Earth's body like a mass grave. Urgently always it was waiting there, for all souls blanked-out, void of Grace. It was there when one lost one's finer touch and became gross, arrogant, subservient, fearful; it was there in treachery, corruption, filth, in the million devisings of human deceit; it was there when one turned a furtive corner. But, ever and abidingly, it *was there*. She felt the pull-down force of it, its sheer tamasic ancient strength; she apprehended it as the gravity of the soul. And with it she was sinking far below the earth.

6

Evelyn was not getting on with herself: she would have to cut-and-run, but she was loath to leave. Tristan at this point, not quite equidistant, was going through a crisis of his own. He had gone back to Patmos ('St John's Isle') and tried to pick up his previous persuasion. But somehow, for him also, the link was lost: the vertical-veridical track of his mind had veered off somewhere and become imprecise. He was left with stray impulses, non-cogent firings, a confused lexicon of isolate etyms, which actually amounted to global FA. He took out his Bible and read from St. John ('In the beginning was the Word'), but even his Original's peerless Logistics could not restore him to his former pitch.

Then, out-of-the-blue, came two letters from Emma, the second one first, as Randomness allows. Her hand, though cool, was firm and strong, and he felt again her leonine presence. Then the truth of what she wrote sank into him: the Pit, the Zero, which Brewston had become. Of course, he could never go back again. The whole place had been from the first, for him, blazing, the beginning of his journey of exile on earth. And now, though he had travelled, he still felt adrift - as if a major

192

connection were missing, some native and endemic Place of Peace. It was there, inchoate, in Emma's cool hand, but this he pushed from his mind: she was remote. He got back on track to Evelyn, her olive-limbed body and frail-of-nature ways. Everything he saw and could see in her expressed itself in oxymorons: strong-weak, forceful-yielding, unfaithful-true. He knew he had to get back to her.

Are both of them travelling from equidistant, disparate points, to converge on the sunset sands of Lesbos? Do we see them in our mind's eye, entwined and entwining, sand pumping, sun throbbing, hear the silken violins? Is the anatomy of their fulfilment complete? Gentle reader, you have jumped the gun.

Let us take Evelyn's journey first. She avoided a nocturnal doubletake to Piraeus, catching a fortunate morning ferry, which got her in about 6p.m. She fully intended to go straight on to Lesbos, but there was some kind of Mediterranean muddle with boats, so that she was left with the expedient of taking a hotel room and coming down to the port every day to check departures.

- Ochi! she was told. Nothing doing today.

Her life at this point was the mirror-image of all our lives: she was waiting for Death. It might come quickly or slowly - who knew? - but the certainty was that it came one day. And perhaps it was this fatal substratum, this agony of suspension, this existential Void, which made waiting, even of the humdrum type, such an angst-filled torment for everyone.

It made all the difference to Evelyn. Overcome with the fag and the drain of it all (the minuscule time it takes to be told 'no'), she took to the consolations of the city: the juice, the weed, finally cocaine. She didn't even bother going down to Piraeus, just lay on her bed in her hotel room, splayed out on the Rack, the screws tightening inch by inch. She didn't even *look* good any more.

It was one of those lapses in the seasons of the soul, which happen to all lovers, however keen, and which the Romantic Illusion tries to patch up. Evelyn's nasal membrane was inflamed - worse, it was getting to the point of dissolution - when she realised she must move on or die the death: the corrosive deliquecence of the flesh was at hand. Quaking from withdrawal but determined all the same, she made her way to the port again. It wasn't going to be so easy: above the reach of wharf to which she came a sign had been affixed, saying: SERVICE DISCONTINUED. Her attempts to improve on this information were greeted with leers, jeers and pointers to the sign. A feeling of 'in extremis' submerged her.

'A miss is as good as a mile,' they say. If Evelyn had arrived just a few minutes earlier, not only would she not have missed Tristan, she would actually have boarded the same boat as him, the last of the season which went straight to Lesbos. Now, of course, she was way out of synch., while our noble hero, ignorant and sailing, made haste across the waters, eager to touch base. He had no thought but of her luscious loins, the Acres of Felicity he had been born-and-bred up to and which now, in a few short hours, he would enjoy. He saw himself, in his specious-ideal way, completing the circle of his life so far, living out and living through to the Space Beyond. He was still, in a sense, all apollonic streamlining, gracious through the wind but, my God, *down there?*

He clipped into Lesbos at the appointed time, faintly aggrieved not to find Evelyn there and waiting. Now it was *his* turn on the Rack. He roamed around and felt the weight of waiting - as if the walls of space-time were pressing in on him. It was Mallia with a difference, the way it was at first: the room, the purlieus, the crash of sea on rock.

He went for long walks along the narrow coastal strip, seeking always to nullify the Ache, which came to him now with the Sirens off the Sea. Autumn was gradually settling in, with its cloud-banks like snow at first, softly unawares. It was blurring out the hard lines of summer, the dust and the glare and the harsh white light. Not like an open oven any more, the sky had taken on a gentler texture, cushioning, absorbent, holding in the sound. It reached him from out-of-sight of the sea: the rhythmical utterances of the waves, their high call to heaven echoed back and out. It stirred in him also with the insistence of desire: the groundswell of the waves, with their open, tippling mouths. He was in and of them - they worked in him - as he strode along in his gangling way. Clothed in seaweed, they were singing to him, calling him out from his odd, spare self. Wreathed, blonde and lovely, their breasts up-tilted, they were running sea-fingers over him, the salt-water running from their bodies onto his. He felt umbilically connected to them, as if they sang always and only for him ...

He didn't realize how far he had walked (the Sirens' song had faded now), when he came to the blank end of himself. He wasn't in a contorting Hall of Mirrors but wholly at large in the natural world: a narrow, stony spit of land pushed out, point-like, to a dull blob of sea.
- This is the Indicator, he said to himself.
He realized he had come to a nullity - the Blank within oneself which only Love can cure. He had striven for years, had Visions, known Angels and climbed up the back of his own spine's Ladder to that place where the Light shone, crystalline-bright. But he needed the other side of the equation, dionysiac downflight, the dark body of the Night; he needed it with Evelyn Rodd. In this meeting and melting, exclusively, lay any hope of his getting it right. It wasn't a mere matter of volition and drive - these he had had and pursued to exhaustion - no, it was

something enfolded in waiting more like dwelling at home, patiently. Could he hold on through the excruciating interim?

Tristan sank into the Pit of Waiting, the necessary aspect of Not-knowing, and, as days and further days went by, he began to languish visibly. It was 'loves me, loves me not', 'black sails, white', as he blew some imaginary dandelion-head. The black sail, bellying and round, he liked, as it ploughed its way through the serpent sea. But the other sail was heady, thrashing, fraught, it pitched and tossed to an unhinged end. If only he could embrace the Dark, he would feel himself healed and restored at source. He began to feel, however, that this would never be: he would wait, spent and wounded, on the blistering Rock for a boat which, if it came, would be sick, white and wrecked. He didn't know what to make of it: there was no news of any boat from Piraeus, no message either, not even a card.

Yet, oddly, he felt rooted as he hadn't felt before, awaiting the return of Evelyn, the Bride. She was the one - he knew it now - whom he had craved and needed all these years. Beyond and between the movements of their bodies - strictly endemic, as it were, there had arisen in him a force of focus, which showed him exactly what and whose he was. He could not live a light-struck existence; he needed deep integration with Earth and with Night. She would come to him, surely, his Night-in-Day, his living Moment of dark, bright Flame.

But she did not come as the days went by, ferry-traffic, anyway, dwindling down to zero. She was obliged, in the end, to negotiate a deal with a tour-operator ('Aegean Adventures'), who was prepared to take her, if not to Lesbos, then at least as far as the Dodecanese. Not knowing any Greek, she found it difficult to haggle - both price and destination were obscure - and was eventually helped out by a Belgian businessman, who was wanting to take a late-season trip and had, by dint of travel, learnt some Greek. Then Evelyn wondered about him, too, but on learning that he was an aristocrat and being shown photos of his wife and children, she decided, perhaps naively, to take a chance and came up trumps: a man-of-honour through and through. Indeed, his company was a solace to her, as the company of older people often is. They talked of many things, and his courtesy and charm helped bring her round to some sense of trust; she was starting to come back again from the dead. Her face, with the aid of a little discreet make-up, was losing its hollow, haggard look, and there was some slight rounding of her limbs by night. Yes, she told herself, it would all be all right.

But all was not all: there was Tristan. She gulped inwardly at the prospect of their meeting. Lovers' partings are always dire, however impregnable the love-knot may seem. We leave with the last scene in our mind, the great golden moment we would like to last. We feel transfigured for a time, ourselves-not-ourselves, in a deciphered New World. And then, by some dull osmotic penetration, the Greyness seeps in through the soles of our feet, rising gradually, swamping every cell, till all that is left is some artificial memory, like a light-bulb swinging on a gusty sea-front, behind it the Deep-drop, the Sea of the Void.

Evelyn still loved and wanted Tristan, but she was unsure, after her recent Trough, whether she had the capacity for love. For there are laws of emotional entropy, just as there are laws of physical fact. And she wondered now, in the mellow afternoon, if the strings of her being weren't too stretched, too wrought and worn-thin to produce a sound. To a body as rich and resonant as hers, bearing down to its root like a fine-tuned guitar, it felt like a heartburn hollowness, a lesion. The sought-for Continuum had been broken: everything would have to be remade from the start. Did she have the strength for it?, she asked herself, leaning over the bows to the blue Aegean, polite conversation in pleasant play. The Baron, who was in mature middle-age, treated her obviously like a daughter, and she couldn't help wondering how her life might have been, if she had had a man such as this for a father. In him might have been a refuge of strength, a genial place in the wicked flux of life. For always and always she had had to struggle - from the very first moment, the moment she was born. Nothing had come easily, without an invoice attached. And even human love had its limits, its points where one faltered and couldn't make the grade.

Time put an end to these lugubrious reflections, as, though it doesn't heal, it often will. They were approaching one of the smaller islands on the 'Aegean Adventures' special itinerary, from which, so the tour Operator assured Evelyn, she could get a boat next morning to Lesbos. That was really all there was to it. The tour-party would be spending the night in a hotel - naturally, she was welcome to join them - and carrying on the next day at first light. Their luggage was off-loaded by the small, ragged crew and dumped in a heap in front of 'The Dark Night'.

Evelyn was happy to dine-and-dance with her Baron whom, by this time, she was calling Claude. He was obviously such a gentleman, a gentleman to his fingertips. He knew how to take her across the floor in a smooth, unhalting, swirling step, which left no part of himself behind; he knew all the right things to say to a woman to make her feel she was the only one. And gradually Evelyn felt released from herself, momentarily absolved from the traumas of her past. Even from Tristan she felt freer, lighter: she was now no longer the fated Bride, recipient and redeemer of his cathartic drives.

Was it Claude himself who had smuggled in the claret, which now stood rubily shining between them, in place of the predictable, resinous retsina? 'Might well be,' thought Evelyn, but she felt it gauche to ask him outright. She simply sipped it, enjoying the taste, the easy, fine, full-bodied palate. A number of local musicians were playing and a man got up and danced alone, picking up and holding a table aloft. Others joined in with rhythmic clapping - arms round shoulders now, moving in a body -, till the whole room partook of that fruity fluidity, which is the proper ripe resonance of Greek folk-music.

Evelyn wouldn't have gone that far - no, really, she reflected later - had not some special effect of the night released her into an easy Space, which made everything seem possible and nothing remiss. In fact, a time-gap had opened up for her - as if her whole life, linear and contiguous, had receded on the instant to reveal a glade, summery and murmurous, to which they two alone had access. What, then, more natural than to take the two-three steps, which would carry them over that innocent threshold?

Claude was hesitant at first, relinquishing himself reluctantly. But Evelyn wanted to give herself, not out of gratitude - because he had ushered in the Moment - but quite gratuitously, from the depths of herself: an existential throwaway. No-one would understand it - they would all call her 'whore'; Tristan, sweet Tristan would be stymied, nonplussed - but she could see further, couldn't she?, further than these stifling bourgeois parameters. She could see out and perfect to the first, spinning Place and, so long as this Image persisted in her, she was obliged, somehow driven, to actualize it. What man - and a gentleman at that - doesn't feel, when such a woman desires him, that gallantry itself impels the response? Claude, however, did think twice, thought about his home and his eight bonny children, the forty flawless years of happy married life. Somehow, he was about to nullify it, and yet that was the last thing Evelyn was after.

Perhaps it was a mark of her desperation that she walked so easily onto that Ground; perhaps she was simply the plaything of Fate. She pinnacled out on her prone, podgy Baron, bringing to life through his skirting skin unused erotic channels, pale crushed portals, the existence of which he had never suspected through all those years of settled intercourse.

From one world - it's true - we are abruptly in another, the White Rose of Heaven opening up. Somehow the dross is left behind, and we glimpse for a second the further Shore. So it was with the nuptial baron, that night-of-the-dark-light, Evelyn coming. He saw for a second what his life might have been, had he chosen to live it otherwise. He had known the steady pleasures, the gratification, the luxury, fulfilment and achievements of life. And yet here was something totally different, a Gate through which he had never passed, a dark cellar Door he had never come upon. Now, this night, it had opened briefly, only, most surely, to close again. Evelyn held him close to her breast, as he wept out tears he never knew he had.

The March of the Day is merciless: it was back to sun-upright, rules and roles. 'Aegean Adventures' were leaving early, and Evelyn awoke to find Claude gone. A peek from her window told her all: the small, ragged crew were back on the quay, with a shouting and a bustling and a loading-on of bags. Claude was already anonymous; she watched for him going, felt him gone.

Later, when she was down at breakfast, alone amongst the deserted tables, she was served by the sole surviving waiter, who brought her on a tray, with her coffee and rolls, a small white envelope and a curled red rose. She opened the envelope and withdrew a neat card, on which was printed, black-on-white: 'Avec les Compliments du Baron van Rijk'. Back to Form's immutability: the High Dice lay splintered and broken on the floor.

Worse was to come - there was no boat out. The assurances she had had from the Tour Operator, lost from sight during the past twenty-four hours, now showed up for the hoax they were: no boat for Lesbos ever left from there. She walked up and down the tiny quay, inhaling the scents of the morning air: the tarred nets drying against the wall, the fresh salt breeze, the oily tang of fish. Why not stay here? But how could she? She was compelled, come what may, to meet her fate. Those Subterranean Ladies had been spinning out her thread, day and night, as they do for all of us.

Eventually, she negotiated a passage to Lesbos with a fisherman who, knowing she was without recourse, extorted the maximum fare from her. He was a taciturn man with a flaring beard, but a good sailor, no doubt, and a no-nonsense character. She felt, at least, she would be safe with him.

But safety and security are provisional, at best: usually the Rope is too taut or too slack. Here she was again, awash on the Sea, with the sail flapping strongly, heaving to the breeze. She knew she was going to her nemesis, and yet it pleased her that she travelled thus, tanned and wind-blown, holding the yard. She had abandoned all hope, save what through Tristan could be salvaged for her from the ruins of Time. Even that she couldn't bank on. Though the boat glided firmly, sharp and white against the sea, the human interval had been unmade; it hung there somewhere, straggling, entropic: everything would have to be built up again. She knew it in the pit of her stomach, her guts; she wanted to escape the trial of it. Nothing was given in this world, nothing; everything had to be done from scratch. She wished, as the wind and the sea were in her, as the boat cut forward, claiming the sea, that this, only this, could go on for ever, that the human resumption would never be. She regretted her lack of tender indifference, that technique people have for staying alive; she wished the whole outcome didn't mean so much. And yet it did: it meant everything.

It was early November, the season of storms, and several times the weather got up and they were forced to land provisionally on one of the smaller, unmapped Dodecanese. 'Captain' Droussos swore it was O.K., but more than once Evelyn had her doubts. Fierce Aegean north winds forced them south-east, and on one occasion she was sure she saw the vertical finger of a minaret. 'Turkey!' she gesticulated to the captain, but he simply said it couldn't be and grumbled on about Greece's mortal grievance. With these country contradictions she had to be content, turning her attention, with a child's blenched prayer, in what she thought was the direction of Lesbos.

The island and its women had been her obsession for seasons now, for months and years. In her Lesbos-of-the-mind she had sought refuge - back there at Trentside, a million miles away - and now she was approaching the reality of it, as, stark and white in a glare of sun, those hundred-metre cliffs stood stiff and sheer. They were like some inchoate Parthenon, some ramrod infinity of Uncarved Light. She shrank and turned from them, shielding her eyes.

Tristan was aghast at the prospect of the Light, the white presence destined from across the sea. Long had he stood there, bleak and alone, awaiting the moment when dark Evelyn would return. But, when she didn't come, his walks and his waiting began to take on an hallucinatory glare: he stared down at the rocks, sun-bleared, jagged, asking; he thought of Evelyn's fainting and Sappho's suicide.

He wandered there often and, truth to tell, most people just thought he'd thrown himself off. Others, more pious, thought it might have been a fall. In any event, he was lost without trace, which meant that both theories were ultimately unfounded, there being no body or circumstantial clues: blood, torn clothing, even a broken fingernail The explanation for this wild occurrence lay in the unduly squally weather, which had washed him out to sea and a watery grave. There *were* precedents, and that was that.

Once this patent half-account had been repeated often enough, it gained credence with the people and they left it at that. What's the point, after all, of getting stirred-up and probing the mysteries of Uncertainty? Why not leave it to the Visiting Experts? Nothing in Tristan's personal effects gave any indication of nearest-and-dearest, much less an address or contact-point; even his passport, on closer inspection, turned out to be already out of date. There were, of course, Emma's two letters, but these were headed simply, cryptically, 'Brewston'. One way or another, the consensus was that, wherever he belonged, he had come out here to die: finally, his lifeline had run out. Dire and fatalistic as this may seem, it was, *qua* theory, comforting enough: everything had its causal niche. It would have been much more demanding, altogether too much trouble, to find out what really *had* happened to Tristan. Nor was Evelyn equal to the task.

7

'The light is hard and merciless here; it takes away every last nuance of protection. I am vulnerable now, as I have always been. We come into the island, with its staggering portents, its unscaleable cliffs of peerless strength. I cannot look at them: they blind my eyes; they rip out my eyes and fry them to extinction. I look down, I look around, I put sunglasses on. That's better, faint soul, better soothe your eyes.

'The soothing, however, is merely momentary, external: I cannot beat off the inner glare. I shall take a taxi back to the old hotel; there I shall be forever his Bride. I pay off 'Captain' Droussos on the quay - he's taken me for every penny he could get. Tristan has no money, either. Here I have arrived now, penniless and drained.

'Dropped off at the hotel, I stand in the blare, the unseen glare of those terrible cliffs. Time, which is waiting, will wait no more: it is leading me out with an inexorable Hand. Those blinding, light-struck cliffs are in my brain.

'Check in, passport, all's awash . . . why isn't he here to meet me, help me out? Why must I always do everything alone? I'm avoiding the porter, because he'd want a tip.

'"Mr.D. gone," they say when I enquire. Mr.D.? O, yes, Deakin - wasn't that his name? I never heard him use it once. Strange how a person you thought you knew suddenly sticks out an unsuspected branch - puts you in a different position, somehow. We know, or we think we know, but we don't. How not-to-know; that is the question.

'"Gone where?" I ask. "Ne, Mr.D. gone." I'm taken up to what they call *his* room, a room we didn't share before. It's stripped, struck bare, like my brain inside, with the same hallucinatory stasis, its order worse than any amiable chaos. It's obvious he hasn't been here for days.

'"Did he say *where* he was going?" No reply. I go to my own room, to rest for a while. But the attempt is futile - there's no rest here, no let-up in the march of murdering Circumstance. I have to get free of it; I have to *know*. I go out and mess about, as one can only as a child, but it's just a device, an evasion: I come back. "Let me see that room again!" I say in my most authoritative voice. They agree. Why not? They must remember 'those two'.

200

'No messing this time, I go through his things, itemizing them one by one. I open his case and that daft bag he carried. Just the usual masculine sparenesses, the poor, nude, stripped-down skeleton of life. They think they can live better and freer without us, but they can't: without us they're down to bare bones. Only a woman puts the marrow into life, fills out the flesh, puts the shade round the bulb. A man on his own's like a walking stick.

'What's keeping me going is a sense of Dread: that I have come, am coming to the final Blank. There's a peculiar fascination in the Horror, and gradually moving closer to it is like peeling an onion, strip by strip. It will reveal itself soon in its ultimate Zero; I am going through all his stuff, piece by piece. They've simply rallied everything together: clean shirts, striped vests, soiled underpants and socks - work for a body that doesn't need them any more. It's up to me to get to the bottom of it.

'I'm getting warm; in fact, I'm getting hot. These papers down here, among the junk and dirt. What's this? - Translated from the German: The Soul-outpourings of an Art-loving Monk. That's him to a T. Love-loving, too! Anything else, in the pocket at the back? Unmistakable Airmail, crinkly and blue. I want them. No. I want them. Yes, I do.

'I'm guilty of a violation, the destruction of privacy, which is also mine. But I can't just stay and read them here: walls have eyes, as well as ears. I shall walk upon the cliffs and read them there. Gently close the door, lock it and go down.

'The sun is waiting; it's hot again. How come I forgot it so easily? It waits at the Apex of Nudity, its Eye unsheathed, like a judgement on me. I knew it would come to this, finally.

'I steer myself away from the cliffs, towards what looks like a patch of green land. There I will sit me down . . . No, I won't. The cliffs are piping strange organ music, the sun's diapason working in them. It soars, peaks, bevels, cuts into my soul. No place here, either. What has *happened* to him?

'I sink down, caught, on the shadeless earth and wrench the letters from my cleavage. They have stuck in my sweat and one page tears. Too bad, too bad - I can read them, anyway. What does it matter, ultimately? A woman pays always, pays with her body, even in something as trivial as this. A man shrugs it off; he gets off scot-free.

'I recognize the hand-writing instantly: Emma, my beautiful creation, my Dream. You didn't, in your earth-soul, have to do anything; just live and be there - I did the rest. I made you up, my solar darling; I made you what you weren't, like Pygmalion. Don't turn me into one of your mediocrities!

'You were still a girl, when I was a woman; I was a star, when you were nothing. All the same, I melted like butter; I was like butter melting in

201

your mouth. I came to myself a different person, and here I am a different person now.

'None of us really changes, though: we modify, go on, become plastic to Circumstance. None of us has the coinage of Truth. We climb a little way, and then the whole castle crumbles; our whole inner edifice falls apart. That's why I'm torn to shreds inside, having lost everything and nowhere to go. No, it's more that I've become a waif again, a soloist on a deserted stage. The theatre's empty, of course; the people have gone. And, like a besieged soldier, my bread-and-water's running out.

'Em.'s letter is just . . . but wait a minute. She wants to share it - ye', that and the rest! She wants to *share* it with him - I'll bet she does! Be plenty of sharing there, all right! Best bib and tucker, then on with the job!

'I wouldn't be surprised if they're not 'sharing' now, back in Ol' England, with me here like a fool. Who knows, anyway, what people will do: they're such hypocritical, self-seeking gits! Tristan I trusted, really I did'; I wanted him, God, I was his night and day. Now he's gone off, the unfaithful bastard, faithless like all men - all men are bastards. And she, what is she, whom I made in my image, built up to be a great dancer like me? She's with him, I know she is; I know she's betrayed me, though it's me she has to thank for everything. Such creatures are women, the more innocent the more deadly, of which there are two kinds: whores and bitches. Whores are more honest - they just do it for money. Bitches screw the heart out as well.

'My energy's failing, though, that's the real problem; I haven't the volumes of energy left. Time was, the sun was hot in me for creation; now it's melting me down, cell by cell. I went too fast, too far, I think ...

'Is that them there, in the blinding sun, walking together, Bastard and Bitch? Have they come back to tell me their secret griefs, to make confession of their deceitful souls? There's nowhere for me to receive them here, not even a tree or a blot of shade. What's more, I'm all dishevelled, like a sack: my make-up's smeared, my hair's like rats' tails.

'They're coming towards me . . . No, they're not: they're dissolving back into the rock. They have no place for me here on earth, as they have no place for me in their hearts. They have disappeared in a pillar of rock, blinding and brutal like the day itself. No place of shade here anywhere: only the wind's, the blinding sun's home. The sun was my lover once-upon-a-time; now he's feeding me psychic meltdown. I can feel myself going out and down: he wants me to know whose alone I am.

'Lord and Life are Bastard and Bitch, but the Two will never meet as One. It's too much to ask of Nature and of Man: there's too much rupture and agony here. The birds have their nests and - what is it? - beasts their lairs, but what the fucking-hell have *I* got? Not even a drachma to lay across a straw.

202

'Already the two have melted out, dissolved, gone missing ..."We regret to inform . . ." There's nothing left but a soft spot on the rock, a vestige of sweat against the hot wall. As at Phaestos, where the Serpent emerged, they have gone back and down to the Underworld: they have gone to rejoin the world-as-it-was.

'Why shouldn't I also, in my priestess-soul, go out, back and down to the Better Place? Why shouldn't I fly? (I was a dancer, too.) The rocks are summoning me, haughty and hard, lifting up their faces with the broken teeth. Tristan is down there, blond Voice of the Sea, and Emma is writhing in the coils of the waves. Betrayed! Betrayed! My words hollow out; they disappear in the sickening sea. Then I pull myself forward - shall I rise again? - I drag myself to the merciless Edge . . .'

Three days later Evelyn's body was found.

# VOLUME THREE: MEMPHIS

## BOOK SEVEN: THE FLIGHT INTO EGYPT

They fuck you up, your mum and dad.
They may not mean to, but they do.

Philip Larkin

1

Not all the Freud family settled in London as a consequence of the
'Anschluss' of 1938. Quite a number of them, actually - more than one
might think -, struck a path north to what some call The Wastes:
Dewsbury, Batley, Halifax, Fartown. Such a one was Adalbert
(subsequently Eddie), who was barely twenty when he came over to
England and whose family connections were with the woollen trade.

He was, naturally, the pride of his mother's life, her only son, a
weakling as a child. She cosseted him and poured over him the pent-up
affections of a wretched bourgeois life, spent ministering mainly to a
husband of no worth. In the early days, of course, in Vienna there *had*
been something, but for a long time now it had degenerated into that
war-and-peace of habitual attrition, which is the common course of
settled married life. There *had* to be a highlight somewhere, something
more than the paralytic bleakness. And Waltraut found it in her love for
Eddie, whom she continued to the end to call 'mein kleiner Adalbert' and
whose every move she monitored like some all-seeing predator.

Adalbert could do nothing right. When he was reading, he ought to be
doing the garden; when he was out in the garden, he should really be
studying. And so he was perpetually out of joint, like a dislocated piece
of machinery. She was on him like a flash if he lolled about reading,
when the Sunday Wienerschnitzel was about to be cooked. The tender
rumpling of her face and the look of pity she cast over him were enough
to tell him without equivocation that he should be up and doing, much
more than he was.

- Bitte, Adalbert, was all she said. But, then, that was all she needed to say: 'bitte, Adalbert' was the psychological needle that could be guaranteed to make him jerk. And he responded automatically, dully, wishing he were a million miles away.

This sparring, which always gave Adalbert the feeling he was coming off second-best for the umpteenth time, was such a feature of life at home that, in a quirky way, he became attached to it. It proved his existence, so to speak.

This circumscription corresponded to his eyesight: he had been myopic from the first. When he walked in the woods - and who doesn't in Vienna? - he saw just that: Woods only, no Trees. Trees became stumbling-blocks for him, since he always saw them (or so it always seemed) too late for him to know 't' other from which. Which is where Mother made the fatal insertion, in the in-between space where he couldn't hide.

His father and sister were, more or less, an irrelevance; Kätchen was a baby, his father was grey. They lived out an unformed, marginal existence on the periphery of the mother-son Terrain.

From 3 September, 1939 onwards, Eddie Fretstone (Adalbert Freud's deed-poll remake) might have expected to see military action. As things were, he wouldn't have minded, but, as it was, he didn't go. In spite of the family's gracious testimonials and the world-wide reputation of Uncle Sigmund, he was still regarded as a 'bloody foreigner' - what with his funny, crumpled face and moony eyes; and his English was not up to that much, either. Then there was the question of his shortsightedness - not much of a recipe for Glory, that. The best he might get would be Ack-ack duty, sitting it out by the dams above Sheffield. But even this was less than realistic, and he was sent to a farm like a common POW.

Oddly enough, the farm itself sat above the dams near Upper Bradfield, crouched like a sheep beneath a nestling wall, on the very fringes of the moors. Between Moor and Pasture, heather and grass, it heaved its gritstone bulk into view, as the family send-off he couldn't avoid drove its old-banger way up the rough rubble track, that cuts back off the road as it swings on to Strines. His father and sister were with him in the car - and, of course, his mother, inevitably. She was pressing flannel underwear on him, which he knew he might need but refused to take.

- Ach, Adalbert, du kannst einfach nicht . . .
- I shall be all right, he said surlily.

Even the German language was part of her weaponry.

-There's Mr. and Mrs. Mellors! he said with relief, as a couple appeared in the doorway of the house and hailed them, seeing the car draw up.
- You'll have time for a cup of tea, said Mellors.

- Just a quick one, then, said Eddie's father. Must be back before it gets dark - this black-out, you know.

- Ah know, said Mellors. Ah s'll be glad when this bloody war's ovver.

But it won't be over, thought Eddie to himself; it won't be over for a long time yet. And even when it is, it won't be.

Mrs. Mellors was, or had been, a lady, who had married her husband when he was forty or so and whose deepening passion had come out as love, almost as an afterthought. As he, at first, had taken hold of her and brought her to sexual ecstasy, so she, more gradually and inwardly, had moulded him later from backwoods disgruntlement to the kind of man-and-farmer she knew he could be. He still had rough edges - bound to have - but he was now free-standing and independent, not the bundle of reaction he once had been. They had sung to one another like two mating birds, and the palpable presence of their song held the air. Eddie was alive to it and felt at home, as he never had at 12B, Vale Close. He was beginning to breathe a different air.

The War intensified its grip. In December, 1940, the City of Sheffield was ablaze, as other cities were, both before and after. Eddie sat it out on the fringe of things, wishing against wish, as any refugee must, that he could get one back at the Teutonic aggressor. The bombing targets were Samuel Fox's, Davy United and other heavy steel plants, while railway lines and, here, the dams were singular objects of attack and concern. Oddly, perhaps, it was the latter which evoked most trauma in people's minds: no-one had forgotten the century's great dam-burst, and the threat of another was subliminally present, like the threat of an earthquake in San Francisco. Ack-ack personnel were everywhere.

Eddie lived in at the farm with the Mellors, at the edge of the moors, between Pasture and Wild. He lived with them and with their daughter, Cloë, who as Mrs. Mellors said, had been a love-child. She was fifteen now and she bore about her the bloom of a love lived out in the Wild. To see her come in on a fresh May morning was to see Spring herself walk in through the door - not as an allegory, leaved and flowered, but, her black hair framing a flushing face, as the living embodiment, the Touch of the Spring. She made all things new, beginning with herself. No sooner had she entered a room than it glowed; there was a pressing radiance and warmth about her. When all was said and done, she had come to actualize the love-in-the-dark-wood her parents had enjoyed.

There is sadness, there is gladness in the seasons of the soul. This was a time of expansion for Eddie, with the bombs crashing round them and the City ablaze. On 12 December, 1940, it was as if the sky itself were on fire (Walsh's was gone, and C&A on Snigg Hill) and two days later, apart from standing shells, there was only rubble left: the buildings had been gutted. Eddie witnessed all this with the kind of still passion one usually reserves for engagement with life. Not that he was unsympathetic towards people - he even wept when he read the accounts - but over and above that, and quietly behind it, was a glowing and coming observation of Life in all its vast beauty and absurdity. The War, as he had hoped it might do as a soldier, was releasing him from the myopic view of Life as a narrow, closed, fixed, mechanical System, in which he could do nothing but walk straight ahead. No, now he was opening out to the world, with its universal hatred and sorrow; he was beginning to look for Derivations, beginning to perceive what moves darkly, in-between.

And all the time there were the Moors, hailing and calling him out of himself - to roam, to wander, to be single and free in. An old drove road led out between the heather, and he would walk along it to the earth's rim, enjoying the kiss of the rippling wind and the skylarks' rising and piping to the sky. He was looking for some final ecstasy, a confirmation of his widening scope.

All this, however, was on the Edge, at the fringe of the tract of his daily life. The rest of it was prose as usual: the early rising, the milking by hand, then, after breakfast, the mucking-out, the fieldwork. Mellors had over two hundred acres, a good catch thereabouts, though it was all down to grass. The land dipped down between its dark walls to the fir plantation round Agden Dam, then back in a swath up to Harecliffe Rocks. Plenty of land to walk and wander in: to breed sheep for wool and mutton, cattle for beef and milk.

The lambing season from February to April was counterpoised by the more random calvings, which seemed to take place almost any time. Often, indeed, it was best left alone, and Eddie and Mellors would stride out of a morning to find a cow calved in a sheltered hollow, the wee beast wobbling, barely licked clean; or, up in the pen, they would hear a ewe bleat and come back to find she had given birth to twins.

It was a life of wandering and wondering for Eddie, poised, as he was, between Peace and War. Down there, in the City, and even closer, was the calamity of the bombing, a mini-doomsday; and here, quite adjacent, not slumbering but watchful, was the peaceful country idyll which had always been. And why, indeed, should it ever end? Why be sucked into the loathsome hellishness? And yet he had a Bridge to cross, one which at present he had no means of foreseeing. His strand of meaning was linear.

This strand of meaning, like a silken thread, he wove into the texture of his friendship with Cloë. They walked, they laughed, they read poetry together. And always she looked on him as a friend, with that immediate decidedness which girl-women have and by which they choose whom they will have. Not that Eddie wanted more. Although well-stocked with

Freudian libido, he was also a foreigner and tentative, realizing, for all his acceptance here, that love-and-marriage were quite a different thing. People gossiped, of course - in 'The Lion' it was rife -, but that didn't alter things a single jot. In his own eyes Eddie was in the Land of the Gentleman, and anything short of the impeccable was out. Nor did Cloë, for all her virgin-spring, have what he wanted or could possibly supply: that state of suspended, multiple indwelling, which is the craft and secret of the In-between.

More often than not he went out alone, taking the track behind the house, which joined up with the grassy drove road. There he rarely, if ever, met anyone. He could sing or shout his poems to the sky, to the sun which, in summer, hovered long, diffused red - and no-one to hear him but the rooks, as they gathered below among the sycamores. They, too, like messengers, were bringing it back: the lost, the high, the ancient Message, the one that was lost with the ancient Pharaohs. They, too, were intermediaries between Heaven and Earth - more than he was, more perfectly.

For all that, he wanted to be a Poet, to bring down and bring out in plastic, living language those intimations of Truth he felt obscurely. Cloë was his catalyst. She talked, she listened and she wrote poems herself - so much so that, in his mind, they were a literary partnership, a team together. And yet there was an untouchable quality about her, as if her freshness had an invisible fence. It seemed to be part of her self-definition, which all of us have, consciously or not. And Cloë knew it from the start - not cerebrally, but in her blood. She was one of those people who are mature from the start, who already, at the age of sixteen or so, have levelled out to their final form and will not be altered by their life's experience.

For Eddie it was vastly different; though older than her, he was more unmade. One might say, of course, that he had greater potential - certainly he had further to go - but the felicity of it, karmic or otherwise, was that they met precisely when they needed to and that they fuelled and fed each other from the first. Cloë, nonetheless, was guided by Eddie, since he was older and had seen and read more. She deferred to him in little ways and thought of him rather as a teacher, a role he was happy enough to play and which, later on, he seemed destined to fulfil.

2

One day, when the lambing and calving were over - it was getting on for Whitsun by now - they decided to take a long walk to Stanage, several miles distant across the moors. Connie and Mellors waved them off from the door, and Eddie took a mental snapshot of them there, which he compared with the one he had taken when he came. 'Chapter

Two', he said to himself, in the way poets have of transposing experience, remaking it already like bronze in fixed form.

The day was fresh, with scudding cloud, and they walked strongly, with the north-west wind at their backs. The sun came through occasionally, touching the grass in little patches, glancing off the pools which lay among the peat; the heather was showing up purple already. Eddie carried their small haversack. Chapter Two was called: 'Walking out with Cloë'.

After two or three hours they crossed the Manchester road, by a bleak, black house which seemed built to resist. A rubbly track led down to the road, which itself looked bleak and deserted. Wartime. Eddie was talking incessantly, rhapsodizing over this and that. Cloë was quiet; she was really his foil.

A different scene opened up before them now, as somewhere they crossed the county boundary into Derbyshire. The dark head of Win Hill came into view on the right, while spreading before them, from their height on Stanage End, lay the verdant and serpentine Derwent valley. Strangely, though, for hill country, it was not a landscape of verticalities: no mountains to speak of, just rising pasture-land, and then, cutting off the view with a horizontal rift, the sailing, unstoppable gritstone edges - Stanage, Bamford, Higgar Tor, Burbage -, while in the right-distance, like a dark giant dreaming, the tawny peat-mass of Kinder Scout lay. A man had got lost there recently, muddling the lookalike, ash-black paths, and they had found his body six weeks later. Statistics lied with their 2,000 feet: it was as hostile a place as any on earth.

They walked on above the intermittent face which constitutes Stanage, the longest edge in Britain. On the slopes below it the bracken was growing, with elongating, curl-topped thrusts, while from the woods a cuckoo called, still far away, among the birches and the boulders. A rill ran down to the greening land, and down there somewhere - a mile or so, at least - was the house that Charlotte Brontë had used for Jane Eyre. Eddie was all for going to find it, but to Cloë it just seemed a madcap adventure, one that would put the whole day out of synch. And, for once, he deferred to *her*; she had only to say:

-We'd lose height, wouldn't we?

Soon they were by that break in the edge where the Roman road had once run through, tracking up northwards from the Camp at Brough. A few rough paving-stones showed where it had been.

- I wouldn't like to be a Roman, said Eddie.

- How could you be? Cloë asked.

- I mean, a Roman at heart.

She gave a little, 'what's-he-on-about-now?' kind of laugh. Her own life-and-art mode was so much more straightforward.

- Road-builders and law-makers, I mean, said Eddie. I'd much rather be an Egyptian or a Greek.
- My name's Greek, said Cloë, it's all the same to me.
- An Egyptian, then.
- A Pharaoh, of course?
- In his nuptial Night-boat, coming out of Memphis.

And he pictured himself, all golden and shining, prepared for his Journey across the waters of the Nile. He was speechless, sublime, like the Rams of Amun-Ra; he was, as they were, both less and more than human. And the straight-pencilled River had richness, depth, Dimension.

- Our civilization is circumscribed, he said. It tries to reduce everything to a small, lit pool. It sets up precepts, then tries to live by them. But there's always something left out of account.
- Like what?
- What's above, what's below, what's in between. We have the structure of meaning but not the space.
- I don't understand what you're on about.
- Nor do I. It just seems we've lost something precious, that's all, a feel for something that doesn't cede to reason. If it doesn't cede to reason, we kick it out. And that way we lose the other half of Life.
- What other half?
- The half between the lines, the half that isn't stated but is crying to be heard. We fuck ourselves up with too much statement. Too much plain statement kills the soul.
- That's true - I've always thought so, now you come to mention it.

They looked out over the burgeoning land.

- Here it's abundantly obvious, he went on. You can even feel it bursting through the land. There's a unitive thread in Nature, somehow. Why isn't it there in the human brain?
- I don't know, but don't bother yourself with it - we're too young.
- I can't help bothering: it churns me up.

And he stood, disconsolately looking out. Behind him was the City, civilization and its folly, before him the sailing edges and the ever-patient Land. It was as if the ancient Cord between Heaven and Earth had been severed at that moment, and that it was so. Rationally, reflectively it had been gradually frayed, till its proper real tension had disappeared for good. That was how the mind explained it to itself, giving itself thereby a certain mathematical comfort. But deeply, inwardly, existentially even, it was a Gash and Ruin of enormous pain. The bombs out there were proving it daily. The inner came first, then only the outer: first the fatal stabbing, then the gush of blood. And there it was, hanging before his mind's eye, the Cord which had broken for him also.

210

He let the Knowledge of it sink in for a while. Some things, at least, seemed stable and constant: the land, the generations, the seasons, human love. Not everything had gone to the dogs - not yet. They found a hollow beneath the rocks, where the sun shone directly and the chilly north wind passed over their heads on its invisible journey. They ate their sandwiches and drank some tea from a flask. No-one came by but the odd walker overhead, and, as if by way of consolation, they kissed and cuddled in that grassy, sunlit hollow, not a stitch removed, innocent like children.

Then it was time to be off back again. Their day had found its Fulcrum, its Poise, that true point of purpose which all days have. And, as is usually the case, the way back seemed shorter. They were soon at the bleak, black house again, with the road winding westward over the Snake. It still looked like a tarred mausoleum; it made Cloë shudder as they walked past. Nothing to do now but set off downhill, till the final incline brought them to the farm.

- Now, what have you two been up to? said Mellors, seeing the flush on Cloë's face and her dark hair disarrayed.
- Just walking, dad, said Cloë, flushing further.
- A likely tale! said Mellors, enjoying her discomfort, which seemed to offer proof of what she was disclaiming.
- Why, if ah'd been out wi' a lass like thee . . . !
- What would you have done, you farty old fool? said Connie, reducing him to sad-phallic order.
- We', ah 'd 've . . .
But everyone was laughing: it was already too late.
- Men love to brag about their prowess, she said to Cloë, when the two of them were alone together later. Even when they have none, or have none left. But it was good, wasn't it - with Eddie, I mean?
- Mother, it isn't like that.
And she blushed again.
- You don't have to lie to me, darling, you know that.
- I'm not lying, mother.
But Connie wondered, just the same.

The ribald spirit of the older generation came as quite a shock to the youngsters, who thought of life as their own invention. And in a sense, of course, it was: they are there as authors of themselves. Connie and Mellors had been Nature's Outsiders, living beyond society's Pale, deriving their strength from the defiance of convention. But their Outsiderness had become a kind of norm, and they had made of it a general law, rather than simply a law of their own being, so that they had to confess themselves, in turn, a little shocked to come upon a couple, both young and lusty, diligent and well-made, who didn't fuck on sight.

211

They had made the mistake all generations make, which think that those who follow will want to be like them.

What, however, could not be gainsaid was the love that united Connie, Mellors and Cloë; it had an eternal quality. It rested on the Perfection of the Three, its ancient stability and pyramidal force. It wasn't even personal, really. Connie-and-Mellors' love had spilled over into Cloë and, though she was free as an individual to take her own form (and virtually had), in another sense, and purely, she was part of the Three, which some call commonly the Eternal Triangle or vulgarly vilify as Rivalry itself. These were *not* rivals: they were Bridges to one another. And perhaps, in the end, this was the reason that Cloë was unable to make a Bridge for Eddie.

In the term and circumstance of their involvement with one another it didn't matter all that much. Most of us know what we need deep down and can pluck the fruit when it's ripe and ready. If it isn't, best leave it on the tree; run around the garden, have some fun. Cloë had a fine sense in this matter: she deleted nothing before it was due. And so she lived, more or less, without regret. She would wait and mould herself into her own form, the moral and sexual person she was. Waiting was part of the law of her being, the necessary maturation of herself.

For Eddie, also, this waiting was right, though he came upon it by stumbly inhibition - being a foreigner born, the dicates of convention - rather than by seeing that it actually was so (men are so much less adept in these matters). And didn't he realize in his heart of hearts that she was *not* the one to take him across? He had the finesse, no doubt about that. What's more, we were only in the early forties: the old Moral Tone still had some shine.

Also, the emphasis of the War had changed. On 22 June, 1941, Hitler put into operation the decision taken the previous December, and Nazi Germany invaded Soviet Russia. It didn't make much difference to the farm, but the bombing of Sheffield diminished considerably. The blackout wasn't lifted, of course - it wasn't till Final Victory -, but there was now less sense, as the War progressed, of Britain being Hitler's special target. When on 7 December, 1941, the Japanese attacked the U.S. Fleet in Pearl Harbour and, four days later, Hitler responded by declaring war on Uncle Sam, the Theatre had extended to global proportions. The WWII all-out Bloodbath was on.

It was a question, really, of relative intensities. The Old Order had given stability (a certain set sense of values and meaning) and this was being blasted for the second time, as minds like Nietzsche's had already been blasted by the terrible, explosive truth of Nothing. It was this that was working from the inside out: first the Dread, then the Pits, the Acts of War.

212

Life went on in all its simple beauty, while Death was raging everywhere. It was a time of ultimate polarities. What, and on what basis, would one choose? Eddie was apt to have chosen death - not consciously, perhaps, but for other, complex reasons, both metaphysical and intimate-personal. First of all, he was a 'Kulturmensch', as any Freud from Vienna must be. Which meant, not only did he love the arts, but he had a deep sense of soul-history: he knew where we were going, so to speak. Though vague, his feeling was unequivocal; it cohered, moreover, with the Great Man's theories: that our western, white male civilization was in the throes of self-destruction. It had come to the end of its terrible Tether. It wasn't just Power and Conflict out there; it was the frantic unleashing of Thanatos in all of us. We were driven by the death-wish, like it or not.

Secondly, of course, there were the intimate concerns, which in his case meant mainly his relationship with his mother. It wasn't that he hadn't freed himself; he had to an extent: he was here, after all. But ever and again he circled back - through letters, through visits, through brown paper parcels - like a homing pigeon, inalienably, to its nest. Thus, he remained at-one-remove, unmade.

Cloë, by contrast, was given over to Life, in all its detail and intimacy. She seemed to have a sense of what was what, simply by being there, being who she was. From this she didn't err; she just focused in on it. The freedom her parents had won and enjoyed came to her naturally, as a right, from the first. It gave her a platform, for which they had had to fight, and, like all children, she took it for granted. And being, as children are, the essence of her parents, she was in no confusion as to means and ends. It was really freedom they had been looking for, and sexuality had been the door to it. This was now their gift and the secret of their bonding, both with each other and with her. She knew this intrinsically, better than they did, which was why their bawdiness somewhat repelled her. Don't parents understand *anything?*

She also felt it incumbent upon her to go-one-further and -better than them. She must quickly, she thought, like an able student, interiorize what they had learned from Life. Quickly, and not go back on it: not make it her dolorous destiny to do the same things all over again. For this was the constant Push of the Elders - well-wishing, wise, intelligent or not. They all universally seemed to want to make one do exactly as they had done. Where is the freedom in that? Tell me!

Hers was a generation which would hold to the right, consolidate and firm up what the previous one had won. That, at least, was how she saw it herself. And Eddie would go away, she knew it.

The farm is stuck now, held in stasis, while the War goes on and the seasons wheel. Eddie is laying a concrete yard, which Mellors certainly

213

could not have done. He is very exact and hard-working, very good. But he has lost some sense of Being Here. Nothing has happened to root him in England, and he constantly dreams of life back in Vienna - schoolfriends, that girl, trains and tribulations. He is going nowhere, that's the impression. He is impatient for the War to end.

3

When it did he went to Sheffield University, having gained a place some years before but deferring it for wild, old, idealistic reasons (also because the War was on). He took digs in the City and left the farm. But he was back again inside a few weeks: Cloë, his one-time poet-friend, was getting married - 'ahead of time', as someone said. It was her first and only moral indiscretion, and patently unimportant; they would have married anyway. Her father, Mellors, gave her away, and two girl cousins from Tivershall were bridesmaids.

Eddie was shyly hovering about, wondering when it would be best to leave, when Cloë came up and touched him on the shoulder. 'Come back and see me sometime,' she said. 'Me,' he thought, 'not us,' and left. And it wasn't until he was back in town that he realized she was unhappy in her match. She had miscalculated somehow, and now it was too late. Inexorably, he and she had missed each other.

For simplicity's sake Eddie studied German, with Psychology as a subsidiary subject. It was a combination he would like to have reversed but, unlike Vienna, the North of England offered little scope for treating hysterics, and he wasn't drawn to the theoretical side. No, he was a pragmatist, a man of action, and he saw himself already in a teaching role, washing away the recent past and introducing students to the glories of Goethe. It was a vision he would have to pay heavily for among the rank-and-file of English youth, many of whom wouldn't accept even him. Nevertheless, it was the right place to be, and he plugged away in the library every day.

He didn't know quite who she was, but he saw her there every time he went in. She was obviously staff - by her age, by her manner. He made up a story about losing a book and asked one of her colleagues who she was.

- O, that's Miss Dakin, said the librarian casually. What book was it?
- Er . . . Steppenwolf.
- Original or translation?
- Original.
- I'll go and see if it's been handed in. You might check the German Section yourself.
- I might.

214

But, of course, he didn't: he'd got the information he wanted. And, though at times he might identify himself with the fictional heroes of German Letters - Harry Haller, Old Werther, Josef K. -, he was in no doubt now that he was on his own track. The latent romanticism of Freud, which he expunged by calling himself a scientist, came rushing to the fore in Eddie. He was twenty-five but inexperienced, and the sexual instinct plagued and fretted him. This Miss Dakin, with her auburn hair, occasional glasses and quiet, remote mien, attracted him strangely, though, truth to tell, she had probably never even noticed him. She wore a pleated grey skirt and a pink wool sweater, and she was neat and trim; she looked self-contained. 'Like Cloë,' thought Eddie, giving himself a start.

He had avoided the rough-and-tumble of going up to University, the promises of orgies and drinking till one dropped. He wasn't gregarious by nature and, though he wanted to be accepted, for a well-bred, refined, 'upper-middle' Viennese, it smacked too much of Anglo-Saxon vulgarity. He was not sure, either, whether these drinkers and talkers actually delivered when it came to womankind. In any case, it all seemed crass and immature.

Not that he was a man-of-the-world: the next few weeks, even months, proved that. He would wait at the entrance to Firth Hall for Miss Dakin, follow her - at a discreet distance, of course - down Western Bank, across Glossop Road and, eventually, down to Paradise Square. And there, in a blackened block of buildings, which seemed exclusively used as offices, she entered a small door and was lost from sight. He stood in the Square by the sombre Cathedral, looking up at the building - a wall of eyes - and, as the year drew on and the nights drew in, he saw two eyes closed by curtains from within. He stood until he was so cold he trembled. And still he stood, looking up at the night.

It was as if she had entered a door marked 'private', on the other side of which lay the Secret of Life. In entering that door she had entered upon something - he knew not what, perhaps just ordinary things; but, for him, they were bathed in a lambent light (the kind of light one puts on in the evening) - and behind her spread that special soft sky, with the white stars emergent, the night-sky of Egypt. She was spreading, her breasts were dipping to the earth, and he was putting forth in his Golden Boat from Memphis. He was upright like the Rams of Amun-Ra, like the Ram himself, who was a figure of God. His entire body-being was golden and luminous, he had come from the Pyramids; he was utterly transformed. She was his blue Cloak, his enfolding dark Chamber, and in her Night-body she drew him upwards to herself. He sailed on and on through the furrowing waters, calling now to her through the acres of the night . . .

- Tha wants to put a co-at on: tha'll catch thi death.

The man was looking him straight in the eye.

- Yes, yes, I must, Eddie stammered.
- Woman, is it? Ah shouldn't bother if ah were thee.
- O, no, of course not.

And Eddie was off. Strange thing, that word 'bother', he thought; Cloë had used it that day on Stanage. 'Don't bother': it seemed to be the national motto. As soon as anything became intense - an idea, a feeling, a formula even - they put the lid on it and snuffed it out; they said 'Don't bother' and killed it dead. No wonder, under these chilling low skies, it was such a dull, grey, drab country. Yet he so much wanted to be part of it!

He took the man's advice and went back to his lodgings, where a hot meal was waiting, punctual as usual. Mrs. Morecombe, his landlady, cooked and 'did' for four young men, which pleased his mother no end. He sat with the others, an alien, apart, though he got through his Lancashire Hotpot with zest. He was still somewhere on the waters of the Nile, looking up at Nut, her enfolding blue Body; he was still a stranger in Paradise Square.


He haunted the library where Miss Dakin worked, finding a million excuses to be there. He even tiptoed after her about the place, as if the very quietness of light tread and whispers were a pact between them, a mute Confessional. She looked at him sometimes out of the corner of her eye but, apart from that, she didn't seem to know him.

It was getting on for Christmas before they spoke and, even then, it was Emma who broke the ice. He had devised a ploy for speaking to her by knocking a book off a shelf as she passed and, while she paused, just bumping into her and then, well then, just bumping into her - as if she were an old friend, so to speak. He knocked the book off the shelf, all right, but he didn't dare bump into her - at least, not physically - and she simply bent down, picked it up and put it back on the shelf. His heart descended through his belly, down through his thighs and was about to reach his boots, when she turned on her heel and said, he thought curtly:
- Aren't you going to speak to me? You've been following me around for a month and a half.
- Two months, actually, Eddie said.

And they both smiled, a frank, straight, open, honest smile.
- I thought you were never going to notice me, he said, as they sat over coffee in a small place off Leavygreave.
- O, yes, I noticed, she said absently. But you see . . .
- Yes?
- O, nothing.
- Yes, there is. Tell me what.
- I was thinking then what I'm thinking now: Don't fall in love with me; you'll only get hurt.

- It's too late for the first, the second I'll find out.
- Not if we don't meet again you won't.
- But we can't not meet, not now . . .
- Yes, we can. I've done much stranger things than that in my life.
- I'll bet you . . .

But he caught himself, boyish, looking up. He knew she was going to be his teacher but, in another sense, they had to be equals. He was loath to become all servility and wonderment - even if, to the present moment, he had done little but follow her around like a puppy.
- I just want to tell you . . ., he began.
- No, don't say it, said Emma, flushing, rising.

And already she had turned and left, leaving magically, or so it seemed to Eddie, the price of her coffee beside her cup.

There was so much of her locked away - and not just behind that door in Paradise Square. She was smarting deeply from some wound, some lost love or agony that Time couldn't heal. Already, in his opulent Viennese way, he had made up a rich-sounding Drama around her. But it wouldn't do; he would have to get nearer.

He got up from the table and paid at the till. People were coming in early for lunch, and each time the door opened a gust of raw air blew in off the street and housed itself there. They stamped the slush from their shoes and boots, and with every person entered there was an increment of black water. The faces and stamps were a blur of movement, a mechanical motion of human flesh. Eddie thought with horror, 'I could shoot them all.' The only face he could see was Miss Dakin's, doe-like, pained, slightly flushed beneath her hair. He realized that he knew nothing about her: he didn't even know her first name. Yet he wanted to take her and ease her pain; he wanted her face to flush with his blood.

There was no going back to the library now; no vigil, either, in Paradise Square. He remembered the poems he had written for her and, on an impulse, he went back to his digs and copied them out in a fresh volume. It was the kind of little book beloved of poets, with silky smooth paper, bound in purple cloth. He copied the poems out meticulously, as only lovers will, who dread every imperfection, and he dropped them through her letter-box in Paradise Square, with a single red rose and . . . No, not 'and': there was no more. But I do know he had thought of sending her a card, with, on it, the words she had forbidden him to say, the words 'every woman wants to hear'. He didn't send it, and he was right - this 'every woman' would have hated it. He might be a 'Minnesänger' on a mediaeval horse but, when it came to superfluity, he had the Freudian touch.

As he walked away across the darkening square, with the pigeons returning and the cathedral lit up, he saw her in his mind's eye reading his poems and wondering what actually *he* was about. 'Equality, Miss

217

Dakin. Equality.' He said it out loud and, as he did, he thought it might be nice to spend the weekend at the farm.

He had never been like a son to Connie and Mellors, that was the refreshing thing about it. They had never usurped or squatted on his Patch; they had given him what he most needed - Space. He sensed it as soon as he entered the yard; it was there, waiting for him, like a gift. And he felt proud and happy, looking at the yard, which once had been a veritable quagmire, that the place had been improved by the labour of his hands.
- Come in, lad, and take a rest from thi books. Tha looking pale - is it ovverwork?
His eyes were twinkling with innuendo.
- More like an unattainable virgin, put in Connie, with greater insight than she realized.
And, walking through that open door, into the familiar, relaxed, warm place, Eddie realized how fraught he had become. The tension rolled off him, like dirt in a bath.
- I've had a lot of studying to do, he said stiffly.
- Aye, we know, said Mellors, with a smile. Then, more philosophically, he added:
- Tha should learn to live first, then study after.
That, of course, was what Eddie was trying to do. Most of the students were doing the same. Raw, immature, first-time-away-from-home, they were trying different poses: getting drunk, creating m3ayhem in a mild sort of way, seeing what caps and careers might fit them. Nonetheless, it was not a happy time. For many it was worse than adolescence, when, at least, the well-tried family had been there, a cluster of friends, perhaps a church, a football team. All these networks were now breaking down, and at the end of three years - with more knowledge but less substance - a still callow, motley, untried generation would be thrown out on the Sea of Life, to sink or swim.
There was a praeternatural Angst about it, which the matrix of home had never laid bare. Whatever went wrong there had natural causes, like 'being a bad boy' or 'doing something naughty'. Here, however, the picture was different: in fact the Picture itself was exploding all the time. The reassurance of Perspective had gone and, in its place, there appeared new images - fast, tangential, allusive, vacant - to which one could relate but which had no rooted meaning. Death had raked down from the skies (Hiroshima was less than a year ago) and the Image was emerging from the rubble, determined to have a life of its own. Students sensed this and adopted one or t' other, without the benefit of anchorage. Small wonder, then, that they felt adrift and clung to

whatever Flotsam was around. It was a frightening, unhinged, blasted-open world.

When Connie and Mellors had found their peace together, after the cataclysm of WWI, the world, though blighted, had still been intact. Now it was a total Nowhere Land: the inner Fabric, the Terrain, was a Blank.

It was only-too-normal that, by mutual conjecture, they should put Eddie's strain and fatigue down to 'love'. They had themselves guided their ship by it, and it was still the most telling of all criteria. What they didn't realize - and it was partly generational - was that Love itself was undergoing a sea-change: without the promise of Eternity behind it, it was letting in water fast from all sides.

- Who is she, then? asked Mellors bluntly.
- She works in the library, Eddie answered.
- Does she now? But who *is* she?
- She's called Miss Dakin - that's her name.
- You mean, you're not on first-name terms?
- Well, no, not yet. She's older than me.
- Is she, begad? How much?
- A few years.
- An unattainable virgin lady, Connie said conclusively.
- I doubt if she's a virgin, said Eddie.
- Unattainable, all the same.
- I'm not sure; that's what it's all about.

And he laid before them in consummate detail the wandering tale of his last two months.

- Tha should 'a' married our Cloë, said Mellors, for whom the whole business was far too aethereal. She's none too 'appy wi' t' one she's got.
- Perhaps you're right, said Eddie lamely.

But in his heart of hearts it was not so. Deeply he was pushing out, falling as a leaf falls, gently, in autumn, moving in his Golden Boat softly out of Memphis. Miss Dakin was his nuptial Night, the Body of the Night-sky, receiving, enfolding. He was drifting, upright, his gaze locked on her, and she was taking him in like a wanderer.

- I must go over and see her, he continued.
- I'm sure she'd appreciate it, Connie said. As Geoff was just saying . . .

But she didn't finish: she somehow thought it indiscreet.

On the Sunday afternoon he walked down to Lower Bradfield, the village at the bottom where the couple lived. A warm coal fire was burning in the grate and a dog sidled up to him, slimly, through the door.

- Come in, Jim, said Cloë sharply. He doesn't want you.
- He's all right, said Eddie, patting his head.
- Eddie, meet John, she said, bringing him through.

A biggish man, wearing corduroys and a checked shirt, heaved himself out of his armchair by the fire. No Wild Goose this but a plump domestic Duck.

- Pleased to meet you, Eddie said. How are you?
- Can't complain, you know. Do sit down.

And he returned to his armchair and paper by the fire. Life settles on that kind of person, thought Eddie, and thereafter he goes slowly, quietly to his grave.

- Where's the little one? he asked.
- Upstairs, sleeping, Cloë said. Shall we go for a walk, while the daylight lasts? John, dear, would you mind?
- Of course not; don't mind me.

There was a sting in his voice, which he could have shot further.

- He's jealous, said Cloë, when they were outside. He gets at me in little, mean ways.
- O, said Eddie, nonplussed and hesitant.
- He's particularly jealous of you.
- Why? I've given him no cause.
- It isn't that, it's everything you represent: my earlier life - though I've told him there was nothing.
- There wasn't, either, not in that sense.
- I'm not sure he believes me, though. He keeps asking me questions about what we did. Then there's 'the other'.
- 'The other'?
- Poetry. 'Something afar from the sphere of our sorrow.' If anything, he's *more* jealous of that: it's something he just can't understand.
- But he *was* your choice, Eddie said, not unkindly.
- I know - and, of course, I *do* love him, in a way. It's just that everything seems so predictable now, not like it was when we were younger at home.
- You know, said Eddie, looking up at the sky, I always thought you'd marry someone local.
- Why someone local? Why not you?
- It never came to that, did it? And also, I mean, Cloë, I'm a wanderer.
- I couldn't live anywhere but round here, that's true.
- That's what I mean. And I had to go. I couldn't have stayed here - it's part of Fate.
- What was it your father used to say?
- 'Into every life a little rain must fall.'
- That's true, she said, That's so bloody true.
- Kismet, Cloë.

And he held her in his arms.

There was nothing more for them to say. The light was slowly ebbing away into an ocean of cloud that seemed to suck it up. The alders by the stream were black and bare. Then, as an afterthought, Cloë said:
- Do you think there's anything in it?
- In what?
- 'Something afar from the sphere of our sorrow'?
- There might be.
- Where?
- I don't know.
And, oddly, this tail-end of conversation articulated for him, like an echo to its source, the substance of something he had sensed but not *seen*. There was a thread in there somewhere - he had been following it all along - and his obsession with Miss Dakin was part of it. He intuited, he *knew* she had the Secret: she was carrying the seed of his Initiation. Though patently she suffered, she had been somewhere; inwardly she had travelled. She could take him There.
- I think there may be other possibilities, he said finally.
He stayed just long enough to look at the baby, who was gurgling in a carry-cot near the fire. 'How soon,' he thought, 'our lives are decided. Here's Cloë and John and little Tom Haddon. The triangle re-forms, the lines are set, and all we can do is fall in with them. And I go out into the cold, dark night, a wanderer for ever, sans hearth or home.
- I'd like you to be godfather to Tom, said Cloë.
They stood together by the heavy front door.
- I'm not sure I'd be much good at it, said Eddie.
- Please, for my sake.
- That's what I mean.
- O, go on!
Startled laughter, welling tears.
He left abruptly and walked out into the night. As he climbed the lane that links the two villages and then the track up to Birches Farm, he was in no doubt as to what he had forfeited: warmth, home, security, children, dogs and fires - the whole texture and bonding of human continuity. And all for what? He didn't even know. He had wagered it all on one throw of the dice.

Things felt calmer when he got back to University. For one thing, Emma wasn't there. As he ascertained from one of her colleagues, she had been due for a week's leave and had gone off somewhere - where, she didn't say. Calm, said the ship; Doldrums, said the captain. He racked his brain but had to accept it. Failing all else, he got down to study: the Minnesänger, as chance would have it. Was she even thinking of coming back?

As a matter of fact, she had gone to the seaside, to a little place near Whitby she had been to several times. She liked to walk up to the old ruined Abbey and read, adjacent to one of the steps, that poem of Caedmon engraved in stone. She felt she became herself again there; she threw off the slough of the library and work. She had brought Eddie's rose and poems, of course, and they impinged on her and pressed for an answer. She couldn't find one, not straight away.

The trouble was, this boy had a line to her. His poems weren't just fatuous pieces of praise: he had tuned in somehow to the rhythm of her being and had reflected that being in the rhythm of his verse. Put another way, it wasn't just emotion, as his clumsy, failed stumblings had made her think. He had a real intuition of what she *was* and, reflected in his words, she saw herself more whole. Moreover - and this was the astonishing part - it stirred her in a place she couldn't argue with, the place where everything assumes its true form, angularities cease, the dread Edge melts. She had met someone equal, a 'würdiger Feind'.

She took a long walk on Three Mile Sands, then climbed the steps to the ruined Abbey. It was a blustery, clear day and the air was icy; it blew through the stonework and vanished windows as it blew through her brain and made it sharp. She was coming out of her blur, at last.

It was Freud, I think, who first pointed out that Trauma can bury a life for ever. It sets up various automatisms, the function of which is to prevent further hurt, while deep down, in quick-wince, the life withers and dies, unable to escape from its Dungeon of Pain. Some such description might have fitted Emma, as she felt the first snowflakes touching her face and the thrust of recollection made itself felt. She had not been able to look at it before. Oblivion was better. Memory was pain. But the rhythm of the poems was moving in her roots; she could not ignore its silent working. It was like a dark and germinal spring, a subterranean ache, which forced its own focus. The dullness began to recede from her brain, as the east wind quickened - she was at the top - and the flakes fell around her like confetti at a wedding. She was looking though a Zoom at her own broken past, at the beast of it lying there, wounded and dead. And, as she looked, it took on sharp shape, like an ibex on a mountain, sunning himself. It was quickening as she was, Observer and Observed, and its head turned towards her with the nuance of a smile.

No, it had not been easy at all; it had been all ache and agony for a while. Evelyn hadn't come back to her, but she had thought at first she had gone on tour or taken one or other of her unpredictable turns. It hadn't been till much later, in the New Year, that she had heard the news - from Evelyn's mother, of all people. And she had simply not known what to do: the pivotal force of her life had gone. She found herself bleeding constantly; she was anaemic, wretched, no energy at all. She had never thought that it might come to this.

But it had, and there was no analgesic for it: she had to sit with the closing of that World. How little we know about the occasioning of Beauty, how little we suspect that it can ever dry up! In its fulsome flood we float and are joyous; our whole life takes on a different hue. Emma had become so mellifluous with Evelyn: whatever the difficulties, she had been made new. Her hair had grown out lustrous and long; her limbs were lithe, her face aglow. An inner radiance dwelt with her, such as normally only children have. And she cast around her this haloed World. Others felt it; they responded in kind. She had joined the Stream of bodily Perfection, whose greatest explosion had been in Greece; anciently, she had touched on that World. It was not part of history but living now, and anyone who was awake and alert could find it.

Then, at one blow, it had been destroyed. Back in Britain, Emma languished. It wasn't caught and colourful here - a damp climate, mute colours, the volume turned down - it smacked too much of resistance and rain. And she hadn't the skill to carry on alone: she needed a Teacher, as we all do. She realized it strongly as soon as she got back. Dancing on her own was a meaningless business; she was just a novice, always had been. Also, she was still in love with Evelyn.

She wanted the taste of Evelyn on her tongue, the sweat of her body purling into hers; she craved the lost acres of nakedness. How good it had been, the whole thing, how rich! What folly and madness had made her come away? Evelyn was strong, a master, yet a child. She wanted to be overborne by her, to surrender to her in every cell; and then to come back, rich, flushed and renewed, and take her, break her, make her whimper like a child. She wanted the whole range of desire made real. And they would never even see each other again!

It hit her like wave upon wave of the sea - brutally, finally, inexorably. It hit her like a boxer might hit an opponent, knowing he had weakened: can't wait to knock him out. It hit her blindly through every aching pore. That was the first blow, and she bled from it.

The second was subtler, slower, more insidious, emerging like a cloud on an otherwise clear day. It was spreading, nonetheless, getting thicker, going further, blotting out the horizon which rimmed off the Greek sea. Its palling, paralyzing name was Remorse. It entered the mouth where Evelyn's tongue had been and it seeped through every membrane of her body like a poison. She flagged and went flabby, couldn't be bothered any more. She slackened till she fitted the Snot-world of Everyday.

And always it was there, like a glass of flat beer: Why did you leave her? Why did you let her down? She went over in her mind a thousand million times the instance of their parting, her decision to go. Was it enough that she had just thought of Brewston - if she had, in fact, *just* thought of Brewston? Wasn't it their relationship that had mattered above all? She knew that Evelyn was, somewhere, a child; she had sensed and slept with her terrible vulnerability. And yet she had not known how to respond. Instead of assuming her deepest feeling, the one which called for an incalculable response, she had fallen back on 'reasoned judgement' and the concrete parameters of the pragmatic mind. One could always tell oneself later, 'I acted for the best', with all the worn-out complacency the statement implies. Yes, that was how she had joined the Zombies, the mindless many, who never make the Choice. And now she was paying for it, painfully, deservedly, living with the many the zombie kind of life.

College went on - what institution doesn't? - and she accepted it as part of the Inevitable. She left her dancing 'persona' on the shelf, in the form of a snapshot from the Open Space. She went on with the groundwork of becoming a teacher. Gravity had got her. Whom does it not?

If she had had any reply to her two letters to Tristan, certainly she would have thought of following it up. But nothing came from that direction, either. Could he be 'missing, believed dead' a second time? Perhaps. We don't know. What we *do* know is that Emma was looking for a resonance, a wavelength with someone: didn't have to be him.

But gradually she resigned herself, as people do, who have loved mightily and lost. A Rift appeared in the Ground of Being, which until then had been even Flow. And, as one will, she thought it was all hers: no other person had suffered as she had! She carried on with the daily things, which, mercifully by now, were straightforward enough. She did teaching practice at a little school in Wirksworth, where the boys were rough and the girls obtuse, but somehow she sailed through it without demur and, as her supervisor said, she seemed to have the knack. It was true, she had a way with children; they seemed to warm to her right away. On her side, too, it was a help: it took her off her pedestal a bit.

Time passed, as they say, and things took their course. It was looking less likely she would ever break out. The dullness of it seeped into her, as it does into everyone: the growing-down of pain. She would eke out a corner in the Prison somewhere, a place-of-rest and -work, a few friends, a pet dog, and that would be the end of it. Schluss. Was *that* her testament to the volcanic Miss Rodd? It couldn't be - and yet it was.

The Trauma had gone in very deep, cutting through layer upon layer of soul. The pigment of it reared up, red and searing; the Rift in Being seemed ultimate, unbridgeable. It was only now she realized at what depth, with what intensity she had lived with Evelyn. It had been altogether too much for this world ('We weren't born to love one another on earth,' Evelyn had said in one ecstatic moment). And perhaps that very intensity and depth had been the real cause of Evelyn's death. For

224

who could live at that pitch for long, with Beauty streaming and Truth stirring through? None but the tragic, obviously.

And Evelyn had had that capacity for tragedy: it could not have been otherwise with her. Whatever she did - and she did practically *everything* - she never accepted mediocrity. Perhaps that was why she had had to die. The bright, strong Cloak she would always wear, but the grey? No, never; not ever. No. At no time would she have bowed to that. 'And that,' thought Emma, 'is what I'm doing now, gradually greying at the temples, in the heart. I didn't realize how much we were a team, how much I took from and owed to her. Somehow, through it all, I remained proud and single, I stayed aloof; I was just too young. How much better it would have been if we had gone together - we were outcasts, anyway - thrown ourselves together into the fire.' Thus she went on, daily, hourly, working back and forth over the same Terrain, like a farmer over patient earth.

She had, ultimately, to accept her own limitedness as a precondition for carrying on at all. Though she might feel she wanted it with all her heart and soul, she was just not capable of living at depth - not alone, anyway, not without Evelyn. Intensity was something one was born with, like a gift, and when one had a great gift, as Evelyn had had, the intensity was waiting just behind. It had fired and touched her, and she had fuelled it in return. But now that the Power that was Evelyn had gone, it was clear to her that she had been the shadow. She had mingled intensities, like a tributary, but without the Mainstream . . . Pouf! . . . her flame merely flickered on and off. The ashes were apparent: her dancing was a whim.

How could she tell Eddie any of this? And what of the time since then, until now? It was a circus of sheer impossibilities. She was like a rider at the Canyon's rim, looking down into the Void, afraid to descend. Would Eddie, if he *tried,* be able to come with her? Was *she* even sure she wanted to go?

From then on, her life had levelled out a good deal; she had stitched together a competence. In a few years, she knew, she could have got to the Top - the competition wasn't all that fierce. And she was single, which in those days meant dedicated. But she had shrunk from it then, as she was shrinking now, though for other reasons, probably more sound. There was always something nagging at her, telling her this was not enough. It might have been the residue of her time with Evelyn or a distant echo from the Moor; it came down like rain on an early spring day, reminding her of patience and the possibility of flowering. She abjured Ambition at a single stroke. What was it but an unending Treadmill, with His Majesty's Inspectors and the Board of Governors breathing down one's neck at every turn? And then the ranks of complaining parents, with their eternal protective pragmatism:- What are your contingency plans for my daughter, Sonia? Why is she getting B's, not A's? She decided, after five years, to throw it all over: education was something one did for oneself.

This had meant, of course, that she must change her profession. Librarianship was the obvious choice. Her income from the sale of Brewston, plus savings from her meagre teacher's salary, had allowed her to do the necessary training. She was glad of the lessened exposure/confrontation and, duly qualified, she came to Sheffield about the time the War broke out. She had first-hand experience of it during the Blitz: Paradise Square didn't get a direct hit, but the buildings were shaken and windows fell out. Huddled in the basement, she heard the thud of bombs, like the rumbling of wheels on a cold stone floor. And she wished, as others did, that she could get out there and fly. There was no Heaven now, only Hell - above, below.

She joined the City in its resistance to the Germans, and she joined the WAF's a short time later. It wasn't an entirely rational thing to do - more of a reaction to creeping 'embourgeoisement', thirty coming up, the stigma of the Shelf. The body of her life was becoming numb, as if spiders were building their webs in its corners. She dusted them off and put on her uniform. Oddly, she liked it; she hadn't expected to, had seen herself drowned and crumpled-looking in it. On the contrary, however, it moulded to her nicely, stretched across her thighs and tipped up her breasts. She would wear her hair pulled back tight again, as she had done ten years ago, when she began to dance. But this time it was different: it was for King and Country.


The intensity of Death was in the air. And that intensity created another, a thirst for drinking the full Cup at the Brink. Emma knew it briefly, almost without knowing, while the whole Cosmic Battle was going on up there: Asperities and Angels, the Light Force and the Dark, Messerchmidts and Spitfires, the Inferno of the Skies ...

In his blue uniform and calling her 'old girl', Oswald - 'Osie' to his friends - couldn't have been much older than she was, thirty at the most, with a handlebar moustache. He was the first man she had been attracted to, and to this day she couldn't say why. Perhaps it was his carefree, mocking manner, the way he had of making everything light. Perhaps it was the ease with which he moved through Life, his straight-on, unruffled contemplation of Death. Perhaps it was simply his physical grace.

Whatever it was, it arrested her; it made her turn a corner in herself; it broke the seal of her introversion, the corner of narcissism lurking there, which for a long time she had seen as something else. She enjoyed the double-play with the woman, that of being both woman and man. She loved the uniform because of this: it had a self-caressing touch. With men it was so much more physical and coarse - often, for the woman, hardly anything at all. Up and in, and over-and-done-with. With a woman one lingered; it was everywhere and endless.

But this man had engaged the 'animus' in her, the masculine principle, which is part of the Play. Its fine quality drew her on and out. It touched her gently in his voice and in his kisses, which were non-aggressive to a fault. They were like the rest of him, glancing, light. The feel of him was good to her.

It was part of the Height and the Flight of their encounter that they would marry one another straight after the Battle. Osie went up and came back so blithely - with such nonchalance, as if returning from a stroll - there seemed no reason to doubt the favour of the gods in their inalienable Dispensation as to who shall live. No reason at all. By Jove, no!

But the sad fact is that one day in August, 1940, Osie Proctor did not return, and Emma, the bride-to-be, suffered again the turning against her of the Screw of Fate. And what did she do? She imploded; she went under. The anaemia and bleeding started again, and by October she had been given a Compassionate Discharge. She came back to Sheffield and the wireless War. Like the rest of us civilians, she was sitting it out.

All this and more went through her brain, as she stood among the ruins of Whitby Abbey, a person poised between land, sea and sky. Why are we not like the birds, she thought, why can we not bring Messages through? There was, nonetheless, a Breath on the air, a taste of something she could hardly describe, which was like the silence between two sounds or the interval between two musical notes. If focused in on, the gap widened and deepened; it sang its own non-sound to the wind - perceptibly, loudly, continuously. It contained and held All-sound in its key, its fine vibration beyond the ear's ken. It was more real and basic than any of these - the distant waves breaking, the solid earth, the sky - it was the Sound of the Unity of Nature and Life. We missed it entirely in our cluttered world of living (what *we* called living), with its banality and strife. We were not attuned - that was all there was to it - otherwise, we would on the instant go to the No-place, the Space-between. For it was the Gap, the Empty Cup, that gave the music, held the Sound.

Emma, among the ruins of Whitby Abbey, found at that moment a place within herself, which she hadn't known since the days of the Moor. It was coming back to her, easily, strongly, that sense she had had of World-Indwelling. She had forfeited it somewhere along the line; she had put off her vestal nature, had to. Was it now time to assume it again, with a new Investiture, a fresh Initiation? Was it not time she sloughed off her dead-mind, the weary infantry of the recent past? She had miles to go, certainly, but couldn't she fly, accelerate past the standing Roman

Army, avoid Herod's wrath and be reborn in Egypt? She thought she could: it was worth a try.

5

- Your poems, I liked them, she said to Eddie, leaning across the library counter.
- O, I'm glad, he said weakly, blushing, the whole of the library becoming a blur.

It was an oval hall, like a goldfish bowl, and the eyes of the world were on the two of them. At various points there were niches and busts: poets, philosophers, bearded 'great men'. These also cast their gaze on them, with - was it only his imagination? - perhaps just a hint of disapproval. He mumbled something inaudible, then lost himself in a sea of books. He was looking straight at Principa Mathematica. Pulling it swiftly from the shelf, he went back to the counter to catch up with himself. He was thinking of what he would say to Miss Dakin, when a bespectacled young man, who had been arranging the In-shelf, bobbed up quickly - did they *sleep* down there? - and said incredulously:

- That one, is it?
- Er . . . yes, said Eddie. Please.

And before he knew it he was walking through the swing-door, clutching the mighty tome to his chest. Just out of interest, he took a peek inside: it looked like a mass of hieroglyphs, logically arranged, incomprehensible. 'A truly universal work,' he thought. But, as a matter of honour, he had to keep it out.

Nevertheless, the urgency was on him, and he waited in the corridor, which felt less exposed, at about the hour the library staff left. What if she went by with a gaggle of others? But, mercifully, she didn't: she was on her own.

- Taking up maths, are we? she said ironically.
- Not really, said Eddie, blushing, receding. I just thought . . .
- It's all right. Let's go and have tea.

He was going, man-strong, to take her back to that café, but she took his arm and led him away. They dropped down from Western Bank, crossed Glossop Road and were soon in the purlieus of Paradise Square.

- This is where I live, she said.

He felt the edge of her irony and it prevented him from saying, too obviously, 'I know'.

She opened the door with her Yale key, and what had been for him a Secret Realm disclosed itself to him quite naturally - a carpeted staircase, discreet lighting, almost music. It *was* a kind of music to him. He followed it, going up the stairs, and crossing the threshold, he absorbed its tenor, as Emma led him into her Place. Its windows, as he recalled them, looked out onto the Cathedral, and she stepped quickly over and drew the curtains.

- Not that anyone can see in here, she said.

He looked through a chink out into the Square. The Cathedral was backing its bulk onto them and, at the other end, thrusting its spire to the sky.

- It looks like an animal, he said, almost alive.

- Yes, doesn't it? said Emma. Quite alive. They took the stained glass windows out during the War and they haven't put them all back in again yet.

- What's it like inside?

- Search me, I don't know; I've never been in it. I'm not a Christian. Are you?

- Not really. I suppose I'm a deist or a pantheist.

- Oh?

- A deist holds that God is a Force in the Universe, perhaps the Prime Mover, but not personal. A pantheist feels He's present in everything - especially Nature and natural drives.

- Does He help with your blushing?

- Not at all.

- I'm sorry.

She meant, she was sorry for bringing it up, but he took it the other way and said:

- There's no-one to talk to, if that's what you mean.

- I mean . . . oh, it doesn't matter now. My name's Emma, by the way.

She had eked out her ration of tea for two and they sat down shyly at either end of the sofa.

- What do you think? she said, casting around.

- It's very nice.

And indeed it was. Emma had used all her ingenuity to make the Place look better than it was. She had worked on the functional angularities - the joints of wall and ceiling, the too-high space - and brought the eye down to focus on pictures, settle on soft cloth, travel through a doorway.

- I studied some Dutch Interiors, she said.

And indeed there was a sense, rather dulled by the darkness, of the maximizing of Light and Space. She had made a judicious use of lamps. One stood on a bookcase, another on a coffee table, while a third, a standing lamp, was over in a corner. They spread their effulgence, rather than beaming it at one, and were a welcome relief from garish ceiling-lights. An aspidistra stood by the window.

- Is it the biggest in the world?, asked Eddie.

- Not quite, said Emma. It hasn't got the gall.

The sofa backed up against the wall, with a small, low table in front of it. Opposite were the curtained windows, the illumined Cathedral, the now-free night-sky.

- Shall I pour? said Emma.

- You know, he said, I was just thinking, how wonderful it would be if we could step out of your window and fly off together into the night-sky.

- You've been looking at too many Chagalls, said Emma.

- I'm looking at *you*, he said intently.

- I can't fly.

- O, yes, you can. We're going to learn to fly, the two of us.

- Where shall we go to?

- Anywhere you like - Egypt, the Pyramids, Memphis - anywhere.

And that was the prelude to their first love-kiss.


Some time later, when they were flying into Cairo, the darkness peeling back, the stars peering through, she leant over and said to him:

- Do you remember?

Outside on the tarmac the night was warm.

# BOOK EIGHT: TRISTAN'S TOMB

I met a traveller from an antique land
Who said: Two vast and trunkless legs of stone
Stand in the desert . . . Near them, on the sand,
Half sunk, a shattered visage lies, whose frown
And wrinkled lip, and sneer of cold command,
Tell that its sculptor well those passions read
Which yet survive, stamped on these lifeless things,
The hand that mocked them, and the heart that fed:
And on the pedestal these words appear:
'My name is Ozymandias, king of kings:
Look on my works, ye Mighty, and despair!'
Nothing beside remains. Round the decay
Of that colossal wreck, boundless and bare
The lone and level sands stretch far away.

Shelley

1

Why investigate the phenomenon at all? Isn't it sufficient that Tristan disappeared? He did, but how? That is the question. How come it isn't written on a gravestone somewhere: Tristan Dakin, Wanderer, Seeker, Soldier: 1896 - 1942? But it isn't and there's nowhere, and that's the end of it. I think he has simply been suspended, but he's hovering out there, as if he were alive. We can't just bury him and have done - he defies our whittling categories.

2

He had gone through a hole in the Canvas of Reality and now he was trying to speak to us again. So picture, if you will, a scene, a room, not unlike Jenny Alpenstock's in Edinburgh. The curtains are closed and a single globe-lamp smoothes its toned light around the room. The lamp is in the middle of a circular table, round which eight people sit silently. Books of the Art, ouija boards and tarot cards have all been stacked away, and the atmosphere is quiet. They are waiting, as he waits, for the Moment of Entry.

Time stands still, but only for an instant. A rustling, as of a rushing mighty wind, tells the seated company, the Inner Circle, that an event from the Beyond is about to occur. The central séance artist, the Channeller or Medium, sways a little and calls on her connection. He is urging and wanting to bring something through.
- Can you tell us your name? she asks.
- The person wants to speak.
- Does he have a message for any of us?
- He says he knew you, some of you, once. He sends his love and blessings to the Brotherhood.
- Where is he now?
- He says he's nowhere. He needs to rest, he needs to find a cure.
- What is it ails him?
- An unfinished life. He has shed his body, but his soul can't find peace.
- Is that why he has come to talk to us?
- Yes.
They would normally have been making the table turn, but the seriousness of the situation descended on them and made them, for once, reflect on things. How could they, in all conscience, help someone like Tristan, who had assumed the form of his terrestrial life, that of an incorporeal wanderer? They were nonplussed, Sensitives though they were.
They decided, through Marjorie, their Medium, to ask him to tell them the story of his plight. They met, all eight of them, every night for a week, and I'm not quite sure how it came about, but the transcribed material (that which follows) was entitled by the Circle 'Tristan's Tomb'. Perhaps it was a case of latter-day sound-shifting (final -b for final -e) but, more likely, it was just a typing error. It does not affect what he said in the least.

3

'I wander, a stranger, among the spirits of the dead. It's not too different from ordinary human life; in fact, I see everything that's going on. What in earth-terms is thought of as so substantial - the getting-on, the getting-by, driving and arriving - is here no more real than anything else. It's part of the Play, neither more nor less, like watching/ being Hamlet: 'To be or not to be'. I haven't ceased to be 'I' over here.
'What *is* different is my own perspective on things: I've shaken free of the 'meatball mode', that sense one has during bodily existence of being chained to a personal history and to a particular set of circumstances. Here I am wide open; I *see* the world. And, so seeing, the world interpenetrates with me; it allows me to live much more 'at large'. Let me explain in greater detail. The average person in normal daily life is

aware of only a fraction of the Field - the immediate urges, drives, preoccupations, and the persistent need to feel secure. This is his reality. It is impinged on only when external circumstances loom so large they have to be dealt with - a death in the family, the threat of war, the eruption of sorrow on a mass or small scale.

'Here one doesn't live in this limitedness: one, at least, of the Veils has been removed. Here in this world - if 'world' 's the word. - it's really more like a continuum. It's much more obvious how things interpenetrate, how the War out there and the War in here are essentially part of the same Bayeux. A ripple goes out from every thought and creates a propensity somewhere else. One can't ignore it: one can watch the waves. Then just such a wave comes back to you, modified, altered, intensified. There's absolutely no way you *can't* see it.

'That's the main difference between your world and this: here consequences are irremediable and immediately perceptible as such. This makes it a kind of Purgatory - if not outright Hell, which it is for some, when they realise that what they engender they *are*. On earth one can *seem* to get away with things, though this seeming is itself impermanent. Here, behind the Veil, there is no such delusion: every action, projection, intention evokes spontaneously its proper Response. No qualms, no dithering. No Bones about it.

'Linear time makes monkeys of us all - and fairly unintelligent monkeys, at that. Identified with the physical body, we drag our separate carcasses about. And, gradually greying, fighting, decaying, we are pulled more and more to the centre of the earth, which finally absorbs us with our baggage of pain. This slow and inevitable progression is much more obvious from over here - because of the acceleration I was talking about and also because the linear perspective, the mind-in-time, yields to something else. This 'something' is what one might call the Round Moment, the palpable Emptiness which subsumes the world. In it there is a play and counterplay of forces, possibilities, juxtapositions, all of which are visible to the Seer. When there is an intersection between your world and this, the preconditions for prophecy exist. All the Prophets are Seers, actually. What they *see* is something in latent, subtle form, the manifestation of which is not yet. But from the point of view of the Prophets, the World of Vision, it is as actual, axiomatic and real as that apple hitting the ground was to Newton. It is real, because it is *already happening.* The view of events is synchronistic: they touch one another like behaviour and effect. Only in the dull, slow World of Time does one have to wait for 'evidence'. Here seeing is believing - without the belief.

'Refreshing and relaxing I would call it, in a way. Refreshing, because Vision is unimpaired; relaxing, because that Emptiness, that No-thing turns out, paradoxically, to be the Content of All. Is it the human body that is 90% water? The world, our galaxy, all matter, actually, is an infinite speck in the Cup of Nothing. Here one feels it more palpably, without the press and dross of Stuff. It's like lying back - not spare and rigid any more - in the Fluid, the Substance, of which we're all made. And not us merely - everything.

'The Round Moment is the Place-Instant (they're not really separate) where all and everything simply *is*. It isn't a question of switching parameters or changing one set of terms for another: rather, quite simply, of dropping the blinkers, which prevent us from seeing our Original Face. There is a contraction to it, as well as a rounding. By this I mean that the course of one's life shows up (like a film; one can look at it again) in terms of its essential scenes. Nothing is missed that has made a difference, but the weary, incessant tread of the days has been edited out in the cutting-room. One can see again more clearly what went wrong, how the shortfall came, what one didn't do and should have. Astoundingly, this is the way of it: missed opportunities far outweigh our meagre, squalid, little sins.

'And so, dear friends, I must tell you my story . . . I see it all now as purgatorial - not jut here-and-now, but then-and there, too. Perhaps I should begin with the sense of shortfall.

'Those who are familiar with the Findings of Archaeon - and who, in a group such as this, is not? - will recall that he ends with the fateful phrase: 'My psychic shortfall is too great.' This phrase, which I own, I have cherished and pursued, trying to discover what it might mean - not just for Archaeon in the Atlantean past, but on into Egypt and, further, until now.

'As we all know, Egypt was colonized from Atlantis. Those who were wise enough to see the end coming forestalled it by creating an Emissary Priesthood, with a Mayan and an Egyptian Chapter. Wisely, I say, because otherwise the Knowledge, that constant enquiry into interstitial Meaning - synonymous, in fact, with their capacity to move matter -, would have perished along with the Continent itself. But over they came and settle they did. The Nile itself was a concrete instance and perfect metaphor for what they were about: the Death-in-Life process, which is the clue to Rebirth. Every summer the river dwindled and every September it flooded its banks, leaving behind, as the waters receded, a ferment of silt on which anything would grow. And, because of this recurrent and reliable fertility, the bedouin and far-off, foreign desert tribes came regularly to trade and barter for corn.

'Then, adjacent, lay the patient desert, clean, unborn, its hummocks to the sky. Where else but there build the Platform of the Eye, the Finger to Sun and Stars, the Chamber of the Heart?

'There *is*, then, a link between birth and birth, between life and life, between death and death; there is a recurrent Mystery. It is to this that we are attuned or not - as cultures and civilizations, as individuals, even. And the measure of our culture is the measure of our attunement: the failure of the latter implies the deterioration of the former. This, also, we have witnessed in History's cycles; we saw it with the Romans, we are seeing it now. Only when Man is aware of the Mystery, of the life-and-death process at his own heart's core, is he able, by *participation in the Mystery,* to rejoin his own life-source - the secret, flowing Self. As part of this process, he must go through the Cross, his own appointed Place of Nought, the Door or Wall meant only for him. And he goes through it because, like Everest, it is *there.*

'These are some elements of the Understanding, which the Atlanteans brought over and the Egyptians lived out. The rest is popular, often idle, speculation - the more erudite and academic, the more idle, naturally. "How *could* they, in those days, with those methods, etc. . . .?" Yes, I know the mechanics are important, but hasn't somebody somewhere got the simple drift of what the Internal Temple is for? Forget Death Cambers - all that came later. It's a projection of the rectilinear mind, which puts Life and Death in separate compartments. For these people distinction did not imply separation: the wholesome process of dying *was* Life. This is all I have for this time. Good night.'

And slowly Marjorie came back to herself, the Circle held hands and broke up for the night.

4

The following evening they were back again and, as usual, to start with, they held hands.

- The Circle is not just a metaphor, said Marjorie, but the living embodiment of a truth. We bring through something, even with our touch.

Then the session began in earnest. In a short while Marjorie's Familiar was able to tell them that someone was 'coming through'. Tristan resumed:

'As the Findings of Archaeon make clear, the collapse of Atlantis was primarily moral, the submerging of the Continent itself a consequence. They who escaped and came to Egypt kept this ever-present to their consciousness: they had to maintain the dignity and height, without the degeneracy, of their culture. And this is the difficult thing at all times. The High Priests themselves must be above suspicion, beyond corruption, utterly intact. And, of course, for some time they were - in fact, for many centuries. Then the rot set in and Egypt ended.

'We were talking, weren't we?, about psychic shortfall. I wonder if anyone knows what this means - outside the Inner Circle, that is. It's like walking ten, fifteen or a hundred miles and realizing you're exactly where you were, with the same sign pointing in the same direction; it's approaching the dreaded last lip of a climb, slipping and falling and finding yourself at the bottom; it's seizing up in the middle of a speech, the balloon-bubble burst, the mind ablank. In short, it's the pits - and everyone knows that!

'I was back in Egypt, wasn't I? I was praising the spirit that made it great. More, I was saying that greatness of spirit is the essential ingredient in any enterprise - be it personal, national, international, etc. I was trying to show what makes things tick, and why.

'I was part of a College in ancient Memphis, one-time Capital of Lower Egypt. It was normal at that time for Pharaoh, the god-king, to gather round him a body of priests and for these priests - a dozen in number - to be, as it were, his right-hand men, counselling him and even, on occasion, governing the country in his stead. Their office, however, was primarily sacerdotal and they laid no claim to governance. It was only later, when deterioration set in and personal power and glory were his overt aim, that the whole College to a man turned against Pharaoh.

'The first intimation we had of the change was Pharaoh's plans for building statues of himself. Stone is more durable than this weak flesh, as the pyramids, temples and tombs attest. In no time the Palace, a kind of sacred precinct, was swarming and buzzing with architects. When challenged by us, who after all lived there, they said, shrugging their shoulders and clutching their blueprints, 'His Pharoaonic Majesty requests . . .' And that, as they knew, was all they *had* to say.

'Nevertheless, it bred a disquiet, a sense among us that all was not right. Since the ancient of days the role of the priest - and what was Pharaoh but the Chief High Priest? - had been synonymous with Service. "Anonymity: a priest is always anonymous," had been the watchword of Initiation. It still was, so far as we were concerned. No aberration on that score! Had not the mighty Cheops and Kephren, whose names had been used for the pyramids at Gizeh, insisted on strict impersonality? They had: there was no effigy to them anywhere. In contradistinction, they had warned against the dangers of building any kind of cult to themselves, and it was only later, out of laziness and common parlance, that their names became identified with those structures and stuck.

'A sense of alert was in the air, a feeling general and ubiquitous that something was badly out of joint. Some of us sought audience with Pharaoh - alas, it had already come to that -, while others made enquiries among the architects, whose numbers seemed to be increasing day by day. In fact, someone suggested - I forget now who - that Pharaoh was

236

promoting the architects to form a new core group with himself, thus ousting the priests from their time-honoured role. We had no investment in him, you see, whereas the architects, career-men to a fault, had everything to gain from his personal favour.

'It hadn't, however, yet reached a point where they wouldn't tell us what the plans were. They did tell us, and it was worse than we had thought: an enormous statue at Abu Simbel, with Pharaoh sitting with three of the gods; another, also sitting but alone this time, on the plain between the River and the Valley of the Kings; then a third - and this, for me, was the ultimate folly - a third in the Temple of Luxor itself. The man was ensuring that never again would one be able to think of Egypt without seeing him. What monumental, massive desecration! Where was the fine touch of Amun-Ra, who appeared only through his symbol, the sun? Where was Osiris' lightness-of-being, where Isis, his beloved: brother-sister, man and wife? They were being overshadowed, shovelled out, stoned to death by our egomaniac Master-builder.

'Eventually he agreed to speak with us, and all of us met, as we had done so often, in a small council-room at the rear of the Palace. We expressed our alarm at the rumours we were hearing, the ubiquity of architects, the rapid development of things. "Why the haste," we asked, "why the single vision? In the former time we had Anubis and Thoth, Bastet and Horus, all assisting, The god-life in everything moved subtle and quick, like the waters of our beloved Nile. Now you want to set it in stone, in the dominant Statue of a sculpted person. But this is not our culture, our mode: we are not a people of commemorative Form. What we are is intuitive, transformational; everything breathes in us of Life. Why do you want to do this, O Pharaoh?"

'He was a long time considering his reply. He argued suavely about the need for change. It was in the air, he said, the people wanted it - though I'm not sure he knew what the people wanted, unless it was better housing and wages. He said we were approaching a more human age, when the Image of Man - of Great Men - would be important. The forms of the past were good for the past, when man and animal lived closer together and so-called transformation was thought of as natural. How many poems and stories there were, where men were bewitched and turned into deer or frogs, only much later, by an equal enchantment, to be turned back into princes or kings! It was part of the vocabulary of the folk-imagination, and it was easy enough to stay attached to it. But the world was entering a new phase now, when it was Man and the deeds of men that would predominate. It would be considered primitive, even barbaric, to think of animals as the equals of Man, as if they shared an equal earth. The poor dumb beasts, with their delightful ways, were here for our purposes, each and every one. And, however the Creator had fashioned us, He had certainly intended us to have lordship over them.

This was obvious to the most advanced minds. The Architects, for instance, saw it to a man. Was the College of Priests going to drag its feet and be as, unfortunately, so often in the past, the Voice of Reaction and a Bar to Progress? He hoped not; we were all such good chaps, really: wasn't one of us he wouldn't take on board.

'He had obviously prepared himself carefully: he had shifted the ground of the argument from what he was up to personally to the general current and context of History. Perfect! Who can argue with History? And it was so uncouth and fractious of us, even to *want* to dispute things with him! Weren't we all friends together, after all? He also had been though the College, as we had. He was one of us. Was that all for today?

'Like dim-witted fools, we said it was: we were glad there had been no misunderstanding. "Not at all, not at all," he was saying loudly, as we left the council-room in a huddle and two or three Architects burst through the door, absorbing him instantly and completely in their midst. "Any trouble?" one of them asked. "Child's play, child's play," was the taut reply.

'We knew we weren't supposed to hear it, but the mere fact that he said it at all showed the contempt he had for us and the pressure he *didn't* feel under to conceal it. When a few days later word arrived that the eldest Brother was to quit the College (his place would be taken by a younger man, and his few possessions were summarily seized), we knew that the velvet glove was off and we were looking nose-first at the Iron Fist. This was confirmed when his replacement arrived: a sickly sycophant of the first water, whose obvious purpose was to spy on us, report back to Pharaoh and stifle all dialogue. We protested vigorously, but to no avail. We were never to meet again in open forum.

'It now seemed to some of us - me, included - that the integrity of our Culture was at stake. If allowed to carry out his plans, this man would reshape things in his own image and nothing would be left of what we had once known as Egypt. He had to be stopped, one way or another. We got together, some of us, in a small underground chamber beneath the Palace. We meditated, fasting for three days and nights. We were very well aware, throughout this period, of the nature of the task ahead of us: the future of Egypt, which meant the future of the world, would depend on what we decided there. In keeping with our priestly discipline, we observed a strict, unbroken silence. We prayed unceasingly for a Sign.

'On the morning of the fourth day it came. It was swift and drastic, as we had thought it might be: we were being instructed to assassinate Pharaoh! I'm not sure how the Message came. Hotep, who was supine, enunciated it: "Ye are the Chosen," he said, "of your Fathers. Ye shall do this in the name of your Fathers and of Egypt. It must be in no way a personal act. Begin to cleanse yourselves, as of today, of any thought of

238

revenge or murder. Ye are God's Priests, His Own, His Chosen. Do what ye have to do - it is required - but do it in Service, like a daily duty. Don't blench or hesitate - ye are there to *act*. But, however and whenever ye decide to act, do it when your powers are at their peak; otherwise, it cannot work. This is your fated, awaited Hour, the Place which, collectively, ye must all assume. For ye are nothing by yourselves. Wait, then, and watch. That Hour draws nigh."

'Hotep got up, as if from a trance; he was barely conscious of what he had been saying.

- We must be going, he said after some time. It'll seem strange if we're absent for any longer.

And we got up and went our separate ways, clear as to purpose but not yet as to plan.

The plan had, as it were, to come naturally, not just as the consequence of human devising. It was getting dangerous to meet, because, in spite of strict confidentiality, the air now bore a different charge and Sensitives among Pharaoh's retinue might pick it up. We did the only thing we could - go underground. The chamber of our three-night vigil had it, that much we knew: it was latent there.

'I can't really take the credit for it, but it was through my lips that the idea came. I saw Pharaoh walking up the Palace steps on a night of full moon, his retinue dispersed. He had been visiting one of the newer sites. We, the original cloak-and-dagger men, came out like stars from fixed points, all at once. We converged on Pharaoh, our daggers drawn, and left him a bleeding heap on the steps.

'This was it, then; this was our plan. There was very little discussion about it. It was preferable to poisoning for a multitude of reasons - it was cleaner, swifter, more direct. And Pharaoh would die like a sacrificial Victim: it was to be a ritual act, after all. Afterwards, we would go straight to the people, tell them what we had done and why we had done it. We would announce the founding of a People's Republic, with a Conclave of Priests as government. Later we could work out some kind of Constitution.

The new moon rose on all our hopes: it would soon be the end of Tyranny. We would set up a just and equitable regime, rooted firmly in the soil of Egypt's tradition but taking cognizance of modern trends. Pharaoh was right - things had to shift - but *we* wanted to preserve a link with the past, some stratum of Glory which couldn't be gainsaid. We wanted to go with Amun-Ra.

'The tension in the Palace was at fever-pitch. Pharaoh, who was paranoid to the nth degree, sent Eyes of his own out everywhere. They were a special unit, called Intelligence, and they sniffed out trouble like tracker dogs. Fortunately for us, they had no sixth sense, and they couldn't penetrate our network. We remained clued into one another the whole time, sure of our weapons, positions, concealment, saving it all for the fatal full-moon night.

'Pharaoh went out somewhere most days - it was typical of him to be always on the move. Even at night, as we later heard, he betook himself to different rooms, afraid lest the regularity of his resting-place should reach the ears of those who wished him harm. Ironically, there was no-one who did wish him harm: our sole preoccupation throughout had been to preserve what he was destroying. Simple enough. But he had to go.

'The full-moon night came rich and strong, as do nights in all seasons in our fabled land of Egypt. We took our ritual bath in the Nile, then climbed the short slope to the temple on its bank. It was time, as usual, for the evening prayers. There was at the altar, the Place of the Event, a peculiar sense of peace that night, as If all the transformative deities - Anubis, Osiris, Horus, Thoth - were present in a body, looking on. And the atmosphere spread among the people, come in volume because it was full-moon. God-man-animal, the whole creation, was gathered together in that open, moonlit space - almost, it seemed, for the last time, almost as if we were saying Farewell.

'Everything happened in perfect order, without the least hesitation or hiatus. And it seemed, as we blessed the people and they left, that we, in turn, had received their blessing for the deed we were about to do. Weren't *we* the proper link, after all - not this Pharaoh in his terrible Stone? We were the binding element.

'Though every man knew his position and cue, it was, nonetheless, a nerve-wracking business waiting for Pharaoh to return to the Palace. We weren't very sure where he had gone, as he made it a matter of policy nowadays not to tell any but a few close associates where he was going or the time of his arrivals. That way he kept everyone guessing, reducing thereby, or so he thought, the immediate danger to himself.

'But finally, of course, he did arrive back. He seemed to be in considerable haste, as he took the Palace steps two or three at a time. Before he reached the top, however, Hotep appeared, as we had agreed he would, and, brandishing his knife, cried: 'For Egypt and her Priesthood!' And instantly, emerging from doors, passageways, recesses, the whole College moved in and surrounded Pharaoh. "What the . . .?" he began, but it was all-too-obvious. And before any of his Associates could come to his aid - in fact, seeing what was happening, they turned and fled -, we had struck him down to pulp and gore. He lay there, massively broken, bathed in blood.

'I don't think we realized what we had done - at least, not the dreadful enormity of it. We had been solely focused on striking Pharaoh down.

But now the whole country was a different place and we had charged ourselves, by our action, with the responsibility of governing it. We had to get the people together, explain to them the why-and-the-wherefore of our deed and show them that from now on things would be different. They had only to listen to us, it was so. No-one need be afraid, we must say that, no-one else was going to be killed. What we had done was for the good of Egypt, and the good of Egypt was their good, too.

'The very next morning, in the open square, we decided to speak out before the people. Hotep assumed the role of speaker. It was true, he said, what they had heard: Pharaoh *had* been assassinated. Hadn't they all been aware of what he was doing - the statues of himself, the self-glorification? He had wanted to change the Face and Fate of Egypt. Was that what they, too, wanted for their Land? Of course, they didn't! (some cried out, "No!") Didn't they, the people, want more say in their affairs? ("Yes, yes!") And it was going to happen. Now that Tyranny was dead, things would be better: we would be equals, one with another.

'In this way History might have been rewritten and the first Democracy appeared at Memphis, Egypt. As it was, however, Realpolitik, that invention of the human brain way before Hitler, supervened in the form of Pharaoh's son. The astute eighteen-year-old - does it reside in the *genes*? - had overnight, literally, got an army together, which, at the very moment Hotep was speaking, arrived in Memphis, bristling with weaponry. Needless to say, they didn't stop to reason, argue or even speak to the people: they hacked into them with iron force, massacring anyone who stood in their way. The people fled to the open side, where another phalanx of soldiers appeared, stiff and deadly like a sheer rock wall. They gutted people as they ran at them, and soon, between the advancing and the static, there was an open gash a thousand bodies thick. It pulped, it reared, it heaved, it bled inwards; it drained to a turmoil of flailing limbs. Hotep was gone, dragged from the podium, one already with the crimson boiling stream. And, in spite of the violence, there was an eeriness about it, the dense dumb quiet of Inevitability. We had made some dreadful mistake with the world, had thought we could bend it in a good, true way. Yet here it was - bloody, triumphant, unmaskable - showing Power's teeth and Power's naked claw. We were helpless against it, just a bunch of cloistered priests, our dreams of enlightenment broken, bleeding on the ground. And, like the people whose lot we had wanted to improve, who are born and who die in misery, we slipped through any hole in the military barrage and ran for our lives as fast as we could.

'It didn't take long for the Old Regime to establish itself with redoubled vigour. Every man, woman or child who had been on the square that warm spring morning was put to death - axiomatically, without a qualm. But Pharaoh's son - now Pharaoh himself - wasn't satisfied with that: he wanted all the 'perpetrators of this hideous crime' (so it was labelled and bruited about) winkled out and brought to book. Anyone who harboured a 'criminal' (the whole remainder of the College was such) would be publicly flogged and then put to death. There would be no mercy, only slow wrath: the 'traitors' would die a lingering death, to the open taunts and jeers of their compatriots. Never again would the invidious priesthood raise its head in defiance of its king. New priests, appointed by Pharaoh himself and loyal only to him, would take its place.

'We, the few, knew the game was up. It was a matter of a thousand years: we had wanted to perform a millennial act, to put our stamp on the shape of things. And we had failed; obviously, we had failed. There was no group solution any more, though a thread of communication remained. It was now up to each one - not all were still alive - to find out for himself what he should do. You see - and I feel I can say it to this group -, one or two of the College were very high Adepts, whose capacity for self-perpetuation was vast. They decided they would stay 'alive', in bodies well-wrapt and mummified, whose maintenance only they could ensure and from which the heart would *not* be cut out, in tombs down secret channels no-one would ever find. The rest of us would help them in this task, whose broad aim was, as they put it to us, to create a Locus of spiritual Energy so powerful no evil could touch it.

'The world, they said, was in for a bad time. It was all-but-the-end for Egypt now. Pharaoh's new College of Priests was a sham: it would be peopled by self-seeking sycophants, who would debase the Priesthood and make it Black. Out of a desire for self-continuity, these people, also, would be mummified and entombed, fostering and furthering the evil in the world. And at some future date, now far hence, their tombs would be opened by strange people called Archaeologists, who, without knowing it, because they were ignorant, would release on the world the evil held therein. This - and the whole Dream began to be prophetic - would contribute to another millennial Confrontation, compared with which the present one was small, played out on a vastly larger Stage and involving the lives and deaths of millions.

'All this the Master predicted calmly, serenely, with the Light of one who knows himself. His face, indeed, shone with beatific radiance, even while he spoke of the direst things. He was of the High Line, now about to be corrupted, of the Pharaohs and Priests who themselves had been Adepts, for whom mummification had been a rite, an absolution from egohood. Now a man of Stone Visage had shut that out, had ensured by the petrification of himself that the whole Higher Music would be no more heard. For, of course, the Plans were going ahead: the statues would be bigger and better than before.

242

'We laid him to rest at the moment of his choosing, in a place on the West Bank, deep-down, unfindable. He said he would be there - and, even in Dream-terms, it seems an incredible thing to say - he said he would there till the end of the world. "You mean, till the end of the present Cycle?" my equally nonplussed neighbour asked. He looked a non-look of perfect calm, as the radiance of his being welled out and around and his speech, like his breath, withdrew from him. We wrapped his body in fresh-washed linen, laid him in his tomb and took our leave. The Grace of his Being vibrated within us, as we quit the dark tunnel and stepped forth into the daylight.

'It had become a new and terrible Day. Along with eliminating 'the remnant', as he called it, Pharaoh was determined, in all his youthful vigour, to wipe out for ever all traces of the past. The gods, including Isis and Osiris, were to become part of the furniture of History: he alone was the sole God-king. Bow the knee and worship him! And for those who didn't? Exile or death.

'Day One was the day of his accession to the throne, the very day after his father died. The calendar of Egypt was being rewritten, as, with non-stop, high-speed invention, the new man made the country synonymous with himself. It was all sawn-off, reduced somehow, a far cry from our entombed and glowing Master. Ruthlessly rolling, the wheels moved on.

'I had to take my own decision, as all of us did who were left behind. And here I come back to my psychic shortfall, the inability to cross the Lip . . . '

His voice was becoming indistinct; Marjorie, also, was getting tired. It had been a charged and potent session and, at the end, they held hands for much longer than usual.

5

'It presents itself in the form of Choice,' the invisible Dream-time Tristan continued: 'this-that, black-white, neither-nor, up-down.' These are the categories of studied Thought. I wasn't ready then, nor am I now, to see beyond them to a different Ground. What I feel is the *necessity* for such a seeing, and I would like to share this feeling with you. Step out, be urgent; don't waste time!

'Exile or death I took as definitive: there was, for me, no third possibility. I didn't have, as our shining Master had, the capacity to 'live' for a thousand years and more. I didn't have anything but what I stood up in.

'In spite of the spies and the soldiers everywhere, I managed - it's part of a priest's repertoire - to stay out of harm's way for quite some time. It was time pending, of course, not time enjoyed: pending which path I was going to take. I fasted, I prayed, I cried out for a decision, but Heaven had retreated and left me to myself. *I* had to find out - not God.

'The difficulty lay with being alone. I had always thought I cherished it. Wasn't it the acme of spiritual endeavour? But now that I had it I didn't want it; I couldn't even stand it for long! I needed the Bond of Brotherhood. I told myself I shouldn't feel like this, and I pressed myself into a monkish mode. A life of exile was homeless and free: one was attached to no place, nothing, no-one. What held me back from embracing it?

'To tell the truth, I did actually try it. I set off towards the Libyan Desert, with the hot sun rising, the morning aglare . . . No, now I remember, I *didn't* actually do it: I saw myself *in my mind's eye* setting off westwards, the sun rising, etc. But I didn't have the courage for it, I didn't have the Enlightenment - neither the illumination, nor the lightness-of-being. To me it seemed an act of desperate folly.

'At that blinding moment the decision was made . . . I walked out a Priest, and a proud one, to the end.'

6

The Circle met again the following evening, anxious to hear the continuation. What happened, however, wasn't at all what they expected: they had nourished the hope of 'further tales of Egypt', but what they got was, first of all, silence, then a colossal switch to the contemporary world. Tristan was talking, and would talk at length, about the Millennium, Stalingrad.

It was as if he were shuffling to his feet, clearing his throat, about to speak. Marjorie's face had become glazed and vacant, as it always did when the session began. She might have been adjusting a microphone, quelling the audience, pouring a glass of water - anything to ensure that the invited Guest would be at his ease; he would come through O.K.

'I wandered through aeons,' Tristan began, 'popping up in places of special Potential. I almost became a disciple of the Master of Galilee; in fact, I was in his entourage for some time. I could and would have become an Apostle, but something wasn't right in the Chemistry. Even *He* gave me that feeling: that I wasn't meant to follow anyone. I was, nonetheless, attracted by His Presence and drawn into the ambit of Secret Brotherhoods. These, as the Inner Circle is aware, have been the Guardians of the Knowledge from the first. It is only now, in this post-war world, that they have the duty, even the right, to open the Gates and release it on the world. Egypt, in its uncorrupted phase, was the repository of the Eternal Gift. Later, well, it passed elsewhere - into the Semitic, then into the Graeco-Roman World. By then, however, other things had intervened, and it became a matter for the cloistered few.

'If you hadn't noticed, I have the knack of failing, a way of being worked off by the Edge. The Cathars, of course, were doomed from the start: their no-holds-barred freedom was their doom. I was, nonetheless, part of that movement, with its glorious communal love-and-brotherhood. Too much for this world, though; too beautiful. The Pope's men came and got us; we were burnt alive, and another possible Turning-point was missed.

'So my story, in a way, is the story of mankind, in this sense - and I'll put it as a question: "Will we ever be able, at the vital juncture, to push through - as a race and individually - to the point where we reach Regeneration? Or shall we wander for ever, dead souls in Purgatory, looking for the True Ground but missing our cue? I put this to you, the Inner Circle, because this, for me, is what it hinges on and because everyone now with the slightest Intuition should be working for the Greater Goal.

'It's not because I've reached it that I speak, nor that I'm part of the Company of the Elect - far from it: I've made dreadful errors, none greater than during my latest phase on earth. I wanted something, someone, so badly that I turned a wrong corner, and here I am. Here I am, waiting, drifting, asking, hoping against hope that she will speak.'

- Who is she? asked Marjorie.

- Emma Dakin.

- Emma, she repeated. Please carry on.

'I got her letters, finally, some time in early autumn in Greece. "Grieve or grieve not, but don't come back - EVER." That was her final sentence. Mine, too. I was being executed all over again, dashed, cut out from the Land of the Living. I felt it as an inward, existential gash, like that which befell the murdered crowd in Egypt. I wandered out across the blighted island, where I had waited in my starving lusts for the return of the Dark Lady, who never came. For she was not She: she was not coming back.

'The Wall had reared itself, white and sheer, the blank and impenetrable cliff-front, the Drop. I stood looking out over the blistering sea to the sharp horizon. No Black Sail. Of all things wanted . . . it was but a dream. I had such a purgatorial sense of myself, such a feeling of being a light-struck soul, that I pinched myself to make sure I was real. I *was*; I was in a body for real.

'A mood of panic swept over me. I was all-in-pieces, like a shattered glass. What's more - and it was like a blow to the stomach - the breaking of the Dark Connection seemed to sever me bleakly from the world. I was adrift, washed-up, like a fish on the shore. All my normal functions, even breathing, were like a fish's exposed to the sun. Thus fretted and rent, I stood on the top, looking down at Sappho's Rock. I would go down, as she had gone . . .

'God only knows what happened next, but I found myself (Had I passed out? Must have) on a ledge about ten feet from the top. Moreover, there was no way back. I thought at first that I was completely trapped, then I noticed a fine crack, down from the ledge, into which I was able to jam a toe. I lowered myself, using toe and finger jams, to a point where I could swing out and grab a spike, below which descended a scree-like, broken gully. I was still 100 feet above the sea but, paradoxically, this crazy descent - a little suicide of its own - brought me to myself and calmed my nerves. The body had taken on the brain.

'It was a simple matter to reach the bottom and find shelter in a rough rock cave. There I stayed for three days and nights, absorbing the lull of the rocking sea, held by it, as in a womb. And for three days and nights I never even thought of how I was going to get away. The rhythms of the sea breathed into me; they calmed and cleansed me and brought me back to life.

'On the fourth day morning a fishing-smack went by, which I hailed with a shout and a vigorous wave. The boatman was willing, for a small consideration, to row me back to the small harbour. From there I could get off somewhere fairly quickly: didn't matter all that much where. Miraculously, I had - I hardly ever did - stuffed money in my pocket and paid my bill. I would leave it - letters, everything. Now was the time to make the break.

'There was a boat to Patmos leaving that morning. From there I knew I could get back to Athens. Moreover, as I later discovered in a bar, there was a rumour going round about a love-struck foreigner, who had disappeared without trace from his hotel and was said to have perished on Sappho's Rock. His hour had come; they had seen it in his face. A fraught, distraught - a hopeless case. But none of them, for some reason, identified him with me, presumably because, however we get there, nothing seems more normal than sitting in a bar. Nevertheless, I hid myself behind an incomprehensible Greek newspaper.

'Just before mid-day the boat set sail, and I was glad to be away from that disappointed island. Truth to tell, I was getting sick of islands: one soon begins to feel a prisoner on them and to yearn for open space on sea or land. Was I bitter that Evelyn had not returned? It wasn't fated - that was all. I left for Piraeus that very same evening and never went back to the Dodecanese.

'Along with Benares and Jerusalem, Athens was one of the great Centres of the Light. That was in ancient times, of course, though something of the True Light must always remain. It had been overborne for centuries by the Turks, who, with the exception of a handful of

Dervishes, had but little understanding of the Things-which-are. There had, after 1821 and Independence, been a certain resurgence of Interest, but it was difficult to know how/where to locate it. Often there is no actual Lodge, just a Locus of Power, like the Parthenon. But I had been to the Parthenon and found it bleak. What I needed was Community.

'The White Brotherhood traces its lineage back to the biblical Solomon, himself a Gnostic and a White Magician. They met every Thursday at a house on 40 Ekklesion, talked, prayed, channelled and performed their special rites. Indistinguishable on the street from the rest of the populace, it was on the inside that a Change took place. They were networked by a series of esoteric cells to other Brotherhoods throughout the world, including the one-time 'Münchener Kosmiker'. And that's how I came to hear about the NSDAP, whom I had thought of at first as an offshoot of the Brotherhood. They were going to cleanse the world, they said, of all its current filth and confusion; they were going to usher in the millennial Third Reich.

' My impression was, I had reassumed my destiny. I was - and I can see it now - a political novice, far too prone to take things literally. But it sounded good and somehow it accorded with my own ambitions for myself. I felt that, inwardly, I had reached a dead end. I had tried to be fraternal, loving and giving, and at every juncture I had been smashed. You may reason that, from a higher point of view, the whole unfoldment of the soul takes time (what's a life or two here-or-there?), but my endemic feeling was: Enough! I wasn't willing to be battered any more. What is the Divine Spirit, anyway? Is it just some simpering, smiling Form, that bends and yields at every touch and whim? No, it is mighty, powerful, destructive: it brushes lives aside, like mud huts in a flood.

'Was it in a gathering of Brotherhoods of Faith that a new Existence could be born? No, it wasn't like that at all. God came through with fury, with Napoleon. And, like Napoleon, He wrecked, burned and murdered; and then He made things new again. Who could say that a daemonic man of genius was further from God than a cloistered monk? If the religions and cults of the world had failed, as they seemed to have done, to bring about the New Order, perhaps it was time for another kind of strategist, one who stopped at nothing to put things right.

'This is what I was thinking then, as I hung around Athens, homeless again, seemingly shut out from everyone and everything. I didn't want to go back to England: somehow it smacked of neurotic withdrawal. In any case, what would I go back for? Brewston was over - that much was sure -, had been for years now, perhaps for ever. I couldn't remember one single clear day.

'No, it's true, one can't go back. In any case, it was not my mood. I felt I had outgrown the littleness of England - even Scotland had been an advance on that. I wanted to live Life on a larger scale, in some vast

247

metaphor of Good vs. Evil, in which, naturally, I would choose the Good. But what *was* the Good in this fractured age? Would it have been good to die on the battlefield, as my comrades did near Passchendaele - or on the Somme, the Marne, at Verdun, Vimy Ridge? What had I been saved for, finally? To stand on a bank in a cold, lonely village and watch a body being planted in a grave? To wait on a blighted island for a woman who never came? There was no sense to it, actually.

'It was obvious to me, in this nexus of Nothing, that I - and I alone - must choose. Nothing was given; nothing was real. Everything passed in a vast Miasma, like a caravan of camels going by in a mirage. Only when one seized the Moment, literally grasped it and committed oneself, did any semblance of the Real come through. Even this was not totally real, but one felt real in it, and from that one could act.

'I had to arise from the Bed of Mediocrity, in which, so it seemed, I was slowly submerging. Yes, I had to go partway up the Mountain and get, if not a view of the Other Side, at least a wider and clearer view of this one. Thus, gradually, imperceptibly almost, I moved towards Germany, the Eliminator of Ills.

'This, of course, is a potted version, a mimicry of what actually took place. For years I was drifting, wandering, searching, uncertain when and where to put my feet down. It was a matter, mainly, of hanging round Athens, frequenting the Brotherhood, tuning in, picking up work as a tourist-guide and teacher, till the press of events put an end to it.

'The German Campaign in the spring of 1941 faced me with a stark alternative: embrace British nationality and resist, or, taking the larger view of things, choose my option in the global conflict. The whole issue, for me, had now expanded: it was no longer a matter of men and guns. One couldn't decide it at that level, whatever the gut-reaction, the flag-waving, the Press. It was now apparent to anyone who *thought* that, as the daemonic Hitler put it, "A historical revision on a unique scale has been imposed on us by the Creator."

'It was not such folly as it now seems - especially with World Communism waiting at the Gate - to embrace the Führer as the New Deliverer. Even such choice spirits as Heidegger, who had diagnosed Man's dilemma as loss of Being (a view I, broadly speaking, agreed with) were ample in their praise of him. Had he not put Germany back on its feet? Was he not the man whom all revered: sitting on a charger, dressed in White, the epitome of the superior Knight? Surely, heraldic, napoleonic, daemonic, this was the man to save our world. Surely, also, if we didn't support him, Communism, already expanding, would spread through the world like some godless cancer. America might - and, in fact, later did - champion the cause of anti-communism, but where was America in May, 1941? Pursuing Isolation, sitting on the fence, not yet ready to join the Fight. And who could really believe, finally, that, after this bit-of-a-skirmish in the Balkans, the German Army would not invade Russia? Everything was leading up to it. Even I, a self-confessed political novice, was aware of that: I was in the next phase.

'Just one last remark before I pass on: It has become customary now, with the benefit of hindsight, to soften the drama of those days (it's one of the privileges of History). But those of us who were alive then felt the Edge, and we felt it with apocalyptic sharpness. Some of us, for reasons ideological and personal, chose the Right in general and the Führer in particular; others, men of standing, culture and intelligence, chose to work for Russia and the Left. They were not facile fools but men of integrity, who saw the world poised, as I saw it then, between two forms of Global Ideology. Liberalism had had its Day: without the support of religious conviction it was bland, wishy-washy, and it had no Teeth. Better pin one's flag to something strong, the defence of values, the quest for the Ideal. It was not my own choice - it was Destiny's.

'Thus I reasoned, if Reason you can call it: thus my flagging spirit heaved. The Millennial Victory was not to be had: again, it seemed, I had made the wrong choice. Perhaps it was all connected to Jessie, the punishment for an illicit love; perhaps it had something to do with Emma; perhaps I had simply missed the Point. I had pushed out along the ideological line, hoping thereby to empower myself by becoming part of something greater. But that something greater still was *me*. I hadn't solved a thing. I am still a ghost.

'Albeit, some such dream of Millennial Glory must have fired the hearts of millions, when, on 22 June, 1941, we crossed the Russian border and the Campaign began. I was an Infantryman, as I had been in the First War, my uniform supplied by the Waffen=SS. This was the German's main recruiting arm, and highly successful they were, believe me. A million Frenchmen joined up, for instance. Heaven knows how Aryan we all were!'

His voice was getting thinner now, and Marjorie was tiring. The Circle broke up until the next day.


7


'It was a piece of monumental aetiolation,' Tristan said sadly as the session began. 'I had lost my grip on reality. Emma's image swam before my eyes, although I hadn't seen her in years; my stomach was a blockage of thick, tight knots. Whatever promises I had made to myself, it was becoming increasingly clear that I had failed, that the final lining was being removed and all that would be left of me was the shell. I fought against the feeling as the year wore on and we moved deeper and deeper, winning all along the Line. This didn't help, either: it was too much *out there*. What I had left and lost couldn't be won back here.

249

'No, I had allowed myself to freeze inside, avoiding the crux of direct personal relationship. I had considered all that too small a thing, too petty, too low, lacking cosmic Width. In so doing I had made a fatal error; I had given myself over yet again to the Ultimate Cause, the Will of the Other. Yes, aetiolation was the word. It was a dreadful, debilitating self-obliteration, a piece of self-violence, like war itself. It *was* War, going on in me.

'And what could I do about it now? Slogging across the Russian Plain was a vastly different story from digging in in Flanders. Nor were Paris and Calais a few hours away. No, on the second Turn I had really fucked up, and like Hitler and Napoleon I was about to pay.

'No-one who hasn't travelled in that area can have any idea of the terrible terrain. It just goes on endlessly, mile after mile. In the summer, when you're winning, it's just about OK, but, come the winter, it's a desert - worse. For the desert moulds itself to the wind; it ripples and ribs and rolls like the sea. Also, because it is free of Man, it whispers to one ineffable things. But the plains are serried and blank and set: they go on inexorably, till the eye dies. One is carried forward, like a corpse, to another station, a new destination, which turns out to be just one more stopping-point. The enemy is retreating all the time, but he never departs till the last shot, and what he leaves you is a Waste. The heartland of Russia still lies ahead.

'And so, like the land, we went inexorably on, fighting for the Right against the Bastion of Bolshevism. It was a war in which the Angels sang - for us, of course - we marched to their song (they were bearing the heavenly Banner, while we marched on with the Swastika). On the ground, however, it was a different story. In September already the rains began, driving and drenching us to the skin; themselves, they were like an opposing army, now soaking into our sodden backs, now sweeping round to assail us from the front. Feldsoldat Dachskind trudged on with the rest. He was becoming a living metaphor for this dreadful war, this unspeakable century - with its Alienation, Uprootedness and Conflict. But he wasn't merely a metaphor: he was real and alive and in his skin; he was sodden and shivering. The gun-carriers were getting stuck.

'And all across the unending plains the leaves were turning yellow and falling to the ground (ranks of poplars by tiny swollen streams). Their drift was faint, like water in a dream, and Feldsoldat Dachskind was out of himself. He was swaying and shivering with the poplars by the stream, their grey bark his skin, their laughing leaves his hair. The sunshine, emergent, was Dream-warmth of him.

'There was a bunch of us, of various nationalities - odd-balls, all of us, of every shape and size. The officers, obviously, were SS or Wehrmacht. And we pushed on in Dream-time across the plains, as

October deepened and the first snows fell. It was becoming like some unstoppable Adventure, a Figure in the Universe looking for its rhyme, the reason for which had long since disappeared. We were tuned in by field telephone to High Command, but, like anyone asking for directions in Germany, all we ever heard was: "Immer geradeaus!"

'And that, essentially, is what we did - first through the mud, then through the snow. It was darkening into December now, the days getting shorter, the nights cold and long. We realized we were totally underequipped to face the ravages of a Russian winter, and often it was only by staying awake all night, slapping one's arms and stamping one's feet, that we could avoid the misery of frostbite. Soldiers got it, anyway, and in our unit, as in many others, there were a number of excruciating amputations. And all the time the Front went back, beating a retreat into the dying land.

'We survived one winter and were digging in for the next - how near the Nemesis we didn't know then. Our victories, in general, had been impressive: Leningrad besieged, the rich industrial zones occupied and our advanced troops one step from Moscow. We had almost done it - but only almost. We fell back on Stalingrad, preparatory to the winter, and that's where Russia's war-gods turned their fighting flesh on us.

'I remember the hallucinatory snow, the crash and the shatter of the guns day-and-night, our unit's retreating before we were cut off. But that's all I remember . . . I was light-blasted out, I was wandering again in purgatorial Wastes.'

There was silence in the room for some little time, as Tristan's voice, mumbly but evocative, trailed off like a walker in distant snow.

- Anything else for us? Marjorie said, finally.
- For you, no, but . . . for me - is there?
- Ah, yes, there's a message from Emma, your . . . She's perfectly all right, and she says she loves you.

Silence again in the soft-toned room. And a walker in the distance, going on his way, step by soft step, till he reaches the horizon.

- Tristan has gone now, Marjorie said.

# BOOK NINE: NUPTIAL NIGHTS

Es sei, wie es wolle,
Es war doch so schön.

Goethe

1

In 'Moses and Monotheism' Freud proposes that Moses was, in fact, an Egyptian. And isn't it ironical that the Religions-of-the-One-God should castigate the Egyptians for their polytheism, if, as seems likely, the whole thing came from there? Yet such are the vagaries of the human brain - its injustices, foibles, incredible discrepancies.

Atemhotep III, later Akhenaton, certainly believed that it was so: he forbade all worship that was not of the One, removed the idols from the temples and pressed priests into its Service. Thus, there was launched on an unsuspecting world the notion of a God out, over and beyond, having no involvement in human affairs but waiting at the end with the Sword and with Fire. The lesion had occurred, in spite of Atemhotep IV, who did what he could - it was too late by now -, to put back the transformative Texture into Life. The world, pulled upwards from its roots, would never be the same again. Where were Isis and Osiris now?

2

Eddie and Emma were still in bed, having landed in Cairo the previous night and taken a room, small but well located, in a back-street off Rue Mohammed Abagui. The name of the place was Pension de la Tour. It wasn't what they had been looking for but rather where the taximan had had an 'in' (a good 10% by all accounts), and they had settled for it in the middle of the night, happy enough to get their heads down.

Whatever its beginnings, timorous and taut, it had been, in a sense, a whirlwind romance, culminating in a Registry Office wedding, the only possible outcome for a non-believer and a Jew. This had been, all told, an excruciating affair, the coldness of the civic Ceremony being matched only by the effusiveness of the Reception, at which Waltraut's

252

tears flowed like bleak champagne and Emma felt a fool in bridal white. 'Not a success,' she said to herself. And then, more tellingly, 'What's the rest going to be like?' She knew she shouldn't, but she measured herself, and she couldn't help getting a sense of implosion when she thought back to that time she had set off with Evelyn, the two toning each other, bringing out the Fire. Now it all seemed stepped-down, somehow. Not that Eddie wasn't 'nice' - he was. But, then, what was the good of simple niceness? Didn't take one very far.

What she was really dreading (why the comparison came up), was the final decline into 'embourgeoisement'. She feared it more than anything on earth. It was the hushed Deceiver who sucked everybody in, took them to their seats and left them there to rot, looking at Life as if on some distant Screen; it was the voiceless Voice that never spoke out loud, that took all the Edge and the immediacy away, leaving everything dulled-down to Compromise; it was the one who came and sat there, smarmy and oozing, svelt and unbudgable, Satan in a suit. It was easy, so easy, to go that way, especially as one got a little older. And now that she was over thirty, well . . . ! Was it right, was it right even for *him*, to pin her hopes on someone seven years her junior?

What persuaded her to take a chance was her own increasing desperation and the fact that Eddie was so much in love with her. She looked on him still as a bit of a boy, without her experience of love and the world, but there was a certain inalienable quality about him, which had already begun to set him apart and give him, in her eyes, a living dimension. His gradient was definitely up: there was a balance invoked and accomplished there.

Eddie, still, was somewhat like a novice, though they had anticipated the wedding by several weeks. There had been such a struggle going on inside him, between his ardour and his shyness, that he had lost the benefits of both, forfeiting the joy of solitude, which he knew, and failing the ecstasy of passion, which he didn't. The first three nights he had been so shy that he hadn't even kissed or laid a finger on Emma. It was she, again, who broke the Ice. Then he had been all eagerness and excitement, taking her by storm like a bolting horse. After he had come-and-gone she felt vacated, lying there blank, with his head in her hands. He just lay there, breathing, then sleeping on her breast, oblivious to what a woman was.

It was at this totally unconsummated juncture that Emma decided - what the hell! - that she would go ahead with it and marry Eddie. Perhaps the whole thing would come right later; perhaps, in the end, it was more important to be friends; perhaps it would be more like brother and sister. Perhaps, perhaps - who knows what she thought?

She realised there was Ice in her, too: she had never been able to feel free with a man. The woman's world was already intimate, sexuality just

253

an extension of it, the brush of a lip that already trembled. With men there was always the assault-course aspect: they came after one like athletes from some sweaty gymnasium. Theirs was the vocabulary of the obstacle-race, and, in their martial Field-of-Honour talk, men spoke loudly and proudly of their 'conquests' - as if a woman's body were the enemy, which, by subterfuge or force, one had to take. And most women went along with it, largely because they had no choice, but also because they accepted it: there was gratification in getting down.

Emma foresaw the potential disaster of the married state long before she got involved in it. And, of course, Eddie was made of finer stuff: much more sensitive, more aware. Still, he hadn't been able, thus far, at least, to be more than an athlete - and a poor one at that! Time might tell, and so might Egypt - it was a Mediterranean country, after all. Then there was the rest, the mellifluous Nile, the prodigious sweet Flow of the Ancient World. That Breath might dissipate, might utterly destroy the forlorn Ice-stiffness of the 'sceptred isle', which since Shakespeare's time had been gradually cooling and was now down to -273 C. No wonder all its artists since the Age of the Romantics had fled its shores in search of warmth and light. And no wonder, in time present, at that special Conjunction, the morning traffic in thick flow, that they waited for the Sun.

Being a poet at heart, Eddie was looking for a metaphor, some sign or signal from the Beyond, which would put this too-solid flesh in context and make it come alive like a song. It wasn't a representational image, nor anything that remotely resembled *him:* it was, rather, something *between* Emma and him, a form or figure of their love unborn. And, without this figure, he knew they would be flat; they would go through the motions, nothing more. He looked within himself, but it wasn't there: what he found within himself were his own projections, reasonings, memories, helpful hints - but nothing to unite him with the Further Field. Being a Poet, that's where he belonged, and without that Breath he couldn't really live.

Osiris and Isis: brother-sister, man-and-wife. This was beginning to dawn on him. But it was not for a while yet, not till Abydos, that he would actually grasp the Secret of it. It was rippling in him, nevertheless; he was beginning to get a whiff of it. It was somewhere at the intermediate level - societally speaking, between the pharaoh and his people. It was *not* pharaonic - it was gentler than that - and it had nothing to do with Authority and Power. One could even say, it had to do with Grace, for Grace comes gently, on ways and wings unseen.

Emma, of course, had known Meltdown, had felt her body turn to solar gold. But that now seemed a long time ago and, in any case, there was no transfer. No, all loves were utterly distinct (that was their beauty): it was the Mystery again. The trouble was - and trouble *is* - finding the key to that Mystery. It doesn't reside in the books and statistics, nor in the catalogues of 'expert advice'; it isn't a matter of studied fucking, planned variation, tubes and twilight. It is a movement, wide and varied as a river, flowing, never stopping, never damming back. It is reachable only through the Metaphor. And in that River, in its depth and surface-light, exists - as on a scroll, as if already writ - every subtle invention, each last touch of sense.

For Emma it was a question of just such a place, the source the touch was coming from, and hardly a matter of physicality at all. It had to have the sense of the Mystery; then all acts were beautiful in-and-for-themselves: they multiplied each other like the reaping rain, when the rainbow runs in it, fire-fine and fluid. The body danced, as hers had danced, when two bodies hear the same small Tune. Then they know in their blood where they come from, the source of their being, their inalienable Self. They move then, swiftly or slowly, unimpeded, through all the reaches of the Outer Land, travelling upstream to where it inheres, the high Point of Origin, the Start of the Stream. Emma had been There. Could she go there again?

This Matter of Love, of Love's indwelling, hovered above them like a question-mark. It was palpable between them, wielding its sickle, its dark dot bobbing, insecure. They pushed it around from one to the other and wondered what Crop would come of it. If nothing comes, said Emma to herself, we'll just leave Egypt and go our separate ways.

From Pension de la Tour the Tower itself is a twenty-minute walk across a wide bridge. They stood nonplussed on a broad causeway, as an eight-lane stream of traffic went by. They were trying to work out some logical strategy, when a total stranger came up to them and told them to say, 'Insha allah', and just go. Unlikely as it sounds, they tried it and it worked: the traffic parted before them like the Red Sea before the Israelites.

They took the lift to the top of the Tower, and it was from there that they had their first sight of the Pyramids. They almost waved to them - it was a curious temptation -, sitting out there on the south-west fringe of the city. Austere and ancient, they had nothing to do with the scurrying ferment of modern Man. For five thousand years they had stood there, and more. Should they change, or should *we* change because of them?

For Eddie and Emma, who had never left Europe before, it was a strange initiation into non-linear reality, into something beyond the measure of Man. Strange, but oddly fascinating, setting off sparks of wonderment, Release. It was there again in the striding statues or the sitting statues of the ancient Pharaohs, which commanded the eye in the Ethnological Museum. It was there in the uraeus-symbol on the forehead, there behind the head in the hovering Bird and in the eyes, half-closed, turning inwards and upwards. It was the Gateway to another Dawn, an unknown Plethora of Possibilities, which the sawn-off, skin-bound Measure-Man denied. Our whole culture and civilisation was in that trap; had been, essentially, since the time of the Greeks. Wasn't it time, for us and them, to break out?

Eddie and Emma were holding hands, letting the drift of it seep into them, musing along, not really thinking that History was a nightmare from which they must awake. It had pinned-and-fastened down and was telling them who they were - constantly, daily, no interruption - and they had to get up from that Bed of Definition, throw it to the wall and find each other and themselves. Then only would they be able to walk tall, to enter the Chamber, to sweep high and clear. Here, in this Miasma, there was no hope at all. After some time they went back to their room.

Emma's auburn curls were tumbling back, then out and wide, spreading like a fan. She was parting, and her body was beginning to burn. His swift incursion was no troubled thing but a sudden implanting of Intensity, gathered and firm like a Pillar of Fire. It was licking up into her everywhere, touching the walls of her womb like flames. There was no adjustment, no false start; he had penetrated her as of perfect right.

Together they were entering the Open Field. It stretched out before them in easy acres, like the rolling remnant of forgotten Time. She and he could play around in it, could play till Time itself had a stop. But at this moment it had no stop: his pressing inside her had no end. It was like the waves of the sea coming in, pushing to a furl of froth, then rilling back. Her body went under to his push, drew in, like the earth, his sea's insurgence. Then magically, somehow, she was on the Other Side, or rather, she was *part* of the rolling sea. Her own body heaved with the same swelling movement, as if there were only One God, One Flesh. They were not two persons any more but points, places, loci, *plays* of Intuition. Unbounded it was, the seamless Sea.

And then a coral Cavern opened up, a recess that Emma never knew she had, like that limbo of the brain they saw we never use. It had been lying, dormant, in her all this time, a colour-gentle world of soft pinks and blues. And they entered it together, she and he, while the external world completely disappeared. In its stead was the underwater World of the Unconscious, no longer a Prison-house of thwarted Demons, but a nascent, irradiating, dancing Wonderworld, in which the Dragon of Daren't lay dead, self-slain. Yes, suddenly, she had slipped into That; or, rather, they had crossed the Threshold together - not as they had on their wedding-night, clumsily, bulkily, fearing the omens, but subtly, without striving, made fluid by warm water. They were in the Other Place as one, the place where the two rivers converge and flow as one - except that here was no Moorland Meet, but a Stasis of Stillness, with every chill dissolved.

Moving, not-moving, they inhabited that World, that Further Field of unbroken Flow. In it the stars were as plenteous as daisies, and they watched them by moonlight as day turned to night. Emma's body was the Body of the Night, overarching, tippling, her nipples to his lips, and his was the body of the blood-loved earth, as it worked her and brought her close, flowing into him.

The cavern itself was splitting now, and the sea, in a great gush, frothing and flooding, poured over the rocks till they began to burst. The cavern was coming of itself, giving up its coral and its slim tongues of fish. Shoals of them, suddenly, were shooting everywhere, like stars in the night when their destiny is done. They were slipping, silent, through the gateway of their bodies, coruscating, burning, darting through their flesh.

The night itself peeled away from the sky, as if it had always been an occlusion. Buried behind it were the acres of the Sky, like fold upon fold of black velvet cloth, and in them dwelt Unity, Meaning, Enfoldment. One had to penetrate to There, to be oneself open, coming, shining and, at one and the same time, hidden forever, lost to oneself in the Matrix of the Sky. No amount of daylight would do it, no amount of Law-giving and Reason. One had to enter the Chamber of the Heart, the rich, unfathomable Sea of the Dark. Only then would the Wall start to crumble, subtly, imperceptibly, as if not willed.

Emma lay still and felt her heart beating, the blood - her new blood - appeased now and calm. The bird of her soul had flown free again, as it does from the bodies of the Egyptian dead. It was hovering above them, a little way off.

- I don't' think I want to sleep tonight, she said.

And they walked out into the lustrous night, which, even in the city, seemed quiet and soft. It was part of their tender Texture, also, the air which surrounded them, the ambience they breathed. They felt it innately, as part of themselves. Standing on the bridge, they promised one another that there would be no step-down, no breaking of the Bond.

It was an engagement ritual and rich, something to which they had committed themselves in a moment of irreversible daring. Becoming man-and-wife was one thing, a totem, entering into the Mystery, quite another. Now - and now only, perhaps - they were married.

3

They took the city bus out to Gizeh in the early light of a February dawn. The morning was coming, gradually. Around the Pyramid of Cheops a few camel-touts were active already, offering the tour of the

257

pyramids, indifferently. As the entrance to the Chamber wasn't open yet, they walked on past a broken masturba and down some distance to where the Sphinx lay

- What do you think she was for? asked Emma.
- Protection, I should think: she was a Guardian.
- Of what?
- Of the Mystery, the Secret of Life. See how serene and silent she is.
- She's taken some punishment, though, hasn't she?

Her face was badly pocked and pitted, where Napoleon's soldiers had taken pot-shots at her. But, in spite of that disfigurement, she still gave forth, through a million dawns, her sense of Gift, of Place, of Metaphor. Lying there leonine, her face erect, she still had the Speech of fathomless Silence.

They watched as the sun, with its fulsome round body, flung its light across the face of the Sphinx. The animal-human figure responded, with something like the corner of a smile, and in her more-than-human way she spoke thus to the two people who had come to her: 'I am the Guardian of the Secret of Life. Through me all shall pass, who enter here. None knows himself who has not found the Secret, the Atom of Truth, from which everything derives. And the key to this truth is in yourselves; seek it within your own body's Temple What stands here is only a metaphor.'

She was there like a lion, implanting, suggesting, leading them on and restraining them, both. They felt her whole Presence, heavy and mighty; they gathered themselves and walked back whence they had come.


The Great Pyramid of Khufu (Cheops to the Greeks) remained impenetrable for centuries, until in 820 A.D. Caliph al Mamoun ordered a breach to be made in its northern side. He was looking for the supposedly fabulous treasure, hidden inside the burial chamber of the King. And he did, as a consequence, find the original entrance, so cleverly concealed, just off-centre, that nobody not in the know could have found it. Needless to say, there was no treasure trove.

Not in the same place but still in the northern side, the official entrance leads one up a stone stairway and eventually, via the Grand Gallery, to the King's Chamber. And, like all things official, it has its hours of opening. Eddie and Emma were ushered in, along with a legion of other visitors. There was a gaggle and rumour of 'what it was all for', which didn't cohere with what *they* saw and felt. In the middle of the Chamber sat what looked like a sarcophagus and this seemed to provide proof positive that this had been, indeed, a place of burial. But *was* it? That was the question now.

The crowds were milling, turning, touching - not for one split second could they be quiet. Then, as abruptly and brusquely as they had come, they went. And when they had gone the ancient peace returned, that Peace which no human presence could disturb. It was fecundating, solid and sure, substantial as water when it gathers, fluid-thick. It filtered into the heart and lungs, as the air, miraculously, came in through hidden vents.

This was not a place of death and decay: its purpose had been otherwise. It was a Centre to which Initiates had come, when their Moment of Readiness had arrived. Here they drew in the dark Peace of the Night, the rich enfoldment of the World Beyond; here they were taught to decode Meaning, to read in all the ciphers of the world the imprinted Signature of That-which-is. It was *there*, somehow, if one knew how to look, it was even staring one in the face. It was the Interstitial, the Betwixt-and-Between, the eminently readable but now lost Sense. It was palpable as Matter; it was intelligible as Form; it was visible, even, in the dancing glyphs. Could it be, thought Eddie, looking through the Gap, that it was now preparing to be born again?

They stood there briefly, just the two of them, enwrapped in a Meaning not their own, for which they were (or could be) Channels. It was a Moment, subtle, impenetrable, and it wove the fabric of human life. It was not tangential, like an afterthought; it was the stuff of things, definite as daylight. And here it was in the Sacred Centre, the Heart of the Pyramid, pointing to the sky. It was the first and the last, the beginning and the end - but without beginning or end at all. Our historicity, our language, our thought were cloddish impediments to its manifestation, to it fine-tendrilled growth in our hearts and minds. But here, in the Silence, there were no impediments: nothing blocked that calm, free Flow.

The Pyramid itself was the total body-focus, the built bold Essent of That-which-is; it brought it, solidly, immovably, densely into the Field, within the reach of Man. He had only to rise within himself, to lose himself within the Sacred Space, to realize that he was the Centre of Creation, as the Pyramid stood at the centre of the earth. The Pyramid, which had once been powerfully luminous, reflecting the sun from its polished sides, had been built to bring down the Sun into the Heart, to meet, melt and wed it to the Matrix of the Night, and from that Wedding produce the New Man. Those who had been here (had Jesus been one?) emerged as Messengers of a New Dawn for Man, the Dark Sun melted and fused in them.

And could they, in their nuptial nights, in their fecund Finding-of-each-other, come to this? For it was no longer the epoch of the lone Illuminate: it was time for people to come together - as brothers and sisters, as man-and-wife; it was a time for Community, not for strong men and strife.

Emma felt it already in her bones, this timely turning of the hands of Time. True it was that Truth was inalienable and, in this sense, invariably sheer and pure. But there was also the other side of the coin, which had fascinated Man since Time began: namely, how he came to meet it - what were the means, forms, metaphors, sounds, by which he could attune himself. For surely that was necessary work. One wasn't - and, as an ordinary mortal, never could be - free of the circus of Man's struggle. On the contrary, it was one's proper place, the earthbound focus which we all share. And we had to turn and struggle there, perhaps many more times than we imagined. And wasn't it how we did it that mattered, just as the care that went into a meal made the meal as good as it was?

We were entering the Age of Being-together, when differences of class, caste, colour, race, creed would have less importance and basic humanness would be the seed from which new life would spring. One could feel it already: the ground had been cleared by the dreadful upheaval of two World Wars. The Picture would never be the same again - and it was in and with this Picture that we had to live. We were not itemized fragments any more, but living members of the same stock. Those who saw this, what it really meant, must come together from all walks of life - not as one nation meeting another, through or over some prearranged barrier, but openly, frankly, in the living daylight - as brother to brother, like to like. The common Germ, once seen and felt as such, was already becoming a focal tree, a tree in blossom, the Tree of Life. For Man had never tasted of that Tree: he had hung in guilty suspension away from it; it had been reserved, if at all, for the Few. But now we were poised to enter the Millennium, the Golden Time, when not just the few but the whole of humanity could share its Fruit.

It was a question of organic maturity. If that seed of humanness grew in one, it would take care of everything, everything peripheral; it would work its way through each and every ground, every hardness, human or non-. Like a tree bursting through on a solid rock face, it would have its own endemic form-and-force. And it would draw on the rock wall the figure of itself, sharing in the process that generates all life. Thus, being all trees, it would *become* itself.

But, although it was the most natural-sounding thing in the world - and *was*, in fact, the most natural thing -, organic maturity did not come easily. It was thwarted by a million impediments - of background, religion, upbringing, etc. If it was true that our parents fucked us up, then so did the Church, the School, the State. Each was casting us in its mould, firmly, insidiously, 24 hours-a-day. And what emerged at the end of that Line was a State-, School-, Church-thing, whose seed had been squashed. It would take years, if it ever happened at all, for that squashed seed to begin to stir again, to swell and create its own endemic form. More than likely, it would simply live out one or other aspect of its Programme: parental ambition, Church sobriety, State duty. And in this way, for-itself, it would slowly perish, a death more protracted, grey and nightmarish than ever the death of the body could be. It was happening NOW to almost everyone. Why did no-one see it or feel the pain? Obviously, Emma reasoned with herself, because we had grown inured to the pain: it was part of our dullness, our bleakness, our Rift.

Awakening came swiftly on the wind, with the soft subtle sound of the freed bird's wing. It was not a matter of plodding and sweating; that, too, belonged in the menagerie, the barred, fetid Cage of human devising. This was a wild thing - it had never been tamed - and it blazed like blue gentians on a Swiss mountain-side.

Though theirs was a hierarchical society, its beautiful benefits reserved for the few, the Egyptians had had this, obviously: they had lived on the Axis of Transformation, which is the burgeoning of the seed in Man. They had known it was the Secret of Life, at a time when Nature and human nature were parts of one seamless, unbroken Field. Man-as-God had not set himself *above:* the workings of Nature (day into night, the sown into the desert, death into life) were aspects of him; they were his own Estate. He realized by an immediate intuition that it was by such a process that he, too, must grow. He must grow through the death of that fictive barrier, the smooth or squalid Cage, the trap of egohood. That's why it had been reserved for the few: the many couldn't rise to it.

And now Man stood at another Crossroads; another Door had been flung open. Perhaps we would walk through it in increasing numbers - or, perhaps, since we were still inward cavemen, it would slowly swing back and close for good. In spite of the Cold War, she felt it coming: the essential Choice which was open to Man. It was immanent already at secret depth. Would people be able to rise to it - or would inner gracelessness, greed and power-politics sink the bloody lot of us, as it had the Atlanteans? And, like an unsought addendum to these reflections, a further pitch of the fateful ball, a fresh bevy of tourists entered the Chamber, cameraless but clicking all the time. The Arrow was pointing Atlantis' way.

A tawny daylight greeted them through the gritty film of a rising sandstorm. It spread its silence, like snow, over surfaces, infiltrated cracks, blotted out sound; it felt its way into the corners of the eyes, slipped between toes, rubbed against fingers; it stuck its finger up one's nose - with the faintest, finest mineral bouquet. But, more than this, it enfolded one; it enfolded the two of them in its embrace. With their arms round each other they were lost and alone, as all lovers are, in a World of their own. The sandstorm drifted and insulated them, as the Chamber had some minutes before.

261

They drifted with it, back down towards the Sphinx, which now seemed utterly regal and aloof, supine and supreme, at the plateau's edge. Whereas before it had spoken to them, now it was completely quiet, withdrawn. They walked off the site, into a village and drank coffee, but somehow the sandstorm pulled them back. It seemed to possess its own mystique, its whirlwind charge of appropriate austerity. It belonged to the Composition of Place, that somehow synthesis of spirit and matter, which integrates the natures, human and divine. They were aware of it at every touch and turn, holding, enclosing, uniting them.

There was nobody about on the plateau now - even the camel-touts were cowering away. The silence of it was like a tryst, but a tryst without borders, a disengagement from Time. They walked to the Pyramid of Kephren, which was closed, then on to the little one, Mycerinos. One went underground, into several vaults, these also, supposedly, burial chambers. It felt strangely warm now underground, after the buffeting of wind and sand. They were glad, nonetheless, to be out again: it fed their senses, curiously. That Energy was running through life and limb; it was uncompacted, strong and equal everywhere. And whose was the body that would not respond, would not burn equally, touching limb-to-limb?

There was an unreal ecstasy about it, as of something that went on and on. They were, in a sense, still out there in the sand. It had become, as it were, their mineral element, subtly feeling everything out; with every available inch of skin they were feeling its tingling tune-and-enter them. It was both more and less than human penetration: less, because until this moment it had not become a phallic act; more, because in the sand's ubiquity lay every glancing touch of sense. The tiniest grain could not be left out - it was as much a part as the ground's vast heaving, the potent moaning of the wind. The wind and the grain were stitched together in some form or figure which was all their own and which it was left to the lovers to decipher as they may.

Indeed, it became a hieratic act, a reading of the runes which were sifting through the sand, an awakening to membranes and sensitivities deep down. Another storm was brewing up. It moaned and glistened slowly over them, working them with its invisible Power. There was no holding or binding it - it transferred itself in one clean sweep from the plateau of the pyramids to this, their own room. The room itself was suitably vacant: a lop-sided table by the window, a rickety chair and a teetery washstand. Then the two of them, the Eight-limbed, on a mattress on the floor. For, indeed, it would have been hard to tell where one or t'other of them began. They were one flesh, like Isis and Osiris; they were brother and sister, making love.

Eddie had lost his youthfulness and assumed a different phase and face. Though gracious still - *more* gracious, actually -, he had resigned his prick-upright, boyish brightness for a well-warmth glow which stirred from within. It was accompanied by a new self-assurance, such as only a loving woman can give, and which gave him the feeling - finally, finally! - that he would not be an outcast for the rest of his life. The strength of his passion was, hence, partly gratitude. Hadn't she saved him from the worst Prison - himself?

That relief and release in him burst like roses, as again and again he turned to her. Now the wind was beating up again, engraining them with the sensual sand. It was not a pocket, a fucking-sock of limbs, but a surge and grip of teeth, lips, hair, an unendurable throb of waves. It kept coming up from the back of the storm, as if the sand would never cease, as if the storm-winds, searching and shuddering, were cleaning out every fingered hold. As their bodies moved to the Higher Rhythm, suddenly apparent like a brooch unclasped, they knew they had broken some Wall in each other, some Dam of Occlusion, which had always been there. Perhaps it was there in everybody and, try as they might, it wouldn't go. It stuck and would block them, as deep things do.

But, somehow, the Dam had been broken through; they were passing through its space to a different Ground. Deep water was gushing from every sluice and, like the sand in the sandstorm, it multiplied. They were now no longer two spare personalities - in some sense they were not even persons at all -; they had assumed every atom of the Stream of Life and, because they had, leaving nothing out, rejecting nothing in themselves or in the world, they had come to this place of glowing Perfection, this Bed of the Stream, this Being - themselves. Nor was this an achievement, an end; on the contrary, it was always and only the beginning, the first step on a Journey that would never tire.

They did not live in pursuit of the mountain-top, the finishing-line, the vulgar point-score; they had stepped into an element, fluid, amniotic, a Dimension unbroken, a Space-time disclosed. It was no longer just out there, the physics of fact; it was also the intrinsic Skein of things, the finely woven pattern of Consciousness. It was *there*, as visible as trees in strong daylight: it was the Inner Reality which sustained the world. And mutely, lovingly, caressingly, at-onely, they had come upon it, as their bodies came.

- It's strange to discover we're still two persons, said Emma after a very long time.

Eddie was mute still, gazing at her. She had that timeless, waiting look, as if she had been where no man had been and had locked in the secret of that strange Frontier. The repose of deep burning lit up her face, rising, as it were, from the centre of the earth, where everything is molten, turning, fierce. And it had risen and come to rest in her: she was the pivot of stasis of the burning earth.

At times like this she became an Icon, an object of reverence and contemplation for Eddie. Looking straight forward, gently batting her eyelids, she seemed to have no personal connection with anything. All that had been disengaged, washed away, and she lay now, purged, dark, holy, serene, on the further side of an Endless Shore.

The afternoon was dimming down, but the haunting, high day was still with them. It pressed through what passed for curtains at the window, the bleared sun oblique like a neglected dream. They would have got up, certainly; in fact, on the face of it, there was nothing else to do. But something stronger than the daylight was pulling: the Bed they had been in, the Dream beyond desire. It tugged at them, not through the webs of inertia, but through some instinct - physical and more - related, no doubt, to the freed Bird's call. They heard it intuitively, mutely, together, and they turned to one other, to love one another, with delicate, deep, long strong tongue-kisses that set the ancient blood afire. It *was* the call, their own Signature, and it was calling them into the body of the other, away from the screeching street below.

Satisfaction is one thing, ecstasy another. Satisfaction isn't what they sought; they sought the quick listening of the inward Hour, the turn to touch that betokens being free. It was, at the same time, a call and a protection, a call to the Journey, a protection from the Fall. And what responded to it in both of them was the same soul-substance, the sense of being one. They were born, as it were, of the same stock, and they knew themselves to be united at the Root.

For the next three day-and-nights they didn't stir but maintained a vigil in their ramshackle room. They caught snatches of sleep, occasionally - sufficient, with the tea a houseboy brought, to keep them in fettle for the rest of the time. They referred to it later as the Dream-time.

They were out on a limb with one another, at the very limit of the known World. And, like all frontiers, it was no place for the faint-hearted. One might come back from it broken, mad or, like Nietzsche, embracing a horse; one might pay the Price, like a mountaineer. Knowing this, they went there all the same, as hardy Explorers of the Edge might spend a night in the King's Chamber of Cheops. They had just come from there, and perhaps that's what did it.

Eddie wanted the depth of that and he wanted it, not singly, but with Emma, his wife. He wanted the Chalice to come to them. He was aware that it might be an act of 'hubris', to prevent which the gods had laid down laws that it was death-defying and dire to break - people went singly, or not at all, through the Eye. And yet his conviction was much like hers; this was the age of the two-, three- or moresome: things were possible now, which hadn't been before. Outright lovers had always been tragic, from Paolo-and-Francesca to Anna Karenina; they had all been toppled by morality and convention. Perhaps it was time now - *wasn't* it the time? - to fly with the Arrow, not die by it.

This joint conviction, which neither uttered, which neither even knew the other had, gave them the strength to go over the Lip. Just at the moment when the letdown might come, when Satiety vs. Nimiety was being set up, they sprung, as by magic, this Opposites' trap and were off again, travelling, laughing, loving, leaving to rust the Iron Maiden of the mind. They had already touched the Bed of themselves, the River-as-it-runs, the Further Field. Now they were testing the truth of it: to see where, if anywhere, it would end. If it ended they were in for mutual catastrophe, since they had set their solid store by it. By their vow, by their marriage, by their existential commitment, they were now in the Place of No Return.

They anticipated each other's every move, each least craving and flicker of desire. There was no interval between the feeling and the deed, but all was fierce following, quiet insistence, Emptiness. For Emma had assumed a different body (the body of Evelyn had gone away). This one was younger, tauter, stronger; it entered her like a blade of steel. She wanted the feel of it always inside her, to feel the fibre and the strength of him. But this, also, was only an effect, a consequence of the Stream flowing endlessly through. He and she were in that Stream, they were of that Stream; they *were* that Stream. And, indeed, there was a sense that it had always been so and that only itemizing Instruction (what passed, in fact, for Education) had bred in them the illusion of anything else. They were back to each other; they were back to That.

And, relating to That, they played endlessly, drawing on that Source, which is the source of all. Eddie's body became very smooth; there was a laugh beneath his skin, always ready to break out. And Emma's serene features were touched with fire: a flush rose up through her cheeks to her eyes, turning them the colour of hazel flame, as if they burned and shone from deep inside her head. This transformed all their touches and their acts of secret plunder into further and finer excesses of the Play. And the Play went on - they knew it now - for ever, creating and sustaining every living thing. Even the destruction of the world would not end it, for it was the Music of the Universe, humming to itself. They had been blest, they had been lucky; they had been fine enough to hear it. They were living on the One Note, the single pitch of Truth.

4

About eight the next morning they took the train to Luxor. It hadn't been easy to book the seats; in fact, only a considerable augmentation of 'bakshish', both to the houseboy and the travel agent, had managed to get them aboard at all. They stashed their light luggage and sat back for the ride.

The slim green strip of the Nile Valley seemed, that morning, to contain all life. The land was too precious to build walls or fences, but there were paths, banks, irrigation channels and other obvious means of demarcation. On the paths were donkeys, carrying loads or people, much as they had done for thousands of years. Houses were scattered here and there among the date-palms, which seemed to be guarding the dark green, luscious plots - early potatoes for the European market. The road threaded its way through, with lorries, cars and bicycles - and always, of course, the broad swath of the Nile, with its curious, pale blue, steely cast. To right and left, west and east, the Valley ended in a sudden dun burst, where, without warning, the desert began: to the left a succession of dusty-looking rock bluffs, to the right the slow slope towards the Libyan Desert. The whole country hung by a thread, actually.

They were not much for staying in the town of Luxor, when, well into the afternoon, the train stopped there. It had the unfortunate emphasis of small towns with reputations, which give themselves over, 'faute de mieux', to the person or place that has made their name. It might be Shakespeare; here it was the Temple - in fact, two temples, since the monolith of Karnak lies only two miles distant to the north.

Instead, they took the ferry across the Nile, then a taxi to the straggle of a town called Thebes. The hotel they eventually opted for - after a number of enquiries, false starts, haggles - was a little place called 'Zum heimkehrenden Fellahin', which had belonged to a German, recently decamped. The new owner had given it an Arabic name, inscribed in flawless koranic calligraphy, for which, apparently, there was no English equivalent, and the two signs hung there quite amicably together (though the tone and temperament of each was quite different) as some kind of testimony to international accord. On the upper floor were six rooms and a balcony, which looked straight into the forecourt of the Temple of Rameses III. It was a bulky structure, inevitably, lacking the finesse of earlier times. 'What happened?' thought Emma, and the question hung there.

They took a late lunch-cum-early dinner and walked out over the scattered plain. There was a ruined temple not far off, with a monumental, broken stone figure, which had served as inspiration for Shelley's 'Ozymandias'.

266

- What pushes a person to become self-important? asked Eddie, looking at the severed torso. I mean, it's not just pharaohs, emperors, kings.
- Is it the drive for self-perpetuity? We just want to put our stamp on things - while we're still here, before it's too late.
- I don't think that's what *I* want, he said. I want 'something afar from the sphere of our sorrow'.
- Then I fear you must leave me, my darling, my own.
- Not for a single second, he said.

And, as the night with its lights came, enfolding, concealing, he eased her back against the statue's bulk. She could feel the warmth of the stone through her skirt, then the warm stone pushing against her bare thighs.
- Don't ever stop, Eddie; don't stop loving me!
- I won't, he said wildly, never - I swear!

The soft sky of Egypt spread over them, like a blanket covering nakedness. And the night brought the stars in its train to look at them. They were not ashamed and they hardly even moved, so enwrapt were they in their mute contemplation, their temple-warmth of living limbs. It might, with its slow, soft movements like breathing, go on (it did seem so) endlessly, as each of the constellations took its place and the Balcony of Heaven became rich, full and glowing. Eddie's hands supported Emma's back and she thrust her arms up under his shoulders. In this way, she felt, she could pull more of him inside her; she would have had *all* of him inside her, if she could. It was not his movement that she wanted but his stasis: his plenitude of Power, like the Pole of the world. On it and around it she would dance, she would go out; she would feel heaven break as it went in more and more. The stars were the outcome of the piercing of the night; they were everywhere and always, as her head fell further back. It seemed her body possessed the earth's fire, as her head tilted back to hold heaven in her gaze. But heaven was moving - it was part of Curved Space - it was underthrusting her stone-warmed back. And the stars were little points of ecstasy; they kept blinking and twinkling to her, eye to eye. She wanted to scream out, suddenly, to shout to all heaven that it was Fire, but Eddie held his hand across her mouth and, sensing the stars, which were stars of fire, beginning to break and fall in her, he pushed her to the Instant, the focus of all-time. Heaven was breaking away from her now, in the centrifugal forms and darts of its stars - it was tippling and coming everywhere. The milk of it was flowing into her. She pressed herself so close over Eddie, she could feel him shuddering right up inside her and the night, through the back of his head, going out. She was naked through to the core of her being. There was nothing outside the nuptial Night.
- He did have his uses, you see, said Eddie, as they walked back to their hotel from the broken site.

That land still breathes its ancient rhythms, its wandered ways of Death-in-Life: the Magic lies buried beneath the sand. For it had once - and has never quite lost - its sense of a Mystery lying buried in the dark, in the Deep-night we have since learnt to fear and shun. We have set our sights on Light-upon-light, exposing all phenomena to our analytical gaze. We have, in consequence, lost the wee Darkness, that grain of Not-knowing, from which True Life springs. We don't want to know about Death-in-Life, because it is a Mystery too sheer and pure. We would rather live in the circumscribed Light, going round and round like Valentin's clown. Then Death, like Heaven, becomes a thing deferred, or some wilful punishment of a displeased God. Whereas Death weaves in with Life in one single textured Whole: it is not a separate phenomenon at all. Not realizing this, we grow down, we grow grey; we're on the existential Scrap-heap by the age of twenty-five. Thus, going round, growing down, we come to Nullity, which, somehow or other, we have to face. For Death is still waiting at the end of it all, and Death - not Saint Peter - holds the Key.

Eddie and Emma were at that Frontier, on the Striding Edge between Life and Death - that's why their relationship was so intense. It was the Love of the Other that made them burn.


- It's almost a desecration, said Eddie, as they walked round the site in the Valley of the Kings. I wonder why . . .
 - Curiosity, said Emma, who wasn't so keen on sites anyway.
- They didn't know what they were doing, couldn't have. The energies latent and potent here . . .
- What makes you so sure?
- Who can be sure? But the Pharaohs and High Priests weren't buried here for nothing: they weren't just ordinary, low-level stiffs.
- Big stiffs, then. Come on, let's have a drink.
And they walked over to a stand selling soda and iced drinks.

For all she admired him and loved him to the hilt, Emma disliked Eddie's pontifical side - she thought one could easily do without it. Wasn't it enough, just to live and be? Why be for ever going on about Mysteries, Pharaohs, Edges and Altars? Wasn't the important thing what one lived *now?* It was trite and easy to talk, always had been. And talkers ended up talking themselves out or, worse, their public got fed up of listening. It was the living, actual Moment that counted; all else was spurious. Destroy all Mirrors!

Eddie couldn't really countenance this: he was a European intellectual, after all. Words came readily, swiftly to him, and he framed new Logics as he went along. He saw nothing wrong with it - it was just a framework for the nonce, a kind of graph for an Image of Reality, which could be replotted as soon as Reality changed. Everything was Flux and

Flow, anyway; what was wrong with pinning it down, so long as one remembered that the pinning-down was temporary? For Emma this was all gobbledigook: why make an Image - verbal, mental or otherwise - which was inevitably so imperfect it had to distort? Why not just *live with* the Flux-and-Flow, seeing oneself as part of it, easily, detachedly, without intervention.

- But you get caught out, too, said Eddie, when the observer-self is all-too-strong. What about your engagement with the world?

- I've had my engagement with the world. I'm having it now; I'm having it with you.

- Of course you are; then, where's pure observation?

- Pure observation is looking at you.

And she looked at him from her sun-warmed blood, from the marrow of her bones which were melting in the sun. The sun, her eyelids fluttering quickly, caught the iris of her eye and made its colour mutant, changing it from hazel to light sun-yellow. She bowed her head slightly and one protracted tear rolled down her cheek, more eloquent than a million. Eddie put out his hand to her.

- Time for Tutenkhamun, she said.

But it wasn't quite over with the Observer and the Observed; one was on the platform, the other on the train. Eddie could feel it as he up-and-awayed on the theme of Tutenkhamun's life and early death. He had been, he said, a very high soul, and the nine death-casings of his body, which they had seen the other day in the Ethnological Museum, were no exaggeration of his rank. Wealth and diamonds were as nothing to him, for he had found the Diamond of his Self. To break open the tomb of such a man, to make an exhibition of it, like some vulgar spectacle! Emma, feeling a rhapsody coming on and looking at a small plaque with dates on it, said:

- Look, he was twenty-nine when he died.

- Same age as Shelley, Eddie said.

- A little bit older than you are, all the same.

- A little bit older than I *was*.

On the spur of the moment, without reference or reflection, one cannot possibly tell what's moving: the train one is on or the train next to it. But the observer on the platform sees only one train, the one that is carrying her beloved away. Her Reality has come in, closed, condensed: it has passed through all the Motions of the Gyre; and now it sits, folded in upon itself, in the form of a handkerchief, sodden, bleak but focused, lost to all other, waving down the line.

We are actually on the horns of a dilemma here, since pure objective observation is *not* possible - there must always be some impact from the side of the observer. Take the case of Eddie and Emma. Emma's approach was, in some sense, clearer, less 'ad hoc' and quixotic, more coherent; hypothetically, and often actually, it kept her closer to the nerve of things, allowed her to receive them with all their coloration. Eddie's tack was more interpretive, and he was apt to leave out what didn't fit his Scheme. On the other hand, his Scheme was a kind of grid, to which he could cling if the Ground slipped away. She had no grid and enjoyed no such reassurance. Consequently, when she slipped, when 'the observer' fell, she was in her own void; she entered the dark Sea of herself. And to get out of it sometimes took her weeks.

Nevertheless, their basic mood was buoyant, as with newly-weds one might expect it to be. The night-sky breathed its Mystery to them, and at Abydos, to which they went by hired car, joining up with another couple from the hotel, it was revealed to them in divine-human form. For this was the Sanctuary of Osiris, the original Founder of the Death-in-Life rites and still, subliminally, its presiding deity. He was the double-crested one, to whom Pharaoh could turn as an equal and a friend, who, though himself the Initiate of initiates, was Brother to all who sought his aid. He had sailed, so they said, from fabled Atlantis many many millennia ago, and he had settled here, in the middle stretch of Egypt, halfway from the Darkland to the delta of the Nile.

Perhaps if such things existed then, he had intended to unite the Upper and Lower Kingdoms, and that's why he was depicted with the double crown. In any event, he was a Uniter of people(s), one who with a firm and subtle hand brought them together or brought them to themselves. He was depicted, as were others, with the 'ankh', the famous handled cross of ancient Egypt. But in his hands - and especially in his - it became the Key to Eternal Life. For the Noughting, the Cross-point, the Zero of oneself, the vertical-horizontal Intersection was not just a point of arrival or stasis; rather, it was the Eye of Entry, the thin, indispensable locus in oneself of a Change so profound it would alter everything. It was, indeed, the Gateway to Eternity, and Brother Osiris waited there, the Key in one hand, the other on Seti's shoulder, bringing him, breathing him through the Door. For he was at all times the Gracious One, the guide, the Helpmeet and Friend of those who knocked. There was no Semitic violence in him, no blasting Word of Authority, but all was easing, freeing, releasing, going through the Wall of the secret Self. Nature into Nature and Nature reborn: this was his dynamic and his gift. And the bird of the freed human soul hovered there, knowing itself to be forever free, raised out of and above the death of the body, born anew in the deathless Realm.

270

They went through the rooms and the pillared hall, saw other shrines to other deities: Horus, Isis, Ptah, Anubis. But ever-and-again mind and body came back to the central Presence, the Gracious Atmosphere. There was nothing top-down about Osiris: no steps, no parade-ground, no fire-and-brimstone stuff - just a gentle, firm hand and an opening of the Door, a welcome into Worlds unknown. Yes, Osisris was Brother; he was brother to the world. And if people could be brothers, as Osiris was, they could help each other, gently but firmly; they could guide one another over the Threshold. For that, in the end, is what it boiled down to: this capacity, natural and unique to Man, to go beyond the bleak, blank Wall, to find in the Region beyond Rugosities the Source of his Being, the deathless Self. And Brother Osisris held the Key.

'I am Osiris,' the initiate chanted, as he travelled through the nether worlds. More than sacrifice, amulet or prayer, it protected him and kept him safe. For his was a Journey difficult, uncharted, a first prizing-open of the spirit-world. His was a Journey reserved for the Few.

Historically speaking, Osiris had been murdered, then dismembered by his jealous brother, Seth, who had buried his limbs in fourteen different parts of Egypt. He, thus, became god of the underworld, whose presence fertilized and brought forth new life: he was, for the people, their dead-and-risen god. For the Few, he actualized the Journey of the soul, its descent into Death, its resurrection and rebirth. For he was, in person, the image of that Life which lies beyond the mind-and-body shell. Miraculously, he would go with one; he would take one through to a different Field. And, just as the truth of the Field was he, so was it the truth of you and I. To attain to that truth was to attain to him; more, it was to *become* him, without differentiation. For Osiris *was* the truth of one's being, its subtle, fine essence, its potency for Life. And, strange as it may seem, on becoming him, one became more really and truly oneself: the union set up a phase of Potential, which burst the iron fetters of common mortal life.

From Abydos they went on to Denderah, which, though dedicated to the goddess, Hathor, was also a cult-centre for the Osirian Mysteries. The outstretched Osiris, in his mummy-wrapping, lay waiting for his own initiation by the priests. It was a living depiction of the truth of his cult, his own entrancement and passage-through-death. How like him, thought Eddie, to go through it himself, to be, not just god-officiant-priest, but layman, also, observer and observed.

- It's a very receptive place, said Emma, as they climbed the outdoor stairway to a roof. To their view now the sand, which had covered the temple and kept it intact for a thousand years, rose gentle and far to a split rock bluff.

- Why don't we walk over there? said Eddie.

271

- You must be crazy - it's much too far! And, in any case, Don and Doreen are waiting.
- O, yes, I was forgetting them.
They looked once again at the welter of pictures of Hathor, the goddess, the Sacred Cow, then they joined the other couple, who were standing by the car.

It seemed to Eddie, as they were driving back - he mentioned it once but no-one was listening -, that we were due to enter a New Age of Osisris. He was our Brother, our very human Friend, and he was offering us the Key to that New Life. It was a crucial, momentous Turning of the Ways, for since the time of Galileo the initiative in giving Man a direction had come from science, not religion or art. But Science itself had now arrived at the inevitable nemesis of any field of knowledge, where Matter and Consciousness overlapped and one fed into and informed the other. It was getting more and more difficult to talk 'hard science' (though, naturally, there were still plenty who wanted to do it), because Matter was basically a form of Energy and Energy itself related to Space. In fact, if one looked at it objectively, carefully, it seemed more and more that, at every level, things interplayed, interwove with one another and hard-and-fast categories were like hand-tools, at best: good at ground-level, but what of the rest? It all amounted to a considerable Breakdown, not only of the laws of classical physics, but also - more direly and at greater depth - of the Classical-Semitic Rule-of-Law-and-Mind. And this Breakdown was part of Osiris's Key; indeed, it was a necessary function of it. For no-one could go through that 'little death' who had not first shed from his whole body-being the clumsy apparatus of mechanical Thought.
Eddie had made a certain Leap: one might say he was in on the Osiric Mode already, committed to reassembling his limbs. For him it was a matter of the Flowing Field, in which all creatures and things resided. There was nothing outside this One Existence. Its deep-anchored Unity held everything together, as indeed it must, since everything is one. Mystics, musclemen, seaport tarts and fairies - all lived together along the one Sacred Line. Even that person waving the handkerchief - the observer on the platform, looking at the train - even *she* was contained in It, the Prime formal Substance, of which everything is made.
His reverie spun out like a thin red thread, and it fell into place just where it ought to be. It was like coming home, in the taxi coming back; it was like settling back into one's own true shape, adjusting the torque which is our inherited 'grand mal'. He could never, from the deepest reaches of his soul, have explained to anyone what this quite meant, but he knew it as a fish knows its element; he had suddenly, magically, unequivocally turned a corner in himself and left the traumatic past

272

behind. He could see it, as it were, from above his body, as if it had been happening to someone else. There was a slumped, twisted thing lying somewhere there, a thing, yes, a *thing*, in a coil of unlove. She, the Force, the healing Touch of Grace, had slipped through his defences and made him whole. What lay there was his history, a dead thing, a corpse.

- What are you thinking about? Emma asked.

- O, nothing, said Eddie.

They were nearly there.

Back at the hotel, he had another Revelation. We were all going back along the Line of our Creation, back along the Thread which had been spun from the First. It was our true, endemic connection to the Matrix, the single sure Path which linked us to the Spheres. He thought immediately of Goethe and he quoted to himself the closing lines of Faust, Part Two, glad that he knew them off by heart:

> Alles Vergängliche
> Ist nur ein Gleichnis;
> Das Unzulängliche,
> Hier wird's Ereignis;
> Das Unbeschreibliche,
> Hier wird's getan.
> Das Ewig-Weibliche
> Zieht uns hinan.

Yes, that was what it was all about: allowing the Eternal-Feminine to touch one, to draw one onwards and upwards to Itself. It might be in the fashion and the form of Emma, in the Presence behind the human frame. Or, more universally, what could he say? What did he know of the form it might take? It was a Principle, certainly, a Universal Being; and single Emanations like the Blessed Virgin Mary were born of it as Mothers of God. It was the sustaining Power of the Universe, its ever-fecund Receptivity, its deep Fertility and Fullness of Life. The Mothers, in their time, brought the Pulse of Truth through; they conceived it in their wombs and gave it birth. And they, the Mothers, were not remote, were not Sinai-descending Father-figures, who laid it out for us on Tablets of Stone. No, they were part of the Continuum of Substance: they inhabited it as indwelling Form. And, when one once perceived the nature of Form, one was in touch with them, one knew the Mothers. 'Of course, of course,' he said to himself, 'it's been staring us in the face - Isis was a Mother!'

And, indeed, it was as Mother that she was worshipped long after the advent of Christianity; those urgent Desert Fathers hadn't quite been able to demolish her benign and blessing look of Grace. But she had entered the past, as had Osiris, through the gate of an expanding,

Romanized Christian Church. Osiris, the death-and-resurrection deity, was assumed by the historical personage of Jesus, in a piece of politicking (A.D.392) which had all the hallmarks of State Control. From then on we had lost a Friend and gained an abstracted Son-of-God, venerated, worshipped, looked-up to, but having no truck with the Nether World. We were in for a hard time, all of us.

Eddie saw this as the central Crux: could we now take Jesus off the High Cross, cease to glorify, worship or ignore Him, and ourselves pass through that Middle Gate, where Time and the Timeless meet in the Zero? It was an act both daring and uniquely simple; it wasn't 'hubris' any more. On the contrary, Man was here for that: to walk shoulder to shoulder into the Mystery with God, to be his partner, his level-looking friend.

For ages we had been overshadowed by the Lord. He had descended on us, unimpeachable and righteous; there had been no second opinion with Him. But now the whole world was entering a new phase, when it might be possible - and it just might! - for the Phoenix to rise from the ashes of the past. God lay somewhere dead among the ruins of Hiroshima, with all his many levels of Hierarchy and Dread; like Humpty Dumpty he had fallen off his wall. And where was the Isis, in this scattered day-and-age, who would put together lost limbs or comb the world for him?

No, He had been part of the Holocaust Himself. It was notions of Truth descending from on High that had built the platforms for Hitler and Mussolini. They had spoken to the people as if inspired, like Prophets of the soon-to-be Fascist State Millennium. And, for the people, it had filled a psychic void, the Blank Spot a dying god had silently vacated. They had found their Dream. Who, pray, does not?

All that platform rhetoric and remonstrance had originated somewhere on Sinai. We were used to getting Truth (what we *thought* of as Truth) in the form of Stone Tablets, indelibly engraved. What we needed, however - and our need was great -, was not potted truth in a Vessel from on High, but something directly related to *us,* what we are *now,* like food to the hungry. It didn't need to have a Platform or a Programme - a million times better, indeed, if it didn't - but it did need to touch us intuitively, intimately, much as deft Osiris had touched Seti on the shoulder; it did need to take us to our secret Self, down passages and channels as multifarious as the pyramids', through all the stiff phalanxes and squadrons of the brain. It was not in the floodlit arena of the stadium, with millennial ecstasy concatenating like cannons; it was in the deep, dark recesses of the Underworld, where shoots pushed up singly, quietly, nicely, where everything, though silent, was nothing delayed and growth came promptly, like mushrooms in the night.

The secret lay, perhaps, in *not trying:* not trying to become anything that one was not. One stood at the Crosspoint and simply waited. Then, perhaps, because one simply waited, not projecting, not forcing forward, not suing for anything beyond the compass of the Moment, the indwelling seat and focus of All-time, the Door would, of itself, gently open and the Land Beyond come into view. In some way, it was simply a question of patience - but the patience of the plant that grows, urgently.

These reflexions of Eddie's, like the thoughts of Stephen Daedalus, were directed mainly at his own soul. Emma sat them out like a character in a novel, a genteel, Jane Austen, sitting-waiting demoiselle. In the taxi from Abydos-Denderah to their hotel she had been talking quite a lot with the Desmonds. They were on their way back from a long stay in India, where they had visited and lived in a number of ashrams. They had travelled overland, as did many then. And now they were coming back to their own.
- Here it's just relics and ruins, said Doreen. India has this and much more besides.
- More poverty and misery, I've heard, said Emma.
- Yes, that too - unspeakable poverty.
- But you still liked it?
- Couldn't resist. It hit us as soon as we crossed the border, didn't it, Don?
The latter mumbled assent (he was stuffing his briar with Egyptian shag).
- It gave us that feeling - you know how it is when you're travelling - that you've come to the right place at just the right time.
- I think we've got that feeling now.
- It's more than possible, if that's where it fits. One man's fish, as they say . . .
- Quite. My husband's particularly taken with it. Look at him now.
And there he was - gone!
It wasn't until they were back at the hotel that Emma realized she had referred to Eddie as her 'husband' (normally, she simply called him 'Eddie'). What was it about Doreen that had made her want to push up this Pawn of unwonted formality?

The men, suddenly ignited, began to talk, over the early dinner they were having on the terrace. Don was saying, and Eddie agreed, what a fine thing it would be if, after the meal, they were to go over to Karnak and catch the 'son et lumière'.
- Can't cost that much, he said persuasively, as if it were really a question of that.
- O, no, not much at all, said Eddie.

And that seemed to settle it, as far as they were concerned. What they hadn't considered, in their enthusiasm, was whether or not the ladies wanted to go. As so often happens, the men made up their minds and just assumed that 'the wives' would come along. In this case, however, it wasn't going to work. Emma was tired from the day's travelling and sight-seeing, and Doreen simply put her foot down.

- I'm not going, she said flatly.
- Well, I think we can manage on our own, can't we, Ed?
- Er . . . er . . .
- Nonsense, of course we can!

And that *did* settle it. Actually, Eddie was not so keen any more: he would rather have stayed back and been with Emma. But, before he knew it, he had been sucked in by the unpredictable politics of the 'double couple'. The older man had written the script and here he was now, centre stage, with a role. His 'faux pas' in not, at least, consulting Emma was clear to him now (what a boy he still was!), but, equally clearly, the Moment had gone. If he spoke to her now, she would just say, 'Go!', since that was what she would think he wanted; if, on the other hand, he said he didn't want to go now, he would look even more of a petulant child - and one who didn't know his own mind, at that. Don would pass it off, of course - either go by himself or abandon the idea -, but, in either event, it would be *his* discourtesy (or indecisiveness) which had decided things, and that would put them further out-of-joint. It wouldn't make the reckoning right with Emma, either. No, in the end, he *had* to go.

5

As the brief pink twilight flickered all around and the sky lost some of its blue luminosity, to explode in flushed shadings of pale green, yellow, red, the two men stepped out of the 'Fellahin' and got into a taxi, which was waiting close by.

- Like two schoolboys going off on a jaunt, said Doreen.
- Quite, said Emma, with a complaisant smile.

She really wanted to be alone, and she walked through the hotel and back up to the balcony, which ran along in front of the rooms. It was quiet here; scarcely anything moved. A gathering swift darkness and, like a bird on the wing, the trembling twilight, about to disappear; then a touch of it, a veil, against the pillars of the temple, their rough pale sandstone made tender, like flesh. Bats were flitting in and out of them.

- Am I disturbing you? said a man's voice.
- O ... e ...
- Don't worry, darling - it's only me.

And, in an instant, Doreen was beside her.

276

- I used to be a professional mimic, she said. I can talk very deep if I want to, like thhh i i s . . .

They both laughed: her voice was low, like a man's.

The bats were even more numerous now.

- Look at them, said Emma.

- Yes, look, said Doreen.

And she turned Emma's face towards the fading light. In one quick, smooth gesture she had caressed her cheek and pushed her hand in further, beneath her auburn curls.

- I can feel you, she said. I know you're one of us.

- One of . . .?

- Quiet, she said, her finger on her lips.

Emma quivered like a frightened little girl. The man's voice, the bold caress, the finger on her lips had overmastered her completely and her knees went weak. She backed away, feeling for the balcony to support her; she gripped the rounded top of it with her hands.

- I'm married to Eddie now, she said.

- And I'm married to Don, replied Doreen, imperious.

- I've told him everything.

- Now, there's a brave girl.

- I've also told him that it's all over - that, I mean.

- Well, if you want to hurt yourself.

It was the last thing Emma could bear to hear. The flush ran up from her belly to her cheek, and without doubt - she could feel it - it was exploding there: her face was burning, like a day in night.

- Leave me alone. I want to be alone.

- Do you? said Doreen, standing her ground.

Emma could see the little wisps of black hair slipping out from under the other woman's headscarf, which she wore, gipsy-like, wound about her head. Her skin had that slightly oily texture which Evelyn's had had; one could almost see the pores. Her loose clothes (must be Indian) smelt of incense, which gave her a softness her Black Leather stance denied.

- Can't you see I'm tired? Emma said.

- Of course you are; you must come and sit down. Come and sit down for a few minutes with Doreen.

- That isn't what I meant.

- Isn't it?

The staircase was no more than a few feet away. She could reach it in two steps and be down there, in public; she could hide her confusion behind a glass. But Doreen's instincts were swifter, sharper: her Current moved her into the gap.

- I don't want anything from you, she said, just to be with you for a little while.

277

Emma realized she was still where she had been, her back supported by the balustrade. If only she could move a little . . . But, like a hunted deer, she was trapped. She had begun to tremble, visibly. Doreen was powerful, like the night, and the Night put its dark, warm arm around her.

- Come, my darling, she said; it's getting cold. Let's go inside - be warmer there.

Emma let her head fall onto her shoulder, the head she had wanted to hold aloof. And Doreen held her in a strong embrace, her two arms about the crouched imploded figure. She was kissing her lightly about the face and neck, feeling the delicious burning of her cheek against her lips, the soft erectile down beginning to stir.

- I love holding you, she said in that hoarse voice. I love holding and kissing . . .

And she went to kiss her mouth.

- No, not that, please, said Emma, pulling back.

- Just as you wish, my darling, Doreen said. I don't want anything from you, remember.

It was true: she only wanted to be with her, to stand in the dark and feel her skin beneath her lips, to attend to and call forth each second of surrender - and to be there at that moment, the perfect love-kin. Emma's resistance was broken now. Doreen led her by the hand to her room.

It was warm in the room: the heat was trapped there. Doreen burned incense; she said it was for love, she said it kept the mosquitoes away.

- Nice, these rooms, aren't they? she said in that voice. Just right for the two of us to be together.

She again put her finger to Emma's lips, sensing that the other was about to speak.

- I'll do the talking. You're here to be unveiled.

She took a length of coloured silk and wound it three times about her neck.

- This is your Talisman, for the Journey, she said.

She undid the buttons of Emma's blouse and pushed it back, so that her shoulders were bare. Emma herself took off her bra.

- That's my girl; you're learning fast.

She took her two breasts, cupped, in her hands, stroking the nipples with her thumbs. Then the hardening nipples she sucked one by one, as Emma flung her arms around her neck.

- Temples for the boys, eh? Love for the girls!

And she pushed her tongue inside her ear, entirely swallowing the lobe in her mouth. Emma's whole body was pure sensation, then she felt the sensation focusing in. Doreen was holding her from behind.

- Don't come, she said, don't you dare!

And she ran her fingers down the knobbles of her back, like a sitar player tuning up.

- The first lesson of Tantra is self-discipline.

Emma, who was still in the Sphere of Mutuality, wanted to do something for Doreen now. She slipped her fingers up under her headscarf, but Doreen backed away from her, as if she wasn't there.

- I don't want anything from you, she repeated. You are the music, you are the one.

And, in a split second, she had turned Emma on her belly, unbuckled her belt and removed her skirt. Emma, will-less, took off her pants.

- Beautiful! You are the perfect subject. But you have much to learn and very far to go.

- Where are you taking me? Emma asked.

- Back to yourself, where else? Doreen said.

She withdrew the belt from the top of her skirt and slipped the slim end into Emma's mouth.

- Kiss him, she said. He is your Mentor.

She pushed it deeper down Emma's throat, and Emma could feel its live penetration calling up sparks in the backs of her eyes. Her stomach muscles began to contract, and a spasm shot down from her belly to her loins. Doreen swiftly withdrew the belt and flicked her across the shoulders with it.

- Is this what's required of me? Emma asked.

- This - and so much, very much more.

Her voice was like a haunting dream; it carried Emma away on its flow. She realized she knew nothing about the human voice. Doreen did, and she was using it now. But, strangely, Emma felt no fear: it was as if it had been taken off with her clothes.

- You must go to the limit, to the very end. You must know yourself as body and soul - and as something far beyond both. You are very beautiful; you must sense it everywhere - in your body, in your blood, in your heart, in your mind. You must know it so completely that you are in no doubt, for only then will you have the nerve . . .

Her tone was becoming prescriptive, and she stopped. She ran the edge of the belt down Emma's back, like a serpent coiling, hissing, seeking. Her voice became mantric again and she said:

- See, he wants you; he wants your love. But he doesn't know if you're ready. Are you?

Emma, face down, nodded assent.

- He is very, *very* hard, said Doreen.

Emma lay prone, face and belly down, surrendered.

- You can't see how perfect you already are. Pain and pleasure are one, you see.

She took the silk scarf from about her neck and tied it tight across her eyes.

- It is better you see nothing, she said. That way you will be open to measureless sensation.

She pulled her two arms straight out from her shoulders and wedged a piece of soft cloth between her feet. Emma lay spreadeagled, waiting - shorn, at last, of everything.

It was some time before the first blow fell, like water over patient rock. Then, with gathering volume, it began to plunge, to seek out every corner of Emma's body, its unsuspected vulnerabilities. It was teeming and seething into her. At first, it was cool, almost nonchalant, with a view out and back to distant snow. But now it was gathering, flooding, strengthening; it was hot and remorseless, cornering her. Some part of her was pleading: 'O, no! Please stop!', but Doreen bore down inexorably upon her, a mask across her eyes now, ignoring her entreaties.

- To the very end, my darling, she said. It's just the two of us, you and me.

And she thrust her legs a little wider apart, running her hand along the insides of her thighs, preparing the way for the serpent-stroke. When it came it was sharp like the strike of a snake, and Emma flailed and turned, evading it and screaming. Doreen was dressed in impregnable chain-mail, and she held up the lash like a sword to her nose. Then she descended on Emma, winning her by strength, pinning her to the ground so that she could scarcely move, forcing her again to kiss the belt, then savour her own saliva on her thighs. It was hot and hissing, like molten steel. She was giving it to her, more burning than before, and Emma was bursting in her screams, her shouts, her tears.

- Shall we stop now, my darling? Doreen said.

- No, don't, said Emma. Do what you like - do anything, anything you like to me!

- That's my beautiful, brave, sweet girl!

And Doreen threw the belt on the floor. She was looking at her lovingly, the mask and the chain-mail stripped away.

- That is the Initiation of Punishment, she said: an ancient rite from ancient times.

Emma was coiled about the Serpent, purged.

- Kiss him a third time, Doreen said.

And Emma took him deep inside her mouth. Again she felt the spasm in her loins.

- You're much more beautiful than you know, said Doreen.

But she didn't remove the band from her eyes; she took her unsheathed, quivering, now-attuned body and ran her lips lightly all over it, the ears, the soft hair, the shaped shoulder-blades - pausing only to savour the down at the nape of the neck, on her cheeks, above her buttocks - then over, brushing them, hardly even touching, the flesh of her still hot, palpitating thighs, her calves, her ankles, her toes in her mouth.

- This is the Other Initiation, she said.

Emma, the purged, lay limp and inert, as if it were happening to someone else. She was in a dark room and everything was dark. Nothing existed, except at those points where Doreen's mouth moved over her body. She didn't want Doreen to kiss her on the lips - curiously she kept that prohibition in her mind. Doreen caressed the inside of her ankle, the inside of her calf, the inside of her knee . . . Emma anticipated nothing: she had let herself lapse into pure sensation; where there was no sensation there was nothing at all - not even her thought, with its one prohibition.

- You're not really a Spartan, Doreen said, much more of an Athenian, one of us.

Emma was alert, suspended, null; she was beginning not to own her body. Doreen let her abide in patience, in mute suspension from her touch, then she began to stroke her very finely down one side. It almost tickled, and Emma said:

- Is this my reward?

- Just the start of it, my dove.

She wanted to look at that lovely face, through which so much ravaging emotion had passed. She turned her sweetly on her side, then completely over on her back. It was true, Emma's face was almost seraphic: it had the look of those who have been close to death and who come back to us from the Other Side. Her skin was so soft it was almost transparent. Doreen was blinded by her beauty, which ran in a wave up into her cheeks, settling there, high and lovely and burning, till the blindfold sealed her eyes from sight. Now Emma wanted to take off the scarf. She moved up her hand, but Doreen was quicker; she grabbed hold of her wrist and, before she could murmur, she was kissing her widely and warmly on the mouth. Emma felt her strong tongue enter her, and it was like the Serpent coming again: she felt his/her still, silent penetration. The world was going away from her. She wanted to resist - not that, not that! - but she was parting and breaking and coming again.

- You see, said Doreen, every bit of you must go.

- But . . .

- No 'buts'. It's all or nothing now.

And with that, she began, in a flurry of motion, to run fingers, tongue, teeth all over Emma's body. She was looking for the place, that special secret corner, where the hidden Treasure of Emma's body lay. Only then, when it was found, would she release everything. It was tantalizing that Emma still held back. She felt for her beneath her Mound of Venus and Emma, stirring, sensing Doreen's search, eased herself, coiling, around her two slim fingers. But it wasn't just in the physical sensation - the erectile flesh in its bath of juice - or in Emma's surrender to the strength of her. She, too, Doreen, must move on it.

In a matter of seconds she was out of her clothes and was lying naked with Emma in her arms. She pulled the blindfold away like a useless rag. It was like a Revelation to her - the secret of Emma's body was her *eyes*: they looked at one from fathomless depth. They were looking now, straight into hers. And they were burnished, deepened, made sage and restful, like the eyes of one who has seen a Foreign Land and comes back, glorified, to tell the tale. For she had been raked through from bottom to top.

Doreen was quick to realize her and, as if instinctively, her hand went down again. Emma uttered a little 'aagh', as Doreen's digits entered her.

- Lie still, my darling, she said in that voice.

She could tell that Emma was on the Last Wave and she wanted to touch her *everywhere*. Very gently, therefore, almost imperceptibly, she slid the whole length of her body under Emma's; it was as if she were supporting her. Her tongue touched her everywhere, opening her pores, releasing the ache of the aeons through her skin. Emma responded, opening, pliant, feeling Doreen's tongue like a flicker of flame. It was gathering and spreading all over her, and she was lost in it; it was like a Forest Fire. She was consumed by the Fire - it went everywhere at once -, and nothing could stand in the way of it. And it was just like that moment when the flames part and one sees the dark heart, from which the flames pulp, when Doreen parted Emma from behind and thrust her strong tongue into her. The fire was inside her now, it was alive; it was shooting out sparks to the fringes of her womb. Doreen's tongue, fluted like an Ionic column, was firm and soft, rough and smooth at once - it seemed to possess a life of its own, independent of her will.

There was a dark place in the back of Emma's brain, some untouched region related to the past. It was hard and unmoving and could not be reached; no amount of reflection had been able to dislodge it. And it was changing colour as the flames licked up, as Doreen's body melted into hers. The physical sensation was of being impaled, of being worked up and wanting to come. But, at the same time as wanting to come, she knew she mustn't: she must await that other, secret moment when what she had nurtured, unconsciously, for years was also ready to discharge itself. It was changing colour now inside her brain; it was turning purple, it was penetrable like her. It was ceding, also, it was beginning to give, and the smooth fluted column of Doreen's tongue which was working her up . . . She couldn't hold it any more. The world exploded in purples and stars, and she awoke to find herself, alone, in bed. She must have been asleep for hours!

For minutes she lay in two Worlds at once: in the dark quiet world into which she had awoken, and the other, more real, the World of the Dream. She touched herself all over, where she had been touched, but there was no trace of punishment or pain. She was naked, nonetheless - yes, those were her clothes, over a chair. Her shoulders felt cold and she covered them with a shawl, and its loose wool tickled like Doreen's finger-tips. The coloured scarf had completely disappeared; so had the belt - she never *wore* belts -, though, oddly, a length of discarded rope, like a broken sash-cord, lay loosely coiled by the chair. Then there was her mouth, her mouth. She ran her tongue over her teeth, along the row, then she curled the tip back to the soft palate, the hard. No, she would have known it immediately by its traces - no-one had been inside her there. She was inviolate, after all. And she was shocked to discover that this gave her more relief than finding she had not been beaten black-and-blue.

She continued to lie still. It was very quiet now: the night had settled, become its own. She thought of getting up and going downstairs, but it was safe and warm here; the door was closed. The blinding reality of the dream continued to stir and work in her, and yet she felt curiously cleansed by it. It was as if a whole area of herself, which she had been walking away from ever since childhood, had now come up and had its say. She knew herself now by experiential insight as utterly vulnerable, with a strong Shadow-side. And, somehow, the Secret lay there, in the Shadows, and not in the brittle, rude World of the Day. The schemata of the Day didn't really apply there: there it was a matter of being *in touch*. And who said dreams were any less real? It was a different phase of reality, that's all.


Someone - the proprietor, Doreen, the houseboy? - must have told him that Emma had gone up to sleep, because Eddie opened the door very quietly, stumbling over something as he came in.
- It's all right, she said. I'm not asleep.
And, as he still said nothing, fumbling for matches (there was no current in the rooms)
- How was the 'son et lumière'?
- Not bad.
Obviously, he was in a kerfuffle.
- Over here, she said. I'm over here. Come and lie with me a little while.
She had a compelling urge to feel his body, to know his muscle and his strength were hers.
- Who else has been here? Eddie said, sniffing the air like a watchful fox.
- O, just the houseboy with some mosquito-coils.

And, as he bent over and kissed her strongly, pushing his tongue deep down inside her mouth, he was quite sure - they both were - that no-one else had been there.


They went down to an omelette breakfast the next morning, to discover that Don and Doreen had left. 'Early gone,' said the proprietor. And it wasn't until they got back from Luxor (Eddie had wanted to see Karnak by day) that the housebody, evidently well groomed in advance, came up to Emma as she was standing alone and gave her an envelope containing a note:
' Sorry we didn't have time to say Good-bye. Don and I are flying back to Cairo - Hotel Rameses, if you care to look us up. Things *do* look different in different lights, don't they? I've left something for you with the houseboy - just ask him.
Love,
  -D'
Ali was rinsing glasses behind the bar and, at the nuance of the raising of an index finger, he emerged with a loose-wrapped package in his hand.
- Thank you, Ali, said Emma, tipping him, more for his honesty than anything else. She flicked open the paper - it was a coloured scarf!
- Look what Doreen left for me! she announced to Eddie, as she entered their room.
- O, that's nice. Must be Indian.
- Must be: it smells of incense. Smell!
Then she put it on, winding it thrice round her neck.
Does it suit me, Eddie?
- Perfectly, he said.


6


There was not much else for them to do in that area (they had already been there several days) and, like Don and Doreen, they left the next morning. Buses ply regularly between Luxor and Aswan, and they rattled along for four hours or so. The environment changes gradually: there is less and less green as one approaches Aswan. (The weather, however, at that February time-of-year, is pleasantly warm, with softening breezes.) The colour-tone of the people also changes: they become blacker, more African. One feels, and they felt, the Dark Continent begins here.
Aswan has been a winter watering-spot for years, and it still has that air of aristocratic ease and footloose worklessness such places enjoy. Many hotels, a simple 'souk', shops, streets. They eventually found a place within their budget and checked in, initially for two nights.

There was no Nasser Dam yet at Abu Simbel - just, on the two-hour ride to the site, the Aswan Dam, whose grey wall they crossed. The site is concealed behind a rounded sand hill and looks southwards from the border into the Sudan. Rameses II sits there with three gods, in a colossal composition, built back into the hill. They walked down and inside it, then surveyed it from the front.

- What do you think? said Emma.

- I think something's been lost; if one things of the Pyramids and Abydos - all gone.

- What happens, do you think?

- Personal power creeps in: sitting with a god makes you feel like one.

- Don't you think he *looks* like a god?

- Quite the reverse - he makes the gods look like him.

- Creating god in his own image?

- Quite.

- Definitely the end of something, then.

They walked hand-in-hand back up the hill. It was getting ten o'clockish and hotter. Their taxi rolled them back into town, with a camera-stop about halfway. Emma and Eddie didn't have a camera, but the young American and his Swedish girl-friend, who were sharing the taxi, both had one. They leapt out with enthusiasm at the sight of a camel-train, with about eighty camels, going north.

- Where are they headed? the American asked.

- I think, likely, Cairo, the taxi-man replied. The market there.

They watched them go by. The camels moved past them, dun against dun, like a sliver of the desert itself in motion.

- They come up from Sudan, he added.

- How long will it take them?

- How long it takes? A month.

Emma thought of all that could happen in a month: the waxing and waning of the moon, a woman's blood; she thought of what this month was doing for them. Back in the hotel, she said to Eddie:

- You know, it seems we've been here ages. And yet, it's been only - what? - a fortnight.

- O, less - ten days.

- It's been so intense . . . these last few days, particularly.

- Do you know what Don said to me the other night, when we were coming back from the Karnak thing? He asked me if I was prepared to die - prepared in the sense, *ready* to die.

- What a strange question! What did you say?

- I said I wasn't sure. I asked him why he asked.

- And?

- He said there was something . . . but that I should be ready. He put it quite poetically, actually (we were coming back on the ferry at the time).

He said the Pharaohs, like us, used to sail forth in their Death-Boats, across the waters of the Nile. They would put out from Memphis and drift down the river, till they reached some special spot, and there they were entombed. He said their Death-Boats were immaculately golden, made perfect, and, if I wanted to join the Elect, I should prepare.

- You had a vision like that yourself, back in Sheffield. You told me about it, don't you remember?
- That's what's so uncanny about it. It's almost as if he'd read my mind - but not the ordinary, day-to-day mind.
 - No, the deep Mind, the Mind you *are*.
- That's right: he had a line to that.
- Strange - he didn't look the type.
- No, neither of them did, did they? Not at first.
- I wonder what they're doing now?
- O, I don't know; probably talking about us.
- Do you know what I'd like to do this afternoon?
- What?
- Take a boat to the other side.

A loose village spread down to the water's edge and they skirted it in the direction of the cleft of a valley. This led eventually up to a sort of saddle, from where one had a view of the Nile, its ancient, slumbering, blue-elusive waters. It was impossible to think of it as other than nourishing. Even when it flooded - *particularly* when it flooded - it was the gifted embodiment of Nurture, of Life. And here before them was the beginning of the desert, that unfathomable tract of Death-in-Life, with its faintly moving, drifting contours, its wisps of sand spitting softly in the wind. Eddie understood the Desert Fathers now, and why they had come to places such as this. There was no trace of human contamination here, not even the possibility of it. It was a place where one could, not only be alone, but also meet oneself coming back - as God's Beloved, in God's Beloved's form. It was a place of meetings, strange as that may seem, of Meetings with the Miraculous. Such things *did* happen in that special Space, that place uncluttered by human Thought.

The Other Dimension, normally so opaque, usually so hemmed-in, blocked, if not obliterated, here had completely free run and play. It could weave itself into the human skein-of-things from that World which lies very slightly behind this one and from which it is able, at a given Point, to take on appropriate physical form. This entry into the human domain is in no way an 'assumption of our sorrow' but a direct vertical-veridical Intervention, akin to what happens in certain kinds of dream. Down this vertical Channel disclosures can be made, which are not of the texture of the Field of Time. And through it, also, that Presence can manifest, which is sometimes referred to as the Eternal

Youth, or the One who has drunk at the Fountainhead, or He who wears his Sandals on his head - in other words, oneself coming back, oneself in the Mirror, oneself as one *is*.

- Do you think He's here? Emma asked.
- Potentially, always; actually, perhaps. It isn't the way we think it is.
- I wonder what will happen to us.
- To you and me?
- Yes.
- I don't know.

She had taken off her sandals and was kicking through the sand.

- It's strange, she continued, we're blissfully happy, and then one realizes . . .
- Realizes what?
- O, I don't know . . . this utter Immensity. And one's total aloneness in the world.
- Don't you think happiness diminishes it?
- O, not one iota: it's always there. It's like the desert - infinite.
- I thought our being together might change it.
- It is changing some things . . . but it won't alter that.

Eddie went back to his ruminations. It was always in upon himself that he turned.

- Somehow, I still think of Shelley, he said.
- But you *do* give me what men call love.
- I do, and it's great. But what about the rest?
- The rest, my dearest, is beyond our control.

They hadn't realized how far they had walked. A ruined palace lay over to the left and, to the right, a ridge with wrinkled sand. They walked up the hump-backed comb of the ridge, then came running, tumbling, down the open side. They fell into each other's arms at the bottom, and the sand filled their ears with its sibilant endeavour. They were listening to its Secret Sound. It was a high-pitched, metallic, non-existent Note - not struck by reed, gut or vocal chord. It was the single Sound of the Universe. They lay in each other's arms and listened/watched, as the Sound, vibrating and gathering in volume, swelled from a point just above the horizon, to take on and take in everything: the sky, which was becoming light and æthereal; the vast, expanding demarcation of the sand; the sand itself, with its shifting ribbed rugosities; and finally the little world of Man - the broken palace of some once-proud lord; a crouching settlement, beginning to twinkle - and the two of them, curled, locked into one another, receptors still, percipients of the Sound.

It went on at volume, containing everything, drawing everything into It, as into its Source. Then, unstoppably and with the same still motion, It scattered, creating the entire universe. This was not some mirage or mental fantasy, but the atom-truth, exactly and precisely, of *what is*. All things were in It, and It was in all. Indeed, their very being and life was It. And It issued forth endlessly, audibly, visibly, from some deep Well of Being known only to Itself. It defied all description, ultimately. It destroyed all categories, all measure, all plans. It was the one, unmistakable Voice of the Undying, the Sound one heard-and-was before one was born.

And Life, *all* life, came through that Sound, which was *omni*present, while present in every living thing. Indeed, it was its Matrix, its Substance, its last and inalienable secret Soul. God didn't play dice - Einstein was right - he played Music, and his Music was the Universe: not just the universe of sight and sense, of light-waves and matter, people-lives and -deaths, but a totally *other* - what? - Open Dimension, where differentiation had entirely ceased.

This wasn't some spare, remote, abstract revelation; in fact, it wasn't something *out there* at all; it was not in time-terms, however distant, like a spacecraft. No, it *was* right here-and-now, as the Immeasurable Quantum, the atom-truth of This. And just as it was perceptible as Sound, so it was intelligible as Seed, as the invisible Core of everything. The light of one's mind was the Light of That - without gap, residue or knowledge-application. It was *not* in the tangential Play of things, in the ever-expanding, -contracting Rainbow World, nor in the sense that one could go from this to That. No, this was *it*, the Journey was now; this was the still Place, round which all revolved. And, without It, nothing was, that ever had been. And it contained the Rainbow, like a drop of rain.

They lay there for a long time, quietly, unmoving. Little by little the Sound diminished; the sky grew darker: night was coming on.

- We should be getting back, said Emma.

- We should, said Eddie.

Neither of them moved.


It was night by the time they reached the little jetty, through the brief mauve gloaming of the Egyptian dusk. Things had taken on their habitual form, the local people their habitual routines. The glow of evening still hummed about the air, and a few desultory vendors moved through it, selling peanuts; the lights were on in the wooden lock-up booths. Was this It, then, given shape and size? Did It all reduce to this familiar scene?

- Tea, sah? said a quiet voice at Eddie's elbow.

As they waited for the bulky boat to fill up, they drank a sweet brew from fragile clay cups.

7

Nile cruises, then as now, were a popular (if expensive) way of seeing the country. Given the limits of their stay, it was a toss-up between taking river transport or flying back to Cairo and bussing it to Mount Sinai. Not entirely for financial reasons, they decided on the latter course.

- The Jews weren't the first, with their One God, said Eddie. An Egyptian Pharaoh got there before them: he banished all images, all idol-worship. Uncle Siggi did a lot of research on it - for that book of his, you know - he told me all about it once. Apparently, Moses adopted the concept - clever of him, wasn't it?

- If that *is* what actually happened.

- Well, you don't believe the Bible version, do you?

- I'm not sure. I haven't really got an opinion . . . Perhaps he was an Initiate.

- What if he was?

- Half-Jewish, half-Egyptian.

- Well, then?

- Well, then.

Game, set and match! They would *have* to go to Mount Sinai now, stay separately at St. Catherine's Monastery and go up the Mountain, as Moses had done. They took a flight from Aswan to Cairo the next morning, checking in again at Pension de la Tour. In the afternoon they walked over to the Rameses, on the off-chance of meeting up with Doreen and Don. The couple had departed that very day, but they had left a note - the deskboy had it for them - in an envelope, marked quite simply '~ The E's ~':

'Thought you might, but the Birds have flown. Nothing left for us to do here now REPEAT nothing left for us to do. We are out on the night-train to God knows where. Your Journey, however, *only just begun*. All the Indicators point East. Go there soon. Be diligent; be bold. So far as Provenance is concerned:-

Emma, darling: 1. Wear your rainbow Talisman.

               2. Acknowledge the Serpent. Know yourself.

Eddie, dear: Make ready your nuptial Night-boat.

Don't expect to see us on This Side again, but we'll be watching, waiting, working for you. Strange, isn't it, when 'seems' stops and 'is' begins - actually, a New World altogether.

   ~ The D's ~'

They read the note over several times, but they didn't speak till they were out by the Nile.

- My nuptial Night-boat I know about, said Eddie. And your rainbow Talisman must be your scarf. But 'acknowledge the Serpent' - what does that mean?

- I'll tell you later, Emma said.

# VOLUME FOUR: **TURIYA**

## *BOOK TEN: BREAKING OUT*

La vraie Vie est ailleurs.

Rimbaud

1

The Forces of Life were coming back gradually, after the ravages of World War II. There was a trembling-at-the-brink, as it were, an incipient sense of something on the way. Difficult to pin down, actually. Did it all begin in Memphis, Tennessee, or further west in the forlorn U.S.A.? The Spirit of the Age was restless, rootless, looking for something beyond its ken.

Then there was the Cold War going on, with an Orwellian kind of predictability. It settled in like some huge Grey Monster and, before long, it seemed it had always been there. Even in 1956 and 1968, those key years in the saga of post-war Western Man, the clamps came down in Hungary and Czechoslovakia to show us all the Chills still ruled, O.K. The Ferment was active, nevertheless; it was seething like roots after gentle rain.

2

Eddie and Emma came back from Egypt, sure now of themselves and of each other. They were now, in some sense, inseparable, wedded by the Sound, as well as word and deed. The desert, from afar, had spread over them the Mantle of Perfection, its own proper sky. And they looked at one another as at the desert sky - on the level all around, the whole time focally. It wasn't that it moved with them (sharing their rhythm) but rather that they had an objective referent, some overarching intermediate Continuum, from which Being flowed and which actually *was them.*

For both of them it was a delight and a revelation; for Emma, in particular, it was the point of poise, the Still Centre she had somehow been always seeking and which had never materialized - not, at least, in a relationship. They knew the close bonding of heaven and earth, the earth tipping up at its very edges to the sky, and heaven's lip touching it, making it burn. It burned in them, for love of one another.

To be honest, they were never quite sure where they were going - just like the world they were living in. It could be this way or that, then again another. It didn't seem to matter very much - not, at least, from a certain point of view. The linear progression of their lives was secondary: what *was* important was the inner trajectory, the Bird released, the inheritance of Memphis. Theirs was no longer flat-level stuff (a plod of days to an awaited end) but a conscious Spiral, vivid and real, like the ossature of human flesh. It curved, jointed, fit, inhered and was at all points immediately itself. They travelled it like travelling the bones, amazed at every knobble and bend to find a new limb opening up. Who would ever think it, who lives only in Flatland?

This 'vita nuova' became their poem, the incessant cadence at the heart of life. Sometimes it lay dormant like an unshaped line or was elegant and finished like a classical Alexandrine. At others, however, it bubbled along, teeming and frothing like a mountain stream, bursting its banks into unfed lands. Then like them, the lovers, it lay still.

Their bodies, too, were no longer heavy hunks but light, suspended, as if made for flight: 'terze rima' incantations. They composed their love, as a composer might a symphony, building it up from the First Sound. For that Sound lived and loved in them; it was like the marrow of their bones, the seething, deep, invisible Blood, the ubiquitous, tastable, all-dissolved Salt. And it *worked* them from out of the World of Illusion, the flat-gravitational Plane of Everyday: they were delivered whole onto a fresh Shore, and it was there that their inner Ascension began. In a very real sense they did nothing at all, for all was pristine, new and clean here; it bore no resemblance to anything known. And it was simple, utterly simple, and true: it was a Movement, voluminous, in which they were assumed.

Eddie and Emma took their course, followed this one, abiding Flux and were in it and of it, as their element. It was scarcely personal any more: it had taken on the redolence of the Dream. That other Reality moved in them, covering, like snow in the Northern Night, the sore points, sharp angles, rough rugosities. It was moulding them to its own non-end. And the coloured World was present, also; it was there among the Snow like the Rainbow bursting forth, its spectrum derived from a single white-light Source. They could find one another so perfectly now that Beauty was born at that very instant, joyous, effervescent and playful as a child. They had entered a New World, and they were new.

292

Would it last, though? That was the question.

Emma and Eddie went back to Sheffield, she to the library, he to teaching. He started out with a sense of mission, and he laboured day by day as the garbage filled it in. No-one seemed to care about the early Goethe - or any other Goethe, for that matter. Everything went down the predictable channels of graft, muck and brass and 'now't for now't'. Never a peep for 'Heidenröslein', especially when set to music by Schubert!

A foreigner he was and a foreigner he remained - the more so, when some lank-haired lout discovered his name and, by a calculated sleight, metamorphosed it from Adalbert to 'Handlebert'. Youth's prevailing and unfailing viciousness threw up every kind of variant: Handle-Wandle, Wanklebert, Bertrude - even, by some farflung connectedness, 'Flossie'. This forest of sobriquets stalked around like some metaphorical Birnam Wood, moving in to murder him. Dodge as he might, or stay immured in his form-room, there was no doubt about it: they were going to get him. He had only to turn a corner and a shout of 'Wank' went echoing across the brown-tiled walls. 'Handle' spears shot up from the floor and others - latest weaponry - shone ominously along the beams. Then came the writing on desks, the graffiti. This covered the whole range of adolescent fun-and-violence, from the simply inane ('Handlewandle pandles') to the straightforwardly murderous ('Blades up Flossie'). This latter had such an effect on Eddie that when, in a quite different context (boarding a tram in Fitzallen Square), he saw, splashed in red on an innocent wall, 'Up the Blades', he got stomach spasms. The Forest was advancing inch by inch, dense, immeasurable, spitting spikes. Of what use, pray, was his slender shield - 'You will call me, please, always Mr Fretstone' - against such an army of predators?

What happened - and it actually saved his bacon - was that some pimply evil genius came up with a formula, which book reviewers might term 'elegant demystification': it took the plethora of Eddie's nicknames and resumed them all in the one word - 'Puff'. Though this was crude, jejune and utterly untrue, it was sufficient to create a new current of abuse and defuse Dunsinane, at least temporarily. Eddie stood his ground: he wouldn't crack, after all.

He lived, nonetheless, along the fine line of survival. The headmaster, a portly and disappointed man, who sported a certain grinning bonhomie, which he paid for in the coin of a nickname, 'Chesh', was, though ineffectual, aware of Eddie's case and generally sympathetic towards him. He was, in fact, something of an oddball himself, having been, when younger, runner-up in the All-England Squash Championships, then, later, an aspirant to politics. Becoming headmaster had been a sort of compromise, whereby he accepted his talents (with their limitations) and applied them to a job he didn't really like. In consequence, he looked favourably on people like himself who, for one reason or another, didn't quite fit in. This was something of a help to Eddie, who found himself otherwise without friend or ally, the male staff themselves (all stolid local lads) being not averse to a little gibe-and-nudge at the expense of anyone not stripped down to bare fact.

It was an atmosphere simultaneously drab and ghoulish: stone floors, tiled walls, iron classrooms, screaming youngsters. Then the staffrooms - if anything, worse: a large, open acreage of common ground, then, at either end, a men's and women's staffroom, separate. The phalanx of local lads occupied the former, while the latter - little, white, withdrawn - was the scurrying retreat of part-time housewives and professional spent spinsters, with their books and phantasies. Eddie bobbed about in No Man's Land, unable to fit in anywhere. He got on with his teaching; he continued to survive.

3

And then there was a touch on the shoulder, an awakening as from a dreadful dream. It came in the form of a boy called Fenlon - funny name, that, everybody said so. He joined the school at the age of fifteen, having been to a prep. school and then abroad. This, in itself, was enough to mark him out.

One day he said, quite casually, to Eddie:

- One of my ancestors was an alchemist.

- O, really? said Eddie, taken aback.

- Yes, really, a little after Rabelais.

- I didn't know Rabelais . . .

- O, but of course. You don't think he could have written that stuff otherwise, do you? Not the content, I mean, the spirit.

- I don't know; I haven't thought about it.

- Then you should; it's really quite fascinating.

And he stood before Eddie, the Master complete, like Jesus in the Temple at the age of twelve.

A lock of blond hair fell across his forehead, which was high and straight and seemed translucent. In fact, he was blond to his fingertips, with the kind of fair skin one associates with women. He spoke with a natural authority, as if nothing he said came from anyone else, and Eddie, not thinking, blurted out:

- What are you doing in a place like this?

- Simple, really, Fenlon said. I didn't want to go to boarding-school. And my parents are living here - for the time being, at least.

Eddie caught a whiff of something else and said:

- Did you have a bad experience?

- Some bullying and fagging, Fenlon said.

And there were tears in a film across his grey-blue eyes: he had obviously passed through a sharp ordeal.

- Sometimes it takes such things, he said.
- ?
- To show us the reality of what men call Life.
- Is it *always* so bad, then?
- Irremediably.

He was adding inches to Eddie's Tape, at the same time cutting out false frequencies. For Eddie was still a Viennese Romantic, with voluptuous possibilities swimming in his head. This boy, this subtle body, this younger Brother had a mind of honed steel when it came to seeing clear. And somehow, oddly, meeting him here, in this place of sheer pain and alienation, gave Eddie the push, the Mirror he needed, to see himself exactly as he was. He realized that he had been backtracking somewhat: the Horrors of Dullday had absorbed him quite.

And yet it seemed part of the skein of things, some inevitable Portal, a Rite of Passage, a Test. He had simply to *stand* and get on with it, not consulting each little fancy or whim, but building up strength and discrimination against the day of his Putting-forth-upon-the-Waters. For that day was coming, inevitably. It was as sure as the accession to the Natural State had been in the context of his marriage to Emma.

He invited Fenlon home to tea with them, and it must have made a welcome change for him, too, in spite of his seeming so perfectly self-sufficient, in the way beautiful teenagers sometimes do. Emma liked him instantly; she acknowledged him instantly as 'one of us'. One didn't have to explain things to him: indeed, he was often on the move before they were. In appearance, he had the body of a Greek god - slender, unforced, natural, gracious. He was a proper guest for Paradise Square.

It is strange how some youngsters are adults already, as if youthful immaturity had passed them by. Fenlon had the poise of a demi-god, sitting somewhere on a mountain between heaven and earth. It was even present in the way he took tea, quietly sipping, utterly at ease. Somehow, the twin natures had fused in him.

- Does Ed. teach you anything? Emma asked.
- German.
- O, really?
- Yes, but I'm just a beginner.
- A beginner with promise, Eddie said, entering the room with a tray of cakes and pastries.
- Put it down there, darling, Emma said, clearing a space for him among the cups and tea-things.

As usual, when he was moving with both hands full, Eddie was prone to find the needful space missing, the carpet unfurling, a table-leg in the way. The young god, recumbent, knew nothing of this. Beyond the usual aches and pains, he had never known any discomfiture in the world. Paradoxically, it seemed, it had adapted to *him,* so that real things flowed through his fingertips, instead of, as with most of us, their being simply there and we having to find our way round them. In this sense, by his presence, he was already a Creator, one for whom Circumstance was not a dictator but which had, instead, bent its will to his, seeing in him the author of his own destiny.

Sin - what we call sin - is also Circumstance, and it is no accident that in the 'Inferno' of Dante the poet and his mentor descend the *Circles* of Hell. The lower they go, the narrower the circles, the tighter, stronger, more unbreakable the hold, till at the bottom the last, worst sinner is held in a stranglehold - a vice for a vice. It's metaphorical, of course, like Kafka's coffin. But metaphors point to a deeper truth, and the truth of the matter is: Circumstances hold us; they stand around and immure us, literally. And, unless we break their hold on us, they will, like the concentric walls of a castle, decide for us exactly where we can and can't go. We shall remain immured for the rest of our lives, unless and until we see *with our own eyes* the slim possibility, the Chink in the Wall. And then, perhaps, there is no Wall at all - just Open Fields forever, effortless Ease and the utter demolition of karmic Circularity.

And, oddly, that's were Fenlon seemed to be: not that he had been inside and broken out - he had never been inside at all. He was part of the Elysian Mystery. His body stretched out across those Fields, with the sense of belonging there, being at home. Everything about him had a timeliness, a pertinence, an on-cue presence, a correctness like a cat's.

- You must have dwelt on inner states, he said, as if they both knew why he was there. I can tell you, it isn't easy, but, of course, you know that. Often the Way seems impenetrable, blocked by obstacles - one's own and other people's. This is called the Moment of Doubt and it happens to everyone, believe you me. Like Dante at the beginning of the 'Inferno' . . . it's the problem of not seeing the trees for what they are.

Eddie had a flashback to the old Vienna days and saw the cast of his mind as the Wood without the Trees. Yes, it had always been a problem for him, part of his incurable myopia.

- You mean, one needs to get involved in detail? he said.

- *See* it, rather than get involved in it, said Fenlon. It's part of the Correspondence of Inner and Outer, and one of the most difficult things to discern. One has to see it *directly,* you see, rather than through the medium of reflection. There's no end to thought and counter-thought. Our whole civilization is based on it. The trouble is that, at the end of it all, one is left with just that: reflecting surfaces.

296

- How do you know all this? asked Emma.
- I don't know. I think I was born with it. I certainly didn't learn it at school.
- Not at the school we're in at present, put in Eddie.
- Not in any school, with any walls, said Fenlon. I've never been boxed in, you see. But to revert to this matter of the Outer and the Inner . . . They are the exact mirror-image of one another, and I don't think we realize it sufficiently. If we did, it would be a different world. It's a question of Correspondences, really, of what makes and meets what on our solitary Way. But the obstacles are real, and we have to go through them.
- What're they made of, do you think?
  Inner blocks, mainly: stiff stuff from childhood, seemingly irreducible entanglements; then all the cross-wires with which society infects us. The first job is to weed the garden.
- I take it you have weeded yours?
- At first I did; now it weeds itself.
- We weed each other's, Emma said.
  It was getting time for Fenlon to go, but he still couldn't say all that he wanted to: he couldn't quite get to the nub of it. He would have liked to dwell on the inner meaning, turn it over in his hands like a coloured ball; he would like to have seen it in different lights, seen the colour itself intensify and grow dim. He would have liked to sit at the foot of the Mountain, enter the Temple and stay there for good. He had suddenly, on the spur of the moment, a frantic desire to be Elsewhere. There was nowhere here that could contain the Mind, for it was always, inalienably, beside itself, beyond itself, more than itself. It covered and subsumed the Open Field, passing through the Moment as through that Chink in the Wall. It *was* the eternal Continuum, the instant and ever-flowing No-place, from which this, that, the other and everything derived. It was going on for ever and it had always been.
  And perhaps that was the secret, after all: not to explain, make plain, declaim, but to live in the Sanctum of the Mystery, utterly quietly, silently, unmoving. For, beyond the fact that we were born, lived and died, what was there to it but this question of Silence? It was the still, wee Source of everything: words, worlds, reasons, people, places, things - indeed, of all identity. It was the No-thing, the Void, the Zero assumed, the suspension of dalliance before Love began. And somehow, he reflected, he had been born there - not out here in the daily desert of mankind. He had merely been a witness to its awful misery, its conflict and thwartedness, misery and pain. Somehow he had watched it as one might watch a river, incessantly moving, repeating itself; he had seen its squalor and pollutedness. And, as a reaction, he had wanted to help, to pull people out of the running filth. But, mainly, his efforts had been in

297

vain; it hadn't worked out: they had backfired on him. This he had never quite understood, not until now. And yet it was so simple: he had the vision, the focus, the poise; what he lacked was experience and integration. Like Emma and Eddie, he had a Journey to make.

- I really must be going, he said, rising. I hadn't realized how late it was. The trams were shuttling along Leopold Street, and one could hear the metal clanking and see the odd tinder spark. Though it was well past New Year, the night was coming in.

- I'll walk over to the tram-stop with you, said Eddie.

On his way back he stopped in at the Cathedral, which was busy with candles, faintly aglow. They seemed to people the air with their soft, felt presence, to absorb the minor, ministrant activity. Eddie sat quietly in a pew for some time, as if in thanks for a blessing received. Then, on an impulse, he sank to his knees and thanked God out loud for sending him Fenlon

He knew as one knows things intuitively, directly, that meeting Fenlon was a seminal event. In some sense, he felt, he had *deserved* to meet him, and certainly he had needed to. A split had been growing in his life, between the Inner World (at home with Emma) and the World of the Outer (the baleful school). It was strange what it threw up, both with regard to the school and in terms of the marriage-relationship. They seemed to be parallel, unrelated Worlds. At school he could no more have talked of Emma than coach a football team or fly to the moon: he would have considered it a desecration. And at home he rarely, if ever, spoke of school, though frequently he came back drawn and exhausted. Even then, he thought, he should be giving something, and when he had nothing left to give he felt miserable. Also, it was a terrain where Emma couldn't reach him, in spite of her own experience of teaching. When he didn't come forward, she stepped back; she became again the silent witness.

There, thus, grew between them a kind of space, an untenanted ground of non-engagement. By intention they did everything right: they avoided bringing into the sphere of their relationship the banality and dross of workaday life. But this very protection was a kind of isolation, a means of not measuring up to reality in all its unevenness and incongruity. The consequence was that there was a knock-on effect: the separation and distance between the Worlds *became* the estrangement of the two of them from one another. The special World of their relationship was attacked and undermined by the things not said.

The sensitive have this problem, don't they? Coarser natures fight things out and, paradoxically, this can and often does bring them to a different ground. They fuck and get on with it: Ed. and Emma stopped. They were so conscious of their privileged status, the Natural State into which

298

they had grown, that they thought they could put a hedge around it, fence out the cattle and all intruders. But this was folly, a sheer impossibility. It wasn't something one could protect; it wasn't even theirs at all! Unfortunately, in this they reinforced each other's weakness, and neither of them was bold enough to break the glass Hold.

Fenlon had inadvertently stepped into this, not knowing, as one doesn't when one visits someone's home, what ghosts, moths, night-creatures are flitting through the air. He felt, nonetheless, some spare valencies around, as if the bonded couple formula were undergoing change. Nothing was actually *said*, of course: it was all writ in silhouette and shadows on the wall.

But for Eddie the school was a different place now; it had become a place where he could breathe again. He even started enjoying his lessons, instead of simply getting through with them. Of course, since he had started to spend time with Fenlon, the sobriquet 'Puff' had become part of his reality, but he lived with it - they both did, actually - until it ceased to have very much point, its being, in any case, universally applied to any man who so much as carried flowers. The Puritan Ethic is anti-aesthetic and lovers of Beauty the sons and daughters of Sodom.

Even where intelligence is measured as I.Q., it is obvious that children find their own level. Segregate them or put them together, like goes to like in an easy flow. If we are alive at all, we are all the time looking, searching for clues to the vast Conundrum. And companionship is part of the Way.

Eddie and Fenlon found a level together, a focus of mutual discovery, in which forest clearings, gemmed iridescences, prehistoric stone circles all had their place. The latter, in particular, they went looking for, combing the moors of Derbyshire, that entire ancillary southern Pennine swath, which swings in an arc from south Lancashire, through north Cheshire, north Staffordshire, on into south Yorkshire. 'Green Knight' country, Eddie called it, for there were traces in those parts - at least as far as Barnsley - of the language of that clattering mediaeval classic.

Their quest, however, went much further back - to that pre-Christian era when, men said, the Correspondence of Heaven and Earth had been closer. It hadn't been necessary, at that time, to box God up in Church or Shrine: he had been living, palpable and present in the outdoor world of wind, sun and rain. The Circles themselves were not confinements but focuses of energy, Places of Power. Runes ran through them, if one could but see, Messages and Figures of Opening. For they were always and uniquely at special spots, places of transition or proximity: on a hilltop, for instance, now long since cleared, on a saddle between hills, or at a confluence of waters. Doors, lintels, altars, all betokened the Passage from one Reality to another, the solemn Rite of Death-indwelling and the birth into New Life: the Circle-Egg-Womb. Sometimes, indeed, there was a small, oval-shaped stone structure, something like a beehive, into which one had to crawl.

And it was good to roam the moors at weekends, to find, as the land sailed out towards an Edge, the scattered remnant of that ancient time, to sense with the Ancients the pulse of the land, as it surged, dipped, swung and gathered to a point. It was good to be, as they had been, open, the wind and spare sun driving into one's face. It was like going back to the childhood of mankind, when the Earth had been light as a flying ball. What had we done with it ever since, but make it heavy, dead, enclosed? We had drenched it in blood and flogged it with machinery; we had taken the Great Spirit and spat in its Face.

The Circles, nonetheless, still gave a clue: they were open indicators of That Time. One could still tune in, somehow, go back, in and down - to the Belly of the World, through the Hara of Mankind. It was possible then, just possible, to contemplate a rebirth of the Spirit, to see against a clear Horizon the re-emergence of those long lost, innocent Inner Worlds. For they alone brought Plenitude. Mankind was standing, as it were, on the Threshold, ready to step over, if he dared to dare. And that, it seemed to Eddie, was the critical factor. Would we actually be able to catch fire, or would the sheer weight of deadness and fear force us to cling to the paralytic Known? That was the great, perhaps the only real question. To *be* or not to be? Now, as then.

Emma sometimes accompanied them on these weekend forays into Time past: she didn't want Eddie to move away from her. They had known release, bold and magnificent, but there was something missing from the kitchen side - almost as if they had been having an affair. They had thrived on wine but they couldn't take to water. There was somehow a gap between the elements, a hole in the process of the double transformation that made changing water into wine look easy. They were at a different kind of Cana - after the honeymoon, so to speak.

Fenlon had walked into this Middle Ground, unwitting, unassumed, not expecting anything. He had sensed the hung valencies, like loops of spiders' webs, moving in over the untenanted terrain. In another way, it was like the open moors, suggestive, pregnant, throwing up images - but, as yet, no structure, no firm abode: nothing had really taken shape.

4

It was Fenlon who suggested they go to India, as if secretly he knew it was up to him to act as a catalyst, the accelerator of events. On the face of it, this might seem strange, since Eddie and Emma had already had a pointer in that direction. But it's one of those things, isn't it? (you've noticed!) that when a Morass builds, even a small one, we have no eyes for the larger view. It gets blocked in, dammed up, shut out, and the tiny wee Point of Silence in the brain is simultaneously obfuscated, dulled. We can even throw boomerangs; they won't come back.

Emma and Eddie were at some such Station, preoccupied and hence unfree, unable to wed-and-weld together at all levels. It became an irritant between them, a source of friction and misunderstanding. Since they were gentle, they didn't shout and fight, but that didn't help things very much, either.

One evening - it was just the two of them, as usual - Emma said:

- We should go, you know.
- To India, you mean?
- Yes, exactly. It's been difficult for you since we got back.
- Difficult for both of us.
- My work's less troublesome - that's what I was thinking.
- My work's improved, too, over the last few months.
- I know it has, but work isn't everything.

There was an awkward pause: she was entering the Ground. She skirted it quickly, sensing Eddie stuck.

- Will Fenlon be able to miss school, just like that?
- He says he can; he says it doesn't matter: he can always pick it up again later, if he wants. Nothing seems to trouble him.
- That's what I was thinking: he seems unscathed.
- Yes, it's uncanny. He's very rare.
- Too rare, in a way.
- What do you mean?
- Sometimes it's as if he were hardly here at all. He'll have to enter this world somehow, somewhere.
- He's young; there's time. Why box him in now?
- I'm not boxing him in, darling; it's just how it is. Even those who're beyond it all have to have a point of bearing on the world; otherwise, they're ineffectual.
- Then *let* him be ineffectual! What does it matter, anyway?
- It *does* matter, darling, even for him.
- O, I'm tired of the way people step everything down! As soon as they see a beautiful bird, they want to capture it and put it in a cage. He's young, he's a free spirit; for God's sake, let him *be*!
- Darling, I think you're in love with him.
- I love what he *is*. It's not the same.

Emma felt relieved - for the moment, at least - that he was not giving away what he owed to her, and the conversation rested there. But they had come to a point of opposition with one another, which demanded, of itself, a reconciliation.

301

- 'You are luscious, my love, like a fresh pomegranate. The fruit of your flesh is dear to me.'
- When did you write that?
- I'm writing it now.

He wanted a new kind of life with her, to come to a place they had never been before. She *was* ripe suddenly, ripe and burning, as he pushed his hand in beneath her auburn curls. He felt her melt and open to him, felt the past melt away from both of them. They were about to begin their Journey NOW, inchoate and fertile like the loam of the Nile. They were going to find the further Shore.

She wanted him to play her like a flute, so that all that could be heard was the Song of Them: she wanted it, like Solomon's Song. And it *was* that Song, reborn, remade, spilling out now through her open pores, pomegranate-luscious, seeded, red. She wanted her flesh turned inside out. She eased Eddie into her, parting like a fruit; he entered the voluptuous Field of Play. It was every last line and tuck of her: the pucker at the corners of her mouth, her firm, tilting breasts, the pout of her Mound, and that upcreased line below her buttocks. He knew he wanted it - all of it. It was like his Garden, his place of Play. He was the upstanding tree in the middle of her. And she eased around him, serpent-like, drew out of him, coiling, thrusts and contractions, minutest movements, orchestrations. She slithered inside him, as he was in her.

It was something to do with the Moment's telling, some fine, unrepeatable fingerhold of Grace, and it was easing them up to a further ledge, some half-perceived place where Creation dwelt. There was just One Sound, and it *was* them. It rose and swelled in both of them. And, finally, there was no opposition at all, just one slim movement, one Declaration. They were going back to the centre of the earth. It was now as it had been in the Beginning; it was World without end, throbbing and dreaming - before all structure, before all Time. It was Sound, also, the sound of the desert, that One Pulse living and moving in them.

Then she wanted him to be quiet inside her, to still the rhythm down till it almost ceased, till the Sound breathed through them and that's all there was. It was in the feeling before the thought - it was never articulated as thought - but he felt it as impulse in his cells, and he quietened around her, as the night draws down. He was folding over her, sensing her soul, its tiniest touches and intimations, and she cried for the sheer beauty of their quickened souls. They were alive to one another at the centre of the earth, through the Pole that stretches from Earth to Heaven, through all the gushing waters of the tides and seas. They were teeming and tumbling through That World's Eye. They were there, at the heart of Eternity.

Her tears ran down her fresh-flushed cheeks and into the crevices of their loins. They were only moving in the Other Space. In this world they were as still as trees. She wanted more, and whatever she wanted came to her from soul-wave depth. There was no gap between the feeling and the deed. It seemed she could go on opening for ever, that the tender quick in things was moving through them now. She was all expansion, softness, belly-being; he was the flame that kept her burning there. And he hung there, light, suspended, aerial, offered up to her in the nuptial night.

They had gone through a Door down an Avenue of Light. There was no way back. They lay quiet for some time.
- You're my serpent, my snake, she said.
It was true, there was no going back for him. He felt the very music of her inside him, prompting him to further feats. But he had reached his own quietus, was still now, appeased, and yet fulfilled. It seemed her glory swam around him: she had become the music and the flow of things. He remained withheld, scarcely moving, hardly breathing, and yet all seed-seethe was alive in him. It worked her with secret Knowledge and Intent. It was as if she were impaled on him. And she realized his strength was contained within him, that it wasn't hers to have or command and that, held thus, he could go on for ever; he was moving on a different Plane. She had the feeling, for the very first time, that anything she did would be all right, and it was bliss and release in every limb - so much so that she gave way everywhere. She assumed a shape she had never known before, certainly not since her education began, and it *was* her, actually, her own true Form. What she had been struggling for was here revealed - without movement, without action, simply being still. The Tide had begun to turn in her.
For him it was a matter of fine, mute suspension, something of which he could never have dreamt. It no longer ached and urged in him; it had become diffuse, ubiquitous, huge, the sexuality of the entire body-world. He realized it as part of the Secret, the fine fire-spark in every living cell. It was hot now and glowing inside of him; it was resurgent still, unquenchable. He realized that, in holding his strength, he was holding the Secret of the Universe. It was there in embryo inside his brain, and now it quivered through the rest of him. It was this that united him, not in theory, to the living quick of everything - to the night-clouds sailing across the moon, to the fresh and salt sea water, the wind-touched summer leaves. They were all together in potency, in the multiple unfolding of the single Germ. And the Germ lay, not remote, away, out there; it was as actual and present as the breath one breathed. It was closer than breathing, more stable and more real. Breathing, in fact, was a metaphor for this: it was a movement in and out. This alone *was*.
And, being there, he knew he was the focus of Creation: the whole Manifestation moved through him. He *was* simultaneously whatever he

303

saw: the softly glowing lamp, the polished chair, that plant. They were he - their pulse and rhythm were his - and he knew them immediately, as one knows a friend. For, just as the Universe had opened out, become star-stretched Firmament without beginning or end, so also it had homed in to the finest detail, omitting nothing, not the slightest thread. It was backlit, everything, shining from the Heart, as if here alone lay its own proper texture, its simple, single, eternal suchness. It *was* what it was, and it was unconfined. It went on for ever as living truth, as permeated membrane, figure of That. No amount of thinking, reflection, diagnosis could bring one to this point of Seeing-in-itself, which indeed was the denial of acquisitive reflection. It was the Tide turning back upon itself, the double-serpent Coil, the first fruits of the Tree. And it was less than nothing; it was beyond nothing: it was what's left of Nothing, when Nothing dies.

Eddie knew all this in a flash - the stamp of recognition came lumbering behind. In fact, he was gazing all the time at Emma, holding her back, still arched, in his hands. Her eyelids were half-closed and she was smiling faintly, the smile that erupts spontaneously when a lifelong agony has been reversed. Her naked body had a rosy glow, as if she were suffusedly giving out the wine that had been pressed in it all summer long. Tendrils of hair crept over her face, blown by summer breezes, across the deep-blood of her cheeks. Her weight had sunk to the centre of the earth. And she held him still inside her, seething, as the night came in on them more and more. He was her Lingam, her living Lord.

And the night outside spread its vast Trajectory, its non-thought Mode of infinite space. It was going out and away for ever, forever untrammelled by Thought's sweat-and-circumstance. Why say it was meaningless, because *we* couldn't stretch to it, because our brains were so narrow and confined? They were boxed in and bogged down from the moment we were born. And then, with a boxed-in, bogged-down brain, we struggled, fought, thrutched to comprehend it all. By then, of course, the brain itself was the problem: it had become the House of Images, most of them distorted. And what we saw, if we pondered it at all, were merely our own projections against the Wall. Since the Universe didn't shrivel down to us, we accused it of coldness, emptiness, death; we saw it as a Graveyard because it didn't have our norms. But this was our shortcoming, not its. The universe was what it was - with spiral nebulae, comet clusters, Black Holes - it was in-and-for itself a Wonderworld. And because we wanted to step it down, make it fit into our own prefigured plan, we forfeited our place in the universe: we began to destroy everything, beginning there.

Why not, then, lie, as Em and Ed did, quietly coiled abut the Serpent Tree? Why not gather strength within, to see the nature of all this, and go beyond? Why did our whole thought-worn civilization stop short where inward enquiry was concerned? Why, in a word, were we still immature? These questions were never articulated as such, but they threw themselves up against the spinning night as direct, spontaneous, unforced Interrogatives. For it seemed to be the Groundwork of any real Endeavour.

The night revolved, not emptily. It was not the mausoleum of Man's mind. No, it was peopled, dense, intense; it was active and alive with Intelligence. In fact, Intelligence sustained it all: the Universe, the Worlds, all Time-space, This. It was ever-active and, at the same time, always still, growing as a plant grows, from itself. It was there interstitially, like the space between two thoughts; it was the unagitated 'fin fond' of everything. And It had, without one's knowing it, to take one's chattering mind away; it had, like a seed when it germinates, to burst through the crust of the mental mode.

- What time is it? said Emma lazily.
- Night-time, my love.
- Already?
- Always.

They were arched and poised at the onset of the Night. Day's brashness and weariness had fled from them.

- Isn't it strange? I feel I've always known you.
- Isn't it just? I feel I've always known *you*

They were held, suspended, in the ever-flying Night. Eddie's eyes were fixed on Emma.

- Your nose has little wings, he said, and your eyes look dreamily out past me.
- You're out there, too: outside and in-.
- Your mouth, however, tells a different tale.
- I don't know what you mean, sir, she said.

And, very demurely, she moved very slightly, that millionth of a millimetre lovers know. He was up and doing on the precious instant, the fire of her running in a thread to him. The Serpent was alive in both of them.

5

Fenlon was absent form school for some time, and Eddie wondered what was wrong with him. No-one took much notice - what was so special, anyway? - as O succeeded black O in the register. He was hesitant, however, to ring Fenlon's parents (something to do with rarefied Fields) and the days went by in the drab, grey place, which had once had pretensions to classical elegance but had long since drowned

305

in industrial Waste. Without Fenlon there, either, it was back to black-and-grey.

Eventually, Eddie plucked up courage (he *hated* the telephone - that was one reason) and called the family one Saturday morning. It rang and rang, but nobody answered. He tried twice again later, with the same result. 'They *can't* have gone away,' he said to himself. Then he realized it was part of Fenlon's private Precinct that he belonged to a family of orthodox Jews. No travel on the Sabbath, no Gentiles, no phone. He tried again the next day. Fenlon's mother answered:

- This is Eddie Fretsone, Fenlon's German teacher.
- O, well, I've sent a note to the school.
- I was wondering how Fenlon was . . . er, how he is.
- It's all in the note. Are you his form-teacher?
- No, *German* teacher.
- German, eh? You sound as though you had a German accent. Well, let me tell you, we don't like Germans.
- I'm not actually Ger . . .

But she had already hung up. It was the kind of conversation Eddie had been dreading and which telephones seem praeternaturally disposed to produce. He decided to pursue the matter on Monday.

Miss Diabolus, Fenlon's form-teacher, always gave the impression she had no time at all. If one wanted to have a word with her, say about a missing book, an absent pupil or the stock of chalk (which she controlled), it was: 'Catch me later' or 'See you at break.' If one did catch or see her (at the appropriate moment), then, more than likely, she would round on one in her waspish manner with : 'Can't you see I'm busy?' And if one couldn't, and there was no-one even *there*, she gave one the Look, her fundamental witherer, which stated without question: 'No business this week.' Today, however, she was in a good mood and merely told Eddie that, of course, she'd seen the note and that it was now with the secretary, where all such things were kept.

The secretariat had its own sphere and rhythm, its own tea-times, parameters and methods, quite unrelated to those of the teaching staff. In consequence, it became a Herculean labour to find time between classes when someone might be available and the whole filing-system not under lock-and-key. Also, the secretaries had their own hierarchy, and it would have been seen as crass behaviour if, for instance, Eddie had asked the headmaster's secretary to let him see a pupil's note. That was Miss Marshall's area, he would have been told: Miss Marshall, who came and went like a shadow and was never there at all (or so it seemed) when staff were free. Albeit, nothing daunted, Eddie tried his luck, popping into the office mock-casually a few minutes after the end of the morning break, when most teachers could be assumed to be at their posts.

Enquiring after Miss Marshall, he was told that she was out and would not be back shortly; no, no-one else could help: she took the keys with her - after all, it *was* her area. Coarser persons might have asked where she kept them (there *were* rumours going round), but Eddie, the outcast, simply felt defeated, reaching out for help and finding none.

- That boy Maciewicz, the headmaster said, flinging open a door and striding in. Get his file out for me, will you, Eileen.

And his obedient secretary, at no loss for access, slid as if on wheels to the forbidden cabinet, unlocked it nonchalantly, withdrew the file, gave it to the headmaster and slid back again. Her typewriter thrapped out the umpteenth letter of the day.

- Ah, Mr Fretsone, are you free for a moment?

Eddie seemed to have got on track, too, for in no time at all he was in the headmaster's study. It smelled of old leather and stale cigars. He was sure the sash windows had never been opened. A smoky sunlight fell through them, filtered by their dust and moted by the air. There was dust in a film along the top of the window-frame and a gathering of it at the joining of the walls.

- I've been wanting to have a word with you - in private, of course: this is strictly confidential. It's about Maciewicz - you teach him, I think.

Eddie's slow brain had only just registered that the object of their enquiries was the same person, Fenlon. He was just in time to say:

- Yes, I do.

- There've been, well, not complaints exactly, but expressions of concern about your friendship with the boy. It's even been suggested . . .

- ?

- There's been a suggestion . . .

- There's nothing in it.

- I'm sure there isn't, and that it's all decent and above-board. But you *were* in the office a moment ago.

- I was enquiring after his health: he must be ill.

- He *was* very ill; he's convalescing now.

- What was wrong with him?

- The doctor didn't say. There's more in the file here, if you . . .

He stretched out a hand towards the file, then withdrew it.

- Look, Fretstone, I must ask you to put a brake on this friendship - for your sake, for his sake, and for the sake of the school. It may seem prurient to you . . .

- It does.

- But one has to respect the view of others.

- Even if they don't respect yours?

- Even if. You're still quite young; you've got a lot to learn.

- What if I learned some of it with him?

- No, Fretstone, this concerns more than just the two of you. Think of his parents, other people, your wife.
- My wife and he are already good friends.
- Mrs Maciewicz, then: I know she's worried.
- Mothers always worry about their sons.
- And I worry, too; I worry about you.
- That's good of you, headmaster, but there's no need - I'm fine.
- Not in this area, you're not.
- And whose 'area' is it, I wonder?
- His parents', the school's, mine - as well as yours.
- I can assure you all, there's nothing to be alarmed about.
- I don't want to be alarmed, Fretstone. I want it stopped - now!

Eddie could see it was useless to argue: the man wasn't even speaking for himself. The Headmaster Mask had stuck to his face, pressed on by parents, kids, governors, staff stalwarts, maintained by his own inability to break free. If anything, he felt sorry for him.
- We can still *talk* to one another, can't we? he asked humbly.
- Of course, said the headmaster, having won his point, genial again and glad it was over.
- If you want to see the file, just ask Miss Marshall, he said.

Eddie was back in the tiled corridor.

A genuine worry assailed him now: that of the state of Fenlon's health. He had seemed so resplendent and invulnerable, so utterly beyond this Mortal Coil, that Eddie had thought him - well, yes - immortal. He walked down the corridor pensively, past the clear-glass classrooms, cold goldfish bowls. Miss Diabolus was teaching in one of them. Economics, wasn't it? Yes, of course! Every head was bowed, every mouth silent. For Miss Diabolus would tolerate no nonsense. She might have been quite attractive, he thought, with her feline good looks and her red dress on, had it not been that, everywhere she went - everywhere Eddie saw her, at least - there were razor-blades waiting to cut out wrong tongues. It was that kind of day, too - edgy, grey and cheerless.

Fenlon came back eventually, looking still quite ill and pale and drawn. Eddie was quite solicitous for him - overmuch, in fact - till Fenlon pointed out that he was behaving like his mother, which stopped him in his tracks.
- Your mother wasn't very forthcoming, he said.
- She's trying to protect me from strange men, I think.
- Am I *so* strange?
- O, completely!

And they laughed a laugh of immediate complicity. Like a warm drink, it set them up again.

- The Head also spoke to me, Eddie said, He told me I should see less of you.

Fenlon smiled (just the slit of a smile); it was like that one tear, eloquent beyond words.

- It doesn't matter, he said eventually. It's part of the wager; one still has to dare.

- You've lost me, said Eddie. What do you mean?

- The characters in Plato's Cave are convinced that what they are seeing is real. It has all the appearance of reality: it is firm, dark, defined, and it flickers with mobility. The only trouble is, it's just a reflection, but such a powerful one that they're convinced. Also, these reflections throw further reflections: shadows of shadows so to speak. So when they see two people (perhaps turned the other way) walking and talking, they say: Aha! What can those two be up to? And if you tell them, Nothing, of course they don't believe you, because in the Shadow-world every action has a motive. You are what you see - it's as simple at that - and, if what you see is nothing but shadows, you are forced to seek the reason in further shadows. It hasn't occurred to them - and, until it does, this mockery of morality will go on for ever - that the only thing to do is to turn round, because *the Shadow-world has no substance whatsoever.* The trouble is, they 've been sitting there so long - and each generation makes it a little more dense - that the quantitive difficulty is, if anything, greater. Qualititively, of course, it's just the same.

- The same in the sense that the Source is One, the Light is One, the Mind is One. The Eye that sees it is not this eye.

- A third Eye?

- The Single Eye, the Eye that sees itself. Then the whole Picture begins to change. It's as if one possessed another organ, one we've never used before. But, instead of being five, six, nine or whatever, it's one and what it sees is One. This is the Secret of Unity.

- And when we turn . . .

- We turn to That. For That is what we are. Here. Now.

- It's wonderful to hear you talk like this. I thought you might have got depressed.

- Does the Sun get depressed?, Fenlon said.

He was regal and untouched - Eddie knew it now - or, rather, That was regal and untouched, which he annunciated. He had thought it a matter of relative densities, but actually it wasn't: it was this way or that. How magnificent to find oneself again on a peak in Darien with stout Cortez! How immovably assured Fenlon was of his Ground, how little bowing to the murky Stream-of-life! No, he had turned right round, full circle: he had his face turned towards Eternity.

When he had gone off to some lesson or other, Eddie, the enthusiast, kicked himself: he hadn't asked the simplest question, the one relating to

Fenlon's health. Fenlon had spoken as if it didn't matter, but that was the privilege of Youth - to think itself, even physically, immortal. There was no gainsaying the work of Time: at some point or other it always got its way.

Mortality was on him suddenly, with a sense of the brevity and fragility of life. It was there in Fenlon, it was there in him; it was there now, apparently, also in Mellors. He had heard from Connie that he was 'none too well', and it was a matter of self-reproach for him that he had not been over to see them recently, nor even bothered to keep in touch. He was due for a visit, he told himself. He should also take being a godfather more seriously. 'Cloë's kid' - he'd even forgotten the name! Was it Bert or Seth? No, Tom, he thought.

6

The farm welcomed him, as it always did, with its redolence of good, rich times, now gone. How he wished he could be young again and do all the farm-jobs he used to do: milking, mucking-out, calving, lambing, hedging-and-ditching, bringing in the hay. He missed it like a life he might have had, a life left hanging, a possibility passed. He could have settled there and married Cloë . . . But, no, it was a perfect illusion, a sop to his sentimental side. It would never have worked: his Wings had grown; sooner or later, he would have had to break out.

Nevertheless, it was pleasant to dream - even if it was quite unrealistic. It was pleasant to think what might have been, how Time's sweet Leaven might have been maintained. For, certainly, the Land had its own Eternity - its recurrent seasons, its earth-salvation - and to work it was to be part of that. It had a settled rhythm and scope, fixed ways and times, and the kind of patient labour which left the mind free. Academia, by contrast, was a place of agitation, an ambitious, fraught, vicious, unremitting Brain-stew. Here, on the Land, it was constant, it was quiet; life came and went slowly; nervous breakdowns were nil. But Eddie had left it: he was elsewhere now.

Mellors was sitting up in bed, nursing his side, in which a tumour had grown. They didn't yet know whether it was malignant or not, though he had been to the Infirmary for tests. They had told him to rest and given him morphine for the pain. New tests would show if they would operate. He was his old, candid self, asked after Emma and wondered out loud if/when they would have children.

- I don't think so, said Eddie. We've more or less decided not to.
- Well, if you change your minds, said Mellors bluntly, you'd best get on wi' it - she's none too young, that Emma.
- I know she isn't, Eddie said.

310

It was another possibility going by, another of Life's frequencies he would never hear. But just occasionally - and now was one occasion - he did reflect on what he had missed, what Emma had missed, by flying high and wide. It was not that he had taken a wrong path. No, it was the only one available to him, the one he had gone down naturally. But it had defined itself by focus and exclusion, as any path must that leads anywhere. And it was the things it had excluded which he missed: warmth, home, a fireside, dogs, cats and children. Out on the Moor there were none of these.

Also, there was the matter of acceleration. If he had chosen that life (if it had been possible), things would have proceeded at a slower rate, as they do on the land, flowing into one another. Now he was 'out there', literally no-where, without Guide or Compass but with a burning inner drive. And he knew he had to get on with it, whatever that might mean and wherever it might take him. There was no time now, in this post-WWII world, for the gradual development that had been the maturing of old. Things were moving now at a faster rate: we were flying, literally, physically, through the air. And what that meant (though few realized it) was that we had to learn to fly within, i.e. teach our hearts and minds to soar, so that they could grasp realities at present obscured. It was a time for stripping down redundancies, throwing off ballast, chucking out waste. Above all, it was a time of no-holds-barred, no Field protected, no Corner unturned. One *had* to dare it, that was for sure, if one had the faintest inkling of a clue. But there was a price, and the price was here - in the warm, patient household, the slow fires of Home.

Cloë was the other half of the equation, the path not taken, the one who stayed at home. She was glad to see him when he came; she showed him her new baby: they had three children now.

- Tom must be quite a young man by now, said Eddie.
- O, he is; he's off playing football.
- Not much of a godfather, am I?

She said nothing. She was looking at some daffodils, nodding in the breeze.

- What about your dad?, asked Eddie.
- I really don't know, but I fear the worst.
- They don't *know* it's malignant yet, do they?
- They don't - and they're pretty cagey, anyway. But I've got a feeling he won't pull through.
- Come on, you don't *know* that.
- Don't I?, she said.

Eddie realized that she had cut deeper ground, that his own remarks were head-level and spurious. Hers were the fruit of a life lived with the Inevitable, limitations accepted, little ways borne; also, the intimacy one shares with a parent, the lifelong being of the same stock-and-stem.

Here, too, he had displaced himself, become (for valid reasons) estranged, adrift.

He didn't want to talk any more: there was a sadness, palpable and fluid, in the air. It was the downpull and -drift, the inevitable dissolution. He had wanted, had striven to go beyond it, but something in its nature was inalienable. It had its own laws, its own operation. And fly as he might, as the Masters had flown, he, like they, would come back to this: the slow end and break-up, the Physics of Death.

He would have liked to put his arms round Cloë's shoulders, as she stood there by the grass and daffodils, but something in the dignity of her grief restrained him. Nothing could alter the brute, stark fact, the final Pitch, where one was utterly alone. He turned on his heel and walked away. Birches Farm, like Nagasaki, was melting down.

But it *was* spring now, all the same; it was coming. There were lambs being dropped in the sloping fields and, along the ways, beneath the burgeoning trees, violets, wood anemones, primroses and celandines. He decided not to wait for a bus but to walk into town - as far as Wisewood, at least - and enjoy the gathering rapture of the day. There was nothing he could do now, certainly: it was a lesson in total Acceptance, Surrender.

The woods climbed up to the bare green hills and, behind him and beyond, to the ever-singing moors. Down here there were finches and sparrows a-chatter (it was early yet for the swallows and the cuckoo), but up there the skylark rose and hovered; it pinned its song to the clear blue sky. There were dips and hollows along the little path and lichen-covered rocks, with moss in the crevices. Sunlight, through the barely burgeoning branches, came in with a shatter and a splash on rock, dappling the thin trail, coiling its turns. Sometimes, for whole seconds, the path disappeared, lost beneath a scatter of leaves, fresh ferns; then, like a memory half-hidden, it re-emerged, slightly blackened, welcoming, winking through the trees.

The trees themselves were waking up. Standing, watchful, surprised to see him there, they were curious at this customer. And he carried on blithely, as if nothing really mattered - singing even, shouting snatches of his poems - covering in a burst of genuine joy his bottom-line sorrow at the agony of Mellors.

- How was he? asked Emma, when he got back.

- Nothing's confirmed, but he's not too good.

- How is Connie taking it?

- With great aplomb, really. Cloë's more affected. She doesn't think he's going to pull through.

- What do *you* think?

- I try not to.

312

He was right on the Edge, the brink of tears. Yet he couldn't cry: it was buried too deep. Mellors had been like a father to him - better than a father, less governing. He had come and gone at Birches Farm as he had pleased - and always the same welcome, the same warmth, rich and red. In the interstices of his thought he looked for hope, but basically he believed what Cloë said: that he was going.

It is Death that gives the sharp edge to Life, its circumscription and, ultimately, its meaning. We cannot waylay it or put it aside, for it has its own strong current, like a river. It comes unbidden, like the flowers in May, and perhaps, like them, it grows long, deep and darkly. We cannot fathom it, nor are we meant to. It takes on the colour of our own skin - fair to the beautiful, dreadful to the ugly. It is the unseen Thread of Life itself, the discovery of which lays all bones bare. It is the Clue, the Key, without a doubt. We are looking, we are searching, as Em. and Ed. were; we have our hands on it sometimes, but then it slips away; theirs for an instant, but then the Wheel turns.

Easter, however, was in the air, with all its permutations of Death-in-Life, Life-from-Death. It was the Season of the Pascal Lamb. Whenever it was Jesus had actually been executed, the turning of the year was obviously the right time for Remembrance. In Eddie's mind it linked him with Osiris, that slain, dismembered, silken god, whose unitive re-emergence was synonymous with spring's. Obviously, someone in one of the Schools had put two and two together on that score and merged the historical Jesus with the legendary Lover. It was a stroke of genius, poetic and noetic, since it allowed finer spirits (always there were *some*) to recreate in their own Heart's Ground the ultimate epiphany of the Risen Lord. This was the Mystery, the Secret of the Cross, the Time-place of Transcendence, the Nuptial Node. All who could pass through Here now must, take the Journey through the Now, the Needle's Eye. For in this way only the false self disappeared - or, rather, it died to be born again, having cast off its threefold identification: I, you, he-she-it; we, you, they. It was the breaking of the triple mode of consciousness, which the three forms of the personal pronoun denote, the superseding of the three dimensions, in which we habitually live and breathe.

Not that we didn't continue to use them or were any less able to function in this world. On the contrary, with the beginning of the Fourth State, all things assumed their proper shape-and-line, which in three-dimensional reality is always slightly blurred. Things *settled*, so to speak, as one freed oneself of the continual impulse to interfere: they became what they *were*, as one became one's Self. For this was the intimate Chemistry, the hieratic Valency, looking for Itself. And when it found itself there was rejoicing in Heaven, the lost sheep was found, the Field complete. And in that completeness It knew Itself - not in the fractured way men know, with morsels of knowledge like hundreds-and-thousands, but intimately, as one knows one's child. It was not a matter of acquisition, and no amount of acquisition would bring it about: it was a matter of That-which-knoweth-Itself, where there was no gap at all between knower and known. This was the first-and-last Step, the Open Door, the lost sheep counted, the 99 assumed.

And it was really so simple and natural; it was not a matter of self-torment and blood. All that had been hopelessly misunderstood. No god, however great, could die for another, though one might feel it an honour to die for him. He could announce a Path, indicate a Door - and then the actual person had to go through it. For all Worlds met in the Cavern of the Heart, the Place of the Assumption, the Zero of Time. Being born, living and dying was the tripartite skin, the outside of the Orange, so to speak; within was the Sap, the luscious Fruit, the Nutriment. And it could only be tasted when one peeled off the skin, sank one's teeth into the pulp and ate it down. There was no other method, no priest, no go-between. One was alone there always, with the Moment, always NOW. One could refuse it, of course (most people did), but it was still there, like a Constant, turning about itself. And to come home to it, to go through it and beyond, was to say 'Yes' to Life, to be born as one's Self.

Eddie pondered these inner truths, as another might ponder mathematical facts-and-figures. It *was* mathematical - at least, to him: these were the elegant, subliminal forms, the unseen ciphers, God's glyphs and modes. For him it was a scientific search: exact, precise, *observable* and real. In fact, it was the inner heart of things, their infrastructure - First Girders, so to speak. And, just as sometimes it happens in life that an inner truth is revealed in the outer - literally, physically, right before one's eyes - so Eddie thought of those girders above Pond Street, that had been standing there since before the War and were now being fleshed out into a cinema. It was like that; it was *exactly* that: without the inner Form, no content, nothing - no realization of what it meant to be alive.

It was so stark and strong in him it knocked him back; the truth of it was plain, like that naked steel. It was like meeting suddenly, unexpectedly, the person one had fallen in love with and tried to rationalize out of one's existence. One sank to one's knees in mute adoration, while she went by oblivious, golden, dark, a dream. It hit him like that - at all points at once - and the effect of it was irreversible. He *knew* now with a knowledge no-one could teach him that the inner structure, the Vision of the world, lay right there inside him, exactly where he was. It was disclosing itself to him, if he would only listen, through all ways and moments, all encounters, fraught and free.

Sometimes, like music, it was gentle, barely born, but vibrant, pregnant, defining the air - like the chord at the beginning of Beethoven's Ninth. At others, it was starting to move along, like a mountain stream when the snow has gone. Later it was rich, deep, resonant as a river. Then, at times, literally it hammered on the door. It was so much *there* - patent, waiting, active -, so much the necessary Skein of things, that, once one saw it, one could scarcely comprehend how people lived in ignorance of it. It was like thinking a car didn't run on petrol or the body need liquid, or some other absurdity. And yet it did seem possible, in a way, to live one's whole life without reference to it, as Man had been doing since the Modern Age began. It was possible to become, by choice, a Dwarf, a boxed-in Midget, something Less. In fact, it was what everyone was trying to become, as faceless Bourgeois Consumerism seeped through, invading and destroying everything. Even the new housing and housing-estates proved it: 'rabbit hutches,' Mellors called them.

7

The War had shattered everything: the Old France, the Olde England, the Old Europe, finally. Now there was Euratom and, in 1957, the Treaty of Rome, the incipient EC. Stones for bread, indeed, thought Eddie. No amount of breast-beating and politicking could obscure the fact, every day more apparent, that Europe had descended to the status of vassal and the transatlantic Big Brother called the shots. Nor was it just a matter of NATO and borders: the inner Hold of our civilization - fragile in America, to say the least - was gradually weakening inch by inch. It became a Ground incapable of Greatness, where the level, grey, mediocre ruled and where materialism, conformity and sheer palsied fear shut everyone in from the Nightmare outside. And out of this most unpromising Ground, acknowledging the rot at the Old World's core, sprang that young and beautiful Flower-of-the Now, that first-and-final Fling, called the Sixties Generation.

Eddie didn't know he was part of it; nor did Emma: it just caught up with them. Though they were both over thirty, it didn't really matter: it was a question of spirit, anyway. And the spirit they had, right down to their bones, the indomitable urge to say 'Yes', to be free. And then there was Fenlon, still not yet eighteen, who was already, it seemed, its Incarnation. For he moved already like a god through the world, as if the Fourth Dimension were his real Home. He lived here, of course, tangentially; he hung his hat on the peg of the world. But inwardly, actually, his life was Elsewhere. He was born to go to India.

He had to keep it from his nearest that he was off - until his eighteenth birthday, at least. Then he would inherit some money from his grandparents, which would allow him to go for an unspecified time.

Emma and Eddie hung on at their jobs, awaiting the appropriate moment to resign. Finally, they agreed that they would all go together, just after Christmas. The timing seemed right.

# BOOK ELEVEN: HEIDEGGER WAS RIGHT

Je est un autre.

Rimbaud

## 1

It shouldn't be necessary to go to India, if what Eddie was discovering was real. In theory, one should be able to sit straight-backed in meditation and find out for oneself, wherever, then-and-there. What impels one to go that far? Is it the pull of the 'mystic East', with its perennial implication of Worlds unknown? Is it post-Colonial nostalgia? Or is it, more likely, some mute acknowledgement that our civilization is 'botched', to use Pound's word, and that new Seeds and Sources must be sought elsewhere - among the erstwhile 'natives' over there?

It was time to break the mould of Time, to give one's brief Icarean Wings a chance. It wasn't primarily geographical displacement but a search for something other than this Grind, this level, grey, concrete, ubiquitous Vale Close. And it *had* to exist somewhere, here on Earth - not just in fond places of the secret Heart or in wild, uncharted regions of the Mind. That's why one went there, basically: it was a place with a people, a country - India.

## 2

They actually took off without any plans - other than flying to the country of their choice - on one of those drab, cold, wet, stark mornings, which are a feature of Heathrow all year round. In spite of their decision and their real joy in going, there was an air of apprehension about them, the apprehension of people who have committed themselves and who are now in what's called the Pool of Angst. For it was one thing, of course, to have an India of the mind and quite another to set foot there - just as it was one thing to be friends in Sheffield, where, after all, there had been a given order, and now to be setting off into the Unknown. It was like setting up house and home with someone, after being a bachelor for twenty-five years: all the hidden corners would have to be worked out.

317

And, of course, sitting there, incipiently, they had no idea what they were going to find, nor how the situation was likely to evolve. Fenlon was a nice boy, Emma thought, even a nice, *illumined* boy, but he was also a young man leaving home for the first time, with all his life before him, his way to make. This was the reality Eddie tended to ignore in his constant push for the Higher Mode, above all, in his desire to see it embodied in a person. Perhaps it was the difference between men and women: men were, in some sense, much less *here*, less planted in the Planet, more tangential, somehow. A woman had always to get down to brass tacks, to cook and wash up, bear, feed and hold the baby. She couldn't, as Eddie often did, sit and wait for inspiration: she had to move and *act*.

Also, she wondered how *fit* the boy was. There had been that bout of illness some time ago, around which still hung, like cloud upon a mountain, an unvoiced veil of mystery. He hadn't wanted to talk about it and had passed it off, as young men will, part of the reason obviously being that he hadn't wanted it to prevent him from travelling. But it was there, she felt, somewhere about him and could move with quickening intensity, as a flower might burst open on the first warm day of spring; it was there somewhere, sitting with them, their unseen companion, the unwanted guest.

Fenlon himself seemed oblivious, as he chatted to Eddie - he had the aisle seat - and the scheduled departure time went by. Emma was looking out of the window at the mêlée of small trucks wheeling about, wondering what kind of life the men who drove them led. It was the same when she walked through a town in the evening and saw the lights coming on behind closed curtains. Who lived there, she wondered; whose place was it? What was the unspoken Word they lived by? For every household has its own Code, its invisible network of familiar spirits, its peopled density of Ancients and Intimates. We are never alone, she thought, though we may think so, though the common conception is that we are. There is always a Link somewhere, if we can find it and are sufficiently open to make it real. Even in houses that have been demolished it hovers - a wisp of wallpaper wafting in the breeze. Who knows what dramas have been enacted there, in those small plots of space, like vacated graves? What has become of that Eloquence? Thus she was musing, as the plane left the terminal, taxied to the runway, and its engines revved.

For reasons not entirely physical, the moment of take-off is always something special. The engines roar, there's a slight sway-and-rattle, and there you are, hurtling along the runway, for all the world like a racing-car with an improbable cargo of two hundred passengers. Then suddenly, abruptly, the ground falls away and you are pointing upwards:

you are airborne, afloat. This daily miracle takes no-one by surprise, and yet it is something about which Man has dreamt ever since he could think and saw the birds fly. It is the Artificer Daedalus' dream-come-true, our perennial passport to places unknown. And like Daedalus, too, our friends were escaping - from a different island, a different Prison. They were going to a different World.

3

The Fourth Dimension, of which Einstein spoke and which is, nonetheless, a matter of conjecture in the West, is in India the palpable Stuff of daily life. It meets you as you step off the plane, in a whoosh of warm air, which envelops you like a cloud. It is even there, waiting in the crowded airport - and what place in India *isn't* crowded? - among the dust, sweat and dirt and the beyond-that special smell, compounded of bodies, beedies and drying cow-dung. It is all going on simultaneously: some sitting, some talking, some under rows of blankets; others standing, simply standing, and trying to make it count. For they are all on the Road of Evolution, from the first mute cell (or sub-atomic particle) to the Highest Principle, the Brahman, the One. It is a Journey multifarious, never-ending, lives-long, starting as that cell or mute particle and building up through a succession of births, till the human Plane is reached at incarnation 8,000,000! It takes in Darwin perfectly: he's only describing in physical terms and soul-and cell-reality they've known about for years - since the dawn of pre-recorded history, in fact. And here it is, pounding through the aeons down to now, incorporating all in its River of Embrace. Who/what stands outside it, ultimately?

At that time of Commonwealth it was possible for a British subject to stay for ever in India. Eddie and Emma were quickly through Passport and Immigration, but with Fenlon it took a little more time: he got caught for a while in the Indian Fork, that Place where two Irreconcilables meet - a cumbersome, rigid bureaucracy and an incurable fascination with fellow human-beings. A split-second's logic would have got rid of one or t'other, but where is that split-second's logic in India?
The official was looking at Fenlon's passport.
- Unusual name for a Britisher, he said.
- O, yes, said Fenlon. My parents are Polish.
- Travellers like you, sir?
- Well, no, not really. They came over to England at the start of the War.
- Refugees from Nazis?

319

- You could put it that way.

Fenlon was beginning to feel awkward and shy: a queue a mile long had built up behind him. The official sat easy, with the stamp in his hand, about to bring it down, but still looking at him.

- My father joined the Polish Air Force in exile. He was a fighter pilot; he fought with the British.

- Battle of Britain?

- Well, no some time later. Missions over Germany, mainly.

- Ah, Dambuster!

He must have seen the film. Fenlon nodded: the queue, which was mounting, was on his mind.

- You are going, sir?

- To Bangalore, said Fenlon, fearing to appear equivocal.

- Sri Jai Ram Ashram?

- Perhaps.

- Very nice.

With that, he stamped with date and place the virgin pages of Fenlon's passport. And, as if his real work were making conversation and checking and stamping passports a mere expedient, he got up from his chair and walked away, leaving the long queue to wait a little longer.

- Decidedly different, Fenlon said to himself. And that was how he entered India.

Emma and Eddie were waiting for him and had been, in fact, watching the whole thing from a distance.

- No trouble? said Emma.

- O, none at all. He was just intrigued by my name, that's all.

- Cometh the hour, Eddie said. Where do you think we should go from here?

- I told him Bangalore, Fenlon said, but perhaps you'd like to stay here for a while?

- In Bombay? exclaimed Eddie, as if the mere suggestion were preposterous.

- Bangalore it is, then, Emma said.


The connecting flight, which left at ten o'clock, was all booked-up, but if they cared to take a seat . . . Tired from their journey, they acquiesced, not really knowing what the alternative might be and, in any case, resolved not to go into the city. It was the first of many waiting experiences - the stuff of life, some people say - which they were about to have over the next few months and which India is anciently expert in. They sat it out, watching the clock plod on and imagining, as it got nearer ten, that their cut-off point was drawing nigh. 'You'll be fortieth on the waiting list,' they had been told. Which already meant . . . or what *did* it mean?

- Flight going? asked Eddie, getting nervous and somehow thinking that pidgin might work better.
- Flight delayed, the languid lady replied.
And, sure enough, on a small screen above his head, the information was relayed in those very same words.
- What shall we do now? Eddie began.
- Kindly be seated, the lady said.
And another round of waiting began.
About eleven thirty there was a buzz-and-bustle (FLIGHT DELAYED still showed on the screen), as if some unseen Bush Telegraph had alerted everyone to a new possibility. A sign had appeared on a distant counter, with the English capitals NO RETURNING sandwiched between the original wording - above in Marathi, below in Hindi.
- What does that mean? Eddie asked.
- Cash payment only, the languid lady said. Here are your tickets. Better hurry: flight's been called.
- But . . . , began Eddie.
But there was no time for 'buts'. He laid the requisite number of hundred-rupee notes on the desk before him (she didn't keep change) and sped over to the NO RETURNING counter, wondering all the while how a flight could be delayed and at the same time . . . Looking up, he saw the small screen had changed: it now read BOARDING in the same detached way. He joined the indispensable queue.
- Sheer nonsense!, the man next to Eddie was fuming. Absolute bloody absurdity, I say!
- What is?, asked Eddie, now utterly bewildered.
- This new tax they've levied on internal flights. Government chicanery, I tell you, nothing more!
Nevertheless, like everyone else, he moved forward to pay the NO RETURNING fee. Emma encouraged Eddie in a similar direction (it was common knowledge that they overbooked), fearing lest failure to procure the necessary chitty should incur a loss of hours, perhaps the whole day. And Eddie, who, in a moment of insight, had realized that queuing here *didn't* mean waiting, pressed on with the rest, clutching tickets and money, until such time as he could stick out an arm and force his attention on the empowered official. The latter seemed to be deliberately ignoring him, while a forest of brown hands, nimble and ubiquitous, got in, through, under, above and in-between and were off with their blessings, like the experts they were. Eventually, however, looking half the other way, he took Eddie's cash and gave him three cards in return: magic passes to the Land of Bangalore. Ten minutes later they were on the plane.

It wasn't yet clear to any of them why they were flying to Bangalore. Although they had read some of the works of Sri Jai Ram, they hadn't really fathomed them. In any case, Sri Jai Ram was dead, as they discovered when they arrived at the Ashram, a small, clean, whitewashed group of buildings on the outskirts of the city, Jayanagar side.

The country at that time rolled away from the city in folds of fields to the wide horizon. Humps of rock, like camels' backs, rose to meet the sky towards the south-west, and from some of their sides, like sustenance, grey granite was hewn for building and fence-posts. The Ashram looked out across a west-facing valley in the pit of which, at the very bottom, a lake gathered the waters from the falling fields. It was good to roam in them endlessly, among the maize and deep grasses, the bright green paddy-fields. Nonchalant, wee walls divided field from field, but it didn't seem to matter where one walked - either there, or in the government forests, with their acres and acres of eucalyptus trees: it was all abundant; it was rich and colour-lush.

The red Deccan earth deepened to bronze, as the October rains swept across in a veil and the Green came up in a new, late growth. Then, after winter, with the early spring, it became drier, more brittle, drained down to pink; one could kick the solid clumps of it, where a field lay fallow or recently turned. There wasn't a tractor anywhere in sight, but everything went as it always had, with bullocks or oxen and the stick of a plough. Village farmers stroked open the land with it or, further down where the paddy grew, they waded through water up to their knees. Though sometimes very poor, they had enough to eat, and their children (their true wealth) swarmed about the dirt streets, played along the porches and shouted after strangers. It was a source of curiosity and wonderment to them, why all these people had started coming from the West. For what had begun as a trickle was now a stream.

Eddie, Emma and Fenlon took to the place with a beauty of Being that was all their own. It was mirrored to them in this simple land, the perennial cycle of established ways - as a face in a mirror sees itself clear. Their features came up to meet them from the soil, from the immeasurable distance of the sailing sky, as they sat on a warm rock above the Valley and watched the sun, a delineated red ball, sink through the strewn purple haze of the horizon. They were saying 'Yes' from some Ground not their own, from something that was 'out there', as well as 'in here'. It was the affirmation of Being Here, fully arrived and alive and NOW. And this was the condition, the precondition even, for seeing the world as it actually is: not as a figment, a construct, a projection, but as a living body-being, alive as we are.

And when one saw it thus, there was no separation, for intensity was equal everywhere and the observer, the looker *was* what he saw. Not that he turned into or *became* something else, which is Magical Transformation, esoteric Play; no, he *was* that at the level of Being: he was of the same essence, the same blood-and-stuff. He was linked to it all, indissolubly - not even linked: he *was* it, plain and simple. In the words of the text they were just then reading: 'Tat tvam asi'. Heidegger was right.

4

It took very little time for them to settle in and to learn the Ashram's simple way-of-life: early rising, bath, yoga and pranayama, then meditation in the small thatched hall. They were, in any case, just looking, not sure at first how long they would stay.

The Ashram was, by common consent, completely silent for the first three hours (it laid the foundation for the rest of the day), so that, when people come into the long, low dining-hall for their South Indian breakfast of idlis and coffee, they were quiet, alert, fresh; their minds were quiet. Gradually then, like a trickle of water, the conversation began to flow. There *were* things to talk about, obviously: supplies to buy in, the garden to tend (they grew most, but not all, of their own fruit-and-veg.), then a building project, recently begun.

Sri Jai Ram, though not a miracle-worker, had attracted a following, nation- and worldwide, devoted to the quiet, the inner Revolution. After those first three hours the day got under way with a combination of study and work. The texts were the basic Hindu Classics: the Vedas, the Upanishads and the Bhagavad Gita. Sri Jai Ram had always insisted that there was enough in any of them to last one a lifetime, as a Buddhist might say there was enough in the Sutras, or a Christian in the Bible, a Moslem in the Koran. And, though quite eclectic, not a proselytizer at all, he had stuck to the texts he knew and loved, the Music that still in this fallen Age rises and curls, like smoke before dawn, from the hearts and hearths of India.

They sat in a circle - about ten or a dozen -, read something together and commented on it. The text itself was the objective referent, the first and necessary focal point. It brought them together in a Pool of Mind, in which the common looking was paramount. It was not psychological investigation (in which the personality with its learned motives and drives claims the whole Field of Life for itself), but an exploration, first, of 'what the man said', what the Poet meant as he brought the Word through; then only, when they had touched on That, and by that touching become attuned to one another, did they begin to turn, as a Dervish might, counter-clockwise in Involution. They were now stepping onto the incipient Spiral, the practical Ascension, the Assumption of the Self. And in that Ascension through the Zero of Being they would, without effort, without force or violation, begin to heal themselves of their Pain, the fractured Sleep of Forgetfulness which goes with being born on Earth. They would begin - and, naturally, it was only a beginning - to set their foot on the Eternal Path, that leads from the cracked-mirror World to the Real. And on that Path, as they climbed it day by day, they would discover again the personal self, which they had thrown off, discarded, shining in the Sun. They would realize then that the very thing they had been striving for, the very distant thing, was right there beneath their feet. They had only to pick it up and *move* with it, for the Kingdom was theirs, the Secret was inherent. From now on there could be no forfeiture.

All this lay, elaborated at some length, in the Collected Works of Sri Jai Ram, who was still, though dead, the spiritual head of the Ashram and whose portrait, painted a few months before he died, revealed a countenance at once compassionate and austere. For he himself had striven mightily, had given up everything as a very young man and gone out in search of the Supreme Truth. He had walked the length and breadth of the land, living in temples, ashrams, caves, forests, until he had found the one spot on earth from which there was no budging, no going-back. And there he had stopped and waited on Truth, abiding, praying, fasting, scarcely eating, until the Truth - almost by the back door, almost without his noticing it - had dawned on him with its own special Day, its silent infusion of Ecstasy.

He had known it was real, after so much striving, because this time it didn't budge: there was no way, even wilfully, that he could dislodge it. He knew it was real because it wasn't him, wasn't *his*; it had nothing at all to do with him. It had come to him like the rising sun, quiet from a still sky, with no fanfare at all. All his efforts, he realized, had been as nothing; they had had no part in this Revelation of Grace. They had been scribbles-in-the-margin, footnotes, foibles - they had had no tincture at all of the Real. Now it sat with him night and day, like his own Familiar, his beloved Friend. Like the perfect Guest it sat down with him, rose with him from table, was his Shadow, constant, true.

He had realized on the instant that he had nothing to do, that no effort of his was of any value. All the activities, the tirades, the masquerades, were shots-in-the-dark, mere attempts to find the Real. And at how much cost to the Actor, the Player! It was incalculable, the misery and suffering of it! There it was, in every house-and-home, behind every closed curtain, every locked door. And almost no-one was awake to it.

He had realized on the instant that he must sit still. The only thing was to *be* with Being, to sit in a chair or cross-legged on the floor. He had to

324

allow the Percolation of the Light to work in him for its own glad ends. More and more he must put behind him the acquired automatisms of the human brain, all the little wires and connections that make us manikinly what we are, derived.

And so he sat and let the quiet Explosion become a Torrent, a Flood in him, washing out all the dross of existence. The longer he sat, the more real it became - hours, weeks, months, years - it was all indifferent: the clock, like the self, with its image, was smashed. And in its place, very gently at first, came the gathering Sun, the Warmth we all want. It took over every part of him. And it corresponded to him perfectly - in every last cell and substance of his body, as well as in the highest reaches of his mind. For the last had become first, and the first last. That is, everything had, as by a miracle, reverted to its Original Nature, had become again intrinsically *what it was/is.*

In the topsy-turvy world in which we live this is not apparent, because of the binding power of Illusion. Everything is reversed, even visually, so that we can make a mental formulation of it and so function in the World of Everyday. But the World of Everyday is only part-reality, is itself a paradigm, a picture, a model. And the inbuilt deception of the mental mode leads it to think that it can grasp the Whole, whereas what it sees is what it thinks-it-sees: a thought-construct, a version, a shadow-play, unreal. The Real, as Sri Jai Ram discovered, resides in another Dimension altogether, and it was this Dimension which had come to him.

He sat very quietly there, unmoving, absorbed in the unfathomable Assumption of the Self, as if his body were very far away - down there, somewhere going on, very small. The fuss and palaver we made about it, the lengths we went to to keep it looking young! When, at best, it was the thing-of-an-hour and, in any case, perfectly adjusted to the Earth, knowing just what to do, if Thought left it alone. Sri Jai Ram was, for all the World, immune, having given up going where no cat would go, if only he knew he were walking on hot bricks. But, generally, he didn't, and that was the problem: he walked on hot bricks, fell down ditches, drank poison. And all because his World was upside-down: what he saw was a Version; the Vision was elsewhere.

It was such a simple thing, in fact, that S.R.J., as he became affectionately known, could never quite say it as it was, and most of the time he taught through Silence. In the early days, when he had first realised the Self, it was difficult, indeed, to get him to talk at all. Even burning questions he answered with a look or, at most, with a few scribbled words in Kannada. He was conscious, as he later put it, of the dichotomy between vision and word, of the fact that the Seeing, which was with him night-and-day, was, though touched upon, hinted at, *performed,* always slightly betrayed by language, never quite accurately or wholly conveyed. It was like a door which let a slight draught through, whereas, in Reality, it fitted perfectly.

Gradually he returned to the world of men - chiefly, it must be said, at their insistence. A small band of followers gathered around him and he became, without seeking it, their Guru. He came down from the Mountain, so to speak, and in that small, modest place, not far from the city that was set to become a metropolis, he lived, saw and taught the fundamental truths.

At first, it was local people who came, seekers who, by tradition in India, sought the presence, the Darshan of the Holy Man. But, as the small Ashram became better known and visitors and journalists bruited it about, seekers came from all parts of India, from the awakening West, from the world at large. And, every day, Sri Jai Ram received people, as if his sole purpose were simply to be there, which indeed it was: simply to *be*. He had cracked the Nut and sweet was the Kernel.

It was common knowledge (and recounted to this day) that he loved to play practical jokes on people. Some - chiefly Germans - took this very seriously, as indicating a further Wing of his Enlightenment, while for others it was just what it was: a joke. He would walk round the Ashram casually, for all the world like a visitor himself, and if anyone asked him where 'the Master' was he would point them in the direction of the Meditation Hall, with a 'Try in there', then 'Don't be surprised if you don't find him'. Tales (unverified) abounded of moments of instantaneous Illumination, when he had asked such visitors, 'Why seek a Master?' or even, 'Where do you come from?', and it had done the trick.

Everyone had his tit-bit of a story (or a very long story) of Life with S.J.R. For some it had become the sole Axis of their existence, the great, straight Road of Acquaintance-with-the-Man; and with it, in it, they had lost themselves in a more rarefied, yet classic, instance of Bad Faith. For others, more true to themselves, less in thrall, and consequently closer to the ever-present Now, it was the Salt of their days, their immediate Meat; they had no truck with the person-of-the-past.

Our Three became slowly familiar with all this, its subtle variations and shades. They weren't quite sure what it added up to, but they were, admittedly, taken by surprise: they hadn't expected, *in a place like this,* to find the kind of sharkiness they had witnessed everywhere. Like some students who go up to University, thinking they will meet a different breed of men and then are disappointed when they don't, they were made to reflect on baser basic human nature, its perennial persistence, its down-drag, its Doom.

But the days in themselves were rhythmical and lovely, and the place seemed to have a beauty of its own, which persisted in spite of

326

'background noise'. The texts provided Eddie with a whole string of metaphors, to which he could relate his burgeoning growth, while for Fenlon they were more like a confirmation, a crystal-clear expression of what he already knew. Only Emma had difficulty with the sessions, finding them, at times, too abstract, too dry, and feeling relieved when her turn came to share in the cooking duties for the day. For her, the best part of the day was late afternoon, when, work and study sessions over, they could go for a walk among the ancient fields. Then all sense of pressure was gone, all compulsion to understand, and she could walk with the two of them (and sometime with others) along the slender, winding, well-trodden paths.

A trickle of a stream ran down to the lake and there they walked, initially on a track, through a mango-grove, with its fingers of leaves, past a slanting wood of tamarind and thorn, till the track gave out and they came, lower down, to a place of confluence, where two streams met. It was extremely auspicious - a neem and peepul grew together - and, as is usual, a small Shiva temple crouched on the land's lip, in blemished white. They peered inside at the dark deity and caught the pervasive smell of oil. Puja had been performed that very morning, and a sense of Celebration, with its quiet intensity, hung on the air like a neutral welcome. They were part of it, somehow, like the strewn scented blossoms. And always the land, the red land, sang.

Afterwards, the path lost itself between black, basalt boulders and clumps of clay. It was playing with the walkers, dodging in and out, then popping up again twenty yards further down. They crossed the stream, scrambled up a bare hillock, walked through a nursery, then crossed it again. A dried-up ravine came in from the left, and a little beyond it, in a clearing, stood the blackened cottage of a charcoal-burner. He seemed to live in utter destitution, with probably a strung cot, not even a sink, fetching his water from the nearby stream. His most precious possession was a bicycle, which he kept locked up indoors at all times. And from his runnelled hands came the rhythm of work, and from his blackened face, like a broken olive, burst the undying Sound of song: he was singing there, in that broken hovel.

Then the path was off again, across the clearing, back down to the stream. A little further on was a bathing-pool, with smooth, warm, sculpted basalt rocks. The sun, which was in them and had known them for years, was beginning to dip in the western sky - across a land which never knew cold or snow and whose totems of trees were Paeans of Praise. It was the Hour of Return for villagers and birds, the latter (mainly terns) wheeling wide above the water, the former walking their boss-backed cattle with the ancient, patient faces in a jostling tribe. They didn't stop or look up at Our Three, just walked their cattle as they always did, from the bank-side pasture to their meagre stalls, while the terns and swifts cut circles in the air and the path went on in an arc by the lake.

They had turned it now and, like villagers and birds, were slowly making their own way home. There were terraced fields on the mounting side, with sun-crunched, darkened, collapsed little walls. The path was straighter, more pragmatic and austere: it knew where it was going and it led them through the fields. Above these the ground was broken again, with stones, coarse grass, the odd spiky bush. They stopped at the jutting hilltop - there was a neem - and sat down on stones to watch the sun set. It had sunk through its suffusions to a solid red ball and was slowly, very slowly, going down, disappearing as if down a pocket in the cloud (first the bottom, like an inverted miniscus, sinking behind the thick purple veil; then the bulk, like a giant ripened fruit, finished and falling to the earth; finally the top tip, the last, glowing rind, hesitant, dropping, then in a plop gone.)

There was nothing then for quite some time, as the walkers made their way back through the waiting wood. Then the undersides of high clouds were caught - pink at first, with a sharp gold rim, deepening gradually, darkening into red, as if the sun still burnt in some cavern of its own. The sky was burnished a surreal blue, clean as if Venus touched it with her light, before drawing over it the soft Cloak of Night. The trees were gathering into themselves, forsaking the open fling of the day, witnesses now to the walkers passing by, as they rejoined their first path higher up and, beckoned by the Ashram, made their way towards it.

It was the hour when the spirit evens out, when everything, after the effort of the day, returns to its original Home and Place. People had gathered in the Meditation Hall, the evening puja performed, the air heavy with incense. The portrait of SJR was there, and a file of devotees prostrated before it, touching the flagstones with their forehead, which then was smeared with a pinch of sacred ash and dotted vermilion at the mid-brow with powder. Whereafter they, like Our Three, took a straw mat from a corner and sat with the rest.

There was no instruction in meditation - in fact, it was referred to, more modestly, as 'sitting in silence' or merely 'sitting'. But it was an open secret that SJR had spoken, when questioned, on the matter of the Heart as being the Centre of Consciousness, the proof of it being that, to indicate oneself, one pointed to the chest, a little to the right. It was, hence, not the physical heart that he meant but a different Locus, a locus of perception, the seat or centre of the 'I'. And, since all Consciousness flowed through the 'I', since it was what we were from first to last, surely it behoved us to focus there, to look and listen to what was going on. It did, and they did, sitting there without a word.

Things began to take shape for them, to take on the natural rhythm and line of a place to which they were intended from the first. None of the externals (food, clothes, climate) cost them anything in terms of adaptation: they moved freely, ate simply, loved the sun. It cost next-to-nothing to be there, either. The Ashram did not levy charges, but people gave what they could from their means - enough to cover living expenses, at least, - while major industrialists, brewers and distillers considered it a step in the right direction to make the occasional massive donation. The immediate consequence of this, in practical terms, was the laying-on of a special lunch, as following the way-of-life of the Master, the Ashram eschewed the accumulation of wealth. And it had no particular desire to expand.

5

Unique among all countries of the world, India leads us to our destiny. For some, it is the Way of Work, the engagement in activity social and useful, for which there is always tremendous need; for others, it is the Way of Detachment, the total abandonment of the world and its ways. One may walk the land, as SJR had done, and the society supports and encourages it. The ochre robe and the ash-covered body are means of establishing the severance, and one lives then apart - beyond the pale, outside the rules -, allowing and having allowed to oneself all means and modes, all avenues to Truth.

For by that One Inspiration we have lived, by that one slim Note of Ecstasy, the central Pillar which bursts through the Roof. And India alone, among the nations of the world, has built a Courtyard around that Pillar, around that central Quest for Truth. Thus it is, and was with SJR, that ministers, lawyers, doctors, kings came to see him in his simple abode, acknowledging thereby his superiority, his power to love, heal, comprehend, command. For he was the Pivot about which they moved, like Planets round a central Sun, without whose Light they were nothing, they were dead.

It is, after all, a very simple truth, not relative (like light , a Constant) or even related to the World of Things. It is, nonetheless, That-by-which-they-live, That, losing which, the rest falls apart. It does not depend upon the will of Man, nor does it subscribe to his norms. No, it is *there*, like Everest, and, like Everest, one must go to It. It is a Well springing up into Eternal Life; it nourishes, without trying, the inner Man. And at the heart of that Source, at its bubbling Core, is the wee Gram of Energy that turns everything about.

Interestingly enough, this truth about India, this Well from which she draws and lives, is not an enclosure, for her own people only, but is there, abundantly and equally, for all. It begins to operate as soon as one

329

arrives, and the closer one gets to the secret Source, the mercurial Essence of her State - the more one opens oneself, in fact - the quicker the acceleration takes place; the quicker, also, those Way-markers appear, which point us in the direction we are meant to go.

Eddie, Emma and Fenlon had settled down because they had settled into a given routine, one which, admittedly, appealed to them, which they saw the point of and benefited from. But, naturally enough, this was just the beginning, a safe haven, so to speak, while they were still new and strange. Something - they sensed it in the air - was beginning to set them down 'where they belonged', at a Place which they could never have suspected, had they been asked about it before they came. It had something to do with that Bubble of Angst, which was the necessary concomitant of their commitment to travel and, in the resolution of which, by the release of its energy, unforeseeable blossoms were to grow.

Naturally, also, it was different for each of them, as it is always different and unpredictable, when we align ourselves, to whatever degree, with that Ordering Energy, with Cosmos, with What-is. It may, indeed, seem the absolute opposite. For the little, contained order we have known (and which, at the time, was appropriate and right) has now to give way to something greater, of which, initially, we may be quite unaware, feeling only tearing, breakdown, Chaos. They were about to enter this uncharted Land, this further necessary phase of themselves.


It began with an illness, oddly enough, the recurrence of which should have come as no surprise. About two-and-a-half months into their stay (it was already beginning to get hotter) Fenlon, who was pale at the best of times, having inherited his complexion from an unusually blond mother, got a touch of fever - like the common cold in India - and was laid up for a day or two. The Ashram doctor told him to stay in bed, drink plenty of liquid, and prescribed aspirin for the fever.

- Soon be all right: in a few days, he said.

But in those few days he had not improved; on the contrary, his condition had deteriorated and he had coughed up blood three or four times.

- Better get a second opinion, said the doctor.

A specialist was called in from Bangalore Hospital, who took one look at Fenlon and said: 'T.B.' This instant, perceptive (though practised) diagnosis was confirmed subsequently by a number of tests. The left lung, in particular, was very bad - badly inflamed and on the point of collapse - that much could be seen or deduced from the X-ray. Dr Alok looked very grave:

- He must have complete rest for a month, at least. And a minimum of visitors . . . you two are his friends?

- Yes, said Emma and Eddie together.
- Apart from t doctor, you only should tend.
- We'll do everything we can for him, Eddie said.

They considered informing Fenlon's parents, but the young man himself was dead against it.
- My mother would want to come over, he said, and it would be awful here, with her grief and agitation.
- Are you sure? asked Emma. She *is* your mother, after all.
- That's just it, said Fenlon with a smile.

They dropped the subject there and then and devoted themselves to looking after him. Emma did most of the practical things; Eddie hovered around with liquids and books, quietly amazed in his heart-of-hearts that this young strayed god who had come into their lives still lived on the Mountain, whatever occurred. Nothing seemed to take him away from himself, in the sense that he became anxious, neurotic, self-concerned. On the contrary, now that he was seriously ill, he became, if anything, more serene, more surrendered, more detached, more calm. 'It's like the wine,' Eddie said to himself. 'In the base-born it brings out their hidden violence, but in the high-born, like Fenlon, only the best.' It was another of the follies of modern Man: to treat everything as causational, circumstantial - as if nothing could exist outside that Circle. And thus, he would always remain a Prisoner, an Inmate of his reductionist Cage, dragging the Ball-and-chain of Cause-and-Effect.

The best things in Life, including its people, were free; they had the Beauty of intrinsic Freedom. That was the quality that made the difference, always. It wasn't a question of weighing-and-measuring or of which came first - Heredity or Environment; it was a matter of *knowing* oneself to be free. That knowledge, which Fenlon possessed abundantly, was, in a sense, available to everybody, was, in the true sense, what they really *were*. And yet they were estranged from it: they had lost the Clue, the Way to Being. Circumstance, certainly, was one of their Gaolers; another was mechanical Cause-and-Effect. These Two, like the thieves on Calvary, weighed on the Redeemer and prevented Man's Salvation.
- How *can* one help people? Eddie asked Fenlon, as he was sitting up in bed one day, feeling better.
- One cannot: it's an illusion, he said.
- You mean, one just watches them going round and round, without even saying, 'Heh!', without offering a hand?
- No, I don't mean callousness, indifference, not caring: I simply mean that everyone must see the truth of the matter for himself.
- But what if they *don't*?
- Then they don't, it's all right. Perhaps they're not ready to see it yet. After all, one has to be part-way up a Mountain, in order to see how small the Valley is.

- But it's *always* small.
- Of course it is! But, if you're in it and of it, you don't see it that way; to you it's everything.
- Until it breaks.
- And what makes it break?
- Suffering, obviously: the sense that one is totally alone.
- Which one was before, of course, but it was hidden. Now one is open, and honest about it. To such a person you can talk.
- It's a matter of losing and finding, then?
- In a sense, yes, like a children's game. The Sufis have a vocabulary for it: they speak of Fana (destruction) and Baqa (what remains).
- ?
- The person who is in earnest realizes very soon that the block to Self-Realisation, Truth, lies in his ego, the conditioned personality. He then sets about in whatever ways he can to break down that central Nub-and-Nut, little knowing what he is about. But the very fact that he has declared himself means that Hurdles will be placed in his path, each of which is a Challenge and a Test. He may choose to avoid them - many do - but, here again, he realizes very soon that evasion is useless: the Test is always there. Gradually, he develops the finesse to discern and the strength to overcome the Barrier before him. And, whenever this occurs, something of him dies, a Veil of Ignorance falls away. The process of this dying-to-self is Fana: the process and also the particular instance. One emerges cleansed from what is often utter turmoil, and one takes another step into the Land of the Real.
- The Land of the Real?
- The Other Dimension. It's like a journey in reverse - and it *is* a Journey, actually. In this material world one builds up ego, and everything (family, nation, career) supports and colludes in this building-up. The fact that it ends in death and dissolution doesn't, apparently, affect the issue, but this can be attributed to the power of Maya. In the Other World, at which the seeker sets himself, this kind of futility doesn't exist. There every gain is a gain of-and-with God: it is by its very nature immarcessible. 'Lay up for yourselves Treasure in Heaven,' said the Master who was free of the clutch of the Thieves. That Treasure is the fruit of dying-to-self, and whoever so dies (the Fana we mentioned) draws closer to the Real, to Truth, to God. In fact, he draws closer to the Object of his search by a mutual process of discarding and disclosure, the second term of which is Baqa - or the Ground of God become more real. It happens both in and out of Time. As growth, development, 'progress' even, one can think of it in terms of evolution. But essentially, intrinsically, it is outside Time, beyond the pale, where all Treasure is - no-one can touch it, actually. It belongs, as *we* belong,

basically, deeply, to the World of Being, from which all Existence derives and into which it is gathered as into its Home.

- How come so few people seek it, then?

- That, my dear, is the Great Question.

- Are you two at it again? said Emma, entering the room with a drink for Fenlon. I bet I know what you're talking about.

- I bet you do! said Eddie, laughing. It isn't as if we kept it a secret.

- I hope not, not from me, she said, putting down the drink and turning to leave smartly.

- Don't forget you're supposed to be resting, she said to Fenlon, as she opened the door.

- I won't, I won't. Thank you, he said.

He took a sip of the drink, then continued:

- One reason is, it's arduous: it takes a lot of patient endeavour - without any apparent result for years. These are the Years in the Wilderness or, as St John of the Cross puts it, the Dark Night of the Soul. One lives and moves with Nothing; one *is* Nothing. One has heard of Jerusalem, so to speak, but the Journey to it is long and lost. Many give up hope at this stage and become cynical and bitter, saying God has betrayed them or, if they don't believe in God, that it's all a sham, a deception, a crime. That's where the Marquis de Sade ended up - and from there, of course, all licence is possible. But licence and licentiousness breed only further reaches of despair, because they have diverted and perverted in us the basic drive, which is the drive for freedom.

- You think freedom's the basic urge in us, then - not libido, not power over others?

- O, much more basic, much more real. A man who sees the vanity of Power does so because Freedom is bursting through.

- Suppose he remains committed to Power?

- Then he hasn't seen that he is destroying freedom - other people's and, consequently, his own. But to Freedom, eventually, all must come, since it's their basic nature and synonymous with Love.

- What makes you so sure?

- O, I don't know . . . the beauty of those hibiscus, perhaps.

Eddie followed Fenlon's gaze, through the meshed window to the falling ground. The hibiscus, slightly pink inside, were pushing their throats up, red like flame. Below and around, holding and supporting, their graceful, dark green leaves stood tall. And in each of them was a solemn rod - upright, pollened, waiting only, firm.

They looked at the flowers and they looked at each other; they were looking as if for the first time, physically. Fenlon's beauty had become almost transcendent, so much was his body wasting and going. His face, which was cream-pale like his mother's, had assumed an aethereal quality, as if light shone up from somewhere inside him. It was only partly the light of the living, for other elements were working there, which brought out the sweat in pearls on his forehead and darkened the look about his eyes.

- They're beautiful, he said, because they simply *are*. They don't have to strive or measure or make good.

- I see beauty in you, also, Fenlon.

- Perhaps, he said, after a pause. I'm tired.

- I should go and let you sleep, shouldn't I?

- Yes, you should, said Fenlon, taking his hand.

Something had passed between them in that moment when they had looked at the flowers and then at one another. It was like a germ or a seed being sown, which neither of them had quite noticed before, which even, indeed, might not have existed. But it had put a different tone in the air, shifted things and established a different level. Fenlon saw Eddie back from the flowers as if he had never looked at him before, as if Eddie had remained somewhere always 'the teacher', from contact with whom he could always withdraw. Now he saw him more as he was: tender, vulnerable, slightly hang-dog and ageing - with an eagerness to get involved and a capacity for getting hurt, which were truly staggering in a man of his age. He wanted instantly, instinctively, to protect him, to offer him what strength was left in his body, to suckle him, somehow, at his breast. For something was so obviously missing from his life, something that Emma could not supply: some deep fertility, a wedding of souls, some sure, warm thing that would nurture him for good. It showed in his face, if one looked carefully: his mouth had involuntarily drawn down at the corners, his lips were becoming thin and pressed, and his eyes were forced and narrowed with strain, as if he were looking myopically, for something he would never find. One couldn't call it sad - it was more than that: something akin to tragedy.

Fenlon wanted to live with it, to *assume* it, somehow, into his being. For it is one of the privileges of youth, not to be able to believe in tragedy. Misfortune, yes, one can see it at a glance, but the Current of the Tragic as inalienable - that comes later, with maturity. Fenlon wasn't yet ready to *conceive* of Life as tragic (perhaps what he was living was tragic enough) but he could see in Eddie, suddenly, the pain and anguish of living-apart, of striving for something which never came good. He was, somehow, Everyman, the Type of his Race - with his piled, dark curls, his frowning, furrowed face and his perennial tendency to take one step back - he epitomized everyone who strove and failed, on whom the Law's Door, as in Kafka's fable, shuts. A flame went through Fenlon (no, he wouldn't *help* Eddie - that would be mean and demeaning for him): he would find a way of *being there* with him, with his laughter and his sorrow, through hibiscus days-and-nights.

334

After some time he began to recover; the Flame of Life came back to him. He had, literally, taken a step into the Beyond, into that Farther Country, from which none return. And he came back like a Guest, like a Traveller, as we are, into this nearer, nether world, which we know. He had a tale to tell then, obviously, but the tale he told was not of Worlds-Beyond, nor of Worlds-within-Worlds, nor of Void-and-Incipience, but of the plain, straightforward world-as-it-is, the one that is with us day-and-night. It had become, he said, for him, translucent, piercingly sharp and beautiful: it was as if every blade of grass had its own special spirit, its own indwelling deity. He *saw* the glory in every living thing - in the thorny bushes, with their flowers like gorse, in the archetypal Form of the mango-trees, whose fruit was just ripening, swelling in the sun, in the easy vision of the hot hibiscus. He awoke, when he woke up, to a Wonderworld, the omnipresent Miracle of the Day, the Nightmare-Prison reversed and sprung. It hadn't wasted a single moment: it was, every bit, luminous and glorious within.

And, Light into Light, he gave himself, through the mantric Power, the OM within. He became strong-radiant, bathed in Light, recovered now from sweat and blood - drenched, cleansed, purified, born anew. He was alive and sensitive to the slightest sound, to any merest Music on the air. He truly *was*, in every pulse and vein, the unheard rhythm of the aching earth. He sensed it in himself, this acceleration, this fresh attunement to Being Here; it was as if he had come down a little from the Clouds and was now in-formed, more earthed, more real.

He looked at the mangoes, with their sticky scent, the blossom all gone over into fruit - at one tree, in particular, with its angling trunk, on which one could sit. He stood and watched it seethe and move, its shining Suchness revealed to him. It was not a thing, a 'res', an *it*, but a living, teeming Node of Being, as real and present and actual as him. In fact, as he looked and penetrated further, he felt more and more the actuality of the tree: the toughness of its bark, the originality of its shape. And, somehow, it lent him grace and strength; it fed its own body-being into his. 'How much we need to come inside,' thought Fenlon, 'and stop seeing the world through Cartesian eyes.' For *that* was the problem, the crux of it: it lay in the subject-object relationship. If consciousness was purely a subjective affair and the rest of the world, the non-I, objective, then the I-in-the-Box was an operant, a scene-shifter, but never part of the scene himself. This meant that, with seeming impunity, he could wreak havoc in the world - which was what he was doing. If, on the other hand, he was part of the scene, if, in reality, the tree *was* him, then a totally different relationship was formed - naturally, easily, right there on the Spot. That relationship, then, would begin to work, would patiently undo the Cartesian Knot, and lead us over the intended Bridge from the Jungle of Conflict to the Fields of Harmony.

'Is it all a dream?' he asked himself. 'Am I making it up as a pleasant sensation?' But he looked at the rootedness of the tree, its bearing and being in the earth, and he knew it as one knows a god, who is in one and of one - though different, still the same. He did not tremble or feel ecstatic: it was not an out-of-the-body experience. On the contrary, it was very much this-here Life, this very present, actual Stuff. The difference (if difference there *was*) was that it was the same Life shining, in and through all. That which gave birth, which gave life and strength, was the same pure Energy that fused them now - that tree at the bottom of the falling field and he looking down, brother-born with it. They were (not figuratively, but accurately, really) stem-and-stock of the same pure Fire, its motif , its expression, its throb-and-thrust of Sap. It was, not less, but a million times *more real than the* ugly ghost-shuttle of carping daily life. For it was what Life *was*, not what it thought-it-was. And when one woke up from that dreadful dream, that nightmare version of abundant Life, then all things were as they were in the Beginning (for one was *at* the Beginning), light and clear. It needed, then, no explanation, no blackboard, no instructor, no course material; then everything was luminously what-it-was. And what it was, in its Being, was perfect without End.

Fenlon stood for a long time looking down, wondering less at the Wonder of what he saw than at mankind's perpetual estrangement from it. Why did people pursue such ephemeral ends - and with such automated frenzy, drive and lust? He had never understood it; now he never would.

And then, quite suddenly, it came to him. The fact was, there was no space in the brain: it was congested like a city at five o'clock. From the moment one was born one was crammed with information (who I am, what I am, nation-family-circles) and this volume of lumber filled the House, which, looked at intrinsically, is a Place of Space-and-Light. Everybody had their bit to contribute - chairs and tables, curtains (very heavy), then all the bottom-draw appurtenances (knives-and-cutlery, bed-sheets, towels, all the necessary aids to fight off the climate) - and, before very long, one had become just *that,* that sequence of artefacts, that soft-and-solid Chain. One became the City at five o'clock.

Thereafter one approached the world, this life, with so many filters and predispositions it was impossible for the Light to get through. Even if one turned to it, prayed for it, wept for it, it was always at one remove, never quite *there.* And it couldn't be there among all that lumber, that ruin and clamp of Domesticity. First, one had to clear the House, slowly, painstakingly removing each item (if one did it too brusquely the stuff came back), until, like Miss Havisham's, it cleared itself - once the entanglement, the past grief and pain, had seen its day coming and decided to leave. Then there was room, there was space for the Light; then, hopefully, one didn't go around with a swarm of worry-bees round one's head. For these, also, were part of the House, part of the Message of who one was: it was encoded, genetic, neurological, deep. And, unless one gave one's life to find out, it would never yield its secret up.

He turned from seeing and went back inside - not with any specific intention, other than to escape the hot, mid-morning sun - inside the Ashram, where the others were sitting. He saw them, too, in the same intrinsic Light, as still infusions of Deity - except that the tree was perfect in itself (its being-of-light was synonymous with its shape), while these, though burning deeply, like a Candle-flame, were totally unaware of what they were: they had mostly slack and untrimmed bodies and aural Fields of dimmed intensity. He wanted to say out loud, 'Thou are That,' as if to shake them from the general torpor, especially as he could *see* the Flame, actually burning in each one of them. Each one of them was potentially an Aspect of Being, was, essentially, already That. And yet there was here, undisguisedly, so much unshifting Cloud-and-Vapour, so much unshovelled karmic Shit, that the Flame burned weakly, without definition, and the earth-bound organism went its way.

'It's strange,' thought Fenlon, standing there, 'how much we think of ourselves as one, through the little loophole of Name-and-Form. In fact, we're so many persons at once, so much a spread of moods, impressions, rooted convictions and lodged pleasure-pain that to call ourselves 'one' is the merest illusion. Any of these elements (plus many more) can take the upper hand at any moment, and then *that* is exactly what we are - one day one thing, another the next. It *isn't* a unity at all but a strange, contorted, involuted growth, with no firm contour, no real sense. That is the dreadful, obscure, true thing; it is the living anatomy of our estrangement from ourselves.

- Coffee, Fenlon? someone said.
- O, yes, why not? he said, sitting down.

What he was seeing didn't budge: the ancient, fluid Continuum went on. He himself was part of it, but as an actor somewhere, rather remote. He was on Stage with the others; they were play-acting. The funny thing was, though, he *knew* it was a Play, whereas they seemed to have taken on their roles in such a way as to believe they were real. Someone, for instance, spilled some coffee on the floor and got immediately annoyed - he could see the mechanism, like a jerk, arise in him -, then blamed the servant who came scurrying with a cloth. It was as if engrained reflexes such as this functioned automatically, without the person's volition, and he/she were just the unwitting victim. Everything seemed to work like this, on a predictable, stimulus-response basis. Yet, constantly, the

337

Flame of Being burnt, unseen, detachedly, waiting to explode. And he knew it to be the finest Truth, the veriest Ground, into which one could reach.

The frustrating thing was, there was nothing one could do but *be* there, available, to anyone who came along. It wasn't even a matter of choice. No, Choice itself was another illusion, another false creation of the ghost-grey world. In the Vision of Reality there was no Choice, because everything appeared as it was - eternal. And in this Single Open Field, from which all enemies had fled, the world came through with such unmasked impact, so pristinely, that the Observer was absorbed. He dived into the Lake of his own mind, there to find himself reborn, at every moment instantaneously mirrored, as rocks, plants, flowers, fungi, grass - the whole rich panoply of circumambient Life. There were no two Observers (one on the platform, one on the train) but a single, unending, glorious Movement, in which train, platform, passengers, even the queue at the station were bound along a Line that transpierced them all. And this was the Pearl, the Sacred Thread, the Salt-in-the-Water that never was consumed. Even to speak of finding it was wrong, for who was then there to find such Bliss?

The condition for it was that 'little death', the end of the Usurper, who laid claim to everything. He had taken the Stage for his own, which was false. And now it was clear to him Who he was: he was not this limited, time- and earth-bound thing, but some unclouded distillation, some essence of That. There was another 'I', working in another Dimension, feeding itself constantly into this. It was like the heart pumping blood round the body. It *was* the Heart, in its own sweet way. The world became transparent before it: it was the shining Deep-sun, the Light of the world. And it countermanded all misinformation, sorted out the rammel that had been there from the start. It began its own work, silently, in one; it opened up the Waiting Gates. It happened so quietly, unannounced, that one hardly noticed its operation. It had nothing to do with psychedelic fireworks (pretty as they were) or with founding new religions. It was the simplest, plain-, straightforwardest thing on earth, the natural answer to an artificial world.

This alignment with Truth was the one thing needful, the one opportunity not to be missed. For this life, after all, was so very short. There was only a moment, and the Caravan was gone.

# BOOK TWELVE: THE CONSUMMATION

The box is only temporary.

Sylvia Plath

1

They might have stayed on at the Ashram for good, as many people did, from both East and West: nothing wrong with it, after all. But the throb of events was in their blood, the necessity to go and meet their Fate, in whatever way it presented itself. They couldn't have stayed there; they couldn't say why.

They were, however, prudent enough to wait for April and May to go by, while the sun scorched and the mangoes ripened and, eventually, rain-clouds appeared in the skies. It took only six hours to get to Madras, where they would catch the Ganga-Cauvery Express, which left the city at 5:30 p.m. and arrived two mornings later at Moghul Serai. From there it was a short hop, or so they were told, to the City of Varanasi itself.

They had made a first-class reservation, partly to secure some privacy (trains were always packed to capacity) and partly to safeguard Fenlon's health, which was still somewhat suspect, though much improved. They scrutinized the passenger list, which was affixed to the carriage they were to travel in, and found their berth numbers (51-53) with the unusual appellation: MR. FRETSTONE & FLY.

- Must be us, said Eddie. Who else could it be?

And, indeed, among a bevy of Indian names - Patels, Patwardhans, Shankaras, Arwaris - from every corner of the subcontinent, theirs did stand out. But who was the 'fly'?

- Your good family, with you, a fellow-passenger said.

So *that* was it: Emma and Fenlon were FLY!

The coolie they had hired put their bags in the compartment, and they offered him a note, which he refused. He went on vociferously about being their 'poor man', pulling at their guilt-strings for all he was worth, though they knew it was twice what a Brahmin would have offered. Our Three talked to each other casually, while he sat there on the seat, the note beside him, quite capable, so it seemed, of sitting there for ever. Fortunately, the occupant of the fourth berth arrived, himself a Tamil,

339

and asked him what he was doing. There then began a furious exchange, like machine-gun fire, replete with rrr..s and trrr..s, which made them think there'd be blood on the floor any minute. It was one of those great reinventions of what's-what, which characterize all non-Western societies and which price- and mind-fixing have done away with for good. In this case it went on for what seemed like an age, the two of them shorn of all pretence, till the train, in fact, began to move and the coolie picked up his note and left.

- Have to stand up to them, or they'll fleece you, said the man.

It seemed ironical, all they same: they had walked into a system not of their making, whose societal base they did not condone, but whose norms and rules they were obliged to follow.

- That's what we thought, Eddie said.

2

In no time at all they had quit the city and were rolling north, the countryside beside them. It parted before them, like water to the prow, and was low and level, dotted with palms, the sea in the right-distance moving in and out of view. To their left the sun was going down, with its ancient seethe of scattered red, its slow ball-diffusion of last, spent heat. One could look at it now, through the horizontally barred window, the glass pane slotted and locked above, without its burning too fiercely on one's face.

Emma had the corner seat facing forwards, and the light of the sun spread wide across her face, opening up its leonine aspect. She was golden like the Rams of Amun-Ra, god-to-god breathing, drinking god. Her hair, in which a hint of grey had appeared and which yet retained its virgin auburn richness, glowed about her like a regal mane. She seemed, as some people are sometimes, born to be sitting there, on that day in that place. It was one of those curious Synchronicities, which occur, for instance, when a man speaks in public and one knows what he is saying is meant intimately for oneself, or, on opening a book casually - just because it's there - one reads the phrase, the *one true phrase,* which has been the subject of one's meditation. Thus it was she sat there, in and out of Time, with the sun in its outward aspect going down and as Sun, as Being, glowing from within. Eddie loved her then, as he had loved her in Egypt, as he had loved her since in Paradise Square, knowing her in her own Reality, her blood- and atom-truth beyond personal desire. For what they had touched on was indissoluble: it was solid Stem-and-Stock for the building of New Life.

But a new Imperative had entered his life, in the form of the young man sitting beside him. They had become blood-brothers, by an oath. It had been a strange and unique occasion, the two of them falling into one another's arms and deciding it then and there, without discussion or even words. They had broken off thorny twigs from a bush and slid them under one another's skin, till the blood came gently, drop by drop, and they mingled their blood and were of the same kith-and-kin. This, also, was indissoluble - part of the Promise of the Night-journey -, as conjugal and final as marriage itself. And they loved one another in That Vein, that common thread of Brotherhood.

Emma watched it from outside, seeing that, for Eddie, it meant a great deal: it was his final setting-down-on-Earth, the Prelude to his Journey across the Nile. The relationship with Fenlon was the House of Construction, without which he couldn't have built his Boat, and it had come to him, as if preordained, to allow him to do the necessary Work. For it involved his Journey back to Being, back to the title of himself, to the first-and-last Point of It All, the Consummation. It was something she couldn't have done herself - she knew it - it required another Node and Pulse. And here *was* Fenlon, young, blest (though consumptive), with whom he could solidly, physically, day-by-day, put together the Vessel he was going to need. Wasn't that, after all, what Don had meant, in that strange serendipitous encounter by the Nile? He had actually meant him to put it together, to construct what he needed form his own blood and guts. They hadn't understood it at the time; they had found it all very weird, bizarre. They had also been thinking too literally - as if such a thing could be comprehended at that level. Now it was all revealing itself, with the hidden purpose and the means combined.

She saw it from a distance, coolly, impartially, as she sat on the seat across from them. It was, also, in some sense, her own Reality, the point to which she, too, had come in this eternal Journey on which they were embarked. She had no idea, for herself, where it would lead. But all her love for Eddie was there, in her birthing of him, in his coming-through. For we are all, aren't we?, inchoate, shadows of ourselves, aching and burning to fly into the Light.

It was strictly relevant to the place they were going, the one-time Benares, now Varanasi. For this was the most ancient and venerable of cities, with remains going back to 3,000 B.C., and inhabited continuously since then. Here they would surely find every Presence, every Correspondence, all Ways-and-Worlds combined. For wasn't it literally, physically, That? It was located at the spot where the River flowed back north, returning, as it were, to its Source. Auspicious and blessed from the earliest times, it was now the Point and End of their Journey, the place where they might hope to, indeed *must,* find their last and most daring Revelation. It was this, 'somme toute', that had forced them on.

It sat easily with them, in point of fact, as passages of great intensity do. They took some of the food they had brought with them and shared it with their Tamil travelling companion, who was immensely curious to learn where they had been and what they were planning to do now/next. He had himself, he said, in his younger day gone to Varanasi, shaved his head and lived the life of a renunciate. But he had missed his home, his family, his friends, and had eventually decided to go back south, walking barefoot all the way as a penance. He had subsequently married and lived the life of a householder, and now he was approaching the third 'ashrama', when he would gradually withdraw from society and get ready, again, to give up the world.

- It's easier when one is older, he said. One is less disturbed by the basic drives.

- But what about the energy? asked Fenlon.

Ah, the energy, yes, the energy . . .

It seemed he hadn't thought of it. It was part of the structure of Aryan society that one prepared oneself slowly for Eternity. Only the few - and, of those, the very few - were privileged and able to attain in one bound what took the ordinary mortal many years and lifetimes. He had turned out to be ordinary, after all, though from his first youth he had had the highest aspirations.

- I, too, had to go through life's phases, he said. I couldn't, as some do, as SJR did, make the ultimate Leap and find myself There. No, it takes time.

- Are you sure? said Eddie.

- O, quite sure: time to grow, to mature inwardly. How does Shakespeare put it?

- 'Ripeness is all'?

- Ripeness is all - quite right; that's it. We all have to realize our own 'swadharma', our inner Law of Being, and live by that.

- And does that realization take time?

- The ultimate realization is timeless, but the day-by-day endeavour takes place in Time. It's both, you see, both in and out of Time - that's the fascinating thing about it.

- You're not an advaitin, then? put in Fenlon. You don't believe that only Brahman is real?

- No, not in the way some Southern Mystics do. I think the Manifestation is equally important, the other side of the Coin of God.

- What does your wife think? Emma asked.

- She agrees with me, he said.

It wasn't entirely obvious to her how genuine this character was. In this Land of the Guru, she thought to herself, everyone has his bit of wisdom to impart. And, unlike the West, where one has to winkle it out, here it is offered before one even asks! Everybody has such a clear idea of the

342

way they're *supposed* to think and act that one's never quite sure who's kidding who: the talker the listener, the talker himself - or whether (or not) it's completely authentic.

Emma's days of received wisdom were over. She had taken a vow within herself, no less binding than Eddie's and Fenlon's, that she would never accept what was not endemic, what had not grown from her own Root up. So she listened carefully, more politely than politely, letting the man's words fall into her Field, watching them without judgement to see if they would grow. They might be words of wisdom, after all. On the other hand, they might be clever counterfeits, sleights and tricks to hoodwink the gullible, of which there were thousands coming over now. She would let his words fall, she would be patient, she would watch, above all, *trust herself,* her own intrinsic Ground of Authenticity (which she fostered by that very trust) and allow it its own untrammelled Voice, its perfume of Freedom, its well-sunk Depth. Thus only, she had said to herself, as she took upon herself the responsibility of freedom, would she live from now on - clean, without fear.

The man sat back, having said his piece, and the train rattled on through the coming night. It had been one of the triumphs of the British Empire - aided, of course, by massive local labour - to put together this colossal network of lines (More Miles of Track than any Country in the World), which people used massively every day and which still stands striding, a nostalgic tribute to the durability of the now long-forfeited Thousand Years. They went over rivers reduced to a trickle, where, by day, women washed clothes, and watched the barely discernible hills of Andhra Pradesh come up on the left: it was getting dark. The smoke from small houses rose in a wraith and made a concert with the purpling air. And always, even invisibly now, came the shouts of children playing out-of-doors. How could there not be overpopulation, when children were the Treasure of the Earth, the pride of their parents, their comfort in old age? It had always been so. How should it change? And, as the darkness deepened and the children fled, Our Three went, like the homing children, to their beds.

They awoke the next morning to cries of 'Coffee! Coffee!' from a stray vendor coming through first-class. They took a cup of the oversweet brew and looked for the sun to rise on their right. They were somewhere in the middle of the countryside, hardly moving; sometimes, as now, completely stopped. Their travelling-companion, whose meditative poise was beginning - already, at this stage - to waver, got down from the train and chatted with fellow-passengers. Apparently, there had been a derailment further down, and their train had been rerouted, first south-west, then north; soon it would be back on track at Nagpur. 'Nothing to worry,' an official said. But of course, it put hours on the journey: 39-40-41-42 . . .

It wasn't until mid-day the next day that they finally reached their destination. After Nagpur the train had picked up speed and was even making up time on the stretch to Allahabad. From then on, however, it was a local-train crawl through the greyish, sprawling fields of the Indo-Gangetic Plain, with mauve water-hyacinth growing in every ditch. Eventually (the train had been rerouted again) they were crossing the Ganges by the iron road-and-rail bridge, which spans the river just north of the city. This, too, was a British Monument, built in 1890 or thereabouts, and it continued to carry trains, lorries, cars and bullock-carts in a constant stream across the swirling swath. Not to be defeated, their lugging train (which had, to be sure, its own way of doing things) stopped at Cantonment, then only at City. They had arrived in the sainted City of Benares.

3

It was a hot maze and babble of furious action, coupled with an utterly detached indifference, which characterized this most ancient of places and made it unique among the cities of the world. Like everything in India, its impact was immediate - and it was completely Indian: the same, only more so. There were either twenty swarming coolies or none at all, prices were astronomical or ludicrously low, the people were saintly or total charlatans. It had all the extremes - and the extremes of the extremes. The streets were filthier, dustier, noisier; the dogs were mangier, the wandering cattle thinner. But it also had the most delicious sweets, the finest silks, the most voluptuous courtesans (their Tamil traveller knew about that, too!) There were no law-courts within the city limits, as the City itself, the whole game-shoot, was sacred to Shiva, its Supreme Lord. For in this holiest of cities, where it was 'moksha' to die, human Measure had lost all hold: Reason gave way to Intoxication, Order to Anarchy, Striving to Being. There hadn't, prior to 1911, been any kind of College here, until the persistent efforts of Annie Besant had culminated in the founding of BHU. It was, thus, and *is* the first-and-last Place.

Actually, they were auspiciously lucky: their taxi-wallah was fairly honest (no meter, of course, but still fairly honest) and brought them to a hotel at the south end of the town, where the budget lodgings are situated. It was just a few streets from the River Asi, which delimits the city on the southern side, the northern extremity being marked by the River Varuna - hence, Varanasi.

The entire City faces south-east, across the darkly swirling Ganga waters, to farmland and trees on the opposite bank. Its streets run inevitably to the steps of the ghats, which front the water form north to south and show one at once where the City's focus lies. Always one returns here, again and again - at dawn, at mid-day, in the evening, any time: to see the sun rise and, little by little, cut a pink path across the River; to see the dead bodies, wrapped in white or coloured cloth, carried with rejoicing to the burning ghat and there turned to ashes with a smell of sizzled flesh; to watch fortune-tellers, head- and body-masseurs, card-sharpers and astrologers plying their trade; to witness the light, from incipient to garish, back, in the evening, to mellow and night - the stone still warm from the hot, strong day, the lame and lepers waiting, the beggars in a row; to walk and to be there, simply sit, where the World of the Living, the teeming, multifarious, jostles to a border with the World of the Dead. For the River is the element of both - nurturing, sustaining, flowing, cleansing - but also darkly-deeply bearing away, taking off for ever our mortal slough. Hear it quietly of an evening, drifting, breathing, or, in the early morning, making new. For Ganga is Mother, as well as River; She is the Gift of Shiva, flowing from his Crown. In this way She nurtures, both in Life and in Death: She brings us into being and She takes us away.

They came into this that very afternoon, having washed and changed in their cheap-but-clean hotel. It was one of those moments (a definite lull), when the light is white and the heat fierce, and people are either sleeping out the hours or languidly waiting for them to pass by. They would have hired a boat and rowed on the river, but really it was much too hot to be comfortable. Instead, they backtracked inside the city and entered that maze of ancient alleys, known locally and generally as 'The Gullies'. They are little more than an armspan wide and thus preclude all four-wheeler traffic, which gives them immediately that human dimension, where smell, taste, touch and the milling of bodies reassert their right over the ubiquitous Machine, and familiarity and weaving in-and-out replace street names, numbers, plans, maps and signs.

There were little shop frontages piled high with powder (conical thrusts of ochre, vermilion, black, vibrant purple, brilliant yellow) and others with oils, incense, figurines of gods, beads and necklaces, rings by the score. And, of course, now more leisurely, opening up, like a recessed 4X3 metre box, the tailors and fitters (shirtings and suitings), 'ready by tomorrow, sir,' ready-mades as well. They would come back later they said - 'just browsing.'

It is sometimes difficult to catch the drift, if people are moving on a rhythm not one's own. How many of the rhythms of India remain unspoken, quick-heeled and swift - across fields, up dusty tracks, down narrow lanes. So it was in the Gullies that day, as the crowd moved rapidly, silently, with purpose, to a Focus the outsider could never have guessed but which was, nonetheless, completely real. Our Three felt the rhythm, picked up the purpose and arrived, turning right at a crossing of ways, in front of the entrance to the Viswanath Temple. This is the holiest of all the Temples of Benares, and, even in a country as tolerant as India, none but Hindus may step inside its walls. They could peep in through a side-entrance - that was all - at the literal throng of devotees, approaching, offering their coconuts and flowers, prostrating, bowing, praying, moving, while the perfume of their praise curled aloft like incense and, with the incense, charged the air.

Our Three lost themselves in the Gullies again, amid the sweet-sellers and cloth-vendors. It was time to have some clothes made up, and they went from shop to shop, looking at material - silk for Emma, cotton for the men. She bought several metres of fine purple silk, which she wanted made up into a pyjama-kurta outfit, while they hunted around among the ready-mades, hoping to do the whole thing in one go. It wasn't a good idea - when is it? -, as the fittings and styles were for Indian men, and they ended up with lengths of cotton cloth, looking for a tailor, as was Emma with her silk. They stumbled on a place in an unlikely back-alley, where a goat was standing on a raised ledge beneath a window and, straddling the sky (they said it had always been there), a tree grew horizontally, straight out of the wall.

The tailor, seeing them with their bundles, invited them inside from his open, waiting door. They climbed a flight of stairs to a large, cool room, where the light spread pleasantly across rolls of coloured cloth.

- Nothing to sell, he said, only make up.

He sent out for tea in the handleless clay cups and they drank it, sitting comfortably on the floor.

- Of course, if you *were* interested . . .

- Not at the moment, Emma put in promptly, seeing him already in her mind's eye rolling out miles and miles of cloth, a length of which they would have to buy, just in order to get out of the place.

- Just our measurements, please, she said.

- Of course, he said in his Indian way, asked her how much she had paid for her silk and assured her that, if she had come to him, she would have got a better price - and better stuff, too.

- That's the tourist area, he said. Those fellows over there, they're just out to exploit you. You come to me: I'll give you a fair price.

- Well, perhaps another time, said Emma, thinking that what he said *did* make sense and that they would probably have done better to look around a bit longer. Then again, one never knew. Eventually they managed to get themselves measured, without buying cloth they didn't want. Their clothes would be ready in three days time. They took the man's card, which seemed to round off their acquaintance.

Back in the Gullies, it was somewhat cooler. Some cloud had built up: the rainy season was approaching. They drifted about for some time longer, looking at all the little shops, till their eyes were full, their senses sated. It was still rather inchoate, somewhat unreal - as if they had been dropped from another planet onto this one and hadn't yet made the necessary Connection. They were looking for a link factor amidst the distraction.

It came via one of those casual conversations, which are the meat-and-drink of any stay in India. They were having tea and bafi at a café near the ghats, when the fourth seat at their table was taken by a stranger, an Indian who wanted to know all about them: where they came from, the purpose of their visit, 'how do you like our country,' etc. They answered that they came from England, had so far liked India very much, and were particularly drawn to the spiritual aspect of its culture.

- Then you have come to right place, he said effusively. This is the home of Sri Ananada Mayi Ma.
- ?
- The Holy Mother, a truly Great Soul. Her ashram is here, by Ganga's side. I show you.

And he leapt immediately to his feet.

- Will she be there? asked Emma pertinently, as Eddie and Fenlon began to follow suit.
- O, not today, he said, sitting down again; I was forgetting. But tomorrow is 'bhajan' at five o'clock.
- And anybody can attend?
- O, yes, open to all. I'll meet you and show.
- What, here?
- Yes, here.

And, with that, he rose and left them to their tea, with the alacrity of one who has done a good deed and doesn't want the point of it to be lost - in fact, such alacrity and such a good deed that he didn't need to come to the rendezvous next day!

- What shall we do now? Eddie said.
- O, I think she should be well enough known, said Emma. We'll just ask around; perhaps the café-owner knows.

Fortunately, he did and gave them accurate instructions, though even if he hadn't he could, with equal firmness, have sent them in totally the opposite direction. He couldn't, after all, have refused a service to a guest or allowed him to think that he didn't know his Patch.

It was actually not very far at all, and people were already sitting down, the women on one side, the men on the other. Incense was burning in opulent profusion, while the tampura, tabla and harmonium players were going through an endless round of tuning-up. It was a rectangular hall, without supporting pillars, and had a dais at the end opposite the entrance. Eddie recognized the man who had met them in the café, but it was not a mutual recognition. The man was straining forward in fixed anticipation of the moment when the Holy Mother would appear: 'darshan' of her was all he wanted.

Mercifully, it was a humble and straightforward affair - no introduction, no speeches, no palaver. Ma simply emerged from behind the dais, dressed in a full-length, flowing white gown, her freshly-washed black hair loose about her shoulders, and took her place with the accompanists and singers. The tampura put its 'sruti' note into the air, and gently, as with a tide just rising, the music rippled across the hall.

Bhajan consists in chanting sacred songs, dedicated to God, gods or Guru. They are part of the landscape of Indian life, just as Protestant hymns were once part of ours - except that they exist in thousands, even millions. There seems no end to them, actually, as there is no end to the permutations of Music, and they feed and sustain and raise a Platform, on which the Enlightened One can sit.

Ma sat silent most of the time, receiving the songs which were addressed to her as Guru. When they were sung in praise of Krishna or Shiva, she joined in quietly - she was a 'bhakta' in her heart. The bhajan went on for about an hour, the fragrance of it filling the hall with the sense of a perfume beyond this world. She sat among it and gave it out, but in such a completely impersonal way it seemed to emanate from everybody equally - not as haloes, auras, lights, but as the True Fluid which had given them birth. They were all as if features and forms of Her, the one Shakti-power, the Creative Feminine. And this was what Ma *was*, actually: she was not just a person on a stage - in fact, that in itself was just a form. She was actually, deeply, this living Warmth, this sustaining Element in which one lived and breathed. The formula of living became reversed: what one regarded ordinarily as fixed, concrete, real was now a small-term, last, though present aspect of something infinitely deeper and more real. It was This that was spreading constantly, soaking up distance, Space and Time, bodying itself forth in the bodies sitting there. Love-as-the-primal-Power became real: it was tangible, obvious even, clear. And absolutely nothing was outside It. It was what lived and moved in everything - closer, more *of* it, than it was itself.

This quiet intensity came from Ma: it was because of her perfection that it was there. For that living Truth required a Mirror, some perfected soul through which it could shine. For, while we were part of it, we were not *fully* it. She was - and it was that which made the difference. It was this Lifebreath, this Love sustained the world; it bred it, as we and all creatures breed. And, though quiet, it was strong, it had Energy and Force; it could destroy as quickly as it brought to birth.

The deep Peace spread to every corner of the hall; it filled every nook-and-cranny of the House. 'I abide,' it seemed to say, 'while worlds pass, this material world and others, more refined. I am like the River, which fills its banks and permeates every last morsel of ground. For I do not derive from anything: I am That which flows and which returns whence it flowed.' It abided, once touched, in the secret recesses of the Heart, perhaps ignored for ages, while lives and living passed. But once that nameless chord had been struck, its quivering vibration awakened in the Rose (like dew on summer mornings, sun-brilliant and pure), then it was as if the false signs, jumbled letters, scrambled Codes began to unravel themselves then-and-there. It wasn't a *directed* human action, and yet it was the Consummation of all action. It was the blooming of the Rose which never dies, the beginning of the Journey which never ends and to which all life hitherto is a prelude. Suddenly, one realized, *this is it*, it's not a dress rehearsal; the preparations are over. One was out there, lights up, audience in their seats, and the fumbling and stumbling were part of the past. And, because it was so, one would do and dare, would take the Stage as an atom of the Play and, realizing one was noughted, infinitely Nought, be born again as the Rose made real.

For now it was the Rose itself which lived, and one lived only in and by the Rose. The Rose, of which the essence was the Perfume, existed and grew strongly as oneself. It was intimate Music, this opening of the Rose, a Tale oft told (like dew on summer mornings - sometimes glimpsed, but only rarely perceived); it was a deep-down Music blotted out by Noise. And yet it was easy to turn Noise into Music; it was both the most human and the most natural thing to do: it was what we were here for, actually. Everything else was peripheral. Yet men still went on one Track only - except that now they went by jet-plane, instead of bullock-cart; now they killed with H-bombs, not with clubs and stones. They were flying always out and away, combing the skies above Hiroshima for clues. But the clues they sought were not out there - in the rubble, in the physics, in thought-action wrought and wide. They were *in here*, rather, along the Flow of sattvic Peace, the still Heart's Moment, as It turned about Itself. Here, and here only, did things make sense.

As in-herence, each one of us *was* that Hub-and-Node: the question of the opposites was resolved. For Existence *was* Essence, and Essence was Existence. There was no gap, really, between the two. Each one, richly, was that Being; he had his being in that single Source, the Self. Seen another way (and this was *real* seeing), there was no Two at all, anywhere, but everything was Movement of the single That. And then the new Translation began, in which personal history, fugitive knowledge, loves won and lost all had their place: they had their place because they stopped Here; Here they died and were reborn - not in grey cipher or flat anecdote but as elements, wings, fibres, blood-and-bones of a Life that was *teeming* to be born. It was knocking and asking at all times to be let in. But mostly, because we were travelling away and had lost ourselves in the calculation of the trip, we were unaware of that seething Life, which grew like daisies beneath our feet. Yes, we had only to look and there it was - the Opening of the Rose, the Journey into Space.

The music had reached an ecstatic pitch and was, climaxed, now gently easing out. It no longer tried to penetrate and hold but was rich, recumbent, drifting with itself. Emma was some way away from the men, among the Indian women with their thick-cord pigtails, their wee bobs of flowers, their bangles, their jewellery, their slim naked wrists and their brightly coloured saris. She was herself enwrapped in the music, enfolded, as if it were everywhere. A question-mark had hung in her mind, as to why they had come here and what they would do; it had irritated her like a nervous tic. Now she felt her irritation washed away· she had returned to the everywhere Heart, her Self. It was really so obvious when one opened up a bit and allowed the other Presence to do its work. It came then cleanly, smoothly, unbidden, working its purificatory way. How easy, all the same, it was for one to be carried off somewhere down a dead-end! How easy it was for the ever-urgent Thief to steal in in the night and take the Baby away!

Now, however, Thieves and Vagrants were gone - like so many wraiths before the blazing of the Sun. Its Light was lambent, infused, diverse, and It resumed and transcended all opposites. It defied all categories of meaning: indeed, it established instant-by-instant totally unforeseeable *new* categories, which were more of a Dance than a Definition. It was forever bursting out of Itself, creating fresh, rich forms, unparalleled. It was ploughing and seeding and breaking down; it was demolishing and building; it was New Wine for Old. And it was in the air like an electric charge, like rebraided Bliss, as the music calmed.

Unexpectedly, so far as Emma was concerned, Ma now began to give a talk. Since it was in Hindi, she didn't understand, but she let the words flow over her, treating them as a verbal continuation of the music. From time to time she looked at other people, as if to see, mirrored in their faces, the meaning of the quick, light speech. A man opposite her seemed all approval and consent, making clicking sounds from behind closed teeth, raising arm and hand in an open-lotus gesture, then with the same hand slapping his plump, rolly thigh. 'I wonder what he *really* understands,' she thought. But then, what did it matter, after all? He was part of the Process - that much was real -, as much part of it as anyone else.

Fenlon and Eddie were sitting together, a little further back than Emma (there were more men than women in the hall). They had been encouraged by a man sitting next to them, called Ganeshan, to join in with the bhajan at the more accessible points - choruses, for instance, of which there were many. He was an Indian of the most mellifluous kind, didn't seem to have a stiff joint in his body. Now he was sitting there, one leg across the other, listening like a child to his mother's words, with the kind of expression children have - serious, guileless, totally attentive. Indeed, as they said to one another later, Eddie and Fenlon learned more about Ma's talk - and, above all, what it meant to listen - from looking at *him* than from the talk itself.

Eventually, however, it came to an end. Ma folded her palms in the 'namaste' greeting, rose and quietly left the hall. Some rose with her, others prostrated; all were silent, imbibing her Presence. Ganeshan hadn't budged an inch. They waited for Emma at the entrance and, when she came up with them, Fenlon suggested that they hang on a minute: wait for Ganeshan.

- He seems available. Could be interesting, he said.

He was, of course, and ebullient and flowing.

- Let's go and have some curds, he said. I always eat a light supper, don't you?

They agreed, by default, that they always did, too, and soon they were walking through a maze of streets, ancient like the Gullies, but open to traffic. For it is true to say that, while Benares has streets, some of them broad, they lead where they will, and only the River steers a direct course anywhere. In the event, it didn't really matter, as Ganeshan had promised to take them back to their hotel and they had immediately placed complete trust in him ('provided he doesn't forget,' thought Emma.)

The place he took them to was large and functional and was owned, he said, by South Indian friends of his; he himself was from the South. They washed their hands at a long sink with a row of taps, all of which dripped.

- Bad plumbing, he said, as if reading their minds. Wouldn't happen in South, believe me.

Suddenly, magically, a waiter appeared, bearing a tray on which stood four bowls of curd. He equally suddenly, and silently, withdrew.

- Help yourselves to sugar, said Ganeshan, indicating a fifth bowl deposited by the waiter. Now, tell me about yourselves.

They told him their story from its beginnings in Sheffield, how the thread of their meeting had brought them here.

- And now you're in Varanasi, he said, the City where every Hindu hopes to die.

- I'm sure there's plenty to see and do, said Eddie.

- Plenty: you've already made a start. And I'll show you more, if you'll come with me.

351

They noticed then that he had, in fact, already finished his bowl of curds and was on the point of getting up. They gulped down swiftly their last few mouthfuls (did these people *never* linger over food?) and were out with him in a second on the street.

- What about paying? Eddie asked.

All paid for, said Ganeshan.

And that was that.

It transpired that he was travelling with his guru, having all but abandoned a law practice in Madras. He had a small attic room at the top of a house, while his guru, Swami Satchitananda, was more capaciously accommodated below, and the entire host family occupied the ground floor. Evening was the time when people gathered - not only their host, who was himself a lawyer, but also doctors, professors, engineers - to hear the discourse of the Holy Man, to benefit from his presence, the greatest boon of all. For all had their purpose and their place in life, but the purpose and place of the Holy Man was highest. He it was who made it all work, who assured by his being-there the continued Connection.

It was, moreover, the most beautiful of evenings, such as one only finds in the tropics. For there the end of the day is a blessing, a release from the heat; there is a quick quietness in the air. And on this particular night, across the waters, from the balcony on which the company met, could be seen, slowly rising, the soft orange orb of the fullest full moon they had ever seen. Yes, they had come to the right place again.

Swami Satchitandanda sat very upright on a high-backed wooden chair of colonial vintage. He wore an ochre 'dhoti' from waist to heel and a matching piece of cloth draped over his head, leaving most of his torso bare. He acknowledged the arrival of Ganeshan and his band with a scarcely perceptible twinkle of his eyes. A semi-circle of people were sitting on the floor.

- Cushions, he said to a 'brahmachari', his student, who promptly got up and, from an adjoining room, fetched a cushion each for Emma, Eddie and Fenlon. Ganeshan was already installed on the floor, sitting as if he had always been there, oozing almost into shape.

- No, it isn't wrong, the Swami was saying, to use a mantra, if properly guided. You use it as long as it's relevant, that's all. Then you'll see, when you're ready, what's the next thing to do.

- But Sri Pillaji says: reject all that stuff!, put in one of the small audience.

- Yes, I know what he says. And, of course, he's right - at the level from which he's saying it, it's right. But, unless you yourself are established in That, it may not be so obvious. It doesn't mean you get attached to your mantra, can't see the wood for the trees, etc.

352

Eddie's ears popped up at this: it was the metaphor of his own life the man was using. Had he really resolved it, he reflected, this contrast, this dichotomy between Vision and Detail? Sometimes he thought he finally had, but then some new instance would spring upon him and he realized painfully that he had not. Ferment and torment were working deep down, the roots of which he had not dug out, the process of which he hadn't understood. He wanted to get to the bottom of himself. Could he do it alone? That was the question. Or did he perhaps not need, like Tom Thumb in the Wood, a few grains of corn to find his way? For one thing was certain: it was *his* Wood - not some generalized, codified, straight-rowed Plantation. And, as such, he had to know it in every detail, as Early Man knew each tree by its name, having not yet arrived at the concept 'tree': its virtue, its properties, its uses, its magic. He needed to know himself that way, intimately, immediately - not through thought and word. That was the missing link, he figured, this failed at-oneness and assumption of himself. Would a mantra really help him? Perhaps. It might.

Swami Satchitananda was interested in them and asked them how long they would be staying in Varanasi. They said they didn't know: a certain time. He invited them to come up in the evenings, when others came, and to be with him. He also was a Traveller, he said, and, as a Sannayasi, never fixed in one place. One couldn't help being attracted to him; there was such a quickness and liveliness about him. His eyes, in particular, danced with light, and it really did seem that here was a man who was leaving this world at every moment - its burden, its suffering, its endless strife - to enter the World of Lightness-of-Being: his bearing and demeanour told one so. His laughter boomed about the place, arising from some Well of Joy within himself, as true and real as those stone wells in fields, that nourished and nurtured the land all around. And yet he could be utterly serious; his look pierced through to the heart's core. This was the kind of look he gave Eddie, when he asked him if he would give him a mantra.

- You don't know what you're asking, he said.

He explained how, in the olden days, a brahmachari might approach a Master and ask him to take him on as a student. It might be years before the Master accepted (no acceptance was guaranteed); when he did, however, he took him in, fed, clothed, and sheltered him, gave him everything. There, thus, was forged a relationship, a bond - that of Guru and Sishya (disciple) - which was regarded as total, permanent and sacred. Indeed, it had subsisted at the core of Indian life, a vehicle of transmission without like or equal, from the first Aryan society down until now. It had weathered all storms, calamities and invasions, all divisions of class, caste and kind, and it still stood today on that same solid Rock, strong and immune from the ravages of Time.

353

- Having a mantra is part of that, he said.

It was not, as it has since become, a thing of the market-place, obtainable for cash. Eddie had his answer, his Challenge and his Test. There was nothing to be had, unless one gave something first. And certainly, he reflected, that was right and proper, too. But was he ready? He felt too weak. There was a reticence deep down, like a kind of sorrow, because he *did* know ultimately what was required. He did - and yet there was something failed him, some privileged word he didn't yet know. Acknowledging this, he found he could accept it, catch up his sorrow, so to speak, like a gown: mantra or no, realized or not, he would carry on living; he would continue to look.

He traced his weakness to instability, to that jumble of inputs, confused and contradictory, to which everyone is subject from the first. He had been a stranger in a strange land and, by God, how often he had been made to feel it! It was only through the medium of other outcasts like himself (Connie and Mellors, now Emma and Fenlon) that he had gained any purchase with people at all. In spite of even them, however, the original pain, the ache of deep loneliness attacked him still like an arid wind; it was at his guts like a cold, iron hand. He was always at a peculiar angle to Life, somewhat askew, never straight on. And he realized on the instant, strongly, in a sweat, that it was this that had prompted his request for a mantra: the possession of that sacred word.

For it needed something - that much was clear - to create a balance in his life: something that wouldn't depend on others or be part of some generalized scheme-of-things. It would address itself directly to *him*, and it would have (if he were lucky) the desired effect. Which was, so to speak, to correct his stoop, to make him sit upright, assumed, assured, in that one true posture which was innately his. He would then no longer piss himself out in the exhausting business of wanting-to-be-liked, but would be able - firmly, finally - to come to rest, unhurried, unworried, unflommoxed, complete. He had a whiff of it suddenly, of what it might mean, if he could actually make it so: of all the little niggles ending there, of all the detail sound and sharp. For it was not in the *avoidance* of anything, but rather in the assumption of one's total humanity, that the luminous Track of Freedom lay. Then all things, clearly, would be seen as they were, endowed with their own radiance and grace: their inner being would be one's own. It *was* just a whiff, the merest hint, but it was enough to quicken him and set him alight. It was a Clear-Light Message and he held on to it as such.

It was a natural step from this Moment of Insight to a growing interest in Buddhism. For, after all, among its many splendours, the region was birth-place and cradle of that Path. Bodh Gaya, where Gautama became Buddha (the Awakened One), was no more than a few hours away by rail, while Sarnath, where he preached his first sermon, was within walking distance of the Varuna estuary. This being so, he persuaded the others - his enthusiasm was, as ever, boyishly infectious - to take that ancient, well-trodden way. They crossed the Varuna by a rickety bridge, having taken an auto-rickshaw to Besant College and walked down the lane to the confluence. Dawn was just coming behind pink, barred clouds and they watched it for a moment from the soft-sand shore, the majesty of sunrise still some time away. But the day would be hot - that much was certain - and they wanted to have put some distance behind them, before the fierce orb took to the skies. They scrambled up a bank and walked on to a village, through which a rough road let out in a north-westerly direction.

It must have been some holiday or other, because children were flying kites in the fields, from which a crop of wheat had already been taken. And, early though it was (the trees barely stirring), there was sufficient breeze coming up off the River to keep a kite giddily flying up there, happy as a child's heart, oblivious of cares. The way itself went on anciently, as ways only can in immemorial places, where the original rhythms have not been lost and one feels, as if through the soles of one's feet, the repeated tread of the pilgrims of yore. The buildings they passed belonged to it: the little shrines and temples, the crowded houses, that open, high-walled ruin which had once been an ashram. It bespoke a life that had gone on for millennia, a land that was dusty, worked-out and tired. They turned right along a railway-track, then left along a road, beneath shade trees to the Sarnath site.

It was for all the world like an extended garden, with one enormous, circular, crumble-domed 'stupa', to which pathways led, dominating the view.

- I like it like this, Fenlon said, better than if it were swarming with people.

It had once been a centre of culture and learning, with all the accretions which grow around a Teaching: shrines and temples, universities and colleges, monasteries and religious foundations, etc. There was little left now but excavated places, to which one had access down worn stone steps (corridors and passageways, functional or secret), and the stump of a pillar commemorating Ashok, the first Emperor to embrace Buddhism. Nonetheless, there hovered about the site, with its green-lawn cleanliness and open space, an atmosphere of calm serenity and peace at many removes form the noisy, honking street.

- I feel I could almost *live* here, said Eddie, although it's a relic - in spite of that.

- Yes, it *does* have something, Emma said.

Its emptiness was, in a sense, its perfection - like the Emptiness of the Mind when thinking has gone. There breathed now across this humpy

355

sward, which was like the burial ground of many pilgrims, the Calm and the Height of action resolved, of things turned back and in upon themselves, where there was no need of speech or writing any more. It had seen and known the lives of thousands, from the mighty Emperor to the humble monk. And now, having seen them and buried them all, having taken and put away from itself all the clutter, bombast, book-learning and greed, which go in the name of civilization, it was free at last to live and breathe, to open itself, green and waiting, to the skies and to hear, in a Space untrammelled, unborn, the Word of the Buddha, the First-and-the-Last.

They ate the sandwich breakfast they had brought with them, sitting on a low stone wall adjacent to the entrance, where buses numberless brought their cargo, and not too far from the small museum. This they deliberately omitted to visit, forfeiting its treasure trove of polished stone for a walk again across the open space and a quiet return to the high round stupa, where they performed a 'pradakshina' (right around), turning the prayer-wheels as they went. They were not alone: other visitors, also, and barefoot monks, of whom (brown-habited, shaven-headed) there were quite a number round the site, followed the same circular, oft-repeated path. It was very auspicious, naturally, this clockwise walk round the solid Mill of Silence. It was part of the ancient Tread of Time.

Down an avenue, with flowering bushes on either side, they came to a temple with a large statue of the Buddha. 'How strange,' thought Eddie, 'this human propensity to create models and images and to worship the person. How strange, when Thatagata is really wide open, part-and-parcel of the air we breathe. Yet, there he was, the long-lobed one, whatever the position we found him in - sitting, standing, recumbent, aureoled -, replicated a million times throughout the East. He was bought and sold, this stiff, stone Buddha; he was marketed in wood, bronze, ivory, gold - while the thing he talked about, the Awakened State, was palpable and present before one's very nose. It was out there waiting, it was running through the breeze; one inhaled and exhaled it all the time without knowing. 'How strange people are,' said Eddie to himself, 'and all the time I thought it was *me*.'

He had fought against this strangeness all his life, had tried to assimilate his life to theirs (as an Englishman, a Christian, an orthodox Something), but always this sense of estrangement had remained, like a thorn in his side, a marriage unmade. And always, being a sensitive lad, he had taken the blame upon himself, thinking - the *feeling* was still there - that he was, like Jude, a maladjust, obscure, a freak, a person who should never have been born. But now, in the lucid state, he saw quite clearly that he ('Handle-Wandle', 'Wanklbert', 'Flossie') was the

356

one who was travelling home to himself and that the others, apparently so sure of themselves, were trafficking in whatever fell to hand, the desperate coinage of material exchange (images, approximations, thought-deals) and that, hence, they were always, inevitably, at one remove from their True State. And, when he looked, he could see it in their eyes, this sense of estrangement from their true Self. They, not he, had wandered away, had locked themselves into their mortal Coil, which everyday strangled them a little more. This tremendous sorrow, like the weight of the world, was a Wound discharging in each of them. And it was only now, in moments such as this, when the mind itself was tranquil and clear, that one saw the living enormity of it, the contraction of pain like knotted nerves. It was a seeing, also, without recoil, without reaction or agitation. He simply was there and saw it all, like looking at the world for the first time without blinkers.

4

It was actually only from this point onwards that Eddie began to sort himself out. He realized many things all-at-once: all of the above and also, fundamentally, that he was Brother to this estranged human Stock. Not that this meant that he lived as they did or tried to assimilate his life to theirs (which was, in any case, water-under-the-bridge), but that we were all, however distantly, related and could, along the thread of our common humanity, be reached, touched fetched, even pulled together. *That* was 'Sangha', *that* was Community - not the living-together in exclusive groups, which was outmoded, anyway, a thing of the past. 'And yet,' he reflected soberly, 'it takes good people, always the right people. Without that one can't even make a start.'
After a quantity of haggling they engaged a taxi at what seemed a fair price and were driven back to Varanasi. It was hot by now and after lunch they rested, thankful for the wire mesh across their windows, a protection against the perennial mosquitoes. Emma slept fitfully but Eddie slept well, and he had a dream, which was surprising in the circumstances, triggered possibly by that fleeting mental reference to the nicknames given him at Sheffield School.

He could feel the heaviness of the atmosphere, the constant, slightly sulphurous smell, and the light, as if filtered, yellow and foreign. He was there again; he would have known it anywhere. It was at-the-school, not-at-the-school, the smell of the school, but the building was different: it opened up somewhere onto a park, which was steep and wooded like Graves Park, but with the light green turf of an Indian lawn. He was talking to Miss Diabolus. Oddly, also, they were alone, in a clearing in the wood, and the light had changed. It was clear and, though still

357

filtered, it was clean; it fell like bright glass on the bracken and dead leaves.

- I've dismissed my class, Miss Diabolus said. They've all gone looking for specimens. Come and see what I've got for you.

- He approached her cautiously, still a bit ginger: he though he knew Miss Diabolus of old.

- Come here, silly boy, and sit down by me.

He sat down beside her on a gritstone rock, weathered by rain and now warmed by the sun.

- Here, she said, handing him a small cardboard box. Open it; I've brought it specially for you.

He tried to take off the lid, which seemed too tight for the box, and became in the process all fingers-and-thumbs. Miss Diabolus took the box from him and, as if by magic, removed the lid.

- There, silly boy, what did I say? Just for you!

It was a box of chalks of all different colours - orange, red, blue, purple, yellow and green.

- There aren't any white ones, Eddie said, like a child whose favourite Flavour is missing.

- But you always use white ones; I thought you'd like a change. Wouldn't you like a change, Eddie?

- I'm not sure I would, he answered primly.

- O, I think you would: you've always wanted Change.

She moved up close to him on the rock, and the warmth of her body came through her dress.

- You're the nicest silly boy I've ever known. Why don't you show me how nice you can be? I've always found you so very stiff-and-starchy.

- And I've always found *you* very cold-and-sharp.

- Time to make amends, then, isn't it?

That red dress was all Miss Diabolus had on and, beneath it, her body was firm and brown.

- They call me the Electric Eel, she said.

And, as if the words themselves had mantric power, he was down at the bottom of the sea with her. He was upright inside her and she was all over him: about his neck, his arms, his loins. She was the sea and he was its people, going, thronging, strong through her. She was the obverse of her daylight self, for now she wanted *everything* and was averse to nothing, nothing he could do. In fact, she showed him successively where all her secret places were. She wanted him between her buttocks, firmly, tightly, incisively: she wanted him brushing, erect, against her nipples. And ever, seemingly, the sea rolled on; there could and would be no end to it - the pink coral tipping, the waving flesh transformed.

- You see, I knew you wanted it, she said. I saw it in your eyes a long time ago.

And want it he did, with his last strain of strength.

- You *are* a nice silly boy, she said, pushing him back against the rock.

- You *do* like my hands on your shoulders, don't you?

He was tilted back against the rock, and he was as hard and imperishable inside her as the rock. 'Even now,' he thought, the Observer-in-the-dream, 'she doesn't stop talking; she *loves* to talk.'

- What a nice long, strong boy you are, aren't you?

The sun was shining into the clearing, warm on her buttocks, which he clenched with his hands. Then she wa sitting astride his thighs, her legs round his waist, her arms round his neck, and they were travelling hot-golden as Shiva and Parvati through the folded silences of sensual Sound. For him it was like exploring a tunnel; it was ribbed and dark and juicy and echoing. Every forward flicker of his terrible member brought from her a simultaneous pearly little gush, like the dappled light of summer down aisles of trees. And, as they entered the second phase (the Further Field), he caressed her also till she became ecstatic, spilling sharp cries and seeking his mouth. And his mouth came down upon hers and sealed it; it worked her mouth also to fever pitch. It was hot inside her mouth, as it was hot inside her belly, and she wanted more of him, more and more. More and more and more and more . . .

Then the waves of the sea were rolling back; they were rising up, seething, from the hot sea-bed. Where was the form and where were the bodies? There was nothing here but seething Sea. Miss Diabolus had atomized out somewhere, and all that remained was a red sea-bush, foliate and luscious, growing from the sand. Her brown firm body had become its stem, her lips its petals, her orgasm its explosion.

And what of Eddie? Eddie came. And, when Emma saw it, she set to herself, with all that sense she sometimes had that Eddie was going away from her, and they made love through the still, hot Benares afternoon, as they hadn't done now for some while past.

5

But it was a stay-of-execution, not a real reprieve: Eddie was going, anyway. He had tuned in somehow to the Buddha's High Note and was, consequently, in thrall to it. What he knew of this world and of the currents of desire were just features, aspects of a widening Field, which extended to the End and whatever lay beyond. He was determined now to go to the End. When he centred on the 'hara' in meditation and watched his breathing rise and fall, he saw Worlds innumerable come and go, created on the in-breath, dissolved on the out-. These Worlds - and there were, literally, thousands of them, not just this one solid Planet Earth - passed through him at every instant, as through their own core.

359

He was joined to them in *all* their modes and meanings, as a child is joined to its mother's womb.

He realized he had been conned, we had all been conned, into believing the Flatland version of things, where the Earth is a cooled-down, floating gas ball, on which we grow like bleak potatoes - eyes, ears, nose, organic stumps. But that was a sawn-off, barbaric point of view, and it was having and would have barbaric consequences. Being shrunk and reduced, it was utterly untrue, a dereliction of the Mind's uncircumscribed potential. We could fly to the moon (we would be doing it soon) but we couldn't fly one inch within ourselves, because we looked always through our one little window at the vast, teeming skies and the volcanic earth.

No, this view fell short, it was a total Dead End, though venerated by centuries of 'objective observation'. For it left out the vital matter of the observer: it was based on the cleft between Consciousness and World. What happened, however, when the observer (the subject) became the object of his own search? Did the world then remain this flat, bald place, from which all sap and meaning had been drained? It didn't, it couldn't, it never did! Because what the observer began to see (and Vision was really the crux of it) was something *else* - in fact, completely different from the self-sealed packet of misshapen ideas he had been peddled by professors and other frauds. He began to see that he *was* the world (not the lichen, the mosses, the sea-bottom skeletons), the world as constructed by consciousness. This world was with him day and night, except perhaps when he entered unawares the completely different Sphere of Deep Sleep. No, his was the consciousness of which the world was made - not contiguous, tangential, acting-upon, separate, but in every corner and aspect identical. *His* was the mind of which the world was made, and therefore it turned about him as its core, like planets round a central sun. He was the Focus, the Place of Passage, and therefore his Vision was utterly crucial.

From this instant realization he could move, could begin to see the vast complexity , the interweaving tumult of successive Worlds. Each one had its own dynamic, its own body-being, its space, its criteria, of which the Physical was the last and most dense. Closely related were the Mental and Vital: the Mental a plane of flitting forms, swift incursions, rapid displacements; the Vital a reservoir of lush concordance, aesthetic resonances, strong emotion. They played and interplayed with one another in a Field that was, put simply, the Body's Field. Then there were Worlds and Worlds beyond, of which Eddie had touched an incipient few: what he called the 'Heaven of the Buddhas', for instance, which was virtually non-physical in the sense that it did not pertain to a particular body but was a space, nonetheless, clear and real, through which Buddhas in meditation passed. They were very light, airy, as if

360

adrift, and moved, self-propelled, under a different Law from Gravity's. On 'tankhas' they were depicted as floating on clouds, which gave an appropriate sense of weightlessness. For, though related to the world and its doings, they were of a different material composition. They had a Guardianship function as regards the Earth, much like the hieratic Priests of Ancient Egypt, and they had the power, like them, which they seldom used, of shifting Matter by non-mechanical means.

All this was part of Consciousness, as was all knowledge, all scientific fact-and-method; they were in different parts of the Field, that's all. And all of it was flowing, all the time, moving, changing like a deep, strong River. What happened in the hara was that the Stream ran through - multiply, abundantly, without thinking once. What we did then (what almost everyone did) was to appropriate what happened as self-experience, call it 'mine' and live by that. From then on, the Universe, its vast panoply, was reduced to a shadow-world and we to mere shadows. It started early, of course, right form the first breath: we were building Wordsworth's Prison as soon as he was born. Within its Walls we thought we were safe. But safe from what? Not Death, not Life. For these kept moving, season-in, season-out. They were transformative Agents, the One-as-Two.

Eddie saw all this and his own part in it; he saw the cramp and limitations of his own fear. Yes, it had been there with him from the first; it had been with him in Vienna, before Hitler. He could see it now, out before him like a cloud, greyly wandering but holding him still. At any moment, until now, it could have swooped down and enveloped him. Now, at last, he knew its name, was aware of its hidden prision on him and, because of this, was able to cast it out - or rather, as with the magicians of old, his capacity to know it *by its name* ( the completion of his apprenticeship) meant that the cloud itself dissolved.

It was as if he were moving through the Realms of Dissipation, which are the necessary forerunners of Realization (the cloud must clear before the sun can shine): all the little irks, murks and subtle suppressions had to flower in freedom and have their Day. He knew this now without a doubt; he knew it in the council and conference of his soul. For what happened there *inhered* for ever: it was not a whim or the thing-of-a-day, to be gone on the next impulse or thought or mood. He knew that everything had to be redeemed - from the least, lowest urge to the highest flight of thought - they had to redeem themselves through him, so that they too might give up their prison-selves and become, like the dream of Miss Diabolus assumed, the red Rose on the Sea-bed, their original Self.

And this was true of everything, once the Vision of Reality *became* that Reality. The whole Creation from bottom to top underwent a glorious Escalation - no longer solid, impenetrable, opaque, it had the quality of indwelling Light: it was sheerly brilliant within. The shadows, images, dull approximations, by which we *think* we know (and like to think), are suddenly exploded - or they explode - from inside, to disclose what always they have been in essence: ciphers merely, pointers, coins.

To accede to this was the arduous Path, the Way of unflinching contemplation. The Buddha had laid it out for us: in the Four Noble Truths, the Noble Eightfold Path. More than that, there had been, in successive Schools, endless debate about Buddha-nature: whether animals had it, for instance, whether Enlightenment were sudden or gradual. Eddie wasn't sure about any of this, nor even whether the questions were real, but he did have a Track to the central sense, that of the Light and Space of Mind. He would follow it, develop and intensify his interest.

It was with this in mind that he took the decision to pay a visit to Bodh Gaya. He took the decision off his own bat, rather assuming that his buoyant enthusiasm would be sufficient to carry the others along. In the event, however, it didn't work out. Fenlon's health was beginning to deteriorate, which would have made any journey, even a short one, a folly, while Emma really didn't want to go: Sarnath was one thing, Bodh Gaya another. In any case, it was wrong of Eddie to always assume that his Flights were her own. She was on a Journey, certainly, but her 'modus operandi' was different from his: she let things settle down in her, watched them grow or not grow - whichever -, whereas he hooked into some high Fast-track, then ran hell-for-leather, looking neither left nor right. This tended to put her on the defensive and make her wonder what her own Line was. In this instance, however, she was quite clear: Bodh Gaya-Buddhism was *his* thing.

He felt somewhat sheepish when she told him so; it gave him a feeling of 'having been here before', with consequent rushes of self-reproach. But he *did* want to go (that much was certain) and he quelled the English objection in himself, that he couldn't/ shouldn't go because the others weren't coming. Nevertheless, for reasons which he couldn't quite pin down, there hung about his forthcoming departure a sense of there being more involved than a five-hour train-ride to the next state would merit. What was the substance of it?, he wondered. Was it a genuine premonition - or was it some psychological ghost, conjured up from disappointment at his own lack of foresight and that peculiar angst one gets just before a journey? He didn't know; he never would. But at Varanasi City, where Emma came to see him off, she did something which made him think of her all day: she took her coloured silk scarf from her bag and wound it three times round his neck.

- There you are; it'll bring you luck, she said.
- But . . .

- No 'buts', my darling. Be well.

It was the moment the train begins to roll, like a dinosaur given a new lease of life, heaving and grunting itself into motion. Eddie looked out of the windowless window at Emma receding, approaching the bridge. There was no sun today on her auburn hair, for the sun was a smear and a blear behind cloud. He could see from the bobbing of her head that she was crying, and he almost shouted: Stop!, threw his bag onto the platform and ran after her, to take her in his arms. But he didn't, as - how *could* he have done? He sat sown on his seat with his strange Imperative, this unfathomable Urge to be Elsewhere, and fingered the scarf about his neck.

- Coming from?, asked the man opposite him.

He went through the by-now familiar routine of making himself and his purpose known. Indeed, he often found it quite fun. But today it was irksome like that one mosquito, the one that slips under the net at night and waits until one is half-asleep. He kept trying to flick him away, so to speak, but he kept coming back at him, whirring and obsessive. Finally, Eddie smiled (a disengaged smile), got up and walked down the open corridor, which was relatively free-standing, to the carriage-doorway. From here he could look out at the countryside.

It went on, as it seemed always to have done, for ever, with its nestling villages, open dirt roads, teeming children and sacred trees. Every place looked worn and old, as if it had seen all Life and carried on. It was there in the faces of the people, patiently; it was there in the land, delved and dug a million times. In spite of the poverty, the disease and degradation, there was a Flame burning still in this ancient Land, a Flame licking up from the village hearth to the Top of the Mountain, its fine-diamond Heart. And people gathered around that Flame, nurtured it, indeed, from their own measly treasure, worshipped the deity in Cobra and Banyan and were spanned out uniquely, like beads on a necklace, threaded and wedded by a single Line. It was a Line we had frayed and destroyed in the West, with our picky intellects and industrial Complexes. We had lost the strength to live from within - with passion, at great depth, boundlessly. We had lost the sense of what it was all about - not the individual items, the whole-thing-as-one. And so the bottom had dropped out of our civilization: there was a Hole in the middle and a frenetic periphery, a hard Rind of activity and an empty Heart.

It was serious; it was very serious, thought Eddie. Because that specious way-of-life had its visible attractions: it promised, to thousands, Streets-paved-with-gold. On a daily basis families by the score were moving to Bombay, to seek just that. And they ended up mostly in some filthy shanty-town, a million times worse-off than in the village they had left.

But still the myth of Consumer-Bliss went on. It was the new religion, the god of our time, with its countless altars like supermarket shelves. But these are dead-end gods, thought Eddie, blind, dumb, stymied artefacts. And we worship them in our deadened state; we worship goods, not goodness, having lost the Thread of Truth.

It was so appalling to think of it all (it formed one single ghastly Clump with the wars, the wholesale destruction of forests, the mindless pollution of earth and air), that Eddie was forced, standing there by the door, to shift himself into a different Gear, one where, though he knew he was leaving Emma and the entire godawful world was adrift, he could look out at the fields in the strong sunlight and know, equally well, that he was blest; whatever the circumstances, he was blest, for the Mastery of Circumstance was what it was about. And that was true of all times and places, however and whenever one came upon them. It had been true for the Buddha; it was true for him now.

And that Blessedness reached him from across the Plain. It wasn't the consequence of anything - certainly not of being born, which was viewed, in this country anyway, as the fated outcome of ignorance, the ending of which meant release form birth-and-death; - nor was it any kind of reward. It had come when he saw the Round of Things, his misery and that of the world as one, but not *because* he saw them as one: there was no knock-on, cause-and-effect connection. But it was there in the sunlight across the ancient Plain, it was there . . . nor was it in *spite* of anything. It was part - it occurred to him suddenly - of the Nuptial Night-boat he had been called upon to build - not that it was his, nor that he possessed it; rather, in a sense, *it* possessed *him*. But it wasn't spooky, magical or weird, invoked in the temple or by special rites: it was stuff and substance of him, and he was It.

This also, surely, was the meaning of it, at a deeper, subtler, more real level: not just to put out as a corpse across the Nile but, *while living*, to master Death, that mightiest and most dreadful of Circumstances. That was what the Buddha had taught, and perhaps that was the secret of Enlightenment, too: the Deathless State, the utter Loss-and-Flow, the incorruptible Firmness of dissonance resolved. He thought as much, looking out of that doorway; he felt as much, from the strong sunlight. For, if it were true that Death held the key, as the ankh of Ancient Egypt pictured forth, then not waiting for death was the vital factor, the unmissable Clue to the Mystery. Why wait anyway, when it was there on the doorstep, hovering and knocking and sure to get in? Why not open the door to the Angel of Death, get to know him, perhaps, let him do his cleansing Work? For, however long one waited, he was always there - rich, ripe and ready to take one away.

He had thought of some process, agonized and protracted, like dying of multiple sclerosis or cancer. Of course, it *had* to be a torture and a pain!

But now he saw that it was actually quite different: it was living raised to the power 2. It was Death's breath running in the wild sunlight, it was Death-in-Life weaving through the glancing trees. Death as death-of-the-body was one thing and, as such, organically inevitable, but death as D, as the *meaning* of Death, was so much deeper and more significant a thing, so much less (and impossibly) to be abstracted out, that it was, in the veridical Seeing-of-the-Moment, the very Bridegroom of Life herself, her twinned coiling Lover, her Brother, her Soul. He was the lovely, mercurial Osiris, cut into pieces but always refound. He was the shadow of the moon when the Moon showed her face; he was all Darkness, pouring into Light. And from that Darkness (which was Obverse, which was Earth) came the sustenance of Light and Life. Not only were they man-and-wife, inseparable, but one could not *exist* without the other: they were impossible partners in the same love-match. And loving, living and dying were one; they were not, as we construed it, selected activities, one after the other (Time, gentlemen, please!), but they belonged with, flowed into, *inhered* in one another, sprang out of one another, as the Seed from the Ground.

It was something so peacefully wild inside that Eddie, whose waiting had been long and patient, felt, at last, the Nightmare coming to an end. He was travelling, certainly, very far and very fast, much further and faster than he could ever have imagined. The Indo-Gangetic Plain and all heaven were stretched out, infinite, in front of him. And *they* were moving at their own rate, too, extremely fast, on an unstoppable Trajectory. Everything was moving centrifugally from a point, like the Universe a millisecond after the Big Bang. And it seemed, as he travelled out with the world, became dual, several, multiple, many, that he was also travelling back to himself, to that unitive Essence before anything was. It was the Journey back through Creation, as it were, through all the membranes of the sprouting Seed. And the Secret lay, not in the growing but the dying: it was the thing (the meditation, the Moment) working in upon itself with such austerity that no atom of outwardness remained. And this working (which was real work, real *inward* Work) left not a trace of the Terrain traversed, nor even of itself, as it pushed a passage through: there was no-one there present to say: 'I've done this.' Nonetheless, of itself, the Journey had been made, through risks, masks, upheavals, eternal as the sky.

This was the miracle he was being born into, the daily, precious Miracle of Life. And it lay, not in wealth, accumulation or accretion, but in the exquisite Suchness of Things-as-they-are. For they also were, in some sense, infinite - not as particles, atoms, existents, but as essents. They also were the Universe. And he thought of Zen temples, with their simple repose, their quiet completeness and naturalness assumed. How different from the Gothic Cathedrals of Europe, with their strain and aspiration to be Elsewhere - which meant, really, that they never left the Earth. And one had to leave the Earth, if one was going to live at all; one had to break its gravitational Pull.

Then only could one enter the Sphere, the *natural* Sphere of Balance and Harmony, which was impossible so long as one was attached to the world or, equally, pushing to some imagined Heaven. For the world (which was oneself) was then always out-of-joint: massively indulged or violently suppressed. The answer lay, not in either mode - and what did Western Man have *but* modes? -, but rather in the poise between Heaven and Earth, in the 'I-am-here-ness' of the hara-life assumed, the toned and gracious Buddhist Middle Way. The train he was riding on was travelling to That.

6

Emma felt he was gone for good, though, if asked, she couldn't have said quite why: something to do with his travelling persona, his being, and wanting to be, up and away. She went back to the hotel and looked in on Fenlon.
- Eddie's gone, she said.
- I see.
- How are you feeling?
- Not too bad.
It was true, he seemed to have perked up a bit. The dreadful shadow that had passed across his face, darkening his eyes and making his flesh translucent, had given way to something softer, which gave him rather the look of a child.
- I was thinking I might go out when it cools down a bit, he said.
- Down to the ghats? I was thinking that, too.
- I'll tap on your door, shall I?
- What time?
- About five.
Fenlon really *was* looking quite a lot better, when they met up at five and walked down to the ghats. The evening glow was beginning to spread, a deepening red in the western sky, though the stone still hummed from the heat of the day. It was the hour when activities start up again: hawkers and vendors reappear, the shops reopen; the world's a-stir. They took tea at a small place just back off the ghats, from where they could witness the whole evening scene. The beggars were back, the masseur, that flute player - and another man, turbaned, where no-one could miss him, with a cobra, from whose fangs the poison had been taken, lying coiled inside a basket. He was charging tourists to have his photograph taken and doing very nicely out of it. He played a wee tune on a thin reed-pipe, and the cobra duly reared and spread its hood. Not

366

far away, at a compatible distance, a dancing monkey performed a jig, prancing around on its two hind legs, with a leather collar and little bells about its neck. Every form of human ingenuity was at work, engaged in that most necessary and colourful of pursuits, making a living from the passing crowd, while, lower down, at the foot of the steps, pious Hindus in countless numbers prepared for and took their evening bath, the women fully clothed, the men in a loin-cloth. Around and in-between them small boys dived into the river, seeming to disappear for minutes, then reemerged, spitting out jets of water, and swam back to the steps in a few swift strokes. Young men were exercising further down: one swung his arms backwards like a swallow in flight, his shoulder-blades flexing, his palms touching; another, distinct upon a plinth, swung a kind of mace behind his back, then hoisted it to balance above his head - then down and around, first with one arm, then the other. Boats in a huddle nodded by the steps, their moorings stirred by the bathers and swimmers, while up-and-down the ghats and in-and-out the people the children, Life's Dower, wove their own tapestry.

All along and among them the River ran, catching first fire now, out beyond the shadows. It was no surprise, as it was no surprise now, to see an uncremated body float by - from this distance it looked like a sannyasi (there was a garland over his ochre robe), who was believed to have passed through the Fire while alive and who, hence, had no need to go through it at death. At other times it might be a cow or an ox, with vultures standing on it, ripping at its flesh; or a child, its eyes open, just drifting there, for whom there was no money to buy firewood. Life and Death flowed together here; they were caught, cupped, raised and dissolved in Ganga's waters.

Emma and Fenlon remained speechless for some time, as the scene went on and the sun drew down.

- There's nowhere like it on Earth, said Fenlon.
- No, said Emma.

And, indeed, there is not.

- Nowhere like it to die, he went on. People come here in thousands, just to die. There are ashrams for them; there's one near the hotel.
- Yes, I've seen it. Seems a bit strange.
- Strange, and strangely beautiful. I think I'd like to die here, too.
- What, now?
- Quite soon - it's what I came here for.
- You're talking nonsense, Fenlon. Why, you're looking so much better!
- It's only a reprieve. I know it deep down; I've know it ever since we arrived.
- But that's absurd! You're still so young, you've got all your life before you! Think again.
- It isn't a matter of thinking, Emma.

367

- Then, whatever it is you do, check again. I mean, be more rigorous about your feelings. Are you sure you haven't just soaked up all the tradition, even the *glamour* of the place?

- No, it isn't that, I can assure you.

- I'm very sceptical about special places. Why should one place be more important than another, if this famous Spirit is everywhere?

- It isn't that the Spirit isn't everywhere. The fact is, there are many levels and variations.

- What do you mean?

- There are Adaptations. A mountain and a forest are not the same, for instance: they have different tones, atmospheres, different rhythms.

- Agreed. But how does that apply to Benares?

- There's something very precious here - over and above the special location, where the River turns back north, etc. It's as if the whole place were guarding a Secret. What one sees is just the show, a display

- You mean, all this we're looking at?

- Yes. The very intensity of it conveys something - the bathers drinking the filthy holy water, the chanters of the Vedas, lost to themselves....

- But that's what I'm saying: they were brought up to it. It's just their conditioning, isn't it?

- For me it's more, *much* more than a pageant. All this points to Something Else; it's the Something Else I'm interested in.

- And that's what makes you want to die here?

- That's what tells me I *must* die here. There's a definite Correspondence, you see, a perfect parity between Life and Death. Nowhere else is Death so open.

- Does that mean *you* have to die here?

- It means that I can *assume* my death, in a way I couldn't do elsewhere. I can enter it deliberately, consciously. For five thousand years that has been the Way here.

- But is it a necessity, physically, I mean?

- The doctors seem to think so.

- What doctors?

- Alok. I overheard him discussing my case.

- So it's all up, is it?

- Fairly soon.

The silence of the Knife-edge fell between them. Yet, it irritated her that he kept so cool and, after a few moments' pause, she said:

- Well, it seems a tragic waste to me.

- No, not really.

He was unmoved. She could hardly believe that this stripling of a youth looked on his life as the River flowing by - coolly, detachedly, without emotion. She wanted to shake him, but it was no good; the only effect it would have on her was to make her feel piqued and hot and sweaty, and then disgusted with herself. He just lived and looked on in his cool-glass way, as if it were all a film or a dream and he nowhere a participant.

He seemed always to have lived this 'via negativa', to have been born with it, to have walked it from the start. Life had hardly impinged on him and here he was, all ready to depart. It had been his Way - she saw it clearly now - to pull down every Edifice (book-learning, institutions, tradition, emotion/feeling), as if he had possessed from the very first the key and the means to dismantle all Machines. Their secret had been known to him, and it had taken him only a very little time and there they all lay like machine-bits on the floor, with him the Supreme Master, aloof. And yet this aloofness of his was not complete: there was a hole in it somewhere, a lack of authenticity, as if there were something he couldn't talk about. He was *too* aloof, *too* out-of-it-all; there was a gap between the Master and the human being.

They left the café and sauntered down to the ghats, from which by now the sun had gone. It was pleasant to walk there after the heat and feel a whiff of breeze wafting up off the River. There was, however, a tension between them - as if they had been placed in a Crucible and discovered they were composed of different elements, between which no chemical fusion was possible. It created a hung Valency in the air. The feeling was the same as they strolled through the Gullies, inspecting artefacts, but not really looking, seeing the world as in a Cracked Mirror - sharded, awkward, picked-up and put-down.

They were about to go, silent, to their separate rooms, when Emma, who just couldn't leave it at that, said:

- Don't you think you should inform your parents?
- What about?
- O, come on! What about?!
- I don't think so; it wouldn't do any good.
- Shall *I* inform them?
- No, please don't!

He turned, but his face, his cool-mask face, was crumpling in the shadows along the passageway. She had touched him *there* (it was visible): on his vulnerable spot, in the space-between, the unmade gap between Master and man.

- No, Fenlon, don't turn away, she said.

He half-turned back to her, hesitantly, and she took him quietly, firmly, in her arms. He bent down and kissed her through his tears, which ran down her cheeks and into her mouth. 'So that's it,' she said to herself, 'that's it.'

- There's no need to be afraid, she said.

They moved in a dance through the quiet twilit room, the air a dark purple, quivering. It was still warm, very warm, beautifully warm. He held her neck, his thumbs against her ears. Her upturned face had an expression of wonderment.

- You usually wear a neckerchief, he said.
- I've given it to Eddie - for his Journey.
- O, I'm sorry, I was forgetting . . .
- That's all right; he'd understand.

Her pique and irritation had changed to desire, mixed with compassion, for the dying boy. Somehow the Knife-edge was in there, too, working them both to a Cutting-point. It was the Moment from which there is no going back.

- You're a virgin, aren't you? she said, kissing him.

He looked slightly askance, a bit sheepish, and said:
- Yes.
- So am I, she said with a careless laugh.

And she felt it was true: she had always been innocent.
- It isn't what you think it is, she said.

He couldn't say he didn't have thoughts - he *did* - and, like most young men's, they were bits-and-pieces, muddled. Something a man had said to him once, in a pub in Sheffield off Ecclesall Road: 'Get thi sen a bit o' married, lad; tha can't do better' - it struck him like a dart. He had dismissed it as proletarian vulgarity, but he saw/felt now it had belly-truth. 'They've got evrythin' to give, and tha's got now't too loise.' It sounded coarse and venal, put like that, but what moved beneath it was beautiful and true. Those fumblings-in-the-dark boys bragged about, with eager, athletic, nubile girls (beauty measured in vital statistics: 38-24-36) were nothing but extended masturbations, narcissistic, 'I-am-king' stunts. It took a real woman to take one down, to open up a Gate as real as Death, from which the Army of the Living might sally forth. It took a deep and patient Rose.

He knew without thinking that Emma was She, that she had come to him as Love's Emissary; she had been summoned, somehow, to take him through that Gate. For her it was not an experiment, an extra experience, an off-the-record fuck: it was fact-and-feature of her Priestess-nature, the one she was born with out on the Moor. They were standing on the Threshold, with the secret of the three, the erotic Third, opening up for them. It welled up in them through the purpling night, through all the hidden spaces of their minds, crying, urging, driving to be born. It was the obverse of the Stream of Procreation, for it held and contained a different Seed: it made fecund and pregnant for a different Birth, the endemic realization of what one *is*. In-and-of this Stream they might also move, as the deep, dark Ganga-waters moved, pushing, swirling, opening out. And the River turned north again, back towards its Source.

Emma took him, step by step, through the Dance, as the lights from the street came up and strafed the ceiling and the purple shadows turned to dark. She wanted to savour each morsel of him, each grain and knuckle of his upright Wealth. He had the kind of body women adore (though they rarely admit it) and crave to be near: slim, slightly frail and Shelley-aesthetic, all focus and firmness and smoothness and line. She felt it more and more as she discovered him: his pearling moist hair, his nipples, his navel. It was strange how quiet he was even now, how responsive to her every touch. She wanted him, quiet like that, in her. For already he was the Counterpoise: they were picking up where they had left off. She no longer felt compassion or the emotion of desire, but pure naked physical desire itself, shorn of all feeling like the spring flower's thrust. Unsheathed it emerged, new, daring and keen, and it went for its Equivalent, a body of honed steel.

She knew in her instinct she would not be disappointed; in this respect she was infallible. She had a sense of the 'Yang' in everything (fine, unrestricted, quietly on-the-move) and the Meat-market Mentality was anathema to her. Because of this, she never went wrong: it was never a case of Shall-I-shan't-I?, Hit-and-miss. Because of this, also, she was completely present; she was full-force into him, without overspill. How could he *not* fell her urgency, as she kissed and caressed him everywhere? For already they were seamless and the force of her was such that he fell back, pulling her on top of him. It was as if she had been pushing him from below, through the soles of his feet from the centre of the Earth, and had now dumped him down on the bed, across the sheets. For now she could feel him like honed steel inside her, utterly physical, unsheathed too. She had wrapped her legs around and behind him in a formally original yogic 'asana', which meant that he lay between her thighs, squeezed and taut and slightly raised. He was penetrating her, more and more.

And still, to her, it seemed he was detached, though alert and quick and completely *there*. He was going away from her all the time, as he was from everyone and everything. This made her wild with desire to know him, to be his Intimate, his One-and-only; otherwise, he was going to leave this Earth . . . It all boils down to a quarter-inch of Flame, and that he had lost in his first few weeks of life. She wanted to give it back to him - by every flick and flicker of her hips, in every grasp, lock, twist and plumbing of her loins. But, somehow, he teased her away from him; he put back the space she was trying to close.

Suddenly, there was a noise in the street, quite loud and ferocious, like a home-made bomb.

- Political trouble, Emma said.

- Hindus and Moslems, probably.

The thrust of his penis was gentle in her, so slight, in fact, he scarcely moved. Yet she gave involuntary little groans of pleasure every time it stirred in her. Her body knew him before she did.

371

- Don't be reticent, she said. Don't be gentle.

And, to her own surprise, she felt herself coming, as if from a point in the middle of her thighs. It was like fingers, running and tickling her.

She was laughing and coming uncontrollably.

- You see what you do to me!, she said.

But it was merely the Prelude to the Dance (there was a running and shouting in the street), for now Fenlon knew himself as a man, as a man made man by a woman like Emma. And it gave him the freedom to roam where he pleased, over and through her, down every Track. She felt exalted by his body burst, by this physical passion which overbore her quite: it brought her to the point of annihilation.

And that, in the end, was the Bliss she wanted - not pleasure, not fulfilment, not even love. She wanted, like Eddie, to be out and gone, along and down the River which never ends. Wild.

7

'In my silent Swirl I bear all away - the good, the true, the unjust, the barely born. I make not, neither am I made. Even this ancient, unrepeatable City is a child to me, a stripling, a youth - like that white boy whose ashes I carried away. I *was* before and I shall *be* hereafter, for I am That-which-is and never dies. Come to me, everyone, Bathers, Travellers, for I am That also which cleanses deeply. Ye shall not know sorrow and death any more.

'I rise at Gangotri from Shiva's Crown and am there milk-white, like a glacier. He is my Eternal Lord. His Crescent Moon is a hand under Me; my body is aching for love of Him. From Himalayan Heights I know Myself, I am Myself, the Bliss twice-born. Others come to Me, little-life born. I absorb, contain and transmute them all; I draw them into my Secret Self. And they flow with Me, in Me, *as* Me, for I am the Object of their Search. None shall die who die in Me.

'Your eyes are two but your Breath is one; your odour is Day's fragrance, dipping into Night. And I am that Night which draws you in; I am that Moment, about which you turn. Come to Me, therefore, all you who are weary, and I will bear you along with Me, as I bear the fishing-boats morning and evening, held on my Bosom like a silent sea. See how the light is dawning on my surface, like a mirror of glass, of fine-honed steel. And see how my Body is lush and strong, opening its waters, giving New Life.

'Everything born is doomed to die: that is the eternal Law of Things. But those who are born and who die in Me are the Inheritors of the Treasure, the other 'I'. I am here as the eternal Bearer of that Secret, the Knowledge of Inherence, the immutable 'I-I'. For, scattered here and

372

there on the surface of the Earth, ye are ignorant, tormented, questing, dead. But, lost and found in Me, ye shall inherit, ye shall *live*.

'In Me is Life (for I *am* Life) and those who die in Me shall be reborn as Me, as Life. They shall become, like Me, the cleansing Waters, the River that carries everything away - destroying, purging, making new. And everything shall come to rest in Me.

'I forget not, neither am I forgotten, for *all* my Children are dear to Me. I receive them living and I receive them dead; their limbs and their ashes are all one to Me. I flow on ceaselessly past the City, with its towers, ornate houses, its ghats, its minarets. I bring balm, resolution, coolness, the End: I ease and work out every pain. For, just as I am mighty, I am also sweet, with all the goodness of the planted earth - its seeds, scents, blossoms, honey and wine. I am clad in silks, the spun silks of Varanasi, and my Body, full and luscious, is bursting out. It heaves to the Hand of its Crescent Lord; it cleaves to the bank, rich, colourful and peopled.

'But there is another side to Me - just as I have another, eastern bank. There I am cold, dark, remote and destructive; I am cast-up, without feeling, and I go as I go. Beware of my dreadful impersonality, my obedience to Forces beyond my control. Like that young man who went paddling not long ago - thought he could swim, thought he'd be all right - and his body was washed up three miles downstream. I am like that, too, sheer, blind, implacable, and I long to say to you: Don't come near. I am much too teeming and strong for you. Stay a while longer in your mute mud-hut, with the evening fire burning, the cooking-pots black and the children outside, running with their kites. What happens with Me cannot be gainsaid: I am as dark and austere as a sheer rock wall. Expect no pity, no thanks, no love. For, just as I give all, I take all, too. I wash out everything you thought you were.

'But, then, I am gay, too, lyrical, ecstatic, like the burgeoning spring when the cold snow melts. I am That which comes always and comes again. And I am calling you Home to yourself, to your deep Heart's Cavern, at fathomless depth. For That-which-comes-always, That-which-is, is what you are; only, you haven't discovered it yet. It is waiting for you in Reaches unknown, like the Pearl in the oyster on the salt-sea bed. It is for this I am sweet, I am swirling, I am soft; I throw my arms around you and whisper: 'Ma! Ma!' For, of course, I am Mother and Lover, too; I am all configurations the mind can conceive.

'After Varanasi I pass Rajghat Fort, where the fabled city of Kashi once stood. Sages out of memory sit and walk there, along sun-bedappled paths, to the water's edge. For mine is the Eye that sees all things as Present. And, in this Present, a new Sage stands, gazing longingly, lovingly down at Me - not thinking, not moving, lost to the world. He has immersed himself for ever in the Waters, and my waters have given him richly of themselves.

'My waters are opulent, Seed-time and Harvest; they breed in the world with fecundating strength. Like the sun-soaked land, of which I am part, I am Mother, Provider: I grow and go on. My belly is swelled by the monsoon rains, and the gathering cloud is bounty to Me. I heal all parchedness, barrenness, infertility. Who comes to me and goes away bereft?

'To that ancient site of Kashi a woman comes - not young, not old - and gazes at Me. She stands beneath a peepul-tree, then she walks along the Fort's east-facing rampart. It seems that she is looking for someone, waiting for someone who will never return. For I have borne the ashes of her lover away, and her husband has crossed the River for good. Quickly in her the new seed stirs, and that is why she has come to Me, who am all Mothers in this burning Earth. She is preparing herself and she knows she must be strong, as I am strong who bear all this away - ashes, limbs, filth - to the ever-open Sea.

'At times she wants to come to Me, to throw herself physically into Me and drown. This is Nescience, Ignorance, Ego; it is not the merging I want from her. But behind it lies the true Impulse: to be out, to be gone, to be One in Me. For I am the Illumination of the Heart, the fluid Matrix of the secret Cave, where in ultimate Silence all Walls fall. I am She who moves swiftly at even pitch, easing out all rugosities, dissolving into Nothing the myriad Mountains of Mankind. I shall assume her as my own. She waits, she weeps, she turns back; she is alone. Her very waiting and weeping are dear to Me, for these are the open Portals of the Soul. Her belly is flaming and her heart is taut, but these are Straits of Passage in the Seasons of the Soul, beyond which is New Life, a New Child being born.

'For the former things have no place any more: thought-splits, brain-polarities, antagonisms, hatreds. They shall be washed away - like effluent, like offal. The misery of Man is loathsome to Me; it is a blight and a blemish on the fair Face of the Earth. I want to put my Arm round the suffering, hold them and hug them and squeeze their Pain out. There is, as one enters the Depths, so much Pain, so much the world can do nothing about and yet for which it is directly responsible: the Wars, the Hunger, the eternal Rich and Poor. All this I would heal and so much more - the secret agony of loneliness, the poverty of feeling, the ignorance of Thought. I would heal the common Sorrow of Mankind.

'I go on thickly between my banks, bending eastwards again, gaining Volume and Strength. And, as I go on, I get deeper, too; I reach out and touch more of Mankind's hidden Heart. There's so much that we know nothing about! For Man is a completely unfathomed Creature, washing about on the surface of himself, with his gods, hopes, images, his

374

ancient lusts. He is, to himself, a total Stranger, a blank Sheet, on which he could write the New Poem, with the force and the rhythms of millennia behind it - if only he would look inward to his own Depth, his own real Potential, his infinite Scope. He could then step easily out of the Cage, in which he has been imprisoned for so long, and say to the New Day: 'Lo! I am here'; he could say, more substantively and simply: 'I am.'

'But I don't know if he dares to *be*. Occasionally, on this used and pitted Earth, a person emerges who really *dares*. He/she then realizes how much is against him, how much he has to go against the Grain. Like that lady at Rajghat (once 'tree-fringed Kashi') - she has done and dared, and she is at the Brink. She will, I feel sure, come Home to Me. But she is one of the few, the very few: those who live deeply, truly, honestly, and for whom all half-measures are anathema.

'As I get deeper, my sympathies widen; the Water of my Compassion flows. It is something like kindness (for I love mightily), but it is much, much more - more powerful, more lucid. I have the Eye, which sees, lives and moves. With it - it is strange, to the human mind strange - I become much more aware of lies and duplicity, political manoeuvring, pressure, constraint: I can trace them instantly to their source. This is a further layer of the Sorrow of Mankind, less obvious than that of physical suffering, but in which - at a distance or very near - everyone is caught, as in a spider's web. It is gradually breaking their hearts, also, in a seeping, parasitic, insidious way, a million times more dreadful than the lover's plunge and grief. For it eats away at their Soul-substance, at that untouched Part of everybody's Brain, till the person, caught, confused, *resigned,* caves in meekly and slowly dies. If you want to behold the Devil's Work, do not look merely at Wars, Tortures, Terror, but more softly, smoothly, indulgently at the slow death of millions in their Heart-of-hearts. The Planet is also suffering from this, as it floats - a blue, oceanic-lovely Ball - into the Third Millennium. It is suffering from this more than anything else.

'At Depth, then, I go; my Eye opens wider, and everything, all Life, becomes more intense: the Colours are brighter, the Shadows deeper, the Currents more complex, varied and rich. I have nothing to give but the whole of Myself, and to this Giving I am myself given. In the process I discover new ways-and-means, small as well as great, to make the Whole Thing flow: a hand here, a push there, a gentle suggestion. Only that the hearer, the Walker-on-the-Bank, be open and receptive to my Voice, my quiet Call. For it is always back to himself that I call him, through aeons and acres of his own soul's past. Somewhere, perhaps, he has heard me before, in this present or in a different Form of Mine, for I am Mistress of all this Display. It may be That which comes to him now, quietly of an evening, when he is walking alone - or in the midst of a crowd, calamitous, cut-off, on the downward Spiral of the Nothing of himself. It may be when others are shrieking all around him and he alone, for a thousandth of a second, sees the utter necessity of building from his stock the Boat, the human Vessel, the Conveyance-and-Carriage, which will take him over the powerful Stream. For it needs both, actually (Flowing-with and Holding), a readiness to move with the Current of Life, and an austerity, not to go out and go under in the devious Multiplicity of Maya. Again, he walks boldly, but without self-assertion, who wishes to find himself in Me.

'Then, as he walks continuously beside Me, through the wide and ever-widening Plain, I become to him the Mirror of his Soul, the tiny Atom he had all-but forgotten and which now has exploded and *grows* in him. No longer the plaything of myth, belief and superstition, it is as real to him as the Wall was before, as the Void was before, into which he gazed. For he has *assumed* himself - Wall, Void, Bag-and-Baggage - and now neither he nor they are the same: they have undergone the subtlest of Transformations.

'Now he walks with Me abidingly, along ancient, beaten ways, past villages and shrines. I reveal more and more of Myself to him - because that wee Atom, which before he had ignored, has now become the Cornerstone of his Being. And his Being is mighty, like a Rock; it is the Fortress around which a New Kingdom can be built. And the Content of that Kingdom he finds in Me, in his constant moving and penetration of Me. For I am That which never dies.

'Once - not long ago - he was spare, he was separate; he ate his breakfast and lived his day. He *circulated*, so to speak. And that Circulation was very purposeful, like a busy dog's, always somewhere to go. What he didn't realize, of course, - and, in this sense, *all* Paths are synonymous - is that what he was doing was meeting *himself*, at all Places and Stations, outer and inner. But, because of Externality, the Thief, he took it to be the usual Round of routinely chaotic Activity. No wonder, then, that nothing added up. Then he saw (and everyone who *sees* sees this) that there *were* no others, only himself. What he had taken to be a random Venture, a dislocated Journey, a formless Maze, revealed itself, on closer inspection, to be exactly what he was himself - not vaguely or tangentially, not as-it-were. He was meeting himself, at depth, coming back - and that was when the corner was turned, the Bud of Being was born in him. It was a Passage (not osmotic, not of Time) from the caught, fraught World of Thought-approximation to the True World of Cosmos, of Things-as-they-Are. It was something unimaginable, the like of which had never happened before, the tincture of which is always unique. For Order was there in daily life: it was not some far-fetched, interplanetary Thing. No, it lay under the kitchen-mat, if one wanted to find it, cared to understand. And it is that which flows deeply in Me, also; it is what I am; it is what Life *is*. Once perceived, there is no going back.

'That's how the Seeker can come to Me - through his own direct, personal, unique Quest. For all Seeking is, by its nature, unique: it is the Voice of the One tuning in to Itself, that 'I' which is calling its Prodigal home. To him who is honest, direct, unspoiled I give Myself abundantly; I flow into every Corner and Crevice of his Soul. Whatever he does then is done by Me, for I *become* he, in deed and word.

'Mightily I move and change. I am not the static God of Man, imposed on himself by guilt and fear: I am everloving-quick, like Life itself. Nowhere is my stopping-point. I have seen all, bred all, borne all away: my Waters have healed this hot, heaving Land. And now the Land knows Me as I am known; it rises, rich and recumbent, to meet Me, as I follow my Course to the waiting Sea.

'In my Movement and Being are all Possibilities, created and still uncreated in Me. There are those things which, as yet, have no name, which are living in Me, unconceived, in the Womb. They are myriad, countless, more numerous than the sands, and I ache with Desire to give birth to Them. You have no idea how much I *long* to body forth the massive Potential which is lying in Me. But only a Creator, a Stream-Enterer, who no longer lives in vague Thought-approximations, can call forth from Me what I have to give. For what I have to give is utterly rich, completely original, faultlessly pure. And of such Quality, also, must the Creator be.

'I go, I flow, through the Darkness, through the Light. All Light and Darkness is resolved in Me: the flailing Opposites sink to their Core, the Zero-point, their Beginning, their End. I am not concerned with Effort and Friction, nor with anything that goes in the name of Debate. Such things are fragile and worthless to Me, the spurious concoctions of overheated brains. I let them sink, like heavy metal, to my Bed. For I see only Eternity. And that Eternity is neither bland nor blank, a Place of Angels, nor a Counterpoise. It is a welling Depth of indomitable Strength, a Surge of Substance waiting to be born. I call on you, my Children, to give birth to It.

'The sky is darkening over the Bay of Bengal, as I take my several Ways to the Sea. This Land has known much suffering, and it continues to suffer, as all Lands do. My Redemption has not yet been sufficient. But Grace is with Me, like the Rose of Dawn; Peace is with Me, and a great Beatitude. I move deeply to the Ocean and I move in you.

'May all who travel be certain of this.'